The two stood in the mid[...]
One of them was the guy she'[...]
other one held the glimmering threat of a knife at his side. From behind her, a hand fell on her shoulder. "Hey, lady, you got some spare change?"

"No," Helix said, and turned halfway to face him.

"No?" the one with the knife queried. "You better be lying."

She shook her head and took a step back, but a firm hand grabbed her arm, twisting it behind her. She gasped at the sudden flash of pain. "I don't—" She paused. "I don't know, let me see."

"Aw, don't strain yourself, darlin', I'll do it for you," said the guy without the knife, and he proceeded to slowly unbutton her coat.

He was standing close as he worked his fingers over the buttons, undoing them one by one. So much the better, she thought, as she waited for him to finish with the third button, at waist level.

He undid it, and looking up at her, smiled. "I think that's enough, for now anyway."

She smiled back at him, widely, baring her fangs, and shot her lower right fist through the opening of the coat and into his midsection while she stomped on the instep of the assailant behind her with her left foot....

ACCIDENTAL
ACCIDENTAL
CREATURES
CREATURES

ANNE
HARRIS

TOR®

A TOM DOHERTY ASSOCIATES BOOK
NEW YORK

ACCIDENTAL CREATURES

Copyright © 1998 by Anne Harris

This book is printed on acid-free paper.

Edited by James Frenkel

A Tor Book
Published by Tom Doherty Associates, LLC
175 Fifth Avenue
New York, NY 10010

www.tor.com

Tor® is a registered trademark of Tom Doherty Associates, LLC.

LIBRARY OF CONGRESS CATALOGING-IN-PUBLICATION DATA

Accidental creatures / Anne Harris.
    p.   cm.
"A Tom Doherty Associates book."
ISBN 0-312-86538-4 (hc)
ISBN 0-312-87560-6 (pbk)
I. Title.
PS3558.A64257A65 1998
813'.54—dc21   98-3037
                                                CIP

First Hardcover Edition: July 1998
First Trade Paperback Edition: October 2000

Printed in the United States of America

0 9 8 7 6 5 4 3 2 1

For my mother

Many thanks to Jim Frenkel for his tireless and infuriatingly accurate editing skills; to my agent Virginia Kidd; to Mike Harris, Marta Bennet, Christian Klaver, Jay Brazier, and Ron Warren; to Ric Lane for lending me parts of his Ph.D. brain; to Deborah Crow and June Harris for their contagious enthusiasm; and to Steve Ainsworth, for being such a twink.

ACCIDENTAL
ACCIDENTAL
CREATURES
CREATURES

PROLOGUE

A New and Cloudy Sky

THE sky over Vattown was a dull, flat, grey, and Ada Chichelski walked beneath it. She wrapped the scarf her girlfriend Mavi had made her around her neck and headed through the dingy, yeast-redolent streets to the vat yard, to work.

On a day like this—damp, low cloud cover—even those like herself who'd grown up in Vattown noticed the distinctive funk of growth medium in the air. It made her wonder if the improvements in worker safety she and her fellow vatdivers had secured would make much difference. They were safer in the vats now, but how much growth medium were they all exposed to, just breathing every day?

That would be the next fight, she thought as she walked past age-faded houses and storefronts. Getting the company to use better seals on the growth medium storage tanks. Now that the vatdivers had secured better wages and had their own technicians monitoring safety measures, it would be time soon to press for more.

With their first strike settled successfully just two months ago, a lot of her sisters and brothers in the vats thought the movement had accomplished what it set out to do. Everyone was amazed at how quickly GeneSys management came around. After stonewalling the strikers for just two weeks, they agreed to three out of five of the vatdivers' demands. It was a better offer than the divers had expected. In fact, they'd all expected much worse.

For years Ada had been saying that they had to do something. That too many of them were dying of vatsickness and they never made enough money to stop working. It was obvious. Most of their parents who'd dived were dead. Her younger sister, Chango, was a sport. She was one of the lucky ones, still alive and healthy despite her mutation. Ada knew a dozen other divers with younger sport siblings, and everyone remembered the stillbirths, the miscarriages, and the ones who only lived long enough to know misery.

Finally, at Hargis' wake, it all came together. Hargis was Ada's age. She'd only been diving for five years, but the company's shoddy equipment inspection had passed over a perforation in her divesuit. She was exposed to growth medium, and died within three months.

They all gathered at Josa's Bar after the funeral, and Ada got up on a table to give a toast, but instead she found herself saying that they would all die just like Hargis, and soon, unless they surrounded the vat yard and demanded better treatment from GeneSys. That they had nothing to lose, not even their lives.

The divers' fear of vatsickness and the deadly deformities it brought overcame their fear of GeneSys' retaliation, and they followed her out of the bar and to the vat yard.

They all expected goons, and they had their air tanks with them. They were heavy, and you wouldn't want to get hit with one. But nothing happened. For two weeks, the vatdivers maintained a barrier of bodies around the vat yard. No biopoly was produced, and no goons arrived.

Finally they were approached by a management representative with a contract securing the divers an across the board raise, their own safety technicians, and a moratorium on the hiring of sports, who were genetically predisposed to vatsickness.

Now a lot of the divers thought they could relax, enjoy their gains and forget about organizing further. But she wouldn't forget, and she knew that GeneSys wouldn't either. They had won too easily, and she knew the war was far from over. If they didn't take advantage of their recent success, and press for more, they would gradually lose what they'd gained.

Up ahead Vonda and Benny were waiting for her on the corner. She'd known them both all her life. She and Benny had been in kindergarten together. Vonda was a little younger, her sister's age. She was their crew's new safety technician. They were all the children of first generation vatdivers.

After the sports were born, GeneSys had instituted a sterilization policy, and in a few short years, Vattown changed from a town of working-class families to a community of single adults. There were no more children in Vattown, and with most of their parents already dead, the only family the divers had now was each other.

As she approached, Benny jiggled his lunch box in greeting. "Stuffed cabbage," he said. "I made it last night."

"Cool. If you share, I'll cut you in on Mavi's next batch of moussaka."

"You've got a deal," he said. "Besides, I have a ton of this stuff. It's my grandmother's recipe. It makes enough to feed the Polish army."

"Well sign me up and get me a uniform," said Vonda, making a grab for Benny's lunch box. He skittered out of her way and the three of them walked on until they came to the gates of the vat yard, where they joined a thickening stream of divers arriving for the second shift.

"Hey Ada," shouted her friend April, behind her. "How blasted were you at Josa's last night?"

Ada laughed, turning, allowing the crowd to guide her backwards. "Not as much as you were," she said, cocking her thumb and index finger at April.

They passed through the gate, and the crowd spread out as everyone went to their various stations. She and April, Benny, and Vonda headed for the far right corner of the yard, to Vat House 9. Up ahead Val and Hugo, the remaining members of her dive crew, were walking with their heads bent in conversation.

The round grey flanks of the vat houses soon surrounded them, along with an intensified reek of growth medium. It was like smelling your death, she thought. The overheated, predatory breath of a beast about to eat you.

They entered Vat House 9 to the din of compressor dryers and the shouts of a dive leader to his crew. Sheets of biopolymer lay drying in the racks which bristled along the wall behind the twenty-foot-tall iron vat.

The divers—Oli and his crew—were just decanting their last

sheet for the day. They stood evenly spaced around the platform surrounding the vat, and at Oli's word they began pulling on the cables which hung from a pulley system in the translucent domed ceiling. They lifted out the last grow tray, and its biopoly load hung suspended over them like a new and cloudy sky.

Ada stopped at the door to the locker room and read the production schedule. Hendricks, the vat supervisor, had her crew scheduled for 1000 cubic meters of A-grade biopolymer insulation sheeting today. Oli and his crew had just decanted 800 cubic meters of C-grade consumer fabric.

"We're going to have to add a lot of dodecagon cell matrix to that mix," said Benny, looking over her shoulder. "At least fifty liters if we're going to get that sheeting today."

"And the grow med better be good and clean," said Ada. "Any coagulants left over from that consumer fabric will ruin the whole batch."

"Look at this," said Vonda, pointing at the projected activity chart. "They've got this vat scheduled for more C-grade fabric tomorrow. Why do they do that? If they know they need more consumer fabric, why not make it all at once? We wouldn't need to clean the vat between batches. Now when we get the insulation out, we're going to have to clean it all over again."

Ada nodded. "We'll get the insulation done first, and see how much time we have left. We may have to leave the second cleaning for the next shift."

"Why don't they listen to us and consolidate their batches? It would save time," said Vonda.

"And money," noted Benny.

"And it would save us from having to dive so much, but what do they care? They're not the ones who'll get sick," said Ada. "That's why, in another couple of months, we should make more demands. Strike again if necessary. Something needs to be done about the seals on the grow med storage tanks, and we should have a say in what's produced, and when."

Vonda wrinkled her forehead. "Two months? So soon? Maybe we should lie low for awhile, let them relax. We were lucky the first time."

"Luck had nothing to do with it," said Benny. "We had them

by the short hairs. Vattown is their main production plant. Without us, they have no product."

"But they'll never let us have a say in the production schedule," Vonda protested. "Don't get me wrong. It was a great thing we did. I'm just not sure we should push things so fast, that's all."

Still arguing, the three made their way to their lockers. "How long did it take you to check our equipment last night?" Ada asked Vonda.

She shrugged, opening her locker with a bang. "A couple of hours."

Ada shook her head. "We should have held out for overtime for the safety technicians."

"Hey, you got them to let us do it. And you paid for my training." She put her hands on Ada's shoulders. "It won't all happen at once. We have to be patient."

Ada snorted. Patience. While every day the growth medium leeched into their bodies, while they waited for the next diver to die. She put on the thick polypropylene suit that covered her from head to toe and protected her from the grow med. When she was done she paused to stare at the safety diagram on one wall of the locker room. In bold lettering it spelled out the steps divers must take to ensure that their equipment was working properly. That was GeneSys' idea of safety measures, that and a monthly equipment inspection. She felt better now, knowing that every week Vonda went over all their equipment with a fine-toothed comb.

By the time she got to the tank room, the others were already there. Benny helped her on with her tanks after she checked the valve to make sure they were full. Bending beneath their weight, she made her way to the dive platform with the rest of her crew.

On the platform, they put flippers on their polypropylene covered feet, donned their face masks, and eased themselves into the growth medium. The six of them fanned out across the vat, searching its murky waters for the coagulants that formed like cellular pearls around any scraps of biopoly left behind in the growth medium.

Almost immediately, she knew something was wrong. There was a tingling in her fingers and toes, and it rapidly spread across her whole body. April was right, she'd used Blast last night, and she'd gotten pretty high. But she'd felt fine this morning. As drugs went, Blast had few long-range side effects, and she'd never heard of anyone having a Blast flashback.

Until now. She tried to surface, to make her way back to the platform, but she lost her orientation and found herself diving deeper into the growth medium.

She didn't have any trouble finding agules. To her Blast-heightened senses they appeared as bright blue sparks in the electric green of the grow med all around. The fluid rang against her body, a high vibration matched by the trembling of her limbs. And then she felt it; the silvery, sleek touch of grow med against the skin of her belly. She reached down, and tried to reclose the seal on her suit, but she only succeeded in opening it further, and the fluid rushed in, wrapping her in a velvet embrace.

She tried again to reach the surface, focusing on the lightening of the waters. Her fluid-logged suit weighed her down, and she almost shed it, reflexively—like a snake loosing its skin or a butterfly emerging from its chrysalis. But those images did not apply to her, for the transformation she would make would end in death, not rebirth. Even as she broke the surface of the growth medium and waved her arms for help, she knew she was beginning to die.

1

MOTOR CITY REQUIEM

THIS building is condemned by the WEB Nine Zoning Authority. Please vacate the proximity of this building. This building is condemned by the WEB Nine Zoning Authority," droned a soft feminine voice. Chango paced the genelink fence in frustration. On the other side, the great brick bulk of the Russell Industrial Center loomed like a beached and lifeless whale.

Two days ago there was a rave-in here: fifty or more squatters partying, cooking, eating, and sleeping. Loud music and vivid strips of celluplast streamed from the windows of the abandoned factory, announcing the presence of the rave to anyone in the neighborhood while electrical and coaxial line usage seeped into Cityweb's awareness.

The squatters had picked up and moved on to another party, another building. They left a trail of condemned theaters, hotels, and office buildings behind them in their travels through the city. They were supposed to leave before Cityweb got wind of them, but they weren't always that fast.

Scanning the genelink fence for gaps, Chango made her way around to the back of the Russell, to the parking lot and loading docks. It was no use trying to cut an opening, nothing could cut through genelink except for a molecular saw, and if she could afford one of those she'd probably be able to buy the whole damn building.

On the far side of the Russell there was a walkway bordered by a small strip of patchy, gravel-dusted grass. Chango rummaged in her backpack and came out with a small shovel. Here the genelink had not been buried in the ground but merely stretched across it, and a hole could be dug. Not a very big hole, just enough for her to wriggle underneath.

Once inside, she didn't worry much about sensors. They'd detect her, sure, but this was a condemned building, and clearly marked as such. The zoning authority wasn't too concerned about whether or not it was empty when they came with the disintegrators.

The Russell Industrial Center was really a group of three brick buildings, each covering a city block. A concrete yard between them once gave trucks access to the loading docks, but now its barren expanse was just a home for the hardy weeds that sprang up between the cracks in the paving.

Chango made her way along one wall, keeping to the shadows until she came to a blank metal door next to a freight platform. She yanked on the handle. It was locked, but the simple electromagnetic identification reader was no match for her inertial lock pick—an expensive little piece of equipment, but it got her places. It bypassed the automation on most modern locks and went to work directly on the tumblers, so all she needed to do was keep the system busy or off-line. She didn't need to figure out the protocols of a system and then talk to it, she just had to shut it up.

She opened the door and crept into a long, dark, tiled hallway. At the end of it was an alcove with a freight elevator and another metal door. She took the stairs. She never had trusted the elevators in the Russell, and she had even less reason to do so now. On the tenth floor she stepped out from the stairwell onto the vast floor of a machine shop. The large room was lit by sunshine from the windows all around. The rusting hulks of die-cutting machines striped the cracked linoleum floor with shadows.

Chango wandered in this gallery of disused mechanisms, running tentative fingers across the dusty, corroded flanks of forgotten tools, their intricate purposes a mystery to her. The rave-in had been in the north building, they had never even ventured here, had never laid eyes on these arcane devices, had neither knowledge of them nor desire to find out. To the ravers, an abandoned building was simply a place to hang out for a while. To Chango, each was a world unto itself, a landscape to be savored.

At the far end of the floor she turned around, taking it all in with careful eyes, the angle of the light, the swirls of dust on the floor, the boxy lines of the machines in all their many shades of grey and brown. She absorbed every detail, burning it in her mind. She'd spent days exploring the Russell, and this was her favorite spot, or almost. In a day or so, it would be gone, but she would remember. She had already remembered so many of the old buildings in Detroit; the curving dome of the Bonstelle Theatre, the majestic columns in the lobby of the Fox, the murals on the third floor of the old library. All were gone now except for in her memory, where she kept them.

Chango climbed on top of a machine bench sitting against the wall and crawled out the window above it. An iron ladder was bolted to the outside of the building about six feet away. Gripping the upper casement of the window, Chango shuffled as close to the edge of the window ledge as possible, and then crouched and leapt. Unfortunately she struck the wall first, but managed to catch the ladder before she fell.

Ribs smarting, she climbed six more stories to the uppermost roof of the Russell Industrial Center.

From here she could see the city sprawling out beneath her like the recumbent body of a very old woman; the buildings and streets a map of scars, tracing her history. The clean black lines of maglev highways were fresh and dark against the faded webwork of paved streets. The areas they led to thrummed with activity, alight with cash and electricity. Elsewhere, whole expanses of the city languished in obscurity.

Once this city was a legend. The Motor City. Motor cars were built here, and for a while, a brief and fabled golden age, Detroit was the axle of industry around which the world turned. But the world moved on, and gasoline got expensive, and foreign manufacturers beat the Motor City at its own game. Even before the advent of maglev transportation, the auto industry in Detroit had fallen far from its glory days. And when maglev did come, it was the final deathblow.

But even industry hates a vacuum. Attracted by a cheap and available labor pool, GeneSys moved its headquarters here, to the old Fisher Building, and brought most of its production facilities with it.

The green-tipped tower of the Fisher, now known as the GeneSys Building, rose up against gathering clouds. At night its peak would be lit gold, and red warning lights would flash from its spire. As a child she had called it the Gold Top Castle, and imagined grand parties held there.

Several miles to the south, the towers of the downtown business district reared abruptly from the surrounding two- and three-storey buildings like an apparition, the curving glass walls of the Renaissance Center and the Millennial Building its glittering centerpiece. Roughly eight blocks square, the district was so incongruous to the rest of the city that it had earned the name Oz.

To the west she could see Vattown, once the home of one of the city's largest automobile plants, now the production center for GeneSys. Rows of vat houses shimmered their grey steel shimmer at the noonday sky. They took up several city blocks, and around them, huddling close to the warmth of industry, were the little brick houses of her neighborhood. It was meager nourishment, and dangerous.

Vattown was a small pocket of working-class living standards in the bipolar morass of the few rich and the multitudes of poor. But the workers paid a heavy price for relative prosperity. Swimming in growth medium did things to your genetic structure; things that would catch up with you, sooner or later.

Like they had with her sister Ada. Her death had left a hole in the Vattown community that could be felt to this day. Though as a teenager, Chango had certainly not appreciated her sister's leadership, particularly her efforts to raise her after their parents died.

Chango remembered the last hour of the last day of her senior year in high school. She'd sat in the humid, crowded classroom, her eyes on the clock. Five more minutes and she'd be free, but Ms. Hinkie, the English teacher, droned on, oblivious to her own irrelevance. What could you learn in the last five minutes of four years spent skipping and smoking and passing on the curve? It was a vat school. Chango and her classmates regarded it as four years of vacation prior to diving in the vats for the rest of their lives.

The minute hand on the clock moved a notch—four more minutes. Behind her Vonda Peterby kicked Chango's chair leg and slid a folded piece of paper past her shoulder. Chango palmed it smoothly and opened it on her lap. A smoking joint was rendered in finest number-two pencil, and beside it the words, "Behind Hannah's." Chango pocketed the note and gave Vonda a quick nod.

The last three minutes of her high school career ticked by with excruciating slowness. When the bell rang, Chango was swept along by a surging wave of students which poured out of the school onto the streets of Vattown. After a block the crowd thinned, and Chango slowed to a walk, ambling lightly down the cracked concrete sidewalk, heading west and south, towards Hannah's Eclectic Homestyle Restaurant.

It was a major hangout for vatdivers, and in the alley behind it, high school burnouts like herself and Vonda congregated to smoke pot and drink beer. When she got to Hannah's, Vonda and their friends Coral, Val, and Tashi were already there, clustered around stacks of milk crates and cardboard boxes.

"Hey, Chango, what happened, you get caught in the stampede?" shouted Coral as she approached.

"Here." Vonda handed her a big fat joint.

Chango toked it, drawing the dense, sweet smoke deep into her lungs. "Dang," she said, exhaling a cloud of smoke, "I thought that last class would never end."

"Yeah," said Vonda, "can you believe that Hinkie, trying to cram one more lesson into us, on the last day."

"Like we're gonna need to know the imagery of T. S. Eliot where we're going," said Coral.

"At least Mr. Beaudet let us talk among ourselves," said Val. "He knew better than to try and make us sit through another hour of chemistry."

"At least chemistry has something to do with vat diving," said Coral. "Look at your sister, Chango, she's putting it to good use."

"Yeah." Ada was taking night courses in chemistry and biopolymer engineering, so she could train divers to do their own safety monitoring on the vats. It was part of her unionizing efforts. Divers couldn't rely on the safety standards GeneSys provided. The company considered three fatalities a year an acceptable margin of error.

Tashi fastened an alligator clip to the joint and passed it to Vonda. "Are you really going to take the clerical entrance exam, Chango?"

She shook her head, "Not if I can help it. Ada's dead set on it, but can you imagine me spending the rest of my life shuffling papers for some goon in a suit?"

"At least you'd have more of the rest of your life," said Tashi.

"Yeah, if the boredom didn't kill me."

"Then what are you going to do?" said Vonda, passing the now minuscule roach to her.

Chango hit it, grimacing as she burned her lips. "I don't know. What the rest of you are doing, I guess. Get sterilized and dive in the vats."

"You think Ada will let you?" asked Val.

Chango shrugged. "I'm out of school now, I'm an adult. She doesn't rule my life."

The others nodded vaguely. Since their parents died, Ada had taken it upon herself to raise Chango, and she was determined to keep her little sister out of the vats. Watching them, Chango bristled. They didn't believe her, they thought she'd eventually do just what Ada said. But there was no way she was going for an office job. Even if she could get it, she'd hate it; she'd rather do what her parents did, what her friends would do—dive, and die at thirty-five.

"So when do you guys have your appointments with Dr. Snip?" asked Coral smugly.

"Not until August," said Val.

"July twenty-third," said Vonda.

"July thirtieth," said Tashi.

Coral smiled. "I'm getting done June sixth. I am going to have a great summer."

"You bitch," said Tashi, "how did you get yours so soon?"

" 'Cause my daddy's a foreman, silly girl."

Everyone groaned. Val spoke up again, "So when are they hiring new divers?"

"Not until September," said Coral. "Word is that vats twenty-two through thirty-one need fresh blood."

"Hey, wouldn't it be great if we all got the same assignment?" said Vonda.

"It won't happen," said Coral. "They'll only take three or four new people at a time, so they can learn from veteran divers."

"I hope I get in that Gordon's vat. He is so hot," said Tashi.

Chango snorted. "You're hopeless."

Sunlight slid in patches across the cracked and stained concrete of the alley. The back door of Hannah's swung open abruptly, and DiDi, the dishwasher, came out hauling a trash can, brimming with garbage, and hoisted it into the black maw of the Dumpster. She didn't acknowledge them, her face closed in a busy frown.

Chango leaned against the pitted brick wall of the restaurant, lifting her eyes to the blue and cloud-spotted sky. The conversation of her peers washed over her, their concerns seeming distant and unrelated to hers, even though she'd known them her whole life.

Ada would never let her go to the vats. She'd lock her up first. And truth be told, Chango wasn't all that keen on it anyway. She'd seen her mother and father die within two years of each other, neither of them more than forty years of age, bedridden for the last two months of their lives, their bodies riddled with cancerous tumors suddenly come to bloom. What little she'd seen of life, she liked, she wanted to keep on doing it. She wanted more than forty years of it.

But she wasn't about to take some clerical job for GeneSys. How could she type letters and file reports for a bunch of white-collar geeks whose decisions determined whether or not her friends lived or died? It was like the choice between picking cotton in the fields, or working in the big house. Sure, it was better to work in the big house, but Chango wanted off the plantation altogether.

The shadows in the alley lengthened, the sunlight turned to mellow amber. The conversation had turned from the graduates' prospects to the more immediate concern of where the parties were that night.

"Claudia's having a house party," said Val.

"That bitch?" said Coral, "I hate her fucking guts."

"Oh yeah?" said Tashi with a smirk. "How come?"

" 'Cause Coral's got it bad for Jerome," taunted Vonda, "and she has since before Claudia nabbed him."

Coral's face turned red, and she glared at them, but she didn't deny it.

"Forget that anyway," said Chango. "Josa's is giving free pitchers to graduates."

"Yeah, and the Ply-Tones are playing," said Val.

"Yes!" said Vonda.

"I am staying out all night, tonight," said Chango.

"You'll do nothing of the kind, kiddo." The voice came from the kitchen door. Chango turned to see her sister standing there, tall and strong, her blond hair short and neatly combed.

Looking at her standing there in the late afternoon sunshine, Chango's jaw clenched unwittingly. She'd never seen anyone so fucking perfect in her life. Certainly she would never be like that, no matter what she did. For one thing, she wasn't tall, Ada had strength and weight on her, and she wasn't beyond using them to her advantage, even in front of Chango's friends.

Chango stood, "I'll see you guys later."

"Uh-huh," "Yeah," "Sure," came the dubious replies.

Chango followed Ada in through the back door of the restaurant, burning with rage. They went through the kitchen and took a corner booth in the dining room. They sat down in silence, and Rita brought them coffee. Ada stirred cream in her cup and sipped at it. "You know you can't go out tonight, Chango, you've got an exam tomorrow morning."

Chango stared at the salt and pepper shakers for a long time. "Ada, I'm not going to do it," she said, finally glancing at her sister's face.

Ada stared at her in anger and surprise. "What?"

She shook her head, "I'm not going to do it. You can't make me."

"Why?" Ada shouted, and there was a momentary lull in the surrounding conversations as other patrons turned to look at them, and then returned to their own talk.

Chango took a careful breath. "Ada, I'm not doing it. I won't go be a suit for you, get it? I don't belong there, I'm not one of them."

Ada stared at her, her jaw stiff, her eyes frozen with anger. "Oh yeah?" she said tightly, "what are you then, huh? You tell me."

"I'm a vat—"

"A vatdiver? Is that what you think you are? Let me tell you something, little sister. You won't last. Mom was in the vats for six years before you were born, Dad ten. You already show signs of gene damage. Your eyes, Chango, don't they tell you anything?"

Her eyes: one blue, one green. A genetic anomaly not present in any of her known ancestors, a mutation.

"If you dive," Ada continued, "you won't make it past thirty. You won't even have a chance to start getting old."

"Who says I want to get old?" asked Chango.

Ada shook her head and gazed at the ceiling in exasperation. "I do, you fool, and you know it's true."

Chango licked her lips and studied the tabletop. "Yeah," she said quietly. "But I can't go corporate, Ada. It's like joining the enemy."

"Nonsense. You can be useful to us there. You can work to change management from within."

"Sounds like a nice idea, Ada, only it's yours, not mine."

Ada sighed. "Then what do you want to do?"

Chango shrugged. "I don't know."

"Well, you've got to do something. You can't just go on partying and hanging out with your friends. You've got to make a living somehow. Think of Mom and Dad. They worked so hard. They wanted something better for you. I owe it to them to make sure you take that exam."

Despite all her protests, Ada took Chango home and locked her in her bedroom with the clerical exam study guide. That night Chango crawled out of her bedroom window and went to Josa's, then to the party at Claudia's, and finally ended up passing out at Coral's house and sleeping until noon the next day, after the entrance exams were safely over.

Ada was furious. She tried to lock Chango in her room again, and even boarded up the window, but Chango kept finding ways to get out. They didn't speak to each other for weeks.

Then one day Ada came home from work early. Chango took one look at her face and knew something had happened. "Hargis is sick," she said, setting her lunch box on the table by the door.

"But she's only been diving five years," Chango said, and wished she hadn't. That was how long Ada had been diving, too.

"Company inspection missed a hole in her suit. It'll go quickly for her." Ada sat down on the couch, her arms resting on her knees.

"That seems to be about all I can hope for anyone anymore, that when the sickness comes it will take them quickly." She shook her head. "It's hopeless. I keep telling everyone we need to organize, but they don't listen. I can't save them," she looked at Chango. "I can't even save you."

She almost retorted that she didn't need Ada to save her, watch out for her, lecture her, or do any of the other things which Ada saw as duties and Chango saw as infringements on her liberty. But she stopped herself, shocked to see her sister near tears. "That's not true," she said. "I'm not diving."

"But you will!" Ada shouted, tears suddenly springing forth from her eyes. "Any day now, when my back is turned, you'll put in an application and make an appointment to be sterilized."

"No. No I won't, Ada. I won't be a clerical worker like you wanted, but I promise you, I won't dive either. I'll find another way to get along."

"Really?" Ada wiped her eyes and sniffed.

"Really." Chango sat down next to her on the couch. "I promise."

Ada nodded. "Well, that's something," she said, and managed to smile a little. "But I'm afraid the vatdivers are a lost cause. They're so afraid of what GeneSys will do if we organize. They'll never listen to me. I might as well give it up."

"You can't." Chango stood up again, shocked. "You can't give up. Sooner or later they'll realize they have nothing to lose, and even if they don't, you'll know you did everything you could to change things. If you give up, you'll never be able to live with yourself. You know it's true."

Ada stared at her a moment and then nodded in resignation. "I know. I guess today I just wish it weren't," she said, looking more tired than Chango had ever seen her before.

But all of that was before Ada's death and the suspicion of negligence that darkened her name and discredited the union movement. Everything had changed since then. Now the question of whether or not to dive in the vats was a moot one. GeneSys wouldn't hire sports anymore. It was one of the things Ada had fought for and gained in the movement's first and last strike.

Chango never did decide what she wanted to do with herself, so she, like so many others, led a marginal existence. Exploring old buildings, scavenging, repairing automobiles, cutting lawns, cleaning houses, scanning cash cards. She lived anyplace she could park her car or bum a floor for the night, but for the most part that was still Vattown, those gritty streets and weathered buildings where she remained, obscure in her sister's shadow.

2

THE ODD MARK

RAIN hissed in the magnetic field of Woodward Avenue, rising to a shrill whine with the passing of every gleaming, beetle-shaped levcar. Helix picked her way along the neglected sidewalk, the pothole freckled motor lane a buffer of neglect between herself and the shiny, rain-slick blackness of the levway.

Like twin rivers, the maglev lanes flowed into Oz and out again, leaving the outmoded, the deadwood, in eddies along their banks.

Woodward was the first concrete highway in the United States. Automobiles weren't invented here, but this was where they began changing the world. Now everyone who could afford it drove maglev. It was a big improvement: no pollution, no auto accidents.

Of course, not everyone could afford maglev. Rusting and battered automobiles stood parked along the side of the motor lane—Civics and Geos and Neons, their names fit for a world that had passed them by.

Although the bulk of her life had been spent in Hector Martin's comfortable apartment in the GeneSys Building, Helix had been a pedestrian before. At the orphanage every Saturday; released onto the sunbaked pavement to walk and run to the corner store to buy comic books.

In her memory, the sun was always shining, but that could not have been the case. Was the sun shining the day Matt and Tina had waited for her outside the shop and taken her *Super Neutrino Man* #86 from her? She didn't remember. All she remembered were their vicious faces, their laughter, and the brightly colored pages fluttering torn to the cracked pavement of the sidewalk.

A sidewalk like this one, the metal-screened shop fronts similar, too. She was countless blocks from the tree-lined oasis of prosperity surrounding the GeneSys Building, walking forgotten in a limboland of aging concrete.

Barricaded pawn shops and living-hair clinics gave way to a long stretch of defunct department store, its walls and windows coated with a thick layer of yellowish grey biopolymer paint. Plaint, as it was commonly known, was one of many materials based on matrices of organic cells which GeneSys produced.

The parked cars disappeared and maglev traffic thinned. An aged Ford Taurus rumbled down the pitted motor lane, sending up splashes of rain from numerous potholes. Its movement was labored compared to the occasional blurred whoosh of the levcars.

Helix watched the motorcar pass, lumbering into the distance at a pace still, despite its age, beyond her own. What's more, it was going someplace, which was more than she could say.

She'd left on an impulse, hoping to discover why when she got there, wherever it was she wanted to go. She was continually aware of the foolishness of it, but apparently that didn't matter; she could not get herself to go back. Whenever she thought of it, a hand— an invisible hand that she did not know—placed itself firmly on her heart and pushed her forward through the abandoned streets as it had pushed her out of Hector's apartment door several hours ago.

Woodward led her down through the city, towards the river, past the university and the cultural center: beautiful, crumbling stone buildings shored up haphazardly, halfheartedly, with garish patches of purple and orange MasonBond.

A small group of people passed by, shaggy men and women in weather-faded greencoats and colorful knitted hats; students or squatters, or both. Helix drew in her shoulders and put her head down as they passed, but none of them seemed to pay her much mind.

She stopped in front of the Detroit Institute of Art. Blank, boarded-up windows stared back at her blindly, a line of polybond around each like heavy mascara, outlining their surprise at the theft of sight.

There were supposed to be people living there now, artists. The front doors were padlocked and barred and padlocked again, as if someone wanted very much for you to know you could not go in there. Before this denial brooded the Thinker, too large, too solid, and permanently heavy to steal, but convenient to deface. His full-body tattoo of fluorescent spray-plaint gave testimony to years of flourishing artistic expression.

She walked on, Woodward leading her visibly closer to Oz, through a district of moderate prosperity which supported clothing shops, small offices, and restaurants.

She pulled Hector Martin's faded overcoat around her protectively as she passed a group of office people, chatting unceasingly with one another, oblivious to her presence. On the next corner there was a stoplight, and more people, all the time more people, and Helix took extra care that her mouth was completely shut.

A little girl in a pink biopolymer raincoat with matching hat and umbrella passed her in the intersection. As her father tugged her along, she looked at Helix with bright black eyes and smiled. But Helix didn't dare smile back.

On the next corner the neon warmth of a diner beckoned, "Fine Food," and her stomach growled on cue. It had been hours since she'd left GeneSys, aimless hours of walking. There'd be even more people inside, and in closer proximity, but she was hungry, her stomach as empty as her vacant and searching heart.

The diner smelled of coffee and frying eggs. Helix sat in a red biovinyl upholstered booth at the back of the restaurant, speedily demolishing a club sandwich and fries. It was warm inside, the windows fogged and sweating, but she kept the raincoat on. Nobody, including her waitress, had paid much attention to her. As she reached for her Coke, the waitress reappeared, "Anything else?"

Helix shook her head, and the waitress placed a swiper on the table and walked away again. Helix stared at it as if it were a cockroach that had just crawled out from beneath the napkin dispenser. Its screen showed a total for her meal: $12.67.

A chill went through her and settled in the pit of her stomach. She shivered, despite the muggy air. Sweat stood out on her arms and neck. Hector Martin's raincoat clung to her clammy skin. She'd forgotten about money.

Helix riffled through the pockets of Hector's overcoat, searching for the cash card she knew she'd left behind in the apartment. All she found was a useless data card. She turned it thoughtfully between her fingers, then pantomimed passing it through the slot on the swiper, carefully shielding the card with her palm so an observer would not see that she hadn't actually run it through. She stood up and walked down the aisle, passing her waitress on the way to the door.

Helix was almost past the cash register when the waitress called out, "Ma'am, you forgot to swipe your card!" Helix plunged for the door. "Ma'am! Ma'am!" the waitress cried again, running after her.

Helix slammed her upper palms against the polyglass door, overcoming its resistance with her momentum. She plunged towards the outer door, only to be brought up short by a sudden jerk at her shoulder. She whirled around, expecting the waitress, but instead she saw the corner of her raincoat, jammed in the crack of the door behind her. Helix tugged frantically at the raincoat, but it was solidly wedged in the doorway.

The waitress barreled towards her, a dishwasher waving his hands in her wake. She reached the door and pushed on it. Panicking, Helix pushed back and they stood there, separated by the polyglass, deadlocked. The woman scowled and shoved at the door again. It opened a crack, and Helix bent to free her coat. The bottom button had torn off, and as she stood again the coat gaped open. Turning for the outer door, she caught a glimpse of the waitress staring, her eyes wide.

Helix fled blindly down the street, running at first and then, at the stares of passersby, slowing to a brisk walk. She turned a corner, and another, but heard no footsteps following her. They weren't chasing her. She'd seen that waitress' face. They were afraid of her.

She lifted a hand to cover her mouth, and found that her face was wet. She was crying. Silent tears spilled down her face and dripped off her chin.

Behind a drugstore Helix sat on a milk crate, staring at the pavement between her shoes, seeing not the cloncrete but that waitress' face: her eyes wide, her mouth gaped in shock, in horror. She'd seen. She'd seen what Helix was, and that was why Helix was always so very careful not to be seen.

In her mind she heard the shrieks and cries of her classmates as they surrounded her on the playground, Chet and Carla and Tim and Darron darting in from the circle to each grab one of her arms and then run, around and around, laughing, spinning her until she was sick and her arm sockets were sore. She remembered the whirling faces, contorted with joyous hate, and their voices, like the harsh cries of birds, calling, calling, in monotonous cacophony, "Freak Girl! Freak Girl!" And she, the eye of the vortex, screaming back, wordlessly, just screaming and screaming, her mouth open wide to show all of them her gleaming fangs.

Hector had rescued her. His first visit came the same day as the playground incident. He brought her a comic book—*Clone Avengers* #98. He didn't talk about adoption that first day. On his third visit, he asked her to be his daughter. She'd been floored, mystified, but too desperate to escape her situation to question his kindness, and she never had cause to, after she went to live with him. He worked hard, it was true, and sometimes she was lonely, but he'd given her everything he could. That it wasn't enough was her failure, not his.

He'd been up all night last night, working on some problem, fiddling with equations on his multiprocessor, his face glowing green from the numbers and symbols floating in the air before him. He called them the keys to life. She didn't understand it; remained forever curious, but exactly what it was that he actually did stayed well outside her grasp. All she ever saw was the multiprocessor, his fingers restlessly striking keys—a far cry from the steady rhythm of the data entry work she sometimes did. Of course that was just when he was at home. Most of the time he was at the lab, and she had never been there, even though it was in the very building where they lived. She didn't even have the door number, floor number, or the transceiver extension. He couldn't be disturbed when he was in the lab, she assumed, but she'd never asked, never asked for any of those things, and he had never offered them, either.

And this morning she'd stood in the hallway as he stumbled off to the shower. "Aren't you going to get some sleep?"

He smiled faintly and shook his head. "No, I've got to go in. I'll just get cleaned up and rummage something up for breakfast." His smile turned more wistful still. "Sure wish we had some of those pastries around." He loved the raspberry and cream cheese danishes the bakery downstairs made.

And so she'd donned his coat and made her sojourn down to the public level, walking across the inlaid marble floors, looking up, as always, at the frescoes that graced the arches of the ground floor gallery. She wore Hector's raincoat then, too. She always did, when she went out. She had to stand in line at the bakery counter, surrounded by working men and women, normal men and women, waiting for their morning croissant or bagel or whatever. The clerk behind the counter barely looked up as she spoke. "Six raspberry and cream cheese danishes, two cups of coffee," she uttered with painstaking minimalism, her lips moving as little as possible, to reveal as little as possible.

The raincoat forced her to juggle coffee cups and bag all the way to the elevators and all the way up. An elderly woman in stately blue wool smiled up at her and said, "You need three hands."

"I have more than that," she wanted to say, scream, shout. "I have more, oh, so much more than that." But she only smiled thinly in mute acknowledgment.

Hector was just coming out of the shower when she got back, vigorously toweling his coarse blond hair, his white shirt partially buttoned and sticking to his damp skin. "Hey, where'd you go?" he asked, and then spied the telltale white bag on the table. "Oh, wow, thanks. Raspberry?"

"Yeah, and coffee."

"Good, coffee." He pried off the filmseal on one of the cups and breathed in the rich steam with gratitude.

"I don't know how you do it," said Helix. "You practically live on that stuff."

Hector shook his head and bit into a pastry. "I'm just going to put in an appearance today," he mumbled. "Graham's been paying a lot of attention to the project lately, so I'd better, but I'll come home early and get some sleep."

Helix nodded. Early, that would be before eight. "Still, you should take a vacation. You must get time off, don't you?"

"Sure, but—"

"We could take a trip somewhere, the ocean maybe. I saw a holoclip yesterday, of the pacific ocean, the waves. I'm tired of sitting around here all the time." The truth was she'd felt more and more lately like she should be someplace else, but she couldn't think where.

"Maybe you should attend university."

"I do."

"On the holonet, sure, but maybe you should attend the physical plant somewhere, Mercy or Michigan."

"Why?"

Hector shrugged. "To get to know people, you know, face-to-face." Suddenly uncomfortable, Hector stared at the table. "You're grown now, you know."

"You think I should move out?"

"No! No. But you could commute, to Mercy anyway. I'm an alumnus; I'm sure I could get you in."

"But I don't know what I want to do, and I don't want to waste your money."

"I've got enough."

"It just seems so extravagant, to go to school, when I can have it come to me for free. Besides, sitting in a classroom with all those people, I don't think . . . I'm not ready for that."

Hector gazed at her and said nothing. "Well," he said, "I'd better be going. I'll see you later."

"Okay."

As he was leaving, she said, "Why can't we go on vacation?"

He stopped and looked back at her from the open door. "Because then Graham would assume that I'm through with the project, and I'm not."

The door shut behind him and Helix gathered the empty cups and threw them in the trash, put the bag with the remaining pastries in it on the kitchen counter, and wiped off the table. Then she flopped on the polyhide couch and switched on the holotransceiver. The prism, a thick, triangular column of glass sitting on the coffee table, glittered with reflected light from the transceiver, and the holoweb appeared before her.

She flipped aimlessly through the entertainment sector, catching fragments of old movies, bits and pieces of soaps, sitcoms, and direct-to-network holofilms.

She selected the interactive drama subgroup and dialed in to *We Are the World,* her favorite soap. There was still a slot open for Natasha, and she grabbed it. Natasha was a wealthy business-woman, the creator of Entranced Parfum, and a former wife of Olin Thatcher, the ruthless communications mogul. Natasha knew how to get what she wanted, always.

Today Natasha was meeting with her attorney in the murder case. She was innocent, at least that was what Helix believed. Samantha, the key witness for the prosecution, came out of one of the offices. The two women stood in the waiting room, staring at each other. "I hope you're paying him well, Natasha," said Samantha, "he's going to earn every penny defending your worthless hide."

Helix/Natasha flashed her a tight-lipped smile. "Not only is Walter West an excellent attorney, he's also a man of high princi-ples. He's representing me because he wants to see justice done."

"Justice? You kill a man and then sleep with his wife! You call that justice?"

"You'd like to see me locked up, wouldn't you? That way I'd be out of the way, and you could move in on Amanda yourself. That's what you want, isn't it?"

"You bitch!" shouted Samantha. "I hope you fry!"

Whoever was playing Samantha was a rank amateur, to blow so quickly. They could have bandied insults for several minutes more, but now the confrontation was forced to a climax. Natasha/Helix stepped up quickly and slapped Samantha across the face. Then leaned even closer and whispered, "Don't ever talk to me like that, you little two-bit piece of gutter trash, or I'll—"

"You'll what, poison me? Like you did Lago?"

Natasha glared at her. "Think what you want, I'll have my day in court."

A secretary popped out of the office, "Ms. Ettelle? Mr. West will see you now."

Natasha looked Samantha over with withering disdain. "I have to go now."

"You haven't heard the last of this, I assure you," Samantha said to her retreating back.

By the end of the episode, Samantha was pushing for Natasha's arrest, insisting that she was violent and dangerous. Oops, thought

Helix, shouldn't have slapped her. "Don't worry," said Natasha to her lawyer, "I'll think of something." Of course she, Helix, didn't have to. That was for the poor shlub that played her next.

Guilty over her dalliance, Helix switched over to the educational region and scurried down the menus to the corporate tax law seminar. As she scrolled through the most recent updates on preadjusted deficit deductions, she reached over to the end table, picked up a nail file, and smoothed the rounded edges of her fingernails. She liked to keep her nails in good shape. Sometimes she painted them and sat in front of the mirror in her room, legs crossed, back arched, arms waving like seaweed, hands dancing like schools of little red fish.

An hour was about all she could take of tax laws. Helix climbed back out of the educational well and accessed her mail. A few pieces of direct mail had wormed their way past her filters, too-bland-to-be-real faces assuring her of the benefits of subscription to one or another access group. One didn't even bother with the pretense of personal communication, showing simply a vista of palm trees and brilliant blue surf. A voice-over said, "Isle Oblique, it's better than being there."

Helix dumped these messages and moved on to a letter from a friend, a text file. "Good morning, Helix, it's Night Hag. What you been up to? Call me."

Helix dialed Night Hag's number. Her page circuit was open, but she didn't answer until the seventh beep. "Helix, hi." The holographic image of a slender woman with long, straight dark hair and olive-toned skin appeared before Helix. She was reclining on a white vat-leather chair. She wore black jeans, a black leather jacket, and round, opaque sunglasses.

"How do you like it?"

Oh, Helix liked it. A lot. "It's cool."

Night Hag grinned. "Cool would be what? Menacing? Dangerous? Chilled?"

"Dangerous, tough."

"Oh, good. Tough is good."

The last time Helix had "seen" Night Hag, she was blond and dressed in leopard skins and white silk. The time before that she was a man in spats and a fedora. Night Hag changed constructs a lot. A lot of people did. It was easy; just pick out an image from the zillions of pictures in warehouses all over the net. There were even clubs you could join, Face of the Month, Columbia House, Backgrounds R Us. What you saw when you talked to someone on the net was no indication of what that person actually looked like. Some people felt it set them free to express who they really were. Helix had used constructs a few times, but she hadn't felt that way. She'd felt as if she were hiding, which of course she was. She was always hiding. Kind of takes the entertainment value out of it, and so she preferred a blank mask. Let them use their imaginations; she could be secure in the knowledge that whatever they dreamed up, it would not be the truth.

"So what's up?" asked Helix.

"That's what I was going to ask you. I haven't heard from you in days. You don't write, you don't call. What, you can't pick up the transceiver?"

"There just hasn't been much to say. Nothing's going on, that's all."

"Tsk, tsk, tsk. A young woman like you, with nothing to do. That's too bad. You oughta get out more."

"I don't like out."

"How do you know? When was the last time you actually left that apartment?"

"This morning, actually."

"Really?" Night Hag's construct raised its eyebrows in surprise. "Where did you go?"

Helix pursed her lips. "I went down to the first-floor lobby to buy danishes."

Night Hag's construct shook its head and rolled its eyes. "Oh, Helix. Dear. You have got to get over this. I know you have a good relationship with your father and all, but, you're a grown woman. Get out of there! Get some independence."

"Why should I go anywhere? I've got the whole world right here in my living room."

"No, no you don't. The net, it's lies and illusions, mostly. You think you know me. You think we're friends. But you have no idea what I really look like, and for all you know, I've made up everything I've ever told you about myself. If we were in the same room together talking, there'd be a whole second conversation going on. One that we can't have, not with the constructs, maybe not even with true visual contact. The conversation between our bodies and our faces, the sensation of sharing space and time. That's what's out there, Helix. That's why you have to go, because that's where the truth is."

Helix laughed ruefully. "You sound like my father. He was just this morning talking about me going to school on an actual campus."

Night Hag's construct tilted its head thoughtfully. "School, hmm. Is that what you want?"

"I don't know." Helix sighed with exasperation. "I don't know what I want."

"But you want something, don't you?"

"Y-yes," Helix admitted, "only I don't know what."

"That's why you should get out of there. You'll never know as long as you remain dependent on Hector. Maybe you should get a job. Live independently for a while."

"Oh yeah, jobs are just falling from the sky out there. You checked the unemployment rate lately? It's still holding steady at fifty percent."

"What about vatdiving? They're always hiring people for that. And you live in Detroit, where most of the plants are. I bet you could get a job diving without even using Dr. Martin's influence."

"He wouldn't like it. He probably wants me to do something more, you know, cerebral."

"But the point is not what he wants, it's what you want."

"I don't—"

"Know what you want. I know. So don't look at it as a career, look at it as a stepping stone."

Helix thought about it. Actually, it had a certain appeal. Of course the drawback was that she'd have to be around people, but Night Hag was right, she needed to get over that, too. She couldn't spend the rest of her life in this apartment, living off the generosity of a man who had already given her more than anyone could expect. Helix imagined herself floating in a great vat of growth medium, swimming through the viscous liquid, scooping out impurities and gently harvesting sheets of living polymer. It was dangerous work. Tales of vatsickness were detailed and grotesque, but it was practically the only unskilled labor you could get paid for these days, and if she just did it for a little while, until she figured out what she wanted to do with herself, then she'd probably be okay. Vatsickness mostly struck people who'd been diving for ten years or more. "But you know," she said, giving voice to her fears, "I don't like people to see me."

"I know. But you shouldn't care. There's nothing wrong with you. That bad time you had, before, when you were younger, that was kids, Helix. Grown people aren't that bad, and besides, fuck them. You have to live your life."

"You're probably right," she said with more conviction than she felt. "I've got to go now." Helix switched off her holotransceiver and paced the living room floor, absently scratching her ribs. She went into her bedroom, threw herself onto her unmade bed and stared at the ceiling. She was bored, she realized, bored and itchy, her skin acting up again like it did when she got this way.

Maybe she should go to school, as Hector suggested, but the thought of sitting in a classroom made her blood run cold. Besides, there was nothing she really wanted to do. She took the tax law seminars because Hector had suggested it, and she felt she owed him something.

He had been more than kind to her, opening his home to her, becoming her father. She could never repay that, but she could, at least, refrain from being a burden to him for the rest of her life.

She got up, went into the bathroom, and started running a bath, but the rushing water was not what she wanted either. She turned off the taps and wandered into the living room again, switched on the holotransceiver, but this time she opened Hector's directory instead of her own. She accessed his personal records, called up the adoption files, and opened her birth certificate.

The document hung in the air roughly two feet from her face. She was born at 10:19 A.M. on March 12, 2022, in Harper Hospital. Her biological parents were Mabel and Owen Harvey. Of course she'd heard the story. Hector had told her. She was the child of vatdivers. But Owen had died in an industrial accident while Mabel was pregnant, and economic necessity had forced her to give up her daughter. Helix knew all about that, but somehow, it didn't answer the question of who she was.

That was when she left. She switched off the transceiver, took Hector's coat from the hook by the door, and went out.

* * *

By afternoon, the weather had soured, and Chango, who had dallied the sunshine away at the Russell and in Palmer Field, found herself driving her old Chevy down to the hectic, gaudy streets of Greektown, where she parked under an overpass to protect the eternally top-down convertible from the rain.

She stood under the awning of a pachinco parlor, studying the street from beneath the rim of her secondhand biopolymer rain hat. It was bad weather for scanning, but she was out of cash, and Mavi had just yesterday mentioned how she was running out of food. She planned to crash there tonight, and she felt like something a little better than peanut butter and rice for dinner. Besides, as often as she was over there, Mavi could charge her rent, but she never did, never hassled her to get a real job either. They'd known each other forever, ever since she was a kid, and Mavi was her big sister's lover.

But this street-corner hanging was getting nowhere. With the rain, people were just moving too damn fast to scan them. She'd have to go inside somewhere and hope that the swiper in her coat pocket would go unnoticed.

It was one thing to stand out in the street, catching whatever came your way and dodging the eyecard carriers, but if you went in someplace and got caught, then you had to deal with the proprietor and the police.

Chango crossed the street and went into the Pegasus Hotel and Casino. She stood in the foyer, dripping wet and fumbling with the clasps of her raincoat. The doorman scowled at her. The Pegasus pretty much let anybody in, that's why she was there, but they let you know they weren't happy about it.

Chango shrugged off his glare and went down the steps to the casino, losing herself in the crowd. The scanner in her raincoat pocket bumped lightly against her side as she wove her way through the throngs of gamblers clustered around the tables. The air was a warm, hazy soup of reefer smoke and damp bodies. She made her way to the bar, lit a reefer, and ordered a Coke.

Swiveling in her stool, she leaned back against the bar and took in the action. Someone was on a roll at table five, blackjack. The crowd there was denser than at the other tables, and stiff with expectancy. Hungry eyes surveyed the table as the dealer laid down the second round.

The focus of their attention was the player second to the right of the dealer. Over the craned heads of onlookers Chango just made out a head of feathery blond hair, but that was all. She couldn't see the pile of chips on the table—she didn't need to. The eyes of the spectators told her it was big, and growing. Chango examined the fringe of the crowd. An elderly woman in a gold lamé turban sipped vodka from a fluted glass and glanced periodically around the room—security, the turban was armor. A young man watched the dealer with the patience of a veteran. Two women in matching glitter bodysuits whispered to each other and laughed. And there, beside them, a middle-aged man, his mouse-brown hair receding at the temples, stood rapt, following the deal of the cards, licking his lips as the players called their bets.

Chango set her glass down on the bar half drained, stubbed out her smoke and walked towards him at an oblique angle, her body facing the main flow of the traffic, not looking at him, but moving sideways with each step, her body language damped to a minimum, which was almost as good as being invisible, especially in a crowd like this. Each step brought her closer to her mark as he stared with desperate concentration at the winning player. Chango pretended to lean around him for a better view as she slipped her hand into his overcoat pocket and withdrew his wallet. She slipped it into her own pocket, the one with the scanner, her knowing fingers picking the cards out of their slots and swiping them. The codes could be sorted later, one of them was bound to be his cash card. She bumped against him as she went past, using the distraction to slip the wallet back into his pocket. "Sorry." She smiled at him, and moved away. Glancing over her shoulder she saw him check his pockets and smile, relieved at finding his wallet still there, his cards still in it.

She didn't like to do more than one scan per place, so she moved on, to Rhoda's, the Laikon, Trapper's, Parthenomicon. That was where she saw her: a reasonably tall woman in a battered grey raincoat, her dark brown hair short and spikey with rainwater. She glanced about the crowded room with blank alarm. She was scared, but not in a focused way, only in the what-am-I-doing-here, what's-going-on kind of way that made for an easy mark. Chango began to circle in towards her. As she did she noticed that the woman's eyes were a startling shade of blue, her olive skin smooth and even. If she kept up this noticing, she wouldn't be able to make the score. She stopped looking at her and focused instead on the pockets of the raincoat.

Chango moved up beside her and slipped her hand into a pocket, very softly, very slowly, as if she wasn't moving at all. She wrapped her fingers around a slim, smooth square and then bumped into the mark, actually pushing her away from her card. As Chango jostled her, she felt something beneath the raincoat, something long and rounded. She was carrying a shotgun under there.

The last thing Chango wanted to do was mess around with somebody packing heat, for any reason. "Sorry," Chango said, bending over and pretending to pick up the card. "Did you drop this?" she asked, but she got no answer, the woman was through the door before she had a chance to straighten up. "Shit." Chango glanced at the square in her hand. It wasn't a money card. It was a data card. Chango stared at it for a moment, and then she was out the door herself, glancing up and down the street. She caught sight of the woman turning down an alley over a block away, practically running and heedless of the pair of disreputable figures that shadowed her. Chango hastened in their direction, following them as they followed her failed mark.

Helix fled down the street in a blind panic. There were so many people in there, and someone had bumped into her and felt—they had to have felt it. Helix swerved, barely avoiding collision with a heavily made up transvestite. People, so many people. Suddenly she felt as if she'd crawl out of her skin in order to get away from them all.

It was almost night now, the rain-soaked streets glistening into darkness, reflecting the colors of the neon signs like the rainbow oil slicks of old.

Soon, she'd have to find someplace to spend the night. She couldn't just keep walking forever, despite what her inner urging prompted her to do. She sighed, glancing up at the windows of the Old Laikon Hotel. She had no money for a room.

Suddenly Helix was struck with a longing so powerful it stopped her in her tracks. She wanted . . . what? To find her mother? Maybe. It was the only thing she could think of. She wanted something, badly, but her life with Hector Martin had been comfortable, safe. So what else could she be lacking? Only her mother, surely, and yet, just then, all she could really think of was a large tub of warm water.

The thought distracted her and she nearly bumped into a man with orange hair sticking out from under a polyweave cap. He grinned and stepped even closer to her. Panicking, she darted down an alley to her right. The lights and music of the casino district faded into shadows and the distant drip of a leaking gutter. She walked past hulking waste modules, the peppermint smell of garbage-eating microbes seeping from their seals. Ahead of her, leaning in the shadows of a service entrance, was a man, the faint red glow of his cigarette a beacon to his presence. As she approached he stepped away from the crates, flicking his cigarette into oblivion. Behind her, she heard other footsteps.

She walked on stiffly, as if she hadn't noticed there was anyone back there, but they undoubtedly had noticed her, and as she approached the man with the cigarette he called out to her, "Where you going, honey?" She didn't answer, she kept on going, but they were closing in behind her, too.

Finally, after seconds stretched out by the rasp of her breath, her footsteps stuttered to a halt and she turned to see the two who now stood, side by side, in the middle of the alley, blocking her exit. They were lean young men, with old faces and dirty T-shirts. One of them was the guy with red hair she'd nearly collided with earlier. The other one held the glimmering threat of a knife at his side. From behind her, a hand fell on her shoulder. "Hey, lady, you got some spare change?"

"No," she said, and turned halfway to face him. She stepped back, trying to keep all three of them in view.

"No?" the one with the knife queried. "You better be lying."

She shook her head and took another step back, but Red Hair grabbed her arm, twisting it behind her. She gasped at the sudden flash of pain. "I don't—" She paused. "I don't know, let me see."

"Yeah," laughed the one who'd been smoking, "that's more like it. Why don't we see what you've got. I'm sure we can use it, whatever it is."

"My wallet's in the inside pocket," she lied. "Let me open my coat."

"Aw, don't strain yourself, darlin', I'll do it for you," said Cigarette, and he proceeded to slowly unbutton her coat.

Her breath sounded harsh and loud as he worked his fingers over the buttons, undoing them one by one. He was standing close. So much the better, she thought, as she waited for him to finish with the third button, at waist level.

He undid it, and looking up at her, smiled. "I think that's enough, for now anyway."

She smiled back at him, widely, baring her fangs, and shot her lower right fist through the opening of the coat and into his midsection while she stomped on the instep of the assailant behind her with her left foot.

Cigarette doubled over from the force of her blow. "What the fuck?!"

Meanwhile, the grip on her upper right arm had loosened momentarily. It was enough for her to wrench it free, and shrugging her shoulders, she let the coat fall to her feet. She stretched out her four arms, so there could be no mistake, and turned, so she was facing all three of her attackers, revealed for what she was.

Their faces registered shock, but Knife only hesitated for a moment before he was upon her, driving his blade towards her belly. She grabbed his hands in hers and pulled him towards her, forcing his arms up as she kneed him in the groin. He sagged in her arms and she released him, pushing him from her as he fell to the ground, curled into a tight ball of pain.

Red Hair ducked to one side, dived and rolled and with a quick jerk, yanked at the coat still lying around her feet. The next thing she knew she was on the ground, and Cigarette, recovered, rushed up and delivered a vicious kick to her head. Her vision blurred momentarily, and her head sang with pain.

She rolled away as he was winding up for another kick, but Red Hair was there. "I don't know what you are, but you just made a big mistake," and he kicked her too, in the stomach.

More kicks came, sharp punctuations of pain in her ribs, her abdomen, and her head. She rolled onto her back and grabbed somebody's foot with all four of her hands, twisting his ankle and knocking him off balance. In that brief and partial respite she forced herself to her feet. Red Hair closed in again, grabbing for her arms. She let him have the lower two, and with the others grabbed his head, bent it back and with her jaws stretched wide she sank her teeth into the side of his neck. He screamed and something sharp sank into her side. She released Red Hair and turned, snarling, her mouth smeared with blood, to face Knife. His eyes widened with fear and she used his moment of hesitation to smash a fist into his face.

"Fuck," someone was screaming, she wasn't sure who. "Let's go." She heard footsteps running away, caught a glimpse of their backs as the three of them fled, one limping, one bleeding. She was bleeding, too. In fact, she didn't feel well at all, she thought as she sank to the ground.

She didn't pass out, but only lay there, her face against the dirty cloncrete, staring at a trodden gum wrapper. She should get out of there, she thought, but when she tried to move, everything, and especially that bleeding spot low on the left side of her back, hurt. She put her hand to it. It didn't seem very big, to be producing so much blood. She tried to keep a hand over it, pressing, to stop the flow, but she kept forgetting. All of this reminded her of something, some other time when she'd lain, beaten, on the ground. What had she done then? When? On that regrettable day at the orphanage. But Hector had rescued her from that place, and now she'd left him.

Footsteps, just one set, approached slowly. She tried to turn and look, but pain lanced up her spine and she subsided, closing her eyes. Whoever it was would come, search for a wallet or something valuable, and hopefully leave her alone.

The footsteps stopped, and she felt a hand on her upper right arm. "Are you okay?"

"No."

"I'll call an ambulance."

"No!" she shouted, which made her head hurt. "No doctors, please. I'm all right. I'll be fine. I just need to rest a little, okay? Please, please, just leave me alone."

"But you've been stabbed, possibly in the kidney. You need help."

"No. No, I don't need any help. I'm fine." With the remainder of her strength, Helix forced herself up onto her hands and knees, and then, using the wall, dragged herself to a standing position. Pain arced through her body, and she trembled. "See?" she said to the stranger, who she still had not looked at. "I'm fine. I'm leaving now, see? I'm fine." And she took a step and the pain made her gasp, but she kept her footing, for a moment, until dizziness swooped in from the corners of her vision like the black, confused wings of birds, and she fell into the arms of this stranger, who as it turned out, was not very big at all. Staggering under her weight, the stranger slowly returned her to the ground.

"Okay," she said. Helix still hadn't gotten a very good look at her face, just a quick blur of small pointed features and something peculiar about the eyes. "Okay, no doctors. I've got a car. It's not far. I parked it under the overpass on Monroe. I'll go get it, and I'll take you to see someone. Not a doctor, a friend of mine. Hang on." And she took one of Helix's hands, and placed it over the wound in her side. "Keep that there, you don't want to lose any more blood. I'll be right back."

And she was, with a rag which she tied around Helix's waist. "I shouldn't be moving you at all, but I can't get that boat of a car down this alley. Here, give me your arms." She wrapped Helix's right arms around her shoulder, and with her arm around Helix's waist, gently lifted her up to a standing position and steadied her.

"Wait, my raincoat," said Helix.

"Forget it, you can get another one."

"No, no I need it."

"Then I'll come back for it. Now let's go." And together, they spent the most excruciating ten minutes of Helix's life, getting her out of the alley and into the backseat of the stranger's car. A motorcar, a big old convertible with the top down, ancient but still functioning.

Helix stared up at the sky, the night air chill through the fabric of her celluweave bodysuit. "My raincoat!"

The stranger sighed. "Okay, hang on."

She was back again in a moment, and she put the now torn and soiled raincoat over Helix, tucking it in on the sides. "Just as well, you need to keep warm."

The car rumbled to noisy life and started to move. Helix didn't ask her where they were going, she just gazed up at the night sky, at the stars spinning far above her.

3

LAND OF THE GIANTS

SHE was gone. He knew it as soon as he opened the door and saw the bare hook on the wall where he hung his raincoat. Only then did he notice the tomblike silence of the empty apartment. He checked her room to make sure, but found nothing more than comic books and dirty clothes scattered on the floor.

Hector Martin wandered the vacant apartment, picking up objects and staring out the windows. She was out there somewhere, in that maze of buildings and streets, clouded over now with night.

It wasn't like he hadn't expected it to happen. Hell, he'd hoped it would. But he'd let himself forget it. He'd gotten used to her—attached. Ah, he'd always been attached to her, ever since he'd found her.

He flopped down on the couch and switched on his holo-transceiver. He had several messages, announcements of meetings, biotechnical conferences, and one from Nathan Graham, the research and development project manager. He wanted to see Hector in his office tomorrow, to "catch up on developments in the Tetra Project." Catch up, sure, more like to find out why it was six months past due and $100,000 over budget.

Hector sighed and reached for an untidy pile of data cards on the coffee table. Maybe he could snow Graham with enough numbers to hide the truth of what was going on in the lab for a little while longer, but the most he could hope to buy was another six months. Maybe by then it wouldn't matter anymore.

But the data cards were all from several months ago. Graham would never be content with data this old. He clearly wanted to know what was going on now. For the past two months Hector had been recording everything on one encrypted card, and he knew exactly where it was. It was in the pocket of his raincoat.

Laughing, he got up and went into the kitchen, took the bottle down from the cupboard and poured himself a deep, dark drink. He shambled back to the couch with it and sat down.

He took a large sip of the burning liquid and let it sit in his mouth, the vapors penetrating his sinuses. He swallowed it; a trail of fire down his throat to his belly. He leaned back on the couch, the glass cradled in his lap, his eyes glazed over with memories.

He remembered being twenty and engaged to Eva. He was just starting his undergrad program in cellular biology then. They had a warm summer that year, and he and Eva took off one day for Kettle Point. The kettle stones were nearly all gone; the few that remained adorned the front yards of the houses on the road to the beach. Squat, round blobs of stone, their surfaces rippled, they only somewhat resembled ancient, overturned kettles.

Hector parked his automobile by the side of the road and they walked down to the water. The beach was rocky and the water was cold, but about fifty feet from shore there was a large rock with a smooth, flat top to it. They crawled up on that rock, their skin damp and dimpled with gooseflesh, and they warmed themselves in the sun, kissing and touching each other until they were both blind with desire.

"Do you want to go home?" he asked her breathlessly. "Or back to the car?"

"No." Eva shook her blond head, her green eyes sparkling with the sun. "Let's stay here."

She always was the adventurous one, always urging him to do things he thought were unwise, but he hadn't needed too much persuasion that day. The water, the sun, the rock, it was such a primal setting; he remembered thinking, "This is how the world began." He also remembered secretly hoping to impregnate her. He never told her that, of course; he barely admitted it to himself. But it had been, he acknowledged now, the perfect time, the perfect place, to bring forth life.

But Eva hadn't gotten pregnant, and they went on, with school, with marriage, and then divorce. He had nothing to show for his time with her except for memories and a few regrets.

As for bringing forth life, he'd done that, but not in the usual way, and not with Eva. After getting his master's degree in genetic engineering, he'd gone to work for Minds Unlimited, a small research company on the cutting edge of self-aware concurrent processing. By modifying several homeotic genes controlling development of the central nervous system, Hector created the multiprocessor brains—the first and still by far the best of the organic computers.

With processing power, speed, and storage capacities far beyond anything Motorola or Intel could hope to offer for another ten years or more, the multiprocessor brains hit the computing industry like a bombshell.

At that time, companies like GeneSys were already developing biopolymers for industrial use, but no one had made the leap from using biotechnology for industrial applications to incorporating it into consumer products. If he'd been working for a larger company, marketing conservatives probably would have quashed the project. But Minds Unlimited was small and reckless and had little to lose.

As soon as he developed the neurotranslator to interface the bioelectrical circuitry of the brains with regular electrical and fiber optic transmission lines, they threw the brains out into the market like Lot's daughters to the mob. And they were wildly successful, ushering in a new era of consumer biotechnology.

If he'd been working for a company like GeneSys then, none of it would have happened. Someone like Graham would have got in his way. Just like he was doing now, with the Tetra Project.

Deep in his heart of hearts, Hector hated Nathan Graham. He reminded him of every bully he'd ever encountered, from kindergarten on. They were all the same, making themselves strong through the weaknesses of others.

But Graham hadn't been in research when Hector allowed Anna Luria, GeneSys' CEO, to woo him away from Minds Unlimited. She'd made a strong case for his need to branch out into other areas of research, to not be pigeonholed as the inventor of the multiprocessor brains. She'd been right. If he had stayed at Minds Unlimited, all he'd have done was improve on the brains, making them more powerful and efficient. He wouldn't have created anything really new. Besides, he'd liked Anna; her management style, her vision for GeneSys, and he thought he'd like working for the company she ran.

And he had, until four years ago when Graham became the research and development manager. When Graham swaggered in to his first department meeting, Hector knew they were in trouble. Since he'd been the manager, research and development had changed, becoming ever more profit oriented, and less and less given to pure research. He'd always known that someday he'd be at odds with Graham. Now the confrontation was imminent, and all the years Hector had avoided it had done nothing to prepare him.

"Everything is an animal," Nathan's mother told him when he was six, tucking him into bed in their apartment in the Penobscot Building. "A company is an economic animal. They are giants, made up of people, numbers, networks. We do not control them, they control us. The way to thrive in a company is to understand it, sometimes anticipate it; but only a company can control another company."

He remembered her saying all this in a sweet, soft voice while stroking the side of his face and smoothing his hair, soothing him into sleep with tales of giants.

That was when she was still with Reynolds, before the Coke merger, before she lost everything. Before the giants ate her.

Nathan Graham swiveled in his chair and stared out the window of his office. On the twenty-fifth floor and facing south, he commanded a bird's-eye view of the city, spread like a carpet of garbage until Oz reared up, all glass and steel and soaring stonework, the Renaissance Center its spun sugar centerpiece. If he squinted, he could almost see the flying cars.

Saddled with his mother's failure and educated in the public schools, Nathan had to fight his way through the GeneSys corporate structure in order to enjoy this view. He'd started as a temp in the mailroom, it had taken years.

He was glad GeneSys had made their headquarters here, in the old Fisher Building. It was a beautiful building, for one thing, but beyond that, it stood alone on Grand Boulevard, two miles to the north of Oz, its isolation a proper symbol of its power. No matter what those nabobs down there might think, it was GeneSys, and GeneSys alone, that ran this town. And he was watching them, in case they tried to dispute it. He was familiar with the treachery of Oz, he knew better than to turn his back to it.

The voice of his secretary, Jenet, came to him over the transceiver: "Dr. Martin to see you, Mr. Graham."

"Show him in." Nathan scrolled through project files until he found what he wanted; File #98-4302 Tetra.

The door opened and Dr. Martin stood just inside. A small, thin, greying blond mouse of a man, his unease apparent in the flicker of his eyes and in the way his rigid shoulders arched towards his ears.

"Dr. Martin, I'm so glad you could make time for me. Please, sit down. Can I get you anything?" Nathan crossed to the bar and poured cola into a cut-crystal glass.

"No, thank you."

Nathan returned to his desk and took a long pull from his beverage. He set the glass down on a coaster. "So how's the project going?"

"It's coming along." Martin licked his lips and rummaged about in a beaten-up vat-hide briefcase. At length he pulled out a sheaf of mylar. "I've prepared an update for you," he said, placing the report on Nathan's desk with all the prayerful hope of a Catholic offering holographic effigies to the Virgin.

Nathan ignored the report, and opened the Tetra file on his transceiver. A stack of holographic forms materialized on the desk. "I've been going over your budget invoices. There are a few items here I wanted to ask you about." He manipulated the virtual forms, picked one up, left it suspended in the air, and pointed at one of the lines, highlighting it.

"Plants, Weber Brothers Greenhouses, $2506.29," it read. Graham picked up another form and highlighted that one as well. "High-spectrum Halogen Capsules, DeLight, $2153.45."

Martin fidgeted as Graham continued to manipulate the forms until six invoices hung in the air between them. "Finches, Bird-Town, $6034.65; Classical Music (25 items), Harmony House,

$548.73; Li'l Big Tyke Jumping Gym, KiddyLand, $4522.84;
Hindu Religious Art of Late Antiquity, Files 'n' Stuff, $709.38."

Nathan watched Martin swallow. Right about now he was
probably wishing he'd accepted that drink.

Nathan called up a subtotal for the invoices: $16,475.34.

"You'll forgive me if I fail to understand the necessity for these
charges."

Martin's eyes were wide, as if he had never seen these invoices
before, but he didn't try to deny the fact that he'd approved them.
How could he? There was his signature at the bottom of each and
every one, damning him.

"We felt they were necessary," he said faintly, "to create the
proper environment for the project."

"A vat house is the proper environment for the project!" Graham shouted, pounding his fist on the table. It made Martin jump.
"That's the whole point, isn't it?"

Martin blew out his breath. "I wanted to examine responses to
a wide range of stimuli."

"Why? No, never mind. I know, because you were curious. I
suppose that's what we pay you for, but this project is overdue and
over budget already, and you go out and spend over sixteen thousand dollars on toys!"

Martin spread his hands. "I'm sorry, I wasn't thinking of it like
that." He wasn't thinking of it at all, Nathan guessed. His eyes
kept on darting to the invoices, reading over them as if he were trying to discover something.

"Don't get me wrong doctor, I admire you, I really do. But I'm
a businessman, and it's my job to toe the bottom line, and to see to
it that you do the same. You may not be aware of it, but GeneSys
is in business to make money, not play with Tinkertoys."

Martin nodded. "Actually, I am aware of that."

"Good." Graham erased the invoices, watching Martin watch
them disappear.

Despite his obvious genius, Martin had never played the prima
donna, and he didn't now. He probably could have gotten away
with it, even around Graham. If Martin pulled rank, went over his
head, there would be little he could do about it. Anna would never
consent to losing a mind like Martin's.

It made Graham think less of him, that he would entirely neglect capitalizing on his early career. After the brains, he could have formed his own company and made even more money than GeneSys paid him, but no. All he wanted was another problem to think about.

Graham switched to personnel files. "You granted four transfer requests in February, but never requested replacements. That leaves you with just two assistants, doesn't it? Greenfield and um . . . "

"Slatermeyer," said Martin. "I found it more efficient, easier actually, to conduct research with a smaller staff."

"I see. Well, that may help to offset some of these charges. Very forward thinking of you, I might add, to voluntarily downsize your staff. Most researchers wouldn't do that." He folded his hands on the table and leaned over them. "So when can we expect this project to go online?" he asked gently.

"Well, I don't know exactly. These are just prototypes we're working with now. They're not really suitable for a real-life situation."

Graham laughed and shook his head. "Always the perfectionist, eh, Martin? I noticed you've been keeping your project data in private storage, and that's fine, but why don't you let me judge how unsuitable these prototypes of yours are.

"I appreciate you taking the time to make out this report," he gestured towards the stack of mylar. "I know we keep you busy. I'll tell you what. I'll read this, and then pop down in a day or so to see what you've accomplished. You don't mind, do you?"

Martin sat very still, staring at Graham as if he were a poisonous snake ready to strike, and his only hope for survival was to remain immobile, attract no attention, and hope to be ignored. But he would not be ignored, not by Graham, not now. The expenditures, the staff changes, the private data, it added up to something, something that would not, he felt sure, be in the good doctor's report.

"Well, I don't know that that's necessary, really," said Martin, his hands clenching in his lap. "The report I've prepared should fully brief you, and of course if you have any questions—"

"Questions, well. You know, despite being a bean counter," he smiled at Martin's discomfort over the term, "I have always felt that seeing is believing. I know your lab time is precious, but it won't take long, just a quick little tour. You understand, don't you?"

"Yes, I think I do."

"Great, then I'll see you again soon." Nathan stood and walked around the desk to shake hands with Martin. His hand was ice cold. "Thanks for stopping by."

4

FIVE HANDS

SHE woke from a muddle of thoughts and memories; the recollection of movement and darkness, of being carried into a bright kitchen with a yellow Formica table, a babble of voices, someone saying, "She's in shock," and a thin face framed by long black hair, bending over her with bright dark eyes, asking, over and over again, "What's your name?"

Helix opened her eyes and gazed at a pink, water-stained ceiling. She was in a bed, a twin bed with a lumpy mattress, covered neck to toe with a multicolored afghan crocheted out of some strange, nubby yarn. She turned her head. The walls were pink too; poorly fed plaint flaking away like dried skin. On a small table by the bed stood an old ceramic lamp, its shade yellow and fraying. She heard voices, muffled, from a nearby room. Her head hurt, and she shut her eyes.

She woke again to see light streaming in from the window, filtered weakly by sheer, age-faded curtains. There was a soft knock at the door, and it opened.

A face peeked through the door; sharp little nose, sharp chin, like a bright, friendly rodent. Tawny brown hair fell untidily across her forehead. Seeing Helix awake she smiled and came in. She was small but solid, dressed in a white T-shirt, and a purple-and-yellow patterned skirt. She sat in a chair next to the bed and leaned forward. "You're awake," she said.

"Yes."

Her smile widened. "That's good. We were worried."

"You're the one who found me."

"Yeah, my name's Chango." She put out her hand.

Helix withdrew her upper right hand from beneath the afghan and shook with her. "I'm Helix," she said.

"Oh, you know your name. Thank goddess. Last night we couldn't get you to tell us. Mavi says your wound isn't serious. Somehow, the knife missed your kidney. She dressed and bandaged it, and the bleeding seemed to stop, but what she was really worried about was the concussion. See, you went into shock, in the car, and you were more or less unconscious when we brought you in. We couldn't wake you up. You're not supposed to go to sleep if you have a concussion."

"A concussion?"

"Yeah, from when those guys were kicking you. Mavi says you have a cracked rib, too, but there isn't much she can do about that except get you to keep still."

"Mavi?"

"The friend I told you about. She's a healer."

"You, you saw those guys?"

"Yeah, and I'm sorry I didn't get involved, but I'm a shitty fighter, we'd probably both be dead."

"You saw me fighting? And this friend, she saw . . . I—" In a sudden burst of shame Helix realized the obvious. Both of these women had seen her for what she was. Her face burned, tears welled up in her eyes. She wanted desperately to be out of the sight of this sharp-eyed person, this person who had already seen too much. She tried to roll over, but the motion sent a lance of pain through her chest and she gasped, pulled at the afghan, and drew it over her head. The strange, nubby yarn was smooth against her skin and oddly comforting.

"Hey, hey, what are you doing that for? Was it something I said?"

"No," Helix said from her side of the afghan.

"Then what are you hiding for? Are you afraid?"

"Yes."

"Because Mavi and me saw you without that raincoat you were so particular about?"

"Yes."

"Look at me."

"No."

"C'mon, nobody's going to hurt you. Look at me."

Helix felt little hands, tugging firmly at the edge of the afghan. She swallowed, and allowed it to be drawn back from her face again. She looked up to see Chango peering closely at her with those strange eyes of hers, and suddenly she realized why they were strange. They were two different colors. One blue, the other green.

Chango nodded, acknowledging her realization. "That's right. I'm one too." She leaned back and released the afghan, but Helix didn't draw it back. "I know this," she waved at her eyes, "doesn't seem like a very big deal to you. But it's enough to give me a label for the rest of my life. Believe me, I've been through lots of pairs of sunglasses."

Helix lay there, staring. She didn't know what to do; she just remained motionless. Finally she said, "I've never met anyone else who was . . . "

"Oh," Chango said quietly, steadily holding her gaze, "that must be weird—to be the only one. I'm lucky I guess. I grew up here, where there's still a few of us to this day. People still treat us differently, but we don't come as a big surprise to anyone."

"Until yesterday, I hadn't been seen by anybody but my father for ten years," said Helix. She didn't know why she said it, it just came out.

Chango took her turn at staring, her mouth hanging open. Silently she mouthed the words, "Ten years?" Then out loud she said, "Goddamn, that's terrible. Shit, no wonder you freaked out." She paced the floor anxiously, glancing quickly back and forth between Helix and the floor.

"Your father . . . he hid you."

"No, not really. He let me hide. I went out from time to time, but always with the raincoat." She tilted her head in some vague indication of the direction in which it might be. "Actually it's his."

"It's his raincoat," Chango repeated, and then shook her head. "Wow, so you just hid out for ten years. Why?"

"Before I went to live with Hector, I was in an orphanage. I was the only sport there, too. It wasn't exactly a good place to be saddled with uniqueness."

Chango drifted back to the chair and sat down. "Yeah." She nodded her head. "Kids suck."

"It was really bad. I remember one year when there wasn't a single day that I didn't wish I were somebody else. That was the last year. Then Hector came along and rescued me, and I guess I just didn't want anything like that to happen to me again." She shook her head. "I can't stand that look. You know that look?"

"Yeah, I know that look. So what happened? How did you wind up where I found you?"

Helix shrugged. "I just left. I felt . . . I don't know, like there was something out there that was meant for me, and I'd never have it unless I left."

"Wow, that's amazing. What an incredible story." Chango fished a pack of reefer cigarettes out of her T-shirt pocket and offered them to Helix.

"No thanks."

Chango took out a cigarette, lit it, and smoked in silence for a few minutes. The smoke made her squint, and Helix thought she could see her the way she would be years from now, an old woman, smoking and thinking. "So how long ago was this?" she asked at length.

"Yesterday. I just left the GeneSys Building, that's where I lived, and started walking around. I ended up in Greektown, I was in this casino. There were people everywhere, and I was starting to panic. Then someone bumped into me. I didn't even see them, but I felt them touch my arm, my lower arm. I just took off, and then I wound up down this alley, and that was when those guys attacked me."

"Welcome to the outside world." Chango laughed harshly. "But then I found you. Out of all the people around there who could have found you, it was another sport. Maybe somebody watches out for us after all."

"Maybe. At any rate, I can thank you for getting involved. I think I would have died out there if you hadn't done something."

"Oh, probably not died."

"Maybe not then. Soon enough, I'll bet."

Chango shrugged and looked at her wordlessly.

"Shit, what am I going to do?" Helix suddenly raised her upper hands to the sides of her head. She'd tried going out, and it had nearly killed her. She didn't have a job, or any prospects of one. Her only friend was a total stranger. What had she been thinking, that she could do this?

But every time she thought about going back, that hand reached up from her gut and pushed her back out again.

"You're going to stay put for a couple of days and let your ribs heal and your head return to its normal size and shape," said a voice from the doorway. A tall figure in a long black dress stood there, her thin face nearly hidden by the unruly strands of her black hair. She walked across the room with understated grace and stood at the foot of the bed. She wore a silver amulet, a five-pointed star inside a circle. She had a long and rather prominent nose which shouldered the main burden of pushing aside her hair. She made an imposing figure there, a long black line parted by a pale slice of face.

Then her hand swept up and pushed back her hair, to reveal a pair of eyes that were warm and deep, and strong lips spread in a smile. "Glad to see you're up; how are you feeling?"

"Better." In spite of herself, Helix slid farther down beneath the covers of the bed.

"This is Mavi," said Chango. "She took care of you last night."

"Thank you." Helix nodded at her awkwardly.

"No problem." Mavi hiked up one bare foot and sat on the edge of the bed.

"Her name is Helix," said Chango.

"Let me take a look at your head, Helix." Mavi moved around the side of the bed and bent over her. Her pendant swung above Helix's eyes as her long, cool fingers probed her skull.

"Ow," said Helix, reflexively jerking her head as Mavi's fingers found the lump on the side of her head. The pendant banged her in the forehead.

"Sorry," murmured Mavi as she gently probed the lump. "The swelling is down some, but it'll be sore for a while.

"She's been speaking coherently?" she asked Chango over her shoulder.

"Oh, yeah. Complex sentences and everything, Mavi."

"Good." Mavi straightened up, nodding her head. "That was the worst of your injuries, actually," she said to Helix. "The ribs will be all right if you just lie still for several days. But I do need to look at your knife wound." She looked at Chango, who was still sitting in the chair, picking at a thread on her skirt.

Chango looked up suddenly. "Oh, you want me to leave." She glanced over to Helix. "You want me to leave?"

Helix looked from Chango to Mavi and back again. If she had her druthers, she'd be the one to leave, but her earlier attempt at rolling over ruled that out. "I guess so," she said reluctantly.

"I couldn't really bandage your ribs," said Mavi after Chango left, "so we just have to do this carefully. Gently she helped Helix roll over.

Despite the pain of moving, Helix was glad to have her face down against the mattress. She didn't have to face Mavi as she pulled back the bed covers to examine the wound in her back. "I have to change the dressing," said Mavi, moving across the room. Helix heard a drawer open and close, and then she felt the cold blade of a scissors against her skin, felt the bandages lifted, and something cool and soothing applied to her wound. "I have you closed up with cellular tape. It seems to be healing clean." She heard the tearing of paper, and then Mavi reapplied bandages and helped her onto her back again, and not once, during any of it, did she say anything about a second pair of arms.

Chango walked up the rickety steps of Hyper's house and leaned against the screen door, shading her eyes with one hand so she could see inside. Squinting, she surveyed the dim interior of the first floor.

Hyper had gutted the place after his folks died, knocking down walls and taking out the front two-thirds of the upstairs, leaving only a small room above the kitchen where he slept—when he slept.

Four metal tables stood bolted to the floor where the dining room had been, heaped with machine and electrical parts. The front part of the house was a maze of books, magazines, and holocubes. And above it all hung the archives of Hyper's past interests. He'd laid steel girders across the rafters, and every time he completed or tired of a project, up it went. Old model airplanes and boats spun lazily in the occasional breeze, along with automated kites, walker robots, rebuilt text processors, and a chemistry set.

"Hey, you home?" she called, her lips brushing against the rusting screen.

Hyper looked up from behind an enormous old cathode ray monitor squatting on the floor by the front windows. He had gutted it and was now putting it back together. His brick-brown skin glowed with perspiration. It wasn't all that warm a day, but Hyper always ran hot. "Chango, c'mon in sister dear, check this out." He waved her in with one hand as he worked an electric screwdriver with the other.

She slid in the door and locked it behind her. "You shouldn't leave your door open," she said.

"Oh, I forgot. C'mere." He gestured for her to sit beside him on the floor. His skinny legs stuck out from paisley boxer shorts that were too big for him. His long toes splayed among screws and transistor chips. The shorts and a faded, stained T-shirt were all he wore except for a head-mounted holotransceiver perched atop his skull like a small black brain parasite, secured by a thin band across his forehead and over his ears. The imaging lens which hung down over his right eye reflected a miniature circuit diagram. To Hyper, it would appear larger, hanging in the air two feet in front of his face. His eyes darted from it to the tube while his fingers sorted feverishly through chips and wires.

"Can you hand me those scissors?" he asked, nodding to the graphite shears by her knee as he uncoiled a length of fiber cable.

"What are you doing?" she asked, handing him the shears.

"If I install an optical receiver in this thing and connect that to a quad board I can program it to display raw visuals in real time. I want to mount it on that go-cart chassis over there, give it infrared and motion sensors and let it follow people around and imitate them. Robo-Mime."

"God, what a pain in the ass," said Chango.

Hyper glanced at her, grinning. "Love those nuisance machines," he said. He fastened a connector clamp onto the end of the fiber cable and turned to face her. "So, how'd it go?" he asked. "I missed you last night at Josa's."

Chango shrugged. "There were complications." She handed him the swiper containing the codes she'd scanned the day before.

Hyper's dark brown eyes widened. "Complications? But you weren't arrested."

"No, not those kinds of complications. At least not yet. I scanned this woman, I thought she was armed." Chango laughed weakly. "When I tried to give her back her card, she bolted. I followed her, and she got jumped in an alley. Turns out she's a sport. She was hurt pretty bad, so I took her to Mavi's."

"You got pretty involved with a failed mark, didn't you?" Hyper said softly, his gaze upon the circuit map only he could see.

"Hyper, she was really hurt. One of her assailants had a knife. What was I supposed to do, leave her to die?"

"Why did you follow her in the first place?"

Chango shrugged, searching for an answer. "When I bumped her, and then tried to give her card back, she freaked. She ran, scared! I was . . . curious."

"You said she was packin'. She shoot any of those guys?"

"No, she wasn't. I thought she had a shotgun, but it wasn't—it was one of her arms. She's got four."

Hyper whistled. "Functional?"

"Yeah! Fully developed, fully functional."

"Wow, impressive."

"See? I couldn't let the sister die."

"Yeah, I guess I can see that. You give her card back, then, or what?"

"No, I didn't." Chango reached into her pocket and pulled out the plastic square. "But get this—" she handed it to Hyper "—it isn't even a cash card. It's data."

Hyper glanced at it. "What's its encryption signature?"

"I don't know. It's nothing I've ever seen before."

"Hmm." He flipped it between his fingers thoughtfully and held it up to the light. A faint pattern glimmered on its surface, and then, as he tilted it just right, bloomed into a hologram. Spiraling curves of burning, electric green wrapping around one another, just discernible as an *S* enfolded within a stylized *G*. GeneSys.

Hyper glanced at her, one eyebrow cocked. "Mind if I keep this and look at it later, when I'm done with Robo-Mime?" he asked.

"I don't know, what if she wants it back?"

"Then I'll give it back."

Chango shrugged. "Okay, I guess."

Chango nudged Mavi's screen door open with one toe and slid through, dumping the hemp fiber grocery bags on the kitchen table.

Mavi was at the stove, whispering over a simmering saucepan. The roiling steam perfumed the kitchen with sage and goldenseal. Her words faded, and she looked over to see Chango. "You bought groceries."

"Yep." Chango reached inside one of the sacks and drew out a package of spaghetti. "Pasta à la me," she said with a flourish of the box. She drew out three eggs and juggled them.

"Ladies and gentlemen, she cooks, she climbs, she produces groceries out of thin air, she's Changini the miraculous." Mavi pawed through the bags. "How did you get all this stuff?"

Chango took a bowl down from the shelf over the sink and cracked the eggs into it. "Through the idleness of fools."

"So that's what you were doing in Greektown last night," said Mavi, returning to her mixture on the stove.

"What else?"

"Oh, I don't know, showgirls, maybe?"

Chango snorted, stirring the eggs with a fork. "What would give you that idea?"

"Your friend."

She laughed. "Oh no. No. A dancing girl afraid to show her body? I think not. Mavi, you've got to get out more."

"Then how did you happen upon her?"

Chango shrugged uncomfortably and began beating the eggs with a fork. "Actually, I'd been following her."

"Following her? But she's not a showgirl."

"Would you stop? Jeez, I can't perform an act of good samaritanism without you trying to turn it into some tawdry little scenario."

"I know you, Chango. Why were you following her?"

"When I tapped her for her cash card, she freaked out and ran. I was curious. There was something about the way she looked. She was terrified. Now I know why. She told me she hasn't let anyone but her father see what she is for the past ten years."

"Oh my goddess, that's . . . that's weird."

"Yeah. If she goes out, she wears the raincoat. I guess I brushed against her arm when I tapped her, she felt it. She thought I knew."

"Does she know you followed her?"

"No, apparently not."

"Then I take it you haven't returned her cash card," said Mavi, pouring her tincture into a jar.

"Well, that's a bit awkward, isn't it?" Chango put the dripping fork in the sink. " 'Oh yes, I'm glad I could help you, and by the way, here's something I stole from you.' No, besides, it isn't a cash card. It's data, from GeneSys."

Amber-tinted liquid spilled on the stove. Mavi set the pan down and looked at her. "GeneSys?"

"Yeah, but I don't think it's hers."

That night Chango brought her spaghetti in bed. Helix sat up, bolstered by pillows. She kept her lower hands under the afghan, balancing her plate with them and wielding a spoon and fork with her upper hands. Chango sat cross-legged at the other end of the bed, holding her plate in her lap.

"So, do you live here?" asked Helix around a mouthful of food.

"Not really." Chango shrugged. "Sort of. I stay here a lot, and sometimes I sleep in my car, or at another friend's house."

"Oh." Helix nodded, trying to think of something else to say. "So how did you find me?" she asked.

Chango stopped chewing and stared at her. "I followed you."

"Followed me?"

"Yeah, you're going to find out about it soon enough anyway. No one around here can keep their mouth shut. I followed you from the casino because I'd been—I'd been trying to scan you."

"Scan me?"

"Yeah, you know, rip off the code for your cash card. Brokers pay good money for those codes."

"Oh. But I don't have a cash card."

"Yeah, I know now, but I didn't then. When I tried to flush you for your uh, wallet, I brushed one of your arms, one of the lower ones, remember?"

Helix remembered going inside the casino to get out of the rain, and then being overwhelmed by the crowd. She remembered the touch against her arm that had frightened her, and then that sharp little face, saying something to her as she fled.

"It was you," she said. "You're the one who touched me."

"Yeah, and you freaked out. It made me curious, so I followed you." Chango was watching her anxiously, as if she feared her reaction to this news.

"So I owe my life to the fact that you tried to rip me off, huh?" Helix smiled. "Thanks."

Chango laughed with relief. "I'm glad you're not mad."

Helix shrugged. "It's not like you knew me or anything."

Chango pursed her lips. "Do you play cards?"

"What?"

"This kind." Chango brandished a deck of playing cards. "Gin, hearts, poker? No?"

Helix shook her head.

"Then you're going to have to learn. You can't be laid up in bed for days on end without at least learning gin rummy."

About halfway through their third hand, Helix brought her lower hands out from under the afghan and started holding her cards in them.

It felt like something that was wrapped very tightly around her heart was starting to unwind. She couldn't help it—she kept staring at Chango's eyes, one blue, one green. They were the visible proof. She wasn't alone.

She liked Hector, she'd been grateful to him, but she'd never felt this comfortable with him. There'd always been some unbreachable distance between them. Each knew the other was different, and somehow she'd always felt he was watching her from the other side of a polyglass window.

Chango discarded the eight of clubs. Helix picked it up with her upper right hand, and lay down the rest of the set with her upper left. She looked to see Chango looking, and their eyes met, and they smiled at each other.

"You've got five hands," said Chango. Helix looked down at the cards she held and laughed, which made her wince.

Chango stepped out into the cool night air, her ancient jean jacket clammy against the gooseflesh on her arms. Helix had gone to sleep, and she was restless. She left the Chevy where it was, parked by the curb in front of the house, and walked to Josa's.

Hyper and Magoo and Pele were hanging around outside the bar. "Hey, what's going on?" she said, joining them.

"Not much," said Hyper, "same old, same old."

"Hey, I heard you've got a houseguest over at Mavi's," said Pele.

"Yeah." Chango glared at Hyper, who shot Pele a look.

"She's got four arms," continued Pele, oblivious or, more likely, unconcerned. "Is she cute?"

"Yeah," Chango admitted, "she's fucking gorgeous."

"Oh, so it wasn't pure altruism, eh?" said Magoo.

"I saw her, she needed help, I helped. Why is everyone trying to twist this around into some sort of bizarre pickup scenario?" she protested.

"Well, you did follow her," said Hyper.

"Oh, oh thanks a lot, buddy."

"You followed her?" said Magoo. "I didn't know that. It doesn't look good for you, Chango."

"Screw you, pink boy."

"Not lately," he said loftily.

"Oh, girl," Pele told him.

"Anyway, you guys have to meet her. You know, she's never met any other sports before."

"Really?" said Pele.

"Well, think about it, she was in this orphanage, where she was the only sport there, and then she got adopted," she looked at Hyper, "by this guy that works for GeneSys. She hasn't been out of the Fisher Building for ten years."

"Ouch, maybe getting knifed in an alley was a good thing for her," said Magoo.

"Well, I wouldn't go that far, but at least now she'll get to know some of her own people."

It was only ten, but Josa's was already crowded with divers off shift for their weekend. The four of them snaked their way through the crowd to the bar. It was still Josa back there, pouring and polishing as she had for the past twenty years.

Chango leaned over the bar with a mylar bill rolled up in her hand. "Josa, a round for me and my friends here; draft."

Josa cast one jaundiced eye in her direction, took the bill, and grunted when she unrolled it. "Four drafts," she said briskly, and went off to pour them.

"Oh look," said Pele, "there's Monkey with Oli. I heard he took Jan's mother's china with him when he left."

"Yeah, but that was after Jan threw his couch out of the window of their third-floor apartment."

Hyper laughed. "Coral told me she saw it go down. Jan had been screaming all morning about throwing that couch out of the window, so by the time it finally happened, there was a little crowd outside, waiting. Can you imagine? That lime-green velour atrocity tumbling through the air and then splat, like a huge upholstered bug."

"That's entertainment," said Magoo.

Chango spotted a lean figure with short dark hair and sideburns coming in the door. "Hey, Benny!" she shouted, waving him over.

"Hey, what's going on?" said Benny, slapping her on the shoulder. "I heard you have a houseguest," he said.

"She's from GeneSys," offered Pele.

His eyebrows went up, "GeneSys?"

"She is not, Pele," said Chango, and then to Benny, "She's not."

"Well, you said her father worked for them," Pele noted.

"That's not the same thing is it? Besides, I was speculating." She looked at Benny again, "She's a sport."

"Oh, yeah, that's what I heard."

"What did you do, Hyper," Chango turned on him, "broadcast it?"

"No," he protested, "I didn't know it was supposed to be a secret, that's all."

"Yeah, I mean, what's the big deal?" said Pele.

"I guess," she said warily, "it's just that she's understandably timid around people, Benny, and when she finally comes out of Mavi's house, I don't want people staring and talking about her."

"C'mon, Chango," Benny said, "this is Vattown, everyone stares, and everyone talks about everyone else."

"Yeah, but she doesn't know that."

"Then she'll have a chance to find out."

"C'mon Benny, at least let her get her bearings. Be cool when I bring her around. No sport jokes, okay? And see if you can't get Vonda and Coral to be a little less their usual selves."

"Oh, you don't ask for much."

"You know you can influence them, if you want to."

Benny raked his hands through his thick hair. "But at what cost?" he cried, looking beseechingly at the ceiling.

"Benny." A young woman with straight brown hair falling to her shoulders walked up to him. Her eyes darted over to Chango for an instant, and then flickered away with a dismissive toss of her head. "Orielle's coming later tonight. Want to go in on a liter?"

"Sure, Vonda," he said. "Mind if I pay you Monday?"

"Yeah, I can cover it until then. Hey, did you see next month's production run? They had it posted this afternoon. They must be crazy if they think we're gonna get all that fiber grown with just the people we have now."

"Overtime," said Benny.

Vonda made a face. "How much overtime do they expect us to work?"

"Hey, it's time and a half."

"Yeah, it's also prolonged exposure." During the course of the conversation, she had slowly turned so that her back was to Chango, who still sat there, staring at her. "Hey, there's Val, c'mon, he'll buy us drafts." She took Benny by the arm and they drifted away. Chango watched them disappear into the crowd, and then she turned around, resting her elbows on the bar.

"Shit," said Hyper, "I can't believe you guys still aren't talking, after all this time."

"What do we have to talk about?" asked Chango, and she drank her beer.

"You used to be best friends."

"Yeah, well, things change, don't they?"

"You don't still seriously believe she falsified Ada's tests, do you?"

Chango shrugged and shook her head. "Not really. I don't know. I know Ada didn't dive blasted, that's all." She drank her glass empty, set it back down on the bar, and left.

For three days Helix sat in "the pink room," as Mavi and Chango called it. She would have been bored out of her mind if it weren't for Chango, who remained at her bedside most of the time, playing cards with her and regaling her with stories of the comings and goings of Vattown.

"I saw Hugo today," Chango said, shuffling the cards. "He lives with Benny, an old friend of my sister's. She and Benny and

Hugo were in a dive team together years ago. Now Hugo has vat-sickness. He's been off work for months. Benny and Hugo are lovers, or at least they were. I don't think Hugo is up for much but lying in bed nowadays. Mavi sent me over there with some morphine for him. That's about all he consumes now, morphine and water, maybe a little soup. But today he was having a good day. He was sitting up, and we watched soap operas on the holonet, the interactive ones. I asked him if he'd like to play a character, but he just wanted to watch."

Helix looked up at the mention of soaps. "Did you see *We Are the World?*"

Chango wrinkled her brow. "Is that the one where the two power bitches are fighting it out over this woman whose husband died?"

"That's it. My character—I mean Natasha, that's the one I like to play—she's going on trial for murdering the husband. Did you see her? What happened? Have they set the date for the trial yet?"

Chango shook her head. "Wow, you're really a freak for that show, aren't you? We only caught the end of it. Something about a couple stranded on an island in the South Pacific."

"Carmen and Peter. They're boring."

"Hugo likes *Tears of Joy.*"

Helix made a face.

"Hey, I think they're all stupid. I mean they may have all those fancy settings and stuff, but as far as pure drama goes, they can't hold a candle to what goes on around here. Why just last week Coral found out that her boyfriend Val was sleeping with her best friend Yolanda. She caught them at it when she went to Yolanda's house to drop off some Blast for her. She was mad at first—she kept the Blast—but now they're thinking of making it a threesome."

Helix raised her eyebrows. "I guess you have a point."

"You bet. Don't worry, pretty soon Mavi will let you out of bed, and you can meet some of these people. It must be really boring for you, stuck in here all day and night."

"Yes," Helix admitted. "But maybe it's just as well. I'm not sure I want to meet anyone."

"Oh, come on. You can't stay in here forever."

That was true. She hadn't really thought about what would

happen when Mavi let her out of here. She thought of Night Hag, who had said almost the same thing to her the day she left Hector's. "Do you think you could borrow a transceiver from somebody? I have a friend on the holonet. I'd like to contact her."

"Oh," Chango said, surprised. "Well, the only people I know who have a transceiver are Benny and Hyper. Benny would lend you his, but Hugo uses it, and I wouldn't want to ask. Hyper . . . well he uses his constantly, but I'll make a strong case for you. Maybe if it's just for an hour or so."

"She always takes my calls. It wouldn't take long."

"I'll try."

The following afternoon, Chango came into the pink room with a self-satisfied smile and something hidden behind her back. "Catch," she said, tossing a headset transceiver at her.

It landed on the bed, and Helix picked it up. "Thanks. Did you have trouble getting it?"

"No, but he made me promise that when you get out of bed, he'd be the first person to meet you."

"Oh."

"Don't worry. You'll like Hyper. He's a sport, like us, and he makes a lot of cool things." Chango handed her the wrist keypad that went with the headset and stood with her arms at her sides, seemingly at a loss. "I guess I'd better leave you alone, so you can call your friend."

"Thanks."

"I promised Hyper I'd have it back to him tonight."

"That's okay."

Chango left, and Helix placed the transceiver on her head, pulled the imaging lens down over her right eye, and dialed Night Hag's number.

"Helix! Where have you been? You haven't been answering my messages," said Night Hag, still using the construct she'd had the last time they talked. Hyper had the transceiver set to visuals, and in her haste, Helix had forgotten to check it. She was sitting up in bed, and had made no attempt to cover up her arms. It was just as well, she thought, she was going to have to start letting people see her.

But Night Hag didn't pay much mind to her appearance. Instead she peered at the peeling walls behind her. "Where are you?"

"That's why I called. After the last time we talked, I left Hector's apartment. I'm in Vattown now."

"Where they make the biopoly. Good. That's good. Have you found a job yet?"

"Not yet. I—I ran into some trouble. Some men tried to rob me. There was a fight. I got injured."

Suddenly Night Hag's eyes focused on her. "Are you all right? How badly were you hurt?"

"I'm okay, still pretty sore, but okay. I had a concussion, some cracked ribs, and a knife wound."

"Who did that to you?" she asked sharply, as if she would kill whoever it was, as if she could.

"I don't know. Just some guys, I guess."

Night Hag stared at her. "You don't know them?"

"No! I was just walking and . . . "

She took a deep breath and nodded. "You're all right now."

"Yes. I—someone found me. Her name is Chango. She's a sport like me. She saved my life. She brought me here to her friend's house. They're taking care of me."

"That's good." She paused, and then added, "Those men that attacked you? Did you fight them?"

"Oh yeah. There were three of them, but one I bit pretty bad, in the neck," she said, and pointed at her teeth, still surprised that Night Hag had made no mention of her appearance.

"I'm glad," said her friend. "People shouldn't want to hurt you. But for some reason, sometimes they do. When it happens, you must fight them."

Helix didn't know what to say to this. "At least I'm with friends now," she said at length.

"And I'm proud of you for leaving Hector. It couldn't have been easy for you. Just don't think that because you were attacked, you made a mistake. There was nothing for you in that apartment."

"Except my transceiver, and Hector's money. I didn't take anything with me when I left."

Night Hag waved one hand dismissively. "Things. Things you can buy after you find work. Are you going to be a vatdiver?"

"I don't know." Helix shrugged. "I hadn't thought about it, but I'm going to need some kind of job."

"Maybe your friends can help you."

"Maybe. But jobs are hard to find, and they've already done a lot. Chango borrowed this transceiver from a friend of hers, so I could call you."

"Everybody doesn't have a transceiver?" Night Hag looked genuinely shocked.

Helix laughed at her naivete. Night Hag had always been the wise one, the experienced one. "No. Everyone does not have a transceiver."

5

WRONGED BY GOD

NATHAN Graham walked to the elevators, suncells in fan-shaped wall sconces brightening at his approach, signaled by his tread on the bioweave carpeting. It had taken research and development years to come up with a bacteria that would put forth a spectrum of light even approaching sunshine. These were the latest achievement, and their bright warm light was gradually spreading through the consumer market, edging out incandescent and fluorescent bulbs.

The elevator doors were covered in etched brass, a holdover from the original decor. Much of the building had been remodeled repeatedly in order to showcase the latest developments in GeneSys materials, but they saved these—oriental etchings of birds and flowers intermixed with geometric designs—and the murals on the first floor.

The doors parted and he stepped inside. "Good morning, Mr. Graham," said the elevator, and Graham rode it down to the tenth floor. In the lobby of the research and development department he asked a vending machine for an apple juice and swiped his card through the pay slot. He downed the juice in one long gulp, and tossed the little can into the welcoming mouth of a motion sensitive trash canister.

Martin's lab was a large, white-tiled affair, strewn with instruments. Martin and his two remaining lab assistants were there: Slatermeyer, a tall, anemic-looking fellow with sandy, badly cut hair, and Greenfield, shorter and stockier, his dark hair receding at his temples. They looked at him like a trio of startled rabbits.

Graham walked along the counter-lined perimeter of the room, glancing at this instrument and that. Everything was gleamingly spotless. Graham had no doubt that Martin had spent the better part of the week preparing for this visit. He had probably also rid the lab of anything he really wanted to see.

"The biopolymer being produced in test vats shows some remarkable properties," said Martin. "Look at these electron holomicrographs." He walked to the holomicroscope. In its viewing platform rested a shallow pan containing a vibrant blue strip of biopoly. He fiddled with the dials of the scope until a three-dimensional holographic schema of the biopoly's cellular matrix appeared in the air: vivid green, yellow, and blue shapes representing mitochondria, endoplasmic reticulum, and secretory granules.

"It's an aromatic amino acid with a fullerian side group—a buckyball with trapped silver ions," said Martin enthusiastically. "It's extremely versatile and has a high rate of synthesis."

"What?"

"It grows fast," said Slatermeyer.

Was that all? Graham rolled his eyes and shook his head.

"And that's not all," interjected Greenfield. "Because of the trapped silver ions, it conducts electricity very efficiently, making it quite suitable for a range of applications where other biopolys have been ruled out."

Hector walked over to the biostat cabinet and took out a tray. "Here, feel it." He lifted out a handful of the stuff and held it out to him.

Gingerly, reluctantly, Graham took the stuff in his hands. It was faintly warm, smelled yeasty, and felt smooth, but what struck him most about the stuff was its color: a bright, deep blue that almost seemed to glow. It had a power of its own, that color. It was the color blood would be, if blood were blue, and there was something at once beautiful and repellant about it.

Graham handed it back to Hector. "Well," he said, clapping his hands together, "what say you show me the vats where this miracle material is being produced."

Hector glanced at his two assistants, and then back to Graham. "I'm afraid that's impossible."

"Impossible? Nonsense, I want to see the vats now. All this lab business is very well, but you must admit, it's a bit off goal for the project. Remember the project? It wasn't to make new biopolys. It was to cut labor costs. Now take me to those vats."

"We can't," said Hector. "We're in the middle of an isolation study. Any interference now would put the project back months."

"An isolation study? What for?"

"To determine the long-range impact on productivity."

Graham gritted his teeth. "When will the test be finished?" he asked.

Martin hesitated. Graham could see him thinking it through before he answered, "By the end of the month."

"The end of the month. And you're absolutely sure it's necessary."

"Oh yes, if we're going to provide you with any figures at all concerning long-term production levels."

Graham nodded. That was exactly the data Martin's report had lacked. He didn't trust him, didn't believe him, but to interfere directly with Martin's research at this stage would only antagonize him. He didn't want Martin going to Anna, telling her that he, Nathan Graham, wouldn't let him do his job. Especially since he had worked so hard to rid himself of his reputation as a heavy operator, a legacy from his production days.

"Very well, Dr. Martin." Graham glanced at his watch. "I'd like to discuss the project with you in further detail, but I have a dinner appointment at the club this evening. Perhaps we can do lunch, tomorrow?" Intense and prolonged attention might cause Martin to disclose whatever it was he was hiding, just to get Graham off his back.

"Lunch? Um, sure."

* * *

Hector threw himself into the back of his maglev and sank into the soft, butter-colored vat-hide cushions which ringed the ovoid riding parlor. He activated the navigation system, and it showed him a holographic list of frequent destinations. He closed the list and called up an area map, keying in the route to his sister's house by hand. The levcar emerged from the parking garage and took a left onto Grand River, heading east towards the I-88 levway. He dialed the stereo for Vivaldi and set the retinal glass of the cabin's windows to transparent.

The traffic was heavy but well behaved. Levcars wove amongst one another seamlessly, guided by the surface of the road. Despite the beauty of the day, the tranquil music, and the lush strands of trees gliding by on the banks of the levway, Hector could not relax. Graham's visit to the lab that morning had left him deeply uneasy. Graham had accepted the excuse about the isolation study, for the moment, but sooner or later he would uncover the truth about the project, and Hector couldn't even bring himself to think about what would happen then.

He had tried calling Lilith, but as usual she would not take his call. Lilith—she was named for the first woman, the one God made along with Adam, before Eve. Created equal to Adam, she demanded equal treatment, and became a demon in the eyes of the religion Hector was born into. A religion he turned to now, despite its faults, for the reassurance of the familiar rituals of the Sabbath.

Bloomfield Hills was a forest of oaks and demi-elms, riddled with small maglev lanes that wove like twisting streams around the ample yards of the houses. Many of the homes here were in the late eco style, barely discernible from the hills and fields surrounding them. His sister's place was one of these, three-quarters underground and surrounded by terraced gardens.

The driveway cut into the hillside. The maglev parked itself, and Hector reached into his suit pocket and took out his yarmulke. It had been given to him by his father at his bar mitzvah. The once-sumptuous blue velvet had faded and taken on a silvery sheen, much like his hair, but the feel of the worn fabric as he slipped it over his bald spot recalled to him the awkwardness of puberty and his nervousness at standing before his family's congregation to read from the Torah.

Setting the memory aside, Hector got out of the maglev and climbed the flagstone steps to the doorway of his sister's house. Recessed in an alcove and overshadowed by the low-hanging roof, the entrance was virtually invisible from the road. He raised his hand to the knockpad, but the door opened before he could strike it.

"Hector, bubulah!" His sister Cerise greeted him with outstretched arms. Hector paused on the threshold to kiss the mezuzah, and entered her welcoming embrace. "Come in, come in," she said, drawing him down the hallway. "I'm so glad you could break away from your busy schedule to visit us."

The roof over the living room was dotted with colored glass tiles which painted the floor and walls with a kaleidoscope of light. Cerise's husband, Paul, was there, and their children, Rachel and Naomi. Cerise brought a tray of vegetables and walnut dip from the kitchen and set it down on the coffee table. "So, Hector," she said, "what's new with you?"

"Oh nothing much," he lied, "working hard, as usual."

Cerise shook her head. "Working, that's all? There aren't any nice middle-aged ladies at GeneSys to go to the movies with or take out to dinner?"

Hector shrugged, "I suppose there are, but—"

"But what? What does a woman have to do to get your attention? Split an atom?"

"Cerise." Paul gave her a warning glance. "And she wonders why you hardly ever visit," he said to Hector. "Would you like a whiskey?"

"Thanks, with soda, please," he said.

The girls showed him the holo pictures they'd been painting, and Cerise told him of the latest happenings at her job at Detroit Edison. "There's a very nice woman in the finance department. She's about your age, Hector, and she's single too. Her name is Ilene, and she's always reading *Scientific American*. I'm sure you two would hit it off. If you'd like me to set something up . . . "

"Cerise." Paul lifted his eyes to the kaleidoscope ceiling, which was growing dim in the fading light. Cerise smiled. "It's time to light the candles."

They went into the dining room, where the sabbath candles stood waiting on the sideboard beside the wine, the kiddush cups, and the challah bread. Cerise lit the candles, covered her eyes, and recited the blessing. "Baruch Atah Adonai Elohanu Melech ha'olam asher kidshanu bemitzvotav vetzivanu lehedlikner shel Shabbat."

Hector's Hebrew was rusty, but he had no difficulty remembering the meaning of those words. "Blessed are You, O Lord our God, source of the universe, who has sanctified us by Your commandments and commanded us to kindle the Sabbath lights."

Paul said the kiddush blessing over the wine, and poured a cup for each of the adults, and smaller portions for the girls. They drank, and then Paul lifted the white cloth covering the challah, and recited the berachah, "Blessed are You, O Lord our God, source of the universe, who causes bread to come forth from the earth." Each of them grabbed ahold of the braided loaf, pulled a piece off, and ate it.

Paul and Cerise then turned to their daughters, "May God make you as Sarah, Rebecca, Rachel, and Leah. May the Lord bless you and care for you. May the Lord cause the light of His countenance to shine upon you and be gracious unto you. May the Lord lift up His countenance upon you and give you peace," they prayed.

Hector prayed too, though silently and not to God. He prayed to one who he knew would answer his prayer, because she had the time before, when he hadn't even known he was beseeching her. She had heard him then, and given him the dream. With all the fervency of a parent praying for his child, he prayed to her, the first person wronged by God, to deliver his project from the arbitrary judgment of Nathan Graham.

They were all there when Graham got to the table; Russ Giacona and Tina Marples and Pauline Zimmerman, all of them sparkling in their suits like the polished crystal goblets on the table. And then there was Kent, leaning back in his seat, his jacket unbuttoned, lazily swirling the scotch in his glass. He didn't sparkle, he didn't have to, he was the chief executive of Detroit operations and he answered to no one but Anna Luria herself.

"Oh good, Nathan's here," said Tina brightly as he approached, and they all stood.

"Hi Kent, it's good to see you again," he said, shaking his hand. "Russ, Tina, Pauline." Everybody shook his hand, everybody avoided knocking over any goblets or candlesticks. As he sat down, Graham glanced surreptitiously at his watch. He was on time, goddamn it. They were early. It was probably Tina's doing, trying to make him look bad. At least they'd had the decency to leave a seat next to Kent open so he didn't have to talk to the man from the other side of the floral centerpiece.

"The waiter was on us like a starved vulture the minute we sat down," said Kent, leaning over and speaking conspiratorially out of the side of his mouth, "so we went ahead and ordered drinks." He waved his hand, and a red-jacketed waiter hurried to his side. "What would you like, Nathan?"

"Scotch and soda," he said to the waiter, who scurried off again. He could have stood a double, without the soda, but it wouldn't have looked good to order the same thing Kent drank.

Kent opened his menu, and everyone else followed suit. "I've heard that the salmon is very good here," Graham told him. Actually, he'd called up the chef this morning and demanded that he have it sent in fresh from Alaska. Salmon was Kent Carlyse's favorite fish.

He pursed his lips, his grey eyes scanning the menu. "Mmm, not really in the mood for fish tonight. Think I'll have the filet."

"They get it straight from Mitsubishi's own farms," said Russ, leaning over his menu, "it's very fresh."

Graham stared at him. The conniving little assassin. He'd probably known Kent wasn't in the mood for fish today and had exploited that knowledge by talking to the chef, finding out where he got his beef, maybe even demanding that he order it from Mitsubishi. Of course he pretended not to understand the significance of Graham's look, sitting there gazing at the menu, smugly, innocently, knowing all the while what he'd done. What was worse was that the chef knew all about it, and had, in fact, sided with Russ. They were probably laughing at him right now in the kitchen. When the waiter returned for their dinner selections, Graham could swear he was smirking.

Pauline had the wild mushroom flan, an appropriate choice

for her position. Tina ordered prawn soufflé, a bit of a risk, but she was a climber. Russ and Kent both ordered the filet mignon, which left Graham in a difficult position. He could stick by his guns and have the salmon, or he could back off and opt for some neutral entree: roast duck or pork loin. There was a nice leek and chestnut sauté on the menu, but a vegetarian choice was out of the question. He didn't know which way he'd go until he said it, "I'll have the salmon."

After dinner they retired to the club bar. To Graham's surprise, Kent took him by the arm and led him away from the others, to the opposite side of the room. They sat on stools, Graham facing the length of the bar. He saw Russ and Tina and Pauline at the far end, in an irresolute little knot, casting pathetic glances of resentment his way. He looked back at Kent.

"They'll find out about it soon enough, let them sweat in their little bean counter undies for one night. I've got a favor to ask."

"Shoot, boss," said Graham.

Kent grimaced. "I've got a situation brewing down in Wichita, that new plant that went in about a year ago. Labor problems. It's not like here, where we're working with second- and third-generation vatdivers, people who, by and large, know what to expect from the job. These greenhorns in Kansas still think we owe them something more than a steady job at a living wage. They're making all kinds of fuss about environmental standards and safety and so on. They've even gotten the IEPA in on the act. Meanwhile the people I've got out there don't seem to know how to handle the situation. I'd like you to go down and show those cowboys how it's done."

Graham's alarm was so great it must have leapt out of his eyes.

Kent held up a hand. "I don't mean permanently, you understand. Just get that jackass Nichols pointed in the right direction. Hell, it probably won't take more than a week. Not for you, with the way you handled that labor movement nonsense we had five years ago. Don't think I've forgotten that. I don't forget anything like that. In fact, it's why I thought of you. I need a reliable, results-oriented man on the job down there."

"I'm not a production manager anymore," Graham said carefully.

Kent waved his hand in annoyance. "I know that, Nathan. I'm

just asking you to do this as a favor to me, understand?" His eyes were flinty and hard, their gleam belying his light tone of voice.

Graham understood. He would go, because to refuse would be to set himself against Kent, and he couldn't afford to do that yet. "Of course." He nodded. "Of course, I'd be happy to help."

"Great," said Kent, shaking his hand. "There's a review meeting with the IEPA Monday morning at eight, but I want you out there over the weekend so you can scope everything out beforehand. I can have my driver pick you up at your place in an hour and take you to the airport."

In his first-class compartment on the GeneSys airliner, Graham poured over the school records, family histories, love affairs, and purchasing habits of Hector Martin's two assistants, searching for a weakness he could exploit.

People could be controlled if you knew their secrets, and companies, as his mother had said, were made up of people. Where she'd been wrong was in thinking there was anything more to it than that. In her obsession with the organism of her company, she had neglected its constituents. She had allowed herself to forget that she was dealing, after all, with people. It was not a mistake her son would repeat.

Henry Theodore Greenfield graduated magna cum laude from Lawrence Technical Institute, did his graduate study in lysis proteins and injection processing at MIT, and then returned to Detroit to work with Dr. Martin in a doctoral fellowship program conjunct with the University of Detroit Mercy College. He broke up with his high school boyfriend while at Lawrence, had three affairs at MIT, and was now seeing a second-year radiology intern at Beaumont Hospital. He had experimented with a variety of drugs over the years, but had never developed a habit for anything more serious than cocaleaf. His mother lived in Dearborn and worked for Blue Cross/Blue Shield. The identity of his father was unknown. There certainly wasn't much to go on with the respectable Mr. Greenfield. Perhaps his colleague Colin Arbegast Slatermeyer would be more forthcoming.

In fact, his file did show more promise. His parents were married, were, in fact, members of the downriver fundamentalist enclave ALIVE! Colin grew up there, attended school in the compound's youth center, and at the age of eighteen was recommended by one of his instructors to be sent out of the community for further education.

Graham raised one eyebrow. Usually such magnanimity on the part of ALIVE! was expected to be repaid, either by returning and benefiting the community as a doctor, lawyer, or some such, or by a tithe of 30 percent of the individual's income. It was contractual, and in fact, Slatermeyer had signed, opting for the tithe. He didn't want to go back, apparently.

Graham pulled up his pay stubs and, scanning them, smiled. Slatermeyer was taking a pretax deduction of $500 off every check and squirreling it away in an escrow account. It would be reported to the IRS as investment income, not earnings, and therefore, it would be invisible to ALIVE!'s auditors.

"Clever, clever," breathed Graham under his breath, and he scanned ahead to his quarry's current profile records. He had an economy model maglev, dark brown. Its navigation module revealed sporadic trips to bars and restaurants around town, an occasional foray up north, no trips downriver whatsoever, and every Sunday, like clockwork, a visit to the Belle Isle Aquarium.

6

A Day in the Life

HELIX woke up in the middle of the night, her head and her ribs and the wound in her back all hurting at once. She lay there for a while, listening to the quiet, looking at the darkness, until her thoughts got round to the day she left Hector's, the casino, and the men in the alley. When she started to think about the playground, she got up, and walked carefully to the bathroom.

To the right of the toilet, beneath a window cracked and peeling with water damage, sat a porcelain bathtub. She looked with longing at the old, claw-footed affair. Wincing, she pulled off her T-shirt and turned on the water. She looked in the medicine cabinet, but there was no kosher salt. You can't have everything, she thought, gazing at the steaming tub, and she eased herself into the warm, delicious water.

Chango awakened blearily on the couch in Mavi's living room. Her head throbbed and her face was mashed into the textured upholstery. When she sat up she carried an imprint of fleur de lis on her cheek. Rubbing it, she made her way to the bathroom on unsteady legs and flung open the door. Something splashed in the bathtub and let out a sharp cry of dismay.

"Gah!" shouted Chango, startled by the movement, and found herself staring at Helix, naked in the bathtub, and staring back at her with bewildered, sleep-filled eyes. "Sorry, I didn't know you were in here," she said, turning to the sink and running the tap. She splashed water on her face, then turned back to Helix. "Were you sleeping?"

Helix sank beneath the edge of the tub. "Yes. Sometimes when I can't sleep, it helps."

"Oh," said Chango, still looking at her.

"I'll be out in a minute, if you could just—"

"Oh, sure, sorry." Chango dried off her face and backed out the door. She went into the kitchen, where Mavi was leaning over the sink, pouring water into the coffeepot. "Guess who I just surprised in the bathroom?"

Mavi looked at her jadedly. "Helix?"

"Well, yeah."

Mavi nodded and set the coffeepot on the counter. "I thought so. It wasn't me and as far as I know, you're not in the habit of surprising yourself. Why didn't you knock first?"

Chango sighed and shrugged. "I wasn't thinking. I didn't expect—Mavi, she was in the bathtub."

"So? She can take a bath if she wants to, Chango. What's the problem?"

Chango leaned closer and lowered her voice. "She was sleeping in there, Mavi, in the water."

* * *

Helix stepped carefully out of the tub and toweled off. Her ribs were still sore, her neck stiff, but her knife wound was almost healed, and the lump on her head was way down. She stepped into her freshly laundered, custom-made four-sleeved bodysuit. The celluweave fabric warmed slightly at the touch of her damp skin, helping her dry off. She wished it wouldn't. Her skin was always too dry, no matter what moisturizers or oils she used. The only thing that ever really seemed to help was soaking in a tub of salt water.

She slipped on her tunic and went out into the hallway and stood there, torn between the security of her room and her curiosity about the house and its neighborhood. She'd been gone from Hector's for three days now, and so far she'd spent most of it in one room. Someone was making coffee in the kitchen. She followed the smell down the hall.

Chango and Mavi stood close together by the sink, their conversation breaking off abruptly as Mavi saw her. "Oh, Helix, it's good to see you up and about."

"Thanks," she said, remaining in the doorway, at a loss for what to do next. Chango and Mavi stood looking at her expectantly. Her cheeks burned, and she realized she was blushing.

"C'mon in," said Chango, suddenly darting across the room to her and guiding her to the table. "Have a seat. You want coffee? Mavi just put some on."

Helix nodded slowly. "Yeah. Yes, thank you."

Hanging from a peg near the door was Hector's raincoat. Just the sight of it made her feel better, more secure. Chango and Mavi had both seen her, seen her arms, seen everything—Night Hag, too, but still she felt naked being anyplace but Hector's apartment without that coat on.

She glanced at her companions. Mavi was stirring sugar into her coffee; Chango was pouring a bowl of raisin bran. "Oh, there's my coat," she said, feigning surprise.

"A little the worse for wear, I'm afraid," said Mavi.

"That's okay. I'm a little cold, that's all." It was true, she usually was cold. She used to keep Hector's apartment so warm he could hardly stand it.

Chango and Mavi exchanged glances as she got up and slipped into the raincoat and buttoned it over her lower arms. "That's better." She smiled and seated herself at the table again.

Mavi poured her a cup of coffee and handed her the steaming mug.

"Want some cereal?" asked Chango.

"Sure, thanks."

Chango poured her a bowl and added milk.

"So what are you up to today, Chango?" asked Mavi, getting up to retrieve a basket from next to the stove.

"Oh, I have a few errands to run. Helix, maybe you'd like to come along, see the neighborhood, get to know a few people."

"I don't know."

"You said you left your father because you wanted to find something for yourself. You're not going to find it hiding out here, are you?"

She was right. She'd left Hector to find out about the rest of the world, and now she was just turning this place into another Hector's apartment: walls to hide behind.

Mavi sat down, pulled a length of knobby yarn out of her basket, and wound it around her fingers. "Fresh air would be good for you, but no adventures." She pointed a long hook at Chango. "Stay in the neighborhood, okay?"

"Yes, ma'am," said Chango.

"What are you doing?" asked Helix as Mavi worked the yarn with her hook.

"Crocheting. My mother taught me, but you just can't find yarn anymore."

"What's that, then?" Helix pointed at the blue-green-red-yellow length of ropy stuff in her hands.

"Oh, they save it up at Vat nine. Every month or so Benny brings me a bag of it. The bodies aren't good for much of anything—"

"Except bouncing balls," said Chango.

"—but I tie the tendrils together and make stuff with them. Pele sells them for me at the Eastern Market. I used to do a lot of afghans, but lately I'm doing hats." She had begun working the yarn into a round. "The hats sell better."

Helix's eyebrows rose of their own volition. "They're—they're that stuff you fish out—"

"Agules," said Chango. "Mavi's a recycler."

"Since you're making the rounds Chango, you want to drop some of these off for me?"

"Sure, but it wouldn't kill you to let sunlight strike your face either, you know, instead of just sitting around in here all the time, smoking and knitting."

"Crocheting. Besides, I've got things to do. Xenia sprained her ankle and needs a sassafras poultice, and Harvey is still trying to come off Blast. He needs more goldenseal tincture. Oh, and stop by Hyper's while you're out, see if he needs more valerian."

"Sure," said Chango, getting up and taking her bowl to the sink. "Helix, will you join me?"

Helix gnawed at her lower lip with one fang. "I don't know. Actually, I should start looking for a job somewhere. Do you know anyplace around that's hiring?"

Chango and Mavi laughed. "Not hardly," said Chango, her smile narrowing to a smirk. "Besides, come with me and you won't need a job."

Helix followed Chango across the street to her motorcar, a yellow behemoth covered with patches of red polybond. It was a warm, cloudy, humid day; the air dense and full of a strange, yeasty smell. It felt soft and damp against her skin, soothing. "Wow, it's nice out," she said.

Chango looked at her incredulously. "Nice out? You must be joking. Days like this, GeneSys should issue everyone in Vattown a divesuit. Smell that? It's growth medium, and it's probably morphing us as we stand." She opened the door for Helix. "You have to get in on this side, the door on the passenger's side doesn't work."

Helix slid into the spacious seat, cracked and shiny with spots of bioadhesive.

They pulled out and rumbled down the street, and Helix leaned back and watched the sky pass above them.

After innumerable turns down narrow streets pitted with erosion and lined with vacant lots and houses in varying stages of disrepair, Chango pulled over in front of a vast field of brick and metal rubble. "All that's left of the Russell Industrial Center," she said, and got out of the car. Helix watched as she ducked under the halfhearted barricade and picked among the dust and stones. She returned with a fragment of concrete. The brief but intense heat of the disintegration process had melted a crescent wrench into its surface like an instant chrome fossil.

"What's that?" asked Helix.

Chango looked at her and then heaved it into the backseat. "It's art," she said, and got back into the car.

"Hey Hyper!" called Chango, opening the screen door. "Why don't you lock your door, fool?"

At one of several metal worktables, a scrawny young black man was busily removing solder from a circuit board. He glanced up at them. "Because then I'd have to get up to let you in. I'll be done here in just a sec."

Helix looked up in wonderment at the ceiling, nearly tripping over a stack of holocubes. There were things hanging up there that she'd never consider hanging from a ceiling: whole computer systems, a fish tank filled with murky water.

The front of the house was furnished with stained cushions, a threadbare beanbag, and a bucket seat from a levcar. Chango flopped down in the levcar seat. Helix just stood there, staring as Hyper's hands flew with soldering iron and vacuum tube. He was right, he was done in just a sec.

"Hi," he said as he suddenly stepped around the table, and then, "Hi!" as he noticed Helix.

"Hi," she said.

"Hyper, this is Helix. Helix, Hyper, a very old, dear friend of mine."

"Hey, Helix," he said, dodging forward to shake her hand. Helix took his hand in her upper right one. "Thanks for lending me your transceiver."

"Hey, no problem. Glad to see you're doing all right, have a seat." He pointed her to the beanbag. "Can I take your coat?" he added.

She looked up at him. "No, that's okay. Thanks."

"Oh, for heaven's sake," said Chango, "it's fucking eighty degrees out today. Aren't you hot?"

She wasn't hot, not really, but the lining of the coat was sticking to her arms and the back of her neck. And she did feel sort of stupid wearing it, when everyone else was in T-shirts and shorts.

She looked carefully at Hyper. Chango had said he was a sport, but she could find nothing out of the ordinary about him except for his bizarre taste in home furnishings. "What's different about you?" she asked.

"My metabolism. It runs high. I have to eat a lot of small meals and I don't sleep too much."

She was disappointed. She'd been hoping for nictating membranes or retractable earflaps, at least a tail. It must have shown.

"I know, it's boring, but it's the only mutation I've got," he said.

She nodded in silence, and as casually as she could manage, slipped the raincoat from her shoulders. It felt good to stretch her arms and feel the air against her skin.

She watched Hyper for his reaction; saw his eyes travel down her body and up again to her face. He was smiling. "Now that's a significant mutation. Do you have complete use of them?"

"Yeah," she said, sliding into the chair, "but my bottom hands are better at fine work, and they don't really lift up to the sides too well, top ones go three-sixty degrees, though." Helix crisscrossed her hands about her knees and rocked self-consciously.

"That is so cool-looking."

"Thanks."

"You know," said Hyper, "she needs to meet Orielle."

"Not Orielle," said Chango.

"Who's Orielle?" said Helix.

"Oh, just somebody who would make you fade right into the woodwork," said Hyper.

"She's a drug dealer," said Chango.

"And a drug inventor, don't forget about that," said Hyper.

"Yeah, but she still makes her bread and butter by selling Blast in this community. It keeps the vatdivers down, keeps them from doing anything about the company. They just do as they're told, and collect their pay and use it to get blasted, that's all."

"It's not just the Blast, Chango," said Hyper. "Besides, you used to do Blast, before—"

"Yeah, but I don't anymore, do I? And you know why, too."

"You always say Ada didn't dive blasted. Don't you believe that?"

Chango glared at him, and finally stood up to walk past them and stare at something hanging from the ceiling. "Fuck you, Hyper," she growled softly.

Hyper shrugged and looked at Helix. "She's a bundle of contradictions, she is. Can I get you something? Water, Kool-Aid, Chromium Fifty?"

"Water, please."

Chango, still standing, still staring at the ceiling, shook her head. "You're going to regret it."

"You want anything, Chango?" asked Hyper, heading towards the back of the house.

"Only your immortal soul," she said, and sat back down in the levseat.

Hyper returned in an instant with a cup of doubtful-looking water and handed it to Helix. She sniffed it. It smelled like solder. Casually she set it down on the floor.

Hyper tapped his foot, rooted around in his shirt pocket, came up with a half-empty pack of Reefer Madness, pulled one out, lit it, and offered Helix the pack.

"No, thanks."

"I'll take one," said Chango.

"So you're new in town, huh?" said Hyper, switching on his holotransceiver and flipping through channels.

"Well, new to Vattown."

"That's what I mean. I heard—I heard you were adopted, by some corporate dink, excuse me, professional man."

"He's a research scientist."

"Oh yeah? What kind of stuff does he do?"

Helix shrugged. "I don't know."

"You don't know? Well, what kinds of projects is he working on? I mean generally, don't spill any trade secrets or anything, for gods' sakes."

She shook her head. "I don't know."

Hyper stared at her. "Industrial ecology, biomathematics, gene splicing . . . "

Helix shrugged again.

"You've been living with the man for, what, ten years, and you don't know. Okay." Hyper drew on his cigarette and pulled the transceiver's imaging lens down over one eye. He glanced at the hologram reflected through the lens, his eyes flickering as he called up new files. He glanced from Helix to the holo several times in rapid succession. "Do think I could—I don't mean to be bold, or embarrass you or anything," he glanced at Chango and then back to her, "would you mind, could I look at your back?"

"My back?"

"Yeah, it looks like you only have one collarbone. I was trying to mount a set of manipulating arms onto the existing armature of this robot I'm working on. I thought I'd have to hang it up, but if I can see how it's been done, with you—"

"Hyper builds robots," said Chango, answering Helix's glance with a reassuring nod.

She felt like she was outside herself as she stood, turned her back to him, and lifted her tunic with her upper arms. Beyond the numbness of her fear she felt a burning curiosity. What would he be able to see?

She sensed him looking, and then felt his hands on her back. She flinched, and then relaxed as they ran, warm and soft, along her muscles and bones. Of course she couldn't see the hologram he was working on, but she sensed he was tracing her.

When he was through, he slipped the transceiver over her head, so she could look through the imaging lens and see what he'd drawn: an anatomical rendering of her back, arms, and shoulders. "What are you going to do with that?" she asked, backsliding into a paranoid fantasy of her image plastered on every building in Vattown, labeled with the words "Look at this freak."

Hyper led her to the work area, to a thing with the lower body of a small tractor and two waldo arms bolted to a steel drum with a hole cut in the middle. A gas combustion engine painted to resemble a face rested on a pivot on top of the drum.

"See, if I mount ball sockets here and here—" his fingers traced the metal struts the same way they had touched her own flesh "—I can support the second set of arms without adding a whole new framework for them."

"What does it do?"

"Well, it's not finished yet. Eventually I want to put a pivot piston in here, and that'll make the head nod up and down as it rumbles and spews smoke. And then it rolls around on the tractor treads, and the arms are operated by radio control and can pick stuff up. I want the extra arms so they can hold this—" He hefted a dented saxophone. "I'm calling it Close Enough for Jazz."

Chango wandered in from the front room. "Do you still need a counterweight for the pivot piston? I may have just the thing."

"Oh yeah? That's cool because I haven't found anything . . . symbolically correct yet."

"It's out in my car, why don't you come out and see."

"Did you get into that data card yet?" asked Chango as she and Hyper walked to her car.

"What? Uh, no. No, It's not giving up easily, and I've been busy with Robo-Mime. Is she asking about it?"

"She did at first, but I think she's forgotten about it."

"Well, she's obviously never read any of it. Unless all that ignorance was an act. She any more forthcoming about her father to you?"

Chango shrugged. "I think his name is Hector. I didn't really ask about him."

"Hector? Hector Martin?"

"That's it," said Chango.

Hyper choked. "Her father is *the* Dr. Hector Martin? Christ!"

"You know him?" asked Chango.

"Know him? I know of him. He's the inventor of the multis."

"Multis." Chango shook her head. So Helix's adopted father was the man behind the multiprocessor brains that ran nearly every major networked system in the world. Maglev, stock market, polymer plants. Shit, even the temperature and ventilation systems in most big buildings. "Jeez." Chango cast her gaze to the tower of the GeneSys Building, hazy in the distance. "Talk about friends in high places."

Hyper gave Chango a crate of DataKleen memory enzyme in exchange for the chrome fossil from the Russell Industrial Center.

They drove to a faded cement-blockhouse surrounded with sunflowers. "Pele's house," Chango said.

The woman who came out the front door to greet them had skin like a painted pony, irregular patches of black on a white background. The color scheme carried over into the cloud of thick hair surrounding her head. She was dressed in a yellow housecoat. "Hey, Chango, I hope you came to fix my truck."

"Actually it was more to make a trade, but what's the problem?"

"It's burning oil."

"Ow. They'll take you off the road for that."

"You don't think I know it? I've got a lot of goods to get to the market this week."

"All right, I'll take a look."

Helix sat on the porch with Pele, drinking iced tea and watching Chango crawl around under Pele's blue pickup truck.

"I still like to watch her fix stuff," said Pele, glancing sidelong at Helix. "What about you?"

"Me? What?"

"Do you like watching her? She's a nice girl you know, but fickle."

Helix looked at Pele in confusion. She was going to ask her what fickle was, but she got distracted by Pele's appearance. "You go to the Eastern Market, to sell stuff?"

"All the time."

"You see a lot of people?"

"If I'm lucky."

"How do you deal with . . . with—"

Pele smiled. "With this?" She waved her hand at her skin, her hair. "I don't ever really think about it, unless someone reminds me. I get that sometimes, from people who don't know me. They always ask me the same thing, 'Are you white or black?' They really don't mean anything by it, they're just surprised, and they say the first thing that comes into their heads. I don't take it to heart, you know? In the end, they have to deal with who I am, not what I look like."

* * *

Chango traded Pele the DataKleen for a cube of holotoys and collected a carton of reefers for fixing the truck. "See?" she said to Helix in the car. "This is how it works. You get by."

"Where are we going now?"

"We'll go to Hannah's. I'm hungry."

"Who's Hannah?"

"Hannah's Eclectic Homestyle Restaurant. It's been around for ages. Used to be a Polish place, but back around '19 or '20 it got bought by Hannah and her husband Ricky. Hannah just started cooking whatever came to mind with whatever was at hand. Menu changed constantly. Her daughter Rita runs it now. Food's still pretty good, but Hannah, man . . . Well, they say Rita's daughter Gabrielle has the touch, and she's almost sixteen. She'll be out of school soon." Chango shrugged. "One can hope."

Hannah's Eclectic Homestyle Restaurant was housed in a brown brick building with a peaked cornice and blue tiles set in at the corners of the doorway. Chango led the way under a red awning and flung open the door. Helix followed her into a large, bright room filled with tables and chairs, humid with the smells of food and loud with the chatter of voices and the rattle of silverware. "Hey Chango!" cried a voice over the din. In the far corner of the dining room a bald young man waved vigorously at them.

"Magnusson," Chango murmured as they wound their way between the tables, "one of my very best buddies." As they got to the table Chango reached across it and snagged a sausage off of his plate.

"Hey!" he protested, but Chango only chortled gleefully and ate it, waving her burned fingertips. "Magoo," she said, ushering Helix into the seat across from him, and sitting beside her, "meet Helix. Helix, this is—"

"Magnusson," he interjected, leaning forward and extending a broad, flat hand. Her fingers brushed the back of it as they shook. His skin was smooth. He had a round head and a round, pudgy body. He was not only bald, she noticed. He didn't have any eyebrows or facial hair either. That's why his skin felt so smooth. He didn't have any hair at all.

"Nice to meet you," said Helix, suddenly realizing with a

twinge that she was staring at him. His eyes were pale, pale grey, colorless, but not red. He looked like a grown-up baby.

"Magoo cooks here. He's gonna get us free lunches, right Magoo?"

He rolled his eyes. "Yeah, sure, long as you don't mind taking my bus shift tonight."

"Bus shift? You're still doing dishes nights? I thought Rita said she'd put you on prep."

Magnusson shrugged. "Sure, she said it. But now I'm doing lunch rush 'cause Octavio got sick, and meanwhile, they still need busers at night. So, I'm busing."

"That sucks. She promised you."

He snorted. "C'mon, nobody believes promises, not from an employer, right?"

Chango nodded acknowledgment. "It still sucks," she added.

"Yeah, well, it can only be so bad you know. I ain't divin'." He softly nodded his head towards a group of five seated in a booth against the other wall. Tank harnesses hung off of their lean, divesuited bodies. Hard men and women, mostly older than them, but there were a few with eyes, it seemed, already darkened by the sight of death, though it stood for them, probably thirty, even forty years away. They were an animated group, smoking and laughing and living it up, partying at the end of their shift. But death hung around them like a cloud of smog that ground its darkness right into their pores so that they seemed steeped in something. Something that would slowly curl around the double helix of their DNA and twist it, twist them, into something else. Helix found herself searching their faces, trying to find, beneath the angled planes of skin, the shape they would become. "Why do they do it," she asked, "if it's so dangerous?"

"For the money," said Magnusson.

"Most of them only plan to dive for five years, take their pay, and get someplace where the living is cheap," said Chango. "Only sometimes they find that five years isn't enough; sometimes they find that nothing is enough."

One of the vatdivers—a tall, dark-haired man—glanced over at them and detached himself from the group. "Oh no, it's Benjamin," grumbled Magnusson under his breath.

He approached their booth with quick strides of his long, lean legs. His vat-leather jacket, still new, crinkled stiffly as he leaned over the table. "How's it going over here?" he asked. He had hard, bright blue eyes.

"Hi Benny," said Chango. "What's new with you?"

"Not much, just snagging goobers." He slid into the side of the booth opposite Chango and Helix.

Grumbling, Magnusson slid his plate over and made room. Benny reached a hand towards the sausages, but Magnusson brandished a fork at him. "Back off, man," he snarled.

Laughing, Benny rested his chin in his hands and looked at Helix. "So, you're the new girl, huh? Nice to meet you."

Helix nodded and leaned closer to Chango. "Hi," she said, her voice cracking. She felt her face grow warm.

"I heard you ran into a spot of trouble," said Benny. "How are your ribs?"

"Much better, thanks."

"She heals fast," said Chango.

"So how do you like Vattown?"

"It's nice," Helix said, "it smells good."

They all stared at her.

"I've heard this place get called a lot of things," said Magnusson, "but good-smelling, never."

"Yeah, top on most people's grudge list about Vattown is the reek of the growth medium," said Benny. "You really like it?"

Helix shrugged. "Yeah, it smells . . . warm."

"Mmm." Benny grunted, then turned to the others. "You hear about the new hiring requirements?" he asked.

"What, you have to be seven feet tall and blond now? I'd think they'd be happy to get anybody they can, these days," said Chango.

"That's just it, they are. They've just loosened up the genetic requirements, so first-generation mutations are okay."

"What?" said Magnusson.

"You heard it, they're hiring sports now. Of course they'll be classified temporaries, so the company can get around giving them benefits, including health insurance."

"Fucking company," said Chango. "This is why we need a union, Benny, to keep them from getting away with crap like this."

"I've never argued with that, Chango."

"No, you just won't do anything about it."

"Aw, give it a rest already, would you? If you're so keen on the movement, become a vatdiver and form one. You can, now."

"I'm not going to throw my life away for a bunch of people who won't even help themselves."

"My feeling exactly," said Benny.

"Where would you go, to apply?" asked Helix.

"Are you serious?" asked Benny.

"No," said Chango. "She's not. You're not serious."

"I was just wondering. He said they were hiring, and I need a job so . . . What is it like—diving?" she asked Benny.

"Well, you put on an anodized rubber suit that makes you sweat, a face mask, breathing equipment, and a forty-pound air tank, and then you go and swim around in a bunch of poisonous, murky water. It's a real giggle."

"I was just asking."

"Well you don't need to know," said Chango, "because you're not going to do it."

Helix stared at Chango, sudden anger lighting her eyes. "I can decide that myself," she said. They went on staring at each other for a moment more, Helix having difficulty keeping her eyes from jumping back and forth between blue and green, and then they both looked away.

"She's right, you shouldn't dive," said Benny, his eyes wandering about the outlines of her raincoat. "Someone like you would be a prime candidate for vatsickness."

Helix studied the place mat in front of her. It had a scalloped border of disinfectant enzyme, pale pink paste that left a little streak of bioelectric neutralizer on the surface of the table every time you moved it. Enough fidgeters, and you'd probably never have to wipe the table down.

"I've got some holotoys for Hugo," said Chango. "How's he doing, anyway?"

Benny shrugged. "About the same. You know how it is with vatsickness. He got up and walked around a little bit yesterday. This morning he only kept water down. He's strong. It's going to take a long time."

"They should just throw him in the vat and let him finish," said Helix.

They all stared at her again. Benny blinked and cleared his throat. "You're probably right," he said.

Chango was glaring at her. "I'm sorry," said Helix. "I don't know why I said that."

"No. I understand. We caught it early; he has a mild dose. That doesn't make it less fatal, it just means it takes longer to kill him. When my time comes, I'm just going to keep diving. If it has to happen, at least it can be quick like with—"

"Don't you even say that Ada was lucky," said Chango.

Benny tilted his head to one side. "In a way, she was, Chango."

"Here." Chango handed him the holocube. "These are for Hugo. You can pay me later. We have to go."

"Chango—"

"See you later."

"Who's Ada?" asked Helix when they got in the car.

"My sister," said Chango, turning the ignition key with exceptional force. She pulled out of the parking space with a burst of acceleration. Helix was waiting for her to calm down before making any further inquiries, but then they drove past the vat yards.

Rows of round metal buildings with glass domes slid by like the silvered flanks of some huge beast basking in the brightening afternoon. The air was filled with the living smell of growth medium. Chango didn't want her to work there, Benny had good reasons why she shouldn't, but Helix looked at those domes and breathed the air, and she knew it wouldn't matter what anybody said.

The knowledge nestled inside her and made her feel light and . . . happy. The sun was coming out, as if the day welcomed her joy.

7

THE DEATH OF ADA CHICHELSKI

CHANGO had been at Josa's when her sister had the accident. She'd been playing up to Pele by putting Otimache Mints on the jukebox and buying her beer.

"Wanna dance?" she asked, swinging her hips and shaking her shoulders. Josa's was nearly empty, it was just her and Pele, a few out-of-work vatdivers lingering in the shadows, and Josa, behind the bar.

"Not until you tell me what you did last night," Pele said, pouting.

"I told you, sweetheart, I got drunk at Vonda's, and Hyper was there, and since he lives right next door, he let me crash at his place."

"Uh-huh." In the dim light, Pele seemed to be there only in patches. "You didn't sleep with him?"

Chango bit her lips and said nothing. It wouldn't matter if she protested her innocence, Pele would know she was lying. She was a lousy liar, and she hated to do it.

Pele shook her head in shock and exasperation. "I can't believe this. I can't believe you! Did we or did we not have a conversation last week in which you said, 'I'm ready for monogamy'? That *was* you, wasn't it?"

Chango climbed onto the barstool next to her and put her head in her hands. "I know, but Hyper, he—I—"

"Oh, don't tell me it's because you were drunk!"

"No. I mean, it kind of was, but, we—"

"Are you in love with him?"

"Not *in* love, I don't think, but— We've known each other for forever."

"*We've* known each other for forever too, and I've known Hyper for forever. We all grew up here, we all went to school together. None of us have ever known more than the same thirty people our whole fucking lives! What has that got to do with anything? Do you love him?"

Chango shrugged. "Yes."

"Fine." Pele slammed her beer down on the counter. "I hope you'll be very happy together."

"But I love you too," said Chango, grabbing Pele's arm as she slid from her stool.

"You can't. You can love Hyper or you can love me, but you can't love both of us." Pele wrested her arm from Chango's grip and headed for the door.

"Yes I can," Chango said to her retreating back. Pele did this every time Chango slept with someone else. Theirs was a relationship of punctuated monogamy. Usually after a couple of weeks, she'd let her back in the house. In the meantime, Chango would have to stay with friends, maybe Hyper.

Chango felt bad though, about telling her she wouldn't sleep around anymore. At the time, she'd really meant it. But then last night at Vonda's, Hyper had been so . . .

"Chango?" It was April, her broad form silhouetted against the bright light from the open doorway. Chango blinked at her, her eyes accustomed to the dimness of Josa's bar.

"April? What are you doing here, it's the middle of your shift."

"Chango." April shut the door behind her and approached her with more eagerness than she would ordinarily express, but not more pleasure. As she came closer, Chango saw the deep lines of worry that creased her forehead. "It's Ada," she said, when she got close enough to speak in a normal tone of voice. "Will you come?"

"Of course," said Chango, sliding from her barstool, feeling suddenly cold, "but what is it?"

April looked at her, and even in the dim light, Chango could see the tears in her eyes. "She got doused."

"No! Oh my gods, no!"

April put a strongarm around Chango's shoulders and gently propelled her toward the door. "She's still at the vat house. I've already found Mavi; she's on her way over there now."

When she got there, April showed her to a small tiled room with a single narrow bench along the far wall. Mavi was there, standing over Ada, who crouched on the bench in a flimsy paper gown, shaking. She'd always been bigger than Chango, but she looked small now—small and pale even under the dusting of biocidal powder that whitened her skin and hair.

"What happened?" Chango said as she walked slowly towards them.

Mavi looked up, her face as white as Ada's, and tight with grief and fury. "Seals came loose," she said through gritted teeth.

Chango breathed in sharply, the air was acrid with the lingering fumes of the chemicals that had been used to wash Ada. "Faulty equipment?"

Mavi shrugged once in sharp dismissal. "They're checking. What difference does it make?"

Ada shuddered and bent over to vomit between her feet. The sweet smell of stomach acid joined the other odors in the room. Mavi cradled her in her arms and wiped her mouth with a tissue.

Tentatively Chango reached out to lay her fingertips on her sister's arm. Her skin was grainy and dry with biocide powder, and cool. Ada's eyes were slits, glimmering with a shifting blue as she looked at her. Her crusted lips parted. "Get me out of here."

They all got a ride in the company ambulance: Coral, Benny, Val, and Hugo carrying Ada out on a stretcher, their faces drawn and blank like pallbearers. They might as well have been. She'd received contact on roughly forty percent of her skin. By vatsickness standards, it would be quick.

Chango remembered the sting in the soles of her feet when she leapt from the back of the ambulance onto the black brilliantine road, to run to the house and open the door, holding it wide as they carried her in. After they'd maneuvered Ada safely abed, Chango and the vatdivers, in silent mutuality, left her alone with Mavi and shut the door.

Coral, Val, and Hugo stood around the kitchen table, like misplaced trees. Benny made coffee while Chango slumped in the doorway. No one said anything. There was only the hiss of the coffeemaker and the faint, soft sound of weeping from the other room, like the lapping of waves on a distant shore.

They were out of reach of that ocean, there in the grim golden glow of the little kitchen, bound and barricaded by a single, overriding thought: "It didn't happen to me." That was the silent conversation they had before the final gurgle of the coffeemaker.

Benny brought mugs to the table with wooden solemnity, his long face still and quiet, his eyes blank as if he were not really there, as if he were thinking very hard of something else.

"How long did she soak?" asked Chango.

Val and Coral shrugged. Benny continued to stare at his hands. "About five minutes," said Hugo.

"Five minutes?" Chango put her mug down. "How is that possible?"

Hugo and Coral and Val exchanged uncomfortable glances. "Apparently she wasn't immediately aware of the leakage," said Coral guardedly.

"Not aware? How could she not be aware?"

"Because she was blasted," said Benny, finally looking up to fix her with a cold hard stare.

"Blasted? At work?"

"I know," Coral said. "I can't believe it either. They must have made a mistake."

"I saw the blood tests. She must have gassed just before her shift," said Benny.

Chango shook her head. "No way."

"Chango, I saw the lab results. I also saw her last night with Orielle." Benny leaned over the table, his hands clenched in fists in front of him. "I hate to say it, but she's been using a lot lately."

"She got blasted the other night at Josa's," said Val, "Thursday."

"Oh, and you don't get blasted there every weekend and most weeknights," said Chango.

Val shrugged. He didn't say anything, but Chango could see him thinking it. "At least I don't take it on the job."

"This completely discredits our movement," said April. "GeneSys will just chalk it up as another example of diver recklessness, another excuse not to take our complaints seriously. If Ada didn't care about her life, why should they? She was supposed to be an example to counter the vatdiver stereotype. She was the spearhead of our movement, and now she's sabotaged us."

Chango shifted on her cushion in the living room of Vonda's apartment and looked at the faces around her, expecting someone to defend her sister, but they were all silent, either in complicity or secretiveness, and no one would return her gaze.

Mavi wasn't there. Mavi was at home taking care of Ada, who they spoke of as if she were already dead. Somebody here had to speak for her, and Chango was the only one who would. "How can you say that, after all she's done? If it weren't for Ada, there wouldn't be a movement. And you wouldn't have the improvements in safety standards that the movement has won."

"She made a mockery of those, didn't she?" said Vonda to a round of grim snickering.

Chango glared at her. "She got you the job of technical analyst,

Vonda. So the divers would have one of their own to administer tests and analyze their results. She paid for you to take the classes from her own pocket, have you forgotten?" Vonda didn't answer her. She wouldn't even look at her.

"Chango's right," said Benny. "Whatever she's done now, we can't turn our back on everything she—we—accomplished. We have to preserve what credibility we can."

"How are we going to do that?" asked Jewel.

"By proving that her accident was a company plot," said Chango.

"Oh come on," said April. "Six of us in this room saw her buying Blast from Orielle the night before."

"So? That doesn't mean she used it before her dive."

"The medical reports say she did," said Jewell.

"Maybe they were doctored."

"By who? Me?" said Vonda, pounding the couch with her fists. "I prepared it, I took her blood and her skin samples, and I carried them to the lab and I did the analysis. There was no one else. If her report was doctored, then I'm the one who did it. Is that what you believe?"

Chango looked away, her eyes burning. She didn't believe that, not really. But to say otherwise would be to admit that Ada was dying of her own negligence, and she couldn't do that. Not when she had to go back to the house tonight and see her, or what was left of her, and the rest transformed into something else. No, whether it was true or not, she would not accept that Ada had brought this on herself.

There was an awkward silence while everyone waited for her to say no, and preserve the fragile cohesion of the group. But Chango didn't say anything.

"I think the best way to move forward is to alter our strategy," said Leo finally, "make a clean break with the past. Let GeneSys know who the leadership of this movement is and what we stand for."

"And who is the leadership, now?" asked Chango.

"Benny, obviously," said April. "He was Ada's right hand."

"Maybe we should have a leadership committee, instead of a president," said Leo. "GeneSys might take us more seriously if we don't appear to be an, um, charismatic movement."

"Or we could have anyone who's interested write an anonymous proposal on why they should be president, and then we could vote on them," said Jewell.

"We could form a committee to evaluate the president's performance."

"Why don't you just form a committee to decide how to vote for the members of the committee that decides which fingers the leadership committee should stick up their asses?" said Chango, and she got up and left. No one noticed her go; they were all offering suggestions and agreeing with one another. Except for Vonda, who watched her go with baleful, injured eyes.

So, amid shame and scandal, Mavi and Chango nursed Ada to her death. She was bedridden from the start. Ada, who'd always been the strong one, the pure one, untainted by the waters of the vats, suddenly needed her sister's help to get to the bathroom. It was as if some secret contract between her and the universe was suddenly withdrawn, she no longer received its protection, and the sun stopped shining on her. She became sallow and gaunt, her body wasting away under the unsustainable demands of her renegade cells.

Her skin became dry and papery, crumbling at the base of tumors which thrust from the deep tissues of her arms and legs, reshaping her with their shiny pink masses, like mountains erupting to transfigure the face of the earth.

Ada always had a spare sort of beauty, the kind that let you fill in the spaces, but now every plane, every angle, every jut of bone and curve of flesh was being reworked with blotches and moles and cysts, transforming her from Bauhaus beauty to medieval gargoyle.

Of course the worst of the changes were on the inside, twisting her intestinal and respiratory tracts so they could barely function, and her heart—she said her heart was thickening, and they believed her. All she consumed now was water and morphine.

Sitting by her side in the pink bedroom, Chango realized that for the first time in her life she didn't envy her sister. She'd always been jealous of Ada; she was beautiful, strong, and a normal person. People liked her. She won them over effortlessly.

Everything with Ada seemed effortless, except for this: dying, losing herself to cells driven mad by growth, alone except for Chango and Mavi. Alone because all those people she'd won over, those vatdivers, people she risked her life for—they never came. Except for Benny. Benny came, standing in the doorway of the room as if coming any closer might put him at risk of catching it.

Chango knew why they stayed away. It wasn't because of the scandal. They didn't want to see her. They were afraid of seeing themselves five or ten or fifteen years from now.

She was in the kitchen when the changes came. She heard Mavi's call from the bedroom and nearly dropped the dish she was washing. She let it slide into the warm, murky water and turned, her hands still dripping as she walked down the hall with a feeling of dread and expectancy knotted in her heart like a fist.

Ada lay on the bed, muttering on and off in a strange, moaning, singsong voice. Her skin bubbled everywhere with new growths, blurring her features into a seething mass of changing tissue. Chango sat beside Mavi and watched as moles and tumors formed and then disappeared beneath new growths, as if her sister were boiling away from inside. There was a pattern to it, she thought. If she could only bear to watch long enough she might see it.

But in the end there was no pattern, no rhyme or reason, just a lifeless, shapeless mass of flesh, no longer identifiable as a human being or anything else. Pure matter, anonymous and silent as a lump of dirt.

Benny opened the door of the apartment he shared with Hugo and stood listening. No sound came from the bedroom. He took off his diving harness and set it beside the door. He walked about the untidy living room, picking up empty beer bottles and spent Blast cartridges. The olive-green carpeting badly needed vacuuming, and the furniture was covered with a film of dust. Hugo was the clean one.

Benny took the empties to the kitchen, set them on the counter amid dirty plates and pans, and got himself a fresh beer from the refrigerator.

He walked softly to the bedroom and peered inside. Hugo was in the bed, but not asleep. His eyes glittered faintly in the dim light as he looked at Benny. His brown skin was tinged with grey, and the bulge of a new tumor ruined the fine symmetry of his forehead.

"How you doing?" asked Benny, sitting on the bed beside him.

"All right," croaked Hugo, his lips parting in the ghost of a smile. "How was your day?"

"Long," said Benny, taking a pull from his beer. "We decanted a thousand and fifty cubic meters of fiber today, and there's another two thousand to do tomorrow."

"I guess they miss me down there."

"Yeah, you bet they do. You always were the best decanter. We lost about forty cubic meters to breakage. That never would have happened when you were on the team."

"They get you a replacement yet?"

"Nope."

Hugo closed his eyes and shook his head. "I've been gone for months now. How can they expect you to keep up with production? And you said the quotas are going up."

"Don't worry about work, Hugo." Benny touched his shoulder—and felt beneath the sheet not skin but . . . scales? There was always something new. He never knew what he'd find when he came home or when he woke up in the morning. It fascinated him, sometimes, when he wasn't just plain scared.

"You have something better for me to worry about?" said Hugo.

"No, I guess not. Hey . . ." He stood up and pulled the memory cube from his jeans pocket. "Chango gave me this for you. Toys."

"Cool." Hugo took it from him with hands pitted with tiny, vestigial fingernails. Vatsickness caused random cell division, mostly tumors of mixed tissue, but every once in a while a cell would get itself together to divide into something specific. Hugo had a tooth on the back of his left heel. Benny dreamed of waking up to find himself sliced and half eaten by his lover's voracious body.

"How's Chango doing, anyway?"

"She's got a new girlfriend," said Benny.

"You mean there's actually someone left in Vattown for Chango to be new with?"

"She's new in town. A sport, but she grew up in the GeneSys Building."

Hugo tried to whistle and failed. "What's she doing down here, then?" he asked.

"Good question, my dear. Good question."

"You think she's spying for them?"

Benny shrugged. "Probably not. Why would they need to spy on us now? Nothing's going on; the movement's been dead for years."

"Maybe they know something we don't."

Benny nodded his head. "Maybe. Probably."

"I hope not, for Chango's sake. She should settle down already. Speaking of which, don't you think it's about time you found a new lover?"

"What?"

"C'mon man, you've been really cool to stick around this long."

"Someone has to take care of you, Hugo. I want it to be me."

Hugo's gaze wandered across the ceiling. "I've been meaning to talk to you about that. I think it's time I moved into Mavi's pink room."

"You can't. It's occupied right now."

His eyes snapped back to Benny. "By who?"

"Helix, Chango's girlfriend. She got mugged down in Greek-town."

"You met her today?"

"Yeah." Benny nodded. "At the Eclectic."

"Then she must be recovering, if she's going out."

"Yeah, but I don't think she has anyplace to stay."

"So what?" Hugo shrugged. "If she's better, she can crash any-where, and if she's with Chango, there'll be plenty of places for her. I'm sick. I need the room. And you—you need to get this mon-strosity out of your bed."

"Stop it!" Benny stood up, turning his back to Hugo.

"Aw come on, you've got to be relieved. Let Mavi help me now. She knows what to do."

"I told you in the beginning. I want to see this thing through with you."

"No you don't Benny. Really, you don't. And more importantly, I don't want you to."

"You don't?" He turned around again. "Why? What did I do?"

Hugo shrugged and coughed. "Nothing, it's just that . . . You're too interested in it—my illness, I mean. You don't say anything, but you watch each new development with this fascinated horror. I just don't want any spectators while I do this."

"So you want to go to Mavi's."

"Yeah. I mean you can visit me and stuff, but that way you won't be involved with the changes on a day-to-day basis. Maybe that'll help." Hugo started coughing again.

Benny went into the kitchen and got him a glass of water. He hated to admit it, even to himself, but he was relieved. Because he hadn't been there for Ada, he'd been determined to stick by Hugo until the end. But if Hugo really wanted to go to Mavi's, then there was nothing he could do about it.

Back in the bedroom he watched Hugo drink in long, painful swallows. His coughing subsided, and he managed a smile. "Do you remember that summer after we graduated, Benny?"

"Yeah, sure I do." They'd just shut down I-75, and it kept flooding. Hugo, Ada, and he had gone swimming there all summer.

"We'd just gotten sterilized, and we were all fucking each other. Except for Ada. She always was a strict dyke. We used to call her the Vagitarian, remember?"

"Those were good times, Hugo." Benny remembered diving into the cool water, surfacing, and rolling over onto his back to see Hugo, Val, and Coral standing on the overpass; his friends and lovers, all young and healthy, innocent of all that was to come. And Ada, poised to dive off the guardrail; a figure of pure potential, so bold and brave. Too brave for the world, but he hadn't known that then, then she'd still been the golden girl, bright and untouchable as the sun.

8

INEXPLICABLE JOY

THE next morning Helix and Chango went out again after break-fast, but they didn't go to Hyper or Pele or Hannah's. They just walked around the neighborhood, pausing from time to time as Chango pointed out some of the many landmarks of her childhood.

"That's where we used to play dodgeball," she said, pointing to a long-disused parking lot overgrown with weeds. "Ada had a wicked throw. I used to just run like hell, but she'd always nail me, right between the shoulders."

As they neared the vat yards, the pungent smell of growth medium intensified. Helix stopped at the fence, peering at the domed vat houses. Her fingers curled around the chainlinks, and she had a sudden urge to climb it.

"Come on," said Chango up ahead. "Let's go, it stinks around here."

Helix looked at her, standing in the middle of the road. "Can we go in?"

"What? No! Why would we even want to?"

Helix shrugged. "To see what it looks like."

Chango shook her head in exasperation and walked back to her. "You're not still thinking of working there, are you?"

She opened her mouth to say yes. But she realized that Chango would only tell her once again all the reasons why she shouldn't, so she settled for a noncommittal shrug.

It was another overcast day, the clouds overhead knotting to-gether to scowl at the city. As they stood there, a first few drops of rain began to fall.

"Shit," said Chango, wiping a drop from her face. "Let's get out of here." She pulled the hood of her jacket over her head and scur-ried for the cover of an awning over a party store.

Helix lifted a hand to the quickening rain. It felt good on her skin, velvet-soft and warm, with a green growingness to it like nothing she'd ever felt before. She tilted her face up to greet it, drops spattering on her cheeks and nose.

"Are you crazy?" Chango shouted from under the awning. "This rain is disgusting and it's bad for you!"

How could that be? How could something that felt so good be bad for her? As if in approval of her thinking, the rain fell harder, growing to a full downpour.

"Helix, get under here!" Chango called, but she didn't pay her any mind. The water felt wonderful. Everywhere it touched her skin it soothed the itching that was as much a part of her daily life as breathing. She threw off Hector's raincoat, lifting her four arms to the weeping sky, letting the fabric of her body suit soak up the rain and hold it close to her skin. And she whirled, whirled and twirled, her feet splashing in puddles like an echo to her own laughter.

Chango stood under the awning of the G&P Party Store, watching Helix dance in the rain. Her total disregard for her own safety, her inexplicable and obvious joy, filled Chango with awe and horror. She realized that she really didn't know Helix much at all. She had no reference point for this odd behavior. Maybe she just liked the rain. Maybe she didn't understand that this rain contained chemicals that would irritate her skin. Maybe, when she woke up with rashes all over her body tomorrow morning, she'd learn her lesson. There wasn't enough grow med in the rain to actually give her vatsickness, unless she stayed out here for hours, which, Chango realized, was possible.

Taking a deep breath and tugging the hood of her jacket further over her head, she plunged out into the rain to haul her friend, bodily if need be, out of the downpour.

Helix didn't see her coming. She grunted with surprise as Chango wrapped her arms around her waist and pulled. "What are you doing?" she said mildly, looking down at her.

"What am I doing? What am *I* doing? What are *you* doing?" Chango sputtered. "This stuff is going to give you such a rash. You have no idea." As she spoke, she hauled persistently at Helix's waist, drawing her at last, with much staggering and splashing, to the shelter of the awning.

"Oh," Chango said with dismay, looking at her. Helix was drenched head to toe in rainwater. "Let's get inside. Maybe they have a towel or something we can use to dry you off."

"I don't want to dry off," Helix said, but Chango ignored her and, taking her damp lower right hand in hers, dragged her inside the party store.

The woman behind the counter—a Mandy-somebody she knew only vaguely—looked up in startlement at the two of them. "So it's raining," she said. "It's been threatening to all day."

Chango nodded. "Do you have a towel or a rag or something we can use to dry her off?" she asked, tilting her head towards Helix, who had detached herself from her grasp and was wandering up one of the aisles.

Mandy-somebody nodded, ducked under the counter for a moment and then tossed her a ragged towel.

When Chango caught up with her, Helix was staring at a rack of replacement valves for air tanks. "What are these?" she asked as Chango unceremoniously began toweling her off.

"They're pressure valves, for the divers' tanks," she said, rubbing the towel vigorously over Helix's arms and legs. "We're going to have to get you out of this bodysuit as soon as we get home, and you should take a shower." Chango pulled at her shoulder. "Bend down, so I can get your head."

The shop door jingled as it opened. Chango, struggling to dry the squirming Helix, couldn't turn around to see who came in, but judging from the footsteps, there were more than one of them.

"Oh look, the sports are giving themselves a bath in the party store," said a high-pitched voice, Coral's.

Chango gave up trying to dry Helix off and turned to see Coral standing at the head of the aisle with Monkey, Oli, and Katrice. All four of them wore voluminous grey rain ponchos, which drained puddles at their booted feet.

"It's a nice day for a shower," Chango said, grinning back at their smirking faces. "But then, you guys prefer to soak in it, don't you?"

Coral's smirk wavered. "We know how to protect ourselves. What about your friend there?" She nodded at Helix, who was running her fingers through her damp hair and smearing them over her face. "She trying to get more of it? Doesn't she think she looks weird enough yet?"

Helix stopped rubbing her face and stared at Coral, her arms at her sides. "What did you come here for? Was it one of these?" She plucked a pressure valve from the rack and started walking towards the vatdivers. "Or one of these?" She took a box of cereal from the opposite shelf and waved it at them. "Or did you just come in here to bother us?"

Coral stared at her in amazement, and Monkey and Oli whispered to each other. "What's the matter with her?" Katrice muttered.

"Nothing that you can't fix," yelled Helix. "Get out of here!" She threw the valve and the box of cereal at them. The valve landed behind Monkey with a clatter. The box hit Coral on the shoulder, bounced, and broke open on the floor, spraying pellets of hearty grain goodness everywhere.

"Hey! If you're going to fight, take it outside," shouted Mandy from behind the counter. "Don't destroy my store!"

Coral looked like she was trying to decide how to hit Helix without getting tangled in her arms. Chango rushed forward and interposed herself between them. "We're leaving," she said, grasping Helix's lower left elbow, pushing her along as she sidled past the vatdivers. Helix broke from her grasp and turned once more to face them. "Go outside," said Chango, pushing her back. "Go play in the rain some more. It'll hardly be worse than the beating they'll give you if you keep this up."

Helix hesitated, staring blankly at her as the rage faded from her eyes. She nodded and went outside.

"Sorry," Chango told Mandy as she picked the spilled cereal box up off the floor and took it to the counter to pay for it. As she stood there she was aware of the vatdivers muttering among themselves and staring, but they troubled her no further.

"That was really some stunt you pulled yesterday," Chango said as they sat in the garden behind Mavi's house. "I don't know what got into you. First the thing with the rain, and then that fight with Coral. You know, after what you told me about hiding out at your father's place all those years, I was really worried about what would happen when you had to deal with the vatdivers. Now I'm beginning to think they better watch out for you."

Helix shrugged and scratched her arm in remembrance of the rain's touch. She looked around the garden. The weather had cleared, and it was a bright, warm day, still a little humid as the sun burned off the lingering damp. If there was any growth medium in the rain, it hadn't done these plants any harm. Green, luxuriant growth surrounded them, making the air heavy with the scent of life and death. About a foot from her knee lay a dead sparrow; feet curled delicately against her grey belly. A thin-bodied bee hovered nearby, and flies took turns crawling into its body to lay their eggs. She thought of what would be found in this garden in November, the bones . . .

"What are those?" she pointed at the tall, bushy, silver-leaved plants growing in a clump in one corner.

"That's mugwort, and it's pretty out of control, but Mavi likes it. She says it brings visions."

Helix leaned back on her upper hands. The ground beneath her palms was warm and springy. It was a nice feeling, being enclosed in this sea of green, cushioned in its quiet by the gentle humming of insects. Chango was saying something about marking, or marks, but Helix wasn't listening.

Leaving Hector was not the fiasco she had thought it would be. Despite yesterday's confrontation with the vatdivers, she felt surprisingly light and . . . happy. She liked Chango and the people she'd introduced her to. Mavi, Hyper, Pele—she felt comfortable with them, not like she had to hide at all. And that scene yesterday in the party store was just the sort of thing she'd always dreaded, but it hadn't killed her. It hadn't even shamed or frightened her. In fact, when she thought of the looks on those divers' faces when she started throwing stuff at them, a grin came unbidden to her lips.

"—and so I was thinking, you'd be an ace scanning once you got the hang of it, and in the meantime, you could be the stall." Chango paused to see Helix looking at her blankly. "You know, distract them."

"Distract who?"

"The mark. Are you all right? You feeling okay?"

"Yeah. It's nice back here. Safe-feeling."

"I'm glad," said Chango, leaning closer to her and taking her lower right hand. She cradled it in her own small hand, splaying her fingertips across Helix's broad digits. Chango's hand looked very small indeed there, next to her own, and it was warm and light, like a little brown bird. "Do you know that you're very beautiful?" she asked Helix.

Helix stared at her. Her face felt warm, and her hands tingled. A small smile crept across her lips of its own volition. "Beautiful . . ." she whispered, looking away.

"That's right," Chango said, gently turning Helix's chin so she was facing her again. Chango searched her face, her two-color eyes bright with intent. "Your eyes, your face, your hair"— she glanced down and then up again, and she smiled— "your body; it all goes together, and let me tell you," she said, locking her gaze to Helix's, her face dead serious except for her shining eyes, "it is one majestic fucking harmony."

Helix blinked, and then Chango was leaning over, her face coming closer and closer to hers. Alarmed, Helix tried to back away, but there wasn't much of anyplace for her to go. There was something crashingly immanent in the air around them, but for the life of her she couldn't figure out what it was, or what Chango was trying to do, and then she felt her lips on hers, another mouth, speaking to her mouth in a moist, sweet language mouths know. She lifted her arms around Chango to hold her, to steady her, to feel with curious fingers the fabric of Chango's T-shirt sliding against her skin underneath.

They lay down on the ground together, there in the garden, and somehow they just lost track of whose body was whose. Chango's tongue got into Helix's mouth, a large, slippery serpent, flickering about, and Helix's lower hands found some way under that T-shirt and she stroked her; smooth warm skin covered with fine, fine hairs, all but invisible to her fingertips. When Chango reached her hand up to cup one of Helix's breasts, she jumped at the unexpected jolt which overrode all fear at being touched, being seen, being known—an electric bolt which ran lengthwise through her body, and threw her mind into some other place, where for once she was not at odds with herself, but was just what she wanted to be, and did just what she wanted to do.

9

SHIVERS OF GLASS

ONE afternoon when Chango had gone down to Greektown to scan codes, Helix went on her own to Hyper's house. "Helix," he said in surprise, pushing the screen door open to let her in. "Where's Chango?"

"She went to Greektown," Helix said, stepping through the doorway.

"Oh." Hyper raised his eyebrows meaningfully. "Codes." He turned to his workshop. "Come on in," he said over his shoulder. "I was just rewiring a telephone."

Helix sat on a stool across from him as he dismantled an ancient push-button phone. "I'm not sure what I'm going to do with this yet," said, frowning down on it. "When in doubt, take it apart." His fingers jabbed the buttons idly, producing a ragged tune. "Hey." He looked at her. "If I got three more of these, I could make you a musical instrument. A keyboard only you could play."

Helix made a face. "I don't think so."

"No? Oh well." He shrugged. "So what's up?"

Helix lifted her shoulders to mimic his gesture and bit her upper lip. "If someone were to apply for a job as a vatdiver, how would they go about it?"

"Someone wants a job as a vatdiver?" Hyper leaned forward, staring at her, grinning in amazement. "Are you sure?"

She nodded her head. Hyper's eyebrows arched and he gazed at the ceiling with a long, drawn-out sigh. When he looked back at her it was with a quizzical expression. "Why do you want to dive?"

Helix opened her mouth, but she didn't know what to say.

"You don't know, do you? You just want to do it."

She nodded and then shook her head. "It's a job, that's all. I need a job."

"Uh-huh." Hyper nodded faintly and returned his attention to the telephone. "Well, if someone wanted to apply for a job in the vats, they'd have to place an application with personnel. Someone could do that either by going to the personnel office at GeneSys, or by filing the application over the holonet." His gaze slid across the table to his transceiver headset, then back to her. "You can use it, if you want."

Helix sat in the bare, tiled examination room, clutching a flimsy paper gown about her. The air was chilly, and she shivered.

The door opened and a tall, white-coated figure entered. "Helix Martin?" he said, glancing at a mylar form on a clipboard.

"Yes." She shifted nervously on the examination table.

"Stand up please, and turn around."

Helix turned her back to him and felt his hands exploring her shoulders, her back, her arms . . . "Candidate possesses obvious mutations: quadruple arms and overdevelopment of the canine molars," he murmured into his transceiver. "You can sit down again," he said to her.

She climbed back onto the examination table, and he fastened a monitor to her naked back. "Heart rate slightly elevated," he said, gazing at the readout. "Are you nervous?" he asked her, smiling.

She nodded.

"There's no need to be, it's just a routine examination. I'm going to take some blood now, okay?"

She shrugged. "Okay."

He pricked her finger with a sharp tube that drew her blood up into it, set the tube in a labeled capsule, and handed her an empty beaker. "All I need now is a urine sample. There's a rest room down the hall. You can get dressed first. Just leave the sample on the shelf in the bathroom. The personnel clerk will be getting in touch with you in a few days."

"That's it?"

"That's it. Fill this, and you can go. Not as bad as you expected, huh?"

She shook her head, and after he left, scrambled gratefully into her clothes.

Chango pushed mashed potatoes around on her plate and wondered what could be taking Helix so long. She said she had to run an errand for Hyper, but she didn't say what it was, and when Chango offered to go with her, she refused. For that matter, she hadn't been able to get much out of Hyper about this errand either. He only mumbled something about machine parts and went back to his welding.

They were living with Hyper now. Mavi needed the pink room for Hugo. She and Helix made a bed for themselves among the cushions in the front room, and Chango made sure the door was locked.

"Hey," said a voice beside her. Chango looked up from her demolished plate special to see Helix standing there, still wearing the raincoat, but unbuttoned now. It was a start.

"Hey, what took you so long? Have a seat."

Helix sat down across from her, smiling widely, her fangs poking out from her lips.

"What's got you so happy, huh?"

Helix shrugged, her eyes flickering uneasily over Chango's face. "It's a nice day out. And it's good to see you."

"Huh. I don't know. You've got what I'd call a shit-eating grin on you. You up to something?"

Helix shook her head slowly, then took one of Chango's hands in hers, brought it to her mouth, and started chewing lightly on her fingers.

"Hey, stop it. Not in here." Regretfully she pulled her hand back.

"No? Okay." Helix folded her four hands primly on the table. "So what are we doing tonight?"

"Think you're ready to go to the bar? There's a band playing at Josa's tonight."

"Hmm."

"I'll be with you. And Hyper said he's going."

Helix nodded. "Okay." And then, to Chango's amazement, she took off her raincoat. "You were right, you know," she said. "People aren't as bad as I thought they'd be."

* * *

Chango clung to one of Helix's hands and squirmed through the crowd at Josa's. It was fine for her, she was good at slipping through crowds, but Helix kept getting caught on people. By the time they got to the bar, she'd had the best possible introduction to a fair percentage of the Vattown population and was looking pretty panicky. "Sorry about that," said Chango, "It's kind of crowded."

Helix shook her head and laughed. "That was so weird!" she said, looking more like the victim of a roller-coaster ride than a person actually terrified. She'd left her raincoat at Hyper's, wearing just the green bodysuit and a blue sylk swing tunic they found yesterday behind Clothzillion's. Her color was high, her eyes sparkling. With a twinge of pride, Chango noticed that other people were staring at her, too.

"People were all pushed up against me," said Helix. "No one could really see me. But I felt them." She leaned forward and ran a hand up Chango's arm. "Like I felt you."

Chango's eyes widened. This was a far cry from the person who'd fled in terror because Chango bumped into her in a casino. "I can't believe how well you're handling this!" she shouted as the band started up. "I didn't think I'd get you in the door!"

"Hey, kids!" It was Hyper, popping out of the crowd like a cork. He still had his transceiver on, with a projector lens screwed onto it so he could flash pictures up on the walls when he danced.

The Ply-Tones started playing "Zinc Oxide," and Chango jumped off her stool. "I have to dance to this!" she said.

"Yeah!" Hyper nodded his head at the dark walls of the bar. "I'm with you, sister. What this place needs is a good light show."

Chango shook her head. "We can't leave Helix here alone!"

They glanced at Helix, who stood. "I'll dance," she said, her voice barely audible over the urgent beat of the music.

Hyper danced in a manic jitter, frantically switching channels, providing the bar's denizens with visuals ranging from detergent commercials to open heart surgery. The images flashed and flickered on the walls as his head swayed to the music, but his efforts were in vain. Everybody within eyeshot was watching Helix.

She danced like a temple goddess, her arms waving, her skin glistening with the reflected colors of Hyper's wall projections. Space formed around them as the other dancers slowed and backed away to watch her. When the song ended, they were surrounded by a ring of onlookers who burst into spontaneous applause. Helix stood in the middle of the circle, her eyes suddenly wide with surprise and fear. But then another song started, and her body seemed to take over from her mind, turning and swaying with the undulating rhythms of the music.

The set ended and Helix, out of breath and dizzy from dancing, followed Chango and Hyper back to the bar. Hyper ordered a round of drafts. With just the jukebox playing, the noise in the bar settled down to a dull roar. The door opened, and a discernible ripple ran through the place. The crowd parted to let a stately creature through. She walked with either indolent grace or extreme carefulness, Helix wasn't sure which. She was upwards of seven feet tall, her hair—pure white and fine as spun glass—was swept up over her brows in an elaborate filigree of braids. Her skin was not so much white as it was transparent. She looked blue. Not the black-blue of the night sky, but the softest, palest powder blue imaginable, and even from here, Helix could make out the tracery of veins across her face and hands. Accompanied by her bodyguard, she glided to the back of the bar and softly folded herself into a corner booth.

"The Doctor is in," muttered Chango.

"Who is that?" whispered Helix.

"Orielle," Chango told her. "They say if it weren't for her, there'd be no Blast in Vattown. Of course that's not all she deals in."

People began to drift over to Orielle's table singly and in pairs. They'd sit with her for a time—you never actually saw the money or anything else, but in a little while they'd get up and another set of buyers took their place.

"I think they're getting up," said Hyper, sliding off his stool and nodding at the pair of divers at the booth.

"Hey, what are you doing?" asked Chango.

Hyper looked over his shoulder and grinned.

"You're not buying anything from her, are you?" said Chango.

Hyper shrugged.

"Hyper, with your jumped-up metabolism, you can't afford to go messing around with her concoctions."

"I'm just going to say 'hi.' Don't you want to meet her, Helix?"

"Yeah, I guess so." said Helix.

"Then come on."

Helix followed him to Orielle's table, trailed reluctantly by Chango.

"Orielle, I want you to meet Helix—Helix, Orielle," said Hyper.

The creature lifted her head, and turned towards them a face of finely drawn bones—all sharp edges and angular planes, her skin thin and translucent, like rice paper. And her eyes—red, hot, albino eyes. "I have heard so much about you," she said to Helix, dropping her eyes and waving her into the seat across from her. Her long, silver-painted fingernails glittered and drew figures in the air.

Like dancers, Orielle's hands moved across the tabletop, scooped up a small silver box, and then, by some subtle motion, she held four ampules in her hand like slivers of ice, palest blue. "A little something of my own design," she said. "I call it Shivers of Glass. It has a diazepam base note with highlights of ergoloid mesylate. A tad on the narcotic side, but still I find it quite . . . exquisite." She twirled an ampule between her fingers and broke it, throwing her head back and inhaling the evaporating liquid.

A moment passed with nothing more than bar noises to mark it. Orielle drew her head back down, her eyes glittering. There were still three ampules in her hand. "Would you like to try it?" she asked Helix.

Chango shook her head.

"No thanks," said Helix. Orielle offered an ampule to Hyper, but he refused under Chango's insistent glare. Orielle turned to Chango.

"No thanks," she said.

"Ah that's right, you're the little pothead who doesn't do drugs."

Chango scowled. "What's a little reefer? It's mixed with tobacco anyway."

"Oh, and tobacco isn't a drug?"

"No, and neither is pot in my opinion. They're plants. The stuff you sell, it's all synthesized chemicals. Man-made substances the human body was never designed to handle."

Orielle chuckled softly. "Whatever. Anyway, I haven't seen your friend Benny here tonight. Tell him I've come into a quantity of Blast in liquid form. If he's interested I can give him a good price."

Chango wrinkled her nose. "What would Benny want with liquid? He's not a shooter."

"Of course not. Some people like to make their own blends. He was into it a few years ago, so maybe he'd be interested now."

"Maybe," said Chango, "but I'm not doing your pushing for you. You want to sell him something, you talk to him."

"She's quite cantankerous, isn't she?" Orielle said to Helix. "Is she taking good care of you?"

"Oh yeah," said Helix. "She licks my teeth."

For a moment, silence reigned, and then Orielle's face split apart, shattered and dissolved and reformed itself into laughter. Her voice pitched through the bar in earsplitting peals, and the crowd, perhaps in self-defense, raised their voices in whoops and shouts. She looked at Helix closely. "They say you are the strangest sport since I came along," she said. "Some even have the umbrage to say you are stranger than I am. But—" she smiled a broad thin smile, like a crack in a windowpane "—I think they may be right. Whatever shall I do?" She shook her head sadly.

"Why do you want to be the strangest?" asked Helix.

"Well, I must be something, mustn't I? Especially since I won't be anything for terribly long."

"It seems to me you're pretty accomplished without the goofy chromosomes," Helix said, nodding at the broken ampule laying on the table.

"Yes, but without the chromosomes, without the strangeness, I never would have had the initiative to do any of it. It wouldn't have mattered. Oh, how I pity those unfortunate creatures whose differences are invisible, and no less deadly." She nodded at Hyper.

"You say creatures . . ."

"It is a more noble term than sport. Sport, as if we were someone else's amusement."

"Maybe we are," said Chango.

"Maybe some of us are," said Orielle with a pointed look. "I know I'm not. A creature is its own being. It exists on its own terms. Others may attempt to enslave it, but it will always thwart control. Haven't you seen the movies?"

Chango stood up. Helix glanced at her, then at Orielle. "I guess we're going to go now," she said.

"Very well. It was nice to meet you. Just remember, Helix," she leaned forward, her red eyes staring, "if you're going to be a freak, you might as well be a freak show."

Back at the bar Chango sipped at her beer, sullenly watching the conclusion of a transaction at Orielle's table. Vonda stood up and walked towards the bar, staring at Helix. She walked right up to them, ignoring Chango as usual. "I don't think you know what you're doing," she said to Helix, "so I'm going to tell you. Sports have no business vatdiving, and if you try it, you're going to find that out."

Chango felt as if someone had poured ice water over her. "What are you talking about, Vonda?"

Vonda glanced at her. "You don't know?" She nodded her head at Helix. "She went in and took a physical today and filled out an application."

"What? That's bullshit." She turned to Helix. "You didn't."

Helix looked at her levelly, not smiling, not protesting. She spoke with a calm that reached into Chango and twisted her stomach. "I did. I need a job."

"Don't give me that crap," said Vonda. "I've heard all about you. You don't need a job. Your daddy works at the big office. He can get you a job. A better one than this, believe me. What are you doing down here anyway? Slumming? Go back where you belong."

"You don't know where I belong," said Helix.

"Helix, you can't dive," said Chango, choking on the words.

"Yes I can, and I will. Watch me."

"I can't believe this. We talked about it." Chango took Helix's upper hands in hers. "I told you how bad diving would be for you."

"I know. I know you did, but—"

"But what then? Listen, don't worry, if they accept your application, just tell them you changed your mind."

"I'm not going to do that."

Chango released her hands, staring at her. "Why?" she asked, because it was the only thing she could think to say.

"Because I haven't changed my mind."

"You're going to wish you had," said Vonda.

"She's right," said Chango.

Helix turned from her to Vonda, an odd impassive expression on her face. She looked at them both the same way, as if they were obstacles. "You can say what you want," said Helix, "but if they want to hire me, I'm taking the job."

"Okay," said Vonda. "Okay, but you've been warned. Remember that."

"You can't stop me from working." Sudden anger glinted in her eyes.

"No," said Vonda, stepping closer, "but we can make it hard for you, and we will."

"Vonda. Vonda, don't worry. She won't dive," said Chango, moving to stand beside Helix.

Helix turned to her and put both sets of hands on her shoulders. "Chango, I know you mean well, but this isn't any of your business."

"What?"

"Well, it's my business," said Vonda. "The only business I and the other vatdivers have. And you working means one less job for somebody who needs one, who can really do it. You know they'll pay you less and classify you as temporary so they can get out of giving you health benefits. You're just playing along with them. You're helping them lower hiring standards. It's a dangerous job; we depend on each other in there."

Helix leaned towards her. "Then you're going to have to depend on me."

Vonda bared her teeth and stiff-armed Helix in the chest. "I'm not depending on you. Not only are you a freak, you're insane."

"What she is," said a voice made of crystal and rain, "is none of your fucking business, you little goon. All you need to know is that she is a far more fabulous creature than you could ever hope to be, even on your deathbed. Now why don't you go croak off."

It was Orielle. She had materialized beside Helix as if made of vapor.

Vonda looked sullen now, instead of enraged. "This has nothing to do with you."

"Why? Because you say so? What if I decide it does? What then? Would you like to shove me, too? Why don't you just throw a punch? Go ahead, shatter my jaw."

"Don't be ridiculous, Orielle."

"No, I didn't think so." Her mouth pointed in a wicked smile, and she turned to Helix and Chango and Hyper, encompassing them with a sweep of her gauze-draped arm. "Shall we, children?" and she guided them through the slowly parting crowd of onlookers.

Outside the bar, Chango turned on Helix. "Vonda's right, you are insane," she said.

"Chango—" Helix touched her cheek; her hand was cool. "I'm sorry I couldn't tell you I was applying. You would have tried to stop me."

"Damn straight I would have. Forget all that crap Vonda laid on you. The reason you shouldn't dive is because it will kill you."

Helix shook her head. "I just don't believe that."

Chango looked up at the sky and laughed. "No, that's right. I'm just making it all up!"

"Maybe she'll be okay," said Hyper.

Chango stared at him. "What? Are you nuts too?"

Hyper shrugged. "It's her life, you know."

She nodded. "Yeah, yeah." She stared at Helix, and there were tears in her eyes. "I guess I'm the fool here. I thought maybe you had something to live for," she said, and walked away.

They sprawled on blankets and cushions around the artifact: Orielle's thirty-six-inch television set with a laser disk drive.

"These old laser disks are much better in their original format. I can't even stand to watch the holographic ones. The framing is all wrong," she said, sliding a well-preserved disk into the slot with nimble fingers.

Helix gnawed at her lower lip with one of her fangs. She'd lived a goodly portion of her life in modest affluence, with pretty close to the latest in entertainment technology, but this, this was evidence of a different type of wealth altogether. A rare and highly specialized piece of equipment. Extremely expensive and of no practical use whatsoever. Just to find disks in playable condition would cost a small fortune. It was a remarkable achievement, this television set, a monument to disposable cash.

Orielle folded herself onto a cushion and reached beneath the coffee table for a lacquered box. It was glossy and black, inlaid with mother-of-pearl in abstract geometric shapes. She drew from it a glittering chrome Blast pistol, its fittings and chamber rendered in curving lines like ripples of water. She fitted a white, ceramic capsule into the chamber and twisted it shut. "Would you like to go first?" she asked Helix, the gun resting in her outstretched palm like a pool of liquid metal.

Helix hesitated, then lifted the thing in her lower left hand, cradled it, and slipped her index finger through the trigger guard. She opened her mouth and rested the muzzle gently against the roof of her mouth, squeezed the trigger and jerked her head back at the cold burst of gas against the roof of her mouth.

"Inhale," said Hyper, but Helix gagged against the rush of pressure-released gas and coughed. In defeat she withdrew the pistol and wiped it on her sleeve. "Sorry," she said, handing it back to Orielle. She felt a mild tingle at the base of her skull, nothing more.

"You have to be ready for it," said Orielle. "Here, watch." She replaced the spent cartridge with a new one and drew the barrel into her mouth. She exhaled deeply, and then pulled the trigger, breathing in at the same time. Her eyes closed momentarily and then she put another fresh cartridge into the pistol with automatic motions. When she handed it to Helix, her eyes were glistening and unfocused. "Now try it again," she whispered.

Helix held the pistol in her hand. "What does it feel like?" she asked.

Orielle smiled and her eyes closed again. "Only one way to find out."

This time when Helix squeezed the trigger she breathed in, and felt her sinuses flooded with icy gas. It made her eyes water, and she shook her head, then shivered as the tingling at the base of her skull spread up and out, across her face and over her skin to the tips of her fingers and toes. She felt like a glass of water vibrating with the frequency of some distant chime. She saw a temple, gleaming white on a distant, sunlit mountaintop. Below, in the valley, a river flowed by.

When her eyes refocused, she was left with a lightness in her body. The chime still vibrated in her cells, thinning her physical form, turning her more into sound than flesh. Hyper was taking the gun into his mouth. She watched him release the gas and lean back, eyes closed.

His skin looked very fine and bright. She leaned closer, because she thought she could see gold in the hollows of his cheeks. Her face was inches from his when he opened his eyes—glittering with the reflection of the river. She could feel the sound emanating from his body, to ring against hers, and she leaned closer to sharpen the pitch, to touch his vibrating skin and tune her cells to his.

Chango climbed the steps to Hyper's house in the bright morning sunshine and let herself in the front door. She knew right away the house was empty. If Hyper'd been home he'd have been moving around somewhere, and if Hyper wasn't home, Helix wouldn't be here either. They'd spent the night then, at Orielle's. Chango shook her head to try and rid herself of a headache. She'd gone to sleep on Mavi's couch last night with a hard lump of anger in her stomach. It had climbed into her head while she slept. It was like a ball bearing rattling around in there, and every time it bounced off her skull, she thought of another angry, hurtful thing to say. She pulled one of Hyper's bench stools into the archway, sat down, and waited.

They came up the stairs together, and as soon as she saw them, she knew they'd made love to each other. She'd been all ready to read Helix the riot act about diving, but this distracted her. It was an easier thing to be mad about than Helix's inexplicable death wish. If there was anything she'd learned from Pele, it was how to throw a jealous fit.

"You slept together," she said, as they stood in the doorway, staring at her owlishly. "My girl and my best friend."

"Your girl? Good gods!" exclaimed Hyper.

"Well, it was too late to leave," said Helix.

"No, I mean you had sex."

"Oh, yeah, yeah we did," said Helix. "It was different than with you. What's the matter?"

"Was it better?"

"What?"

"Chango, please," said Hyper.

She ignored him. "Was it better, Helix? Do you like him better?"

"I like both of you."

Hyper spread his hands. "Can't argue with that, can you? Don't tell me Miss Free Love Michigan is going to claim ownership of her lover's body."

Chango put her face in her hands. "I don't know. I just don't know anymore."

"The shoe hurts when it's on the other foot, doesn't it?" said Hyper. "But that's not really what you're upset about. I mean, maybe you are, but what's really bugging you is that Helix is going to be a vatdiver."

"I can't believe you support her in this. Don't you care if she dies?"

"Of course I care." Hyper approached her, and put his hand on her arm. "But let me show you something—"

"No!" Chango recoiled and jumped off the stool. She started gathering her clothes from the front room, stuffing them heedlessly in her backpack. "I don't want any more explanations." She turned to Helix. "You're going to dive in the vats and you're going to die." She looked at Hyper. "And you're helping her. Well, I'm not going to stick around and watch it happen. I'm out of here," she said, and she left, banging the screen door shut behind her.

Helix arrived at the gates to the vat yard at a quarter to eight the next morning. About twenty vatdivers congregated on the street in loose clusters, talking among themselves. A tall, broad-shouldered woman looked up as she approached the gate and muttered something to her companions. They all darted glances at her, their conversation becoming more animated. "Must be crazy," Helix overheard as she passed, and, "What makes her think she has the right?" She quickened her pace, entering the vat yard and searching among the domed vat houses for one labeled 9. Before long a security guard spotted her and ambled up. "Employees only, ma'am," he said.

"I am," she said, "that is, I will be. I'm here for orientation, Vat nine."

He looked at her dubiously. "What's your name?"

"Helix Martin," she told him.

He switched on his transceiver, scanned through a list of names, and found hers. "Okay." He shrugged. "It's the one over there, second from the end." He pointed to the opposite end of the yard.

"Thanks," she said, and made her way across the cloncrete towards it. Inside, the vat house was astir with end of shift activity. Divers filed towards the showers, a pair of porters went by, lugging a plasmic barrel marked "Grow Med. Batch 1234-9896," a supervisor shouted instructions to a team in the vat, her voice ringing clear above the general din and murmur of voices bouncing off the polished cloncrete floor and the glass dome above. It was bright inside, lit by halogens and the morning sky. A balcony ran along the second story, with catwalks connecting to the upper rim of the vat, which filled most of the room.

An ample woman in white coveralls approached her, glancing at a clipboard. A badge above her left breast said "April." "Helix Martin?" She eyed her impassively.

"Yes."

She nodded. "You're early. Come on, there's some forms for you to fill out."

Helix followed her to a small office on the ground floor, where a stoop-shouldered, smiling clerk handed her waivers and contractual agreements and tax forms, and she signed them. When she was done, April took her to the locker room. It seemed to be a vast sea of tile and steam, with rows upon rows of lockers, and divers in all stages of undress. April took her down one long aisle, a narrow bench running its length down the middle, to a locker at the far end, near the wall. "This is yours, number three-oh-two," she said and opened it. "Take off your coat. I have to measure you for a suit."

A small throng of divers hung out at the other end of the aisle with an expectant air. She glanced at April, who stared back with patient indifference. She swallowed and reached for the buttons of Hector's overcoat with trembling fingers. She adjusted her position to put as much of April between herself and the divers as possible, and slowly, with economical gestures, she unbuttoned her coat.

"Na-na-na-na, na-na-na-na," someone sang the tune to "The Stripper," and someone else hooted, and there was general laughter among the audience. Helix's face burned, and she stood there, her coat hanging open, her hair standing on end, sweat breaking out under her armpits. She glared at April, who pretended not to have heard anything.

"Well," she said, "c'mon, you can't dive unless you've got the gear."

There was silence as Helix removed the coat and hung it up in the locker. She turned back to face April and the divers again, her limbs revealed in the polyweave bodysuit and tunic she wore. April pursed her lips and whistled softly. "I don't know," she said loudly, turning to one side so everyone could get a good view. "I don't know if we have a suit that'll fit you." She cast a winking, sidelong glance at the divers, who snickered. "Follow me. We'll have to see what we can do."

The vatdivers dispersed as they approached, wandering off in muttering clusters to the showers or their own lockers. April led her out of the locker room, back onto the vat floor, and then to a room crowded with suits and tanks and face masks. With a sigh she began taking suits off the rack and holding them up to Helix, squinting and frowning. "They're supposed to be skintight, but you're gonna have to take a larger size." She nodded her head, gazing at Helix's lower arms. "You'll have to keep them inside. Less'n you want to forfeit your first five paychecks for a custom job, that is," she added with a smirk. "And I'd recommend against it, seeing as how you may not live that long. Might as well spend the pay while you can."

Helix stared at her. April stared back with blank, implacable hatred. "What do you care?" she asked, finally.

April shrugged. "Only that you're a damn fool on a suicide stunt, that you're liable to endanger my divers, and that you're keeping this job from someone who deserves it. I guess they're looking for cheap labor. They want to see how long you last, see?

If it's long enough, and they can convince more of you to sign waivers on medical coverage and future compensation, why then, they've got fresh, cheap, labor to replace the rest of us with."

Helix nodded with sudden comprehension. "You think I'm a scab."

April snorted. "Shit yeah. Ain't yah?"

She shrugged. "If I am, I don't mean to be. But I am going to dive. And you are going to show me how. Besides, if all of what you say is true, then I'll croak in a month and I'll be out of your hair. Right?"

April raised an eyebrow and a slow, sly smile slid across her mouth. She voiced a single crack of laughter and shoved a suit at Helix. "Try it on, smart-ass."

By the end of her shift Helix felt as if her suit had fused to her body, and her lower arms were painfully cramped. She trudged wearily to the locker room, found her locker, and sank onto the bench. She unfastened the seals of her suit and extricated her aching arms. Propping her upper elbows on her knees, she let her lower arms dangle between her legs, her fingertips grazing the tile floor. They tingled with pins and needles, the pain increasing sharply as blood rushed in and circulation resumed.

Helix was blinking back tears when she heard footsteps behind her. She turned to see four vatdivers sauntering down the aisle towards her. "So how was your first day, sport?" said Vonda, a narrow, sarcastic smile across her face. She threw one leg over the bench and sat down, the others ranged themselves behind her, leaning against the lockers and smirking at one another.

"It was all right," said Helix, sitting up and reaching for her clothes.

"Yeah? Is it everything you dreamed it would be?" asked one of the others, a man with brown skin and dark hair curling on his chest.

"I hope so," said Coral, still in her divesuit, the hood pulled down to reveal her straight dark hair. " 'Cause it's going to cost her plenty."

"Mmm-hmm. What would you give her, Vonda? Six months?"

asked the fourth one, a fair-skinned guy with a broad face and blue eyes.

"Oh, if that long," answered Vonda. Her eyes took in Helix's body with ravenous curiosity. "With a mutation like that, I'd say four months, tops."

Helix fumbled for her bodysuit. She got the limp thing in her hands, only to realize that she still wore her divesuit over her legs, and she'd have to get completely undressed in order to get dressed, and she'd have to do that, apparently, with an audience. She clutched the bodysuit to her breasts and turned around, brandishing her lower arms. "Look," she said, "get a good look, all of you, because next time, it won't be a free show."

They glanced among themselves and giggled. " 'Fraid not, honey," said the fair-skinned man. "You're on our dive team. We're all going to be seeing a lot of each other."

"If you stick around, that is," added Coral.

"And I'd advise strongly against it," said Vonda, standing and putting one hand on Helix's shoulder, pushing her, gently but firmly, into the locker behind her, "Because we don't want you here, and we can make you not want to be here, too."

Helix stared into her hazel eyes and then laughed. "Fuck off."

Vonda's eyes flashed, and she tried to punch Helix in the stomach, but Helix caught her arm with her lower two and, grasping her fist, bent it back against the wrist. She gave it an extra twist before shoving her away hard with all of her arms. The bench hit Vonda on the back of the knees, forcing her to sit down suddenly, nearly falling backwards.

"What's going on here?" said a new voice. It was Benny, down at the end of the aisle, his hands on his hips. At the sound of his voice, the others started drifting away, all except for Vonda, who still glared at her, nursing her wrist, daring her to tell him what happened.

"Vonda and her pals here were just welcoming me to GeneSys, that's all. She was trying to teach me the secret vatdiver hand-shake, and I must have gotten it wrong."

Benny stopped the others. "Wait a minute, since you guys haven't been properly introduced, allow me. You already got Vonda's name, and I think you know Coral. This is Val," he gestured towards the blond guy, "and this is Claude. Everybody, this is Helix."

"Helix?" said Claude. "Her name is Helix? What a joke."

"Yeah," said Helix, "pretty hilarious." She turned her back on them and got dressed.

"Don't you guys have something to, you know, do?" Benny said, and she heard them walk away, their feet slapping against the tile floor.

When she turned around again, he was still standing there. "Sorry about that," he said.

"Why should you be sorry? You didn't do it."

"No, but I could have warned you. Obviously they aren't too happy about having you here."

"Plenty of people warned me already. I don't care. I've had worse."

He shook his head at her and smiled. "This is really important to you, isn't it?"

"Naw, Benny, it's just kicks, can't you tell? I'm sorry. Yes, it is, and I don't know why."

10

ANCESTOR EYES

NATHAN Graham took a candicaine lozenge from the dish at his bar and sucked it in frustration as he returned to his desk to sort through the mail. He had neglected it during the two weeks it took him to settle the Wichita affair. He was behind on his real work, and now there was that out-of-control project of Dr. Martin's to contend with.

He had a message from Brea Jeffries, the lead personnel clerk for production. He remembered Brea. She was diligent, conscientious, and had a fine eye for detail. He'd always had trouble with her. She questioned anything that did not follow strict hiring protocol. He skimmed her letter in annoyance. She was inquiring about some missing application records for a recent hire.

"I'm not in production anymore, dammit," he growled and deposited the letter in his low-priority stack. He checked his watch. It was ten o'clock. In another hour, Colin Slatermeyer would make his weekly pilgrimage to the Belle Isle Aquarium.

Nathan's maglev parked itself beside the aquarium and he got out, admiring the delicate glass structure of the arboretum on the side of the building. He'd been here once before, years ago. They hadn't gone inside the aquarium; they just wandered around among date palms and banana trees inside the arboretum's domes. He remembered the heady musk of orchids and the aridity of the cactus room.

It was a strange place to come to alone, he thought as he ascended the steps to the brick archway above the entrance, but then, you probably didn't get out of ALIVE! without being a little strange.

Inside, the aquarium was cavelike, with black-and-green enameled brick walls, the mortar between them dark with age. Reflections from the display windows in the walls lent the dim light a greenish, watery cast. The air was cool, and his footsteps echoed on the floor with an odd, hollow sound.

The place was nearly deserted. In fact, except for the jaded attendant who took his admission fee from him, it seemed that he and Colin had it all to themselves.

He hadn't seen Colin yet, but he didn't need to. He'd seen his maglev in the parking lot. Nathan strolled slowly along, looking into the tanks in the wall beyond the railing. Everything about this place, including the fish, had an air of the forgotten to it. He paused to stare at a huge gar, grey-green and ancient, its narrow, pointed nose nearly as long as his forearm. It floated there in the softly glowing water, barely moving, contemplating eternity, until he walked past and one eye swiveled to follow him.

He found Colin at the far end of the aquarium, gazing at blind, white little cave fish. He stepped up behind him quietly. "You can still see where their ancestors had eyes," he said.

Colin jerked around, his already wide eyes bulging further when he saw who it was. "Mr. Graham!" he said in alarm, and then quickly feigned pleased surprise. "What are you doing here?"

Nathan waved at the tanks. "Same as you, looking at fish."

He laughed nervously. "That's weird. I've never seen you here before, I come here all the time and—"

"I know."

That shut him up. He closed his mouth, his expression one of studied neutrality, waiting.

"You think I came here to talk to you. You're right. You're a very talented young man, Colin. I've been meaning to tell you how pleased I am to have you on our research team at GeneSys. We're very excited about your doctoral thesis, 'Recombinant Percolation of Basic Proteins in Eukaryotic Sheeting.' I've been discussing it with the people in departmental, and we think it could be big. A whole new direction for development at GeneSys. And since you've done the groundbreaking work on it, well, naturally—" He broke off and shook his hands in front of his face. "Let me just say, for now, that I think the folks back home would be durn proud, that's all." He stopped and smiled, watching him.

Colin stood there, his arms limp at his sides, his mouth open. Slowly he shook his head, his brows knitted together. "What's this all about?"

"You're from downriver, aren't you Colin? That's what I like, a good local boy. Did you know I was born in Detroit? I was. Grew up in Oz, later Roseville. I remember after high school, everyone talking about where they were going to go. It never occurred to me to move away. I couldn't imagine living anywhere else."

"Yeah?" Colin shrugged cynically. "Well, the only thing I miss about home is having Sundays off. That's why I come here; to observe the day of rest."

"You're part of that religious community down there, aren't you?"

"Huh? Uh, yeah. 'Religious community,' that's putting it politely. Cult is more like it."

"Mmm. I take it then that you would not welcome an opportunity to return."

His nostrils flared in alarm. "No, I would not."

"That's good, that's good. We need you here. Dr. Martin needs you, I'm sure. He's very tight-lipped about this Tetra Project and I sense that things are not . . . as they should be."

"I don't know what you mean."

"Oh, come on, Colin." Graham put a hand on his shoulder and leaned towards him conspiratorially. "Why were you demonstrating biopolymer properties to me in connection with a project to lower production costs? Why haven't I seen any agule density ratios on the test vats? Why haven't I seen the test vats?"

Colin stepped away from him. "Dr. Martin is very particular about laboratory conditions. Any outside influence would taint the results of our research."

"And the density ratios?"

Colin stared at him. Graham could see him trying to think of something to say. "If you ask Dr. Martin, I'm sure he'd be happy to provide you with those figures."

"Sure, after he's doctored them to show me what I want to see. No. I want you to tell me—how bad are they?"

Colin was shaking visibly now, unable to make eye contact with him. "I can't give you any information on that," he said, and started walking away.

"That's too bad," said Graham, raising his voice until it echoed off the walls. "Personally, I think you have way too much talent to waste away in that downriver Bible cult, but then, it's your funeral."

That got him. He turned around. "I'm not going back there. I'm never going back there."

"Really? Well, when you lose your fellowship here, and you can't get another job anywhere in the industry, what else will you do? And when ALIVE! learns about how you've been holding out on them, they may take matters into their own hands."

Colin stared at him; his face, at first red with rage, turned pale.

Nathan strolled slowly over to him. "You're at a critical juncture in your career, Colin. Consider carefully. Hector Martin is a great man, I know. Your admiration of him is perfectly justified, but let's face it. He's already had his moment, and now it's passed. For you, it's all to come. Don't cheat yourself out of your full potential through a misguided sense of loyalty. You deserve better than that. You deserve better, quite frankly, from Dr. Martin than to be sidetracked for—what, three years?—on a project that's never going to accomplish its objective."

"Oh, I wouldn't sell Dr. Martin so short if I were you. You saw that biopoly, and if you could see the tetras . . ."

"But that's just the point. How is he, how are you, ever going to get recognition for the work if you don't let anybody see it?"

"You don't get it, do you? You think Dr. Martin cares that a bunch of bean counters know his name. You think that's what I want. That's not it, and it's not the money, either. It's the work. It's fascinating, it's its own reason."

"I see. How nice. But are you so firmly ensconced in that ivory tower not to recognize that if somebody doesn't start cooperating with me, there isn't going to be any project anymore? I can get it canceled, and if I have to put up with much more of this nonsense, I will. Do you think I enjoy running out on my Sundays to little out-of-the-way places for clandestine meetings with lab assistants? Do you think I have nothing better to do?"

"Hey, I didn't ask you out here. You wanted to talk to me."

"That's right, that's right. But now my patience is at its end. Are you going to tell me what's going on with this project, or are you going to start brushing up on the scriptures?"

Colin watched a manta ray glide past the glass at his side, its edges fluttering. His chin dipped in an almost imperceptible nod.

"Why won't Martin let me see the test vats?"

Colin laughed and raised his hands to his face. "That's simple. We can't get in."

Colin Slatermeyer pushed his cafeteria tray down the line, paused to peer doubtfully at the cello molded dessert of the day—piled high with lactose foam and glowing an impossible orange—and made his way to the soda fountain.

He took a seat at the table with Greenfield, Pincus, Utreje, and Johns. "That all you're having?" said Greenfield, eyeing the cup on his tray.

Colin shrugged. "I'm not hungry." He took a long pull on his cola.

"So how's Dr. Martin's project coming along?" asked Johns.

Greenfield shook his head. "I think it's a dead end."

"He's not going to reach his objective?" Utreje said, leaning forward.

Greenfield shrugged. "I don't see how."

Colin swallowed hurriedly. "So what if he doesn't? The research has already provided some really remarkable side dividends. The blue biopoly being produced in the test vats, for instance. It's amazing stuff. With a buckyball side group containing trapped silver ions, it's an electricity conductor, and it's at least as malleable and durable as any of the top-line biopolymers GeneSys is producing now."

"But he was supposed to find a way to cut production overhead, not invent a new biopoly," said Pincus, pouring ketchup on her french fries.

Colin snorted. "So what? Everyone knows that's not the way research works. Most of the time the things you find out while trying to accomplish a particular goal turn out to be more important than the goal itself."

Johns raised his eyebrows. "That's not the way Nathan Graham sees it."

"Nathan Graham is an idiot," observed Utreje.

"But he's a powerful idiot," said Greenfield. "He came by our lab the other day, throwing his weight around, wanting to know when the project would be ready for field testing. He scared the hell out of Dr. Martin."

"What an asshole that guy is," said Pincus, shaking a red-tipped french fry. "He asked me to keep separate records when I was working with Dr. Vine on that base phase bonding thing."

"You're kidding. Really?" said Johns.

"Oh, no. He's always pulling shit like that. What do you expect? He's from production."

"So did you?" asked Johns.

Pincus snorted. "Please. I told him if he wanted a worm, he could look under a rock."

"Ooh, what did he do?" asked Greenfield.

"Nothing. What could he do? He didn't have anything on me. It would have attracted too much attention if he fired me. Dr. Vine would have asked questions."

Colin stared at his cafeteria tray, wishing he had taken the cello after all. It would have given him something to do with his hands. He picked up his soda, gripping it hard, and forced himself to drink.

"Yeah, but you were lucky," said Utreje. "He must have been in a good mood that day, man. I heard about this guy who handed an accounting report in to him late. Graham made him take off his pants and throw them out the window, along with the report."

"Jeez. How can he get away with that?" asked Greenfield.

"Beats me," said Utreje. "The guy was probably too scared to report it."

"Well, if he tries anything like that with Dr. Martin, you can believe Anna will be hearing about it, right Slat?"

Colin nodded faintly and took another sip of pop.

"We're professionals," Greenfield continued, "not vatdivers or grunt office workers. Besides, I'd rather quit than be that guy's toady."

Despite himself, Colin laughed, and squeezed his cellofoam cup so hard it broke, spilling ice and cola in his lap.

11

THE HABIT OF AIR

HELIX trudged down the street to Gate 29, carrying her dive-suit, air tanks, and a battered tin lunch box. It was just like being at the orphanage, this feeling of dread she had as she approached the vat houses. She never knew what she was going to find when she got to her locker.

She'd started taking her equipment home with her after her third day, when she'd found the lock cut and her suit stiff with thickening solution. She missed half a shift scrubbing it clean.

She had wanted this. She had gone against everyone—had ignored Chango's insistent pleas—to dive. Only Hyper somewhat supported her decision, letting her stay at his house after Chango left and started living out of her car again.

But as the odor of the vats hit her, infusing her nostrils with its pungent aroma, her doubts evaporated. It was worth it, worth all of it, to swim inside that smell.

Someone had scrawled the words "mutant sport bitch" across her locker with black caulking adhesive. How articulate, she thought, ignoring the expectant glances and snickering all around her. She opened her locker and got undressed, pumping her lower arms to get the blood circulating through them before wrapping them tight around her ribs and zipping the divesuit up over them.

She joined the rest of her dive mates on the platform. No one spoke to her. They just lowered themselves into the growth medium and started making their rounds, clearing the grow med of agules. During shifts they did their best to ignore her, though they were forced to acknowledge her at certain times, like when decanting. Then the whole team had to coordinate their efforts to lift the sheets of biopolymer out of the vat and maneuver them onto the drying racks. And of course whenever she made a mistake, her dive mates were only too happy to point it out.

Helix plucked a small agule from the fluid and placed it in her collection bag. "Hey, sport," Vonda's voice squawked over the suit's speaker. "You missed a whole network. You can't just pull them out, you've got to check to see if they're connected to others. Didn't we cover that in your training?"

They had, but her upper hands were not as good at fine work as her lower ones, and the tendrils tended to snap in her fingers before she could trace them. Helix glanced around the vat. Vonda was above and to the left of her, apparently at a better vantage point to see the agules in question. Helix swam up and over, located the agule cluster, and dove back down to it. She tried to collect them gently, but they still kept breaking, and she knew Vonda was up there watching her, though she didn't say anything further.

When she opened her locker at the end of the shift, a pile of agules fell out at her feet. "Missed a spot," said Vonda, and laughed.

Helix turned to her. "How did you get inside my locker?" she demanded.

"I watched you work the combination. I've been watching you a lot." She nodded at the pile of agules. "Those are all the goobers you missed today. It's bad enough you have to be diving, but at least you could be good at it."

Helix turned from her and picked up an agule, feeling her face redden. Vonda was right, she wasn't very good. And she'd been so certain she would be. She never even considered any other possibility.

She examined the agule, which was dry of growth medium and perfectly safe to handle. Long tendrils trailed away from its round, lumpy center. There was something oddly appealing about it, she thought, squishing it between her fingers.

When she got home Chango was there, standing behind Hyper as he downloaded her pirated cash card codes. She glanced up as Helix came in, a look of forlorn longing flashing briefly in her eyes before she hardened them and turned to Hyper. "You can pay me later," she said. "Meet me at Josa's." She glanced once more at Helix and then she was out the door and gone.

Hyper shook his head as the screen door banged shut in Chango's wake. "She's so afraid for you. She thinks you're going to get vatsickness and she doesn't want to go through what she went through with her sister, so she's shutting you out, trying to protect herself from getting hurt again."

Helix nodded. It was a reasonable explanation, but she still missed Chango. She needed Chango, to help her figure out how to handle the vatdivers, to take away the loneliness that followed her around like a shadow.

She dumped her gear in a corner by the stairs to the loft. Hyper wrinkled his nose as she came near. "Are you going to take a shower?" he asked hopefully. She shook her head. She'd given up bathing about a week ago, so she could keep the smell of the vats with her all the time. It had its advantages and disadvantages. Her dive mates tended to keep their distance now, conducting their persecution from afar. She didn't have to worry about them doing anything up close and personal, like beating her up on the way home from work. On the other hand, it had put a halt to any romance that might have developed between herself and Hyper.

She realized she didn't really care, that the smell of growth medium was more important to her than human contact. She must be losing her mind, she thought.

Hyper was still downloading cash card codes. His transceiver headset lay on the table beside him amid the scattered parts of a circuit board he'd been disassembling that morning. "Can I borrow this?" she asked, lifting up the headset.

Hyper nodded, leaning ever so slightly away from her. "Go ahead. You're going to call your friend, what's-her-name, Night Hag?"

"Yeah," said Helix.

"Good," he said. "Maybe she can get you to take a shower. Does she have an olofax?"

Helix ignored him, taking the headset with her up to the loft. Today Night Hag was a redhead in a green satin ballgown. "Wow," said Helix. "Going someplace special?"

"No, just having fun."

"Well, good for you." Helix leaned back on Hyper's bed, making no effort to hide her arms, which Night Hag had yet to comment on.

"How's the new job?"

"Awful, wonderful. I don't know, Night Hag, I think I'm going crazy."

"You're not crazy. What's going on?"

"The other vatdivers are giving me a really hard time. My girlfriend broke up with me. I'm not a very good vatdiver, but I love it. Or I should say, I love being near the vats, the smell of the growth medium. . . . Everyone says it stinks, but I love the way it smells. It makes me feel more alive. Isn't that weird?"

"I don't think that's weird at all."

"Then you must be pretty weird yourself."

Night Hag laughed and nodded her head. "Most people would say so."

"Well, it was your idea I become a vatdiver."

"I thought you said you liked it."

"I do. Well, like I said, I like being near the grow med. Swimming around with these," she waved her lower arms at Night Hag, "trapped inside a divesuit all day I could do without. I'm saving up for a custom suit, but it'll be a while, and in the meantime—"

"You wear a suit?" Night Hag interrupted.

"Of course." Helix sat up in surprise. "What did you think? That I swam around in there naked? Growth medium is really dangerous. That's why I can't figure out why it appeals to me so much. Maybe the vatdivers are right. Maybe I'm suicidal. But I don't feel suicidal. I feel like I'm fighting for my life. I wish I didn't have to wear the suit. I could use all of my arms. But I need the suit to protect me from the grow med."

"Maybe you don't need to be protected."

"What? Night Hag, since I've let you see me, have you noticed anything different about me?" She waved her lower arms again for emphasis. "This is not a construct. I'm a sport. If anything, I'm even more susceptible to vatsickness than a normal human being."

Night Hag shrugged. "A sport is what?"

"Someone with a mutation."

"But a mutation is a change in the genetic code. That can be anything. How do you know that besides your physical attributes you are not also mutated to have an immunity to the growth medium?"

Helix shook her head in disbelief. "You know what? You're crazier than I am. Look, I've got to go, I just borrowed this transceiver from a friend. He wants it back."

"Wait, where can I reach you?"

"Don't worry. I'll call you tomorrow. Bye," said Helix and hung up. She lay back on the bed, staring at the ceiling. An immunity to the growth medium. Night Hag obviously didn't know what she was talking about. But wouldn't it be wonderful if it were true? Then she could swim in the vats without the cumbersome suit, touched and embraced by the beautiful green waters. The thought of it rolled around and around in her mind, lulling her to sleep.

At work the next day the dream was still with her, making the reality of her situation even more difficult to bear. She floated in the vat, the murky fluid surrounding her but not touching her. The harsh rasping of her breath was loud in her ears. She propelled herself with a gentle twitch of her flippers, drifting towards a small blot a few feet off.

The coagulant hung suspended in the growth medium; a bundle of replicating cells, pink and blue and fibrous, and already sprouting. They were like weeds. Just one, if allowed to grow, could ruin an entire vat.

Somebody—probably her—had missed this one on the previous sweep. It was nearly the size of her palm, fringed with tendrils that reached outwards, and in at least one case, formed new coagulants.

Helix grasped it in one hand, holding it firmly while she gathered tendrils with her other free hand, trying to be careful and not break any. It would be so much easier if she could use all of her arms. She could hold the body still with her uppers, while her lower hands nimbly drew in the tendrils, which sometimes narrowed to a millimeter or less in width.

As it was she simply drew gently on all of them at once, hoping not to feel the sudden jolt of a break, which she did. She examined the coagulant in her hand, turning over the pulpy thing until she found one long tendril, broken off at the end. She stuffed the agule into her bag and examined the area carefully, searching for the dark spot of another coagulant in the milky green of the growth medium.

There, to her right and a few feet away. She'd been wrong. The agule she'd found had not sent out tendrils and formed more agules, it was the sprout of an even larger one, as big as her head and bristling with outgrowths. Helix's lower arms writhed in frustration as she swam towards it. She unfastened the seals of her divesuit and drew the zipper down to free them.

Growth medium rushed in to touch her everywhere with warm, soothing wetness. She began drawing in tendrils, her lower hands grasping their fleshy strands, tracing them, plucking the agules that bulged at their ends and placing them in her bag. She had the whole complex of agules cleaned up in a fraction of the time it would have taken her with two hands.

Helix moved on, relishing the feel of the growth medium on her skin. This was more like it, more like she'd imagined vatdiving would be. She removed her face mask and thrust it heedlessly into her bag with the agules. She dived deeper, searching for more cells with eyes surprisingly unclouded, only returning to the surface of the vat for air after gathering ten more.

"Hey, what are you doing?" she heard someone shout when her

head broke the surface. Helix ignored the voice, took a breath, and dived to the bottom of the vat, growth medium swirling about her, hiding her from sight. In the depths she heard the muted clamor of an alarm, and looking up, saw the vague forms of divers approaching. There was nowhere for her to go. She relaxed and let the loosened divesuit slip away, its clinging touch replaced by the soft caress of the growth medium. She plucked a nearby agule, its texture pulpy and slick as she rolled it between her fingers. She ate it. Its juicy crunch and salty flavor were more satisfying than any food she'd ever tasted.

She watched her dive mates come for her, shadowy forms gradually emerging from the surrounding haze. She had every intention of going peaceably, allowing Vonda, Coral, Benny, and Val to take her by her arms and draw her up, towards the surface, but the closer they got, the bigger the whole white dry cold world became, and she did not want to leave the emerald-green waters she had found. And they *were* emerald green, and ever clearer as her eyes lost the habit of air. She could see agules dotting the waters like stars, thousands of them, some no bigger than a pinprick, others over twenty feet away. And all over her skin, a feeling like smell only different, the currents speaking to her about where they had been, and how many agules there were there.

She could be such a good vatdiver now. She could clean this vat faster than any of them, and they were pulling her out, and she'd never get to do it again. The waters lightened as they rose, and above, the surface loomed like a rippling sheet of glass.

She pushed out at the divers holding her arms, twisting to free herself of their grasp. She managed to get her lower left arm free, and she used it to pry Vonda off her opposite shoulder. Benny, who still had a firm hold of her upper left arm, recaptured the lower limb and pulled them both back against her shoulder. She put her upper right hand on his head and tried to push him off, but Vonda had rallied and was twisting her lower right elbow the wrong way.

As they broke the surface, the air suddenly erupting with shouts and sirens, she thrashed in their clutches, futilely attempting to remain in the vat. It wasn't until they had dragged her out and pinned her to the diving platform that she remembered to breathe.

She would have jumped up and dived back in, but several

strong arms prevented it. "What's wrong with her?" someone shouted—Coral.

"She's flipped. Where's April?" said Vonda.

"Right here."

Faces loomed above her, but her eyes were still clouded with growth medium. "Let me go!" she screamed, straining against the hands that pinned her.

"Jesus Christ, somebody get a sedative. Everybody stay suited, she's drenched with the stuff."

Helix felt the slick tingle of an epidermal on the inside of her lower left elbow. In a deepening haze, she felt herself carried off the diving platform and into the decontamination showers.

They scrubbed her everywhere with stinging disinfectant soap, and then subjected her to the evaporator until her every pore was desiccated and barren as a desert. It was April who took her out and dusted her from head to toe with acrid biocide powder. Cold, naked, and itching everywhere from her colleague's ministrations, Helix began to weep.

"Don't cry," April told her harshly, "your tears will help the stuff spread. Saline solution's not too far from growth medium as it is. Not that it's gonna make any difference. The way you were wallowing around out there, you've probably swallowed some, and Val says you had your eyes open, so if you wanted to get out of my hair, you took one quick way of doing it."

"I jus' wanted to use my arms," Helix slurred vaguely.

"You just wanted to— So you forfeit your life, so you can use all of your arms, once. I don't even care about you, but you jeopardized the lives of your dive mates as well. Thank God nobody's seals or masks came loose during that tussle, because if they had, it would be negligent homicide, instead of simple suicide, and you wouldn't have a chance to find out what the sickness is going to do to you, because I'd kill you first."

"I'm sorry, I didn't mean to fight. I just didn't want to leave the water."

April shook her head slowly. "I don't know about you. You don't seem to be simpleminded, but you don't show any sense, either."

April abandoned her lecture for the moment and held out a sterile gown made out of paper. "You know how much it costs us to stock these things? Can't use biopolymers, though. They have an, ah, affinity."

"When can I go home?" mumbled Helix. Never, she thought, answering herself, never.

"Well, there's not much point in sending you to a hospital. There's no cure for vatsickness, and with the exposure you got you'll probably only last a few days. Besides, the company won't pay for it. Remember those waivers you signed? You'll be just as well off with the painkillers Mavi buys from Orielle as with any of that doctor shit. I'm just keeping you here until someone comes for you. There's something wrong with you. In your head. You're a danger to yourself and others. I can't just turn you loose."

Besides, thought Helix, if you did, I'd probably try to find a way to get back into the vats, and you know it.

April escorted her to a small cubicle off the decontamination chamber which held a bench, a folding chair, and a table with two ancient and plastic-coated magazines on it. "Now, are you gonna be a good girl and wait here quietly, or do I have to give you another epidermal?"

"No dermal," said Helix, and she sat down on the chair, folding her hands across her knees obediently. "Can I have my clothes?"

"Not until your friends come to get you."

She itched. She itched and she'd never realized how much she'd always itched. And now she would itch for the rest of whatever life she had left. The only thing that she had ever found that stopped the itching had been taken away from her as soon as she found it. I might as well die, she thought, raising her arms at the white walls surrounding her, regarding her own biocide-dusted limbs, caked and dry, as if they were already mummified, "because this is not being alive."

The door opened and Chango rushed through, followed by Mavi. Chango's face was red and streaked with tears. "Helix, we heard what happened! Oh my gods, why?" She rushed forward to hug her, and then stopped short. "Why did you do it?"

Helix shook her head. "It's not catching, you know that."

Chango looked at her suddenly. "No, it's your skin . . . It's started already, hasn't it?"

A shiver went down Helix's spine and she once again regarded her skin. "No, this is just biocide powder. They dusted me with it to soak out and kill the growth medium. It's driving me crazy. It stings. But nothing's happened yet."

Mavi closed the door and walked slowly towards her. She was pale, almost as pale as the powder caked on Helix's skin. She glared at Helix with eyes like two black pits of fire. "Do you have any idea what you've just done?"

"What—what?"

"She doesn't," Mavi said to Chango, "she has no idea."

"Mavi—," Chango said, "please. It doesn't matter now. It's too late." She turned back to Helix and wrapped her arms around her, clinging to her. She started crying again. Helix ran her palms across her back, soothing her. Chango's tears soaked through her paper gown and into her skin, soothing the itching there.

"Oh, for goddess's sake, stop. Chango, you're going to get her wet, quit it." Mavi forcibly separated them. "You know," she said, turning on Helix again, "you I don't care about, not anymore. But you endangered the lives of everyone in that vat. They had to come after you. You fought them. They aren't there by choice. They're there because they have to make a living. And you could have killed any one of them with this suicidal tourist trip you're on."

Helix gritted her teeth, "Can we go now? I want to rinse this shit off."

"You want to— Did you hear that? She wants to take a shower!"

"Mavi," said Chango from the doorway, "let's just go."

"We're going, we're going."

Helix rode in the backseat of the convertible, while Chango drove and Mavi glared at her over the front seat. A sudden wave of uncontrollable shivering overcame her. She thought at first it was because of the wind, but the shaking only got worse, until her muscles were spasming in rapid, jerky motions, and she couldn't stop it, and she couldn't get a decent breath because her lungs weren't working right and the wind kept snatching her breath away, but it wasn't the wind. She could have gotten her breath back if she could have followed it, but something was holding her back by the throat, choking her.

"Holy fuck, she's going into convulsions," she heard someone, Mavi, say. "Haul ass."

Big patches of fog hazed their way across her field of vision, blocking out sight, replacing it with blooms of pattern, moving, changing, a funny grey color that held within it not the hues but the mathematical understanding of every other color, rendered in shifting moire. And in between those patches, in spaces getting smaller now, she saw Mavi's face, looking at her as if from far away.

She was floating in a sea of green.

Chango stepped on the gas and tore off down Riopelle, the car jouncing across potholes, sending up sprays of loose asphalt in its wake. She glanced behind her to see Mavi forcing her vat-hide wallet between Helix's teeth. She was shaking violently, her hair stiff and streaked white, her face crusted with white flakes of bio-cide. Quickly Chango looked back at the road. The sunshine and the buildings and the strangled tufts of grass beside the road looked unreal, like they were nothing more than a painted screen, a holographic overlay, masking the horror of life. But the horror of life was seeping through. Over the rush of wind in her ears she heard a hoarse, hacking kind of moan from the backseat, and Mavi swearing as she rummaged through her bag for epidermals. How could there still be sunshine while this was happening? Eyes wide, she stared down the road and drove.

A great bubble of grief seemed to rise up into her heart and break. Clenching her teeth, she laid on the horn and took the left at Caniff without stopping.

She pulled sloppily up to the curb in front of Mavi's house and jumped out of the car. "Help me carry her," said Mavi, "she's big."

With difficulty they maneuvered Helix, still quaking, up the front steps and in the door. "Put her on the couch," said Mavi, "Hugo's in the pink room." They deposited her on the faded green couch. Mavi knelt over her and peeled back one of her eyelids, shook her head, and stood up.

"What is it? Is she dying?"

Mavi looked at her gravely. "She may be dying, but not of vat-sickness."

"What?"

"I've never seen anything like this in an onset before."

"But her exposure . . ."

"The indications are all wrong. Patients always run a low-grade fever by the time they start displaying other symptoms. Her temperature is dropping, rapidly. And those convulsions, I've never seen anyone do that before, not with vatsickness. It's more like a straightforward, severe toxic reaction."

"To the growth medium?"

Mavi shrugged and looked at her with flat, bleak eyes. "What else? I gave her a clonazepam epidermal, which seems to be keeping the convulsions down a bit, but her system's in shock. I don't know what else to do."

From the couch, Helix let out one of those moans again. Chango shivered. "God, what is that noise she makes?"

"I don't know."

"Get it off me," Helix groaned.

"What?" Chango knelt by her side. "What did you say?"

"The biocide, get it off me," she croaked hoarsely. "It's killing me."

Chango stared at Mavi, who stared back at her. "But the biocide is supposed to help kill the growth medium, Helix."

Helix closed her eyes in exhaustion. "That's the problem." she whispered. "Please, it hurts. If you don't help me, I'll die."

Chango and Mavi looked at each other again, hesitating. "It's not vatsickness . . ." said Mavi, "it could be a reaction to the biocide, but—"

"You know I'm not human," said Helix, staring at Mavi with half-lidded eyes, "or at least you should."

"Let's get her to the shower," said Chango.

Water white with biocide ran down the drain of the tub. Helix rested her head in Chango's lap, half conscious, comforted by Chango's fingers on her scalp, scrubbing away the crusted powder. "I can see why you wanted this stuff off," she said, "it's nasty."

Helix didn't answer her. She was dreaming that she was swimming in a great green vat of growth medium, moving with the currents and feasting on agules. Mavi had been right. She would die, but not from vatsickness; she would die because she had found what she'd never known she wanted, what she'd always wanted, and as soon as she did, it had been taken away from her. She couldn't go back to her pathetic existence as a sport. She wasn't that, now she knew she wasn't that. She'd been born to swim in the vats, harvest agules, and eat them. But she couldn't do that either. After today, they'd fire her for sure.

Helix felt the last of the biocide rinse away, but still her skin burned, still the tremors washed over her. "Fill the tub," she said to Chango, "and get some salt from the kitchen and put it in."

Chango did as she asked, and then sat on the edge of the tub, holding one of her hands. "Is it better?"

She nodded. It was better, better than being coated with poison, but it was a far cry from the velvet caress of the growth medium. She longed for it in her cells. She wondered if she would ever feel it again.

"It wasn't an accident, was it?" said Chango. "You did it on purpose."

"Yeah. I had to find out what it felt like."

"So what did you find out?"

"It's what I'm meant to do, and if I can't, I'll die."

12

CREATION STORY

IN the beginning was the dream, and in the dream Hector was in the laboratory alone. It was late at night, he was in his pajama bottoms. Gooseflesh stood out on the exposed skin of his arms and chest. Light came faintly from a single row of phosphorescents at the back of the room. He padded up and down the aisles on cold bare feet, walking past incubators and microscopes, biophages and growing trays. A multiprocessor was awake, spilling holographic equations into the air with incomprehensible speed. Hector stopped and watched the numbers and symbols stream past. He couldn't make anything out; they were moving too fast. As he stood and stared, the equations flew at him, tumbling into him through his eyes, his ears, his mouth. His head was filled with them, he felt them working their calculations through his bloodstream. He danced and jerked, an arithmetic robot, trying to rid himself of these numbers, these symbols. But it was too late now. They were in him. They were a part of him.

He left the emptied screen of the multiprocessor and moved towards the back of the room, where a large, rectangular tank lay beneath the round saucers of the phosphorescent lights. Inside the tank, like a corpse laid out in a coffin, lay a body, submerged in the faint opalescent sheen of growth medium. As he approached the tank, she stood up. She was tall and strong, with a long mane of black hair, generous breasts, four arms and gleaming white fangs. And as he stood there, staring, she began to dance.

She danced like the Indian women he'd seen on a PBS special once; all rocking back and forth, angular gestures, stamping of feet and bending of knees. She whirled around him, and he turned, trying to keep her in sight. She was a blur all around him now, and he was inside of her, being born by her dance. The equations that had infected him earlier were coming out again now. He spoke them into the whirlwind, and she stopped.

She stood before him, silent, motionless. She was beautiful. He would have liked to touch her, hold her, make love to her. She smiled slowly and nodded her head, once, and then walked towards him. But as she approached she got smaller. Smaller and smaller until she was no bigger than a gum ball, and she hung in the middle of the air, in front of his face. Hector opened his mouth, she climbed inside, and he swallowed her.

The next morning he awoke to the sound of his alarm clock, showered, and went in to the lab. He turned on a multiprocessor and opened his latest notes on the project. In his imagination the equations from his dream lay superimposed over his own, and now he could read them. Hurriedly, he began jotting them down.

Some of them were familiar, some of them were already in his notes. For processing and control of the organism he'd been using a modified multiprocessor brain, tinkering with the mix of NMDA, glutaminergic and GABA synapses, and the balance between excitory and inhibitory neurons, searching for the right combination to give the organism the complexity of neural functioning it would need.

But his main difficulty was with mapping sensory input onto cognitive centers in the brain. Every schema he developed seemed to put the creature's behaviors and thought processes into lock step, leaving no room for adaptation or choice.

Now, looking at these new formulas, he realized he'd been on the right track using neural adhesion factors, chemoattractants, and neurotrophins to direct the formation of synaptic connections, but he'd neglected synaptic *plasticity*. With it, the organism could utilize Hebb's rule of coordinated synaptic activity to reinforce useful connections and inactivate inappropriate ones. Rather than hardwire their behavior, he could allow their environment to mold and nudge them toward their intended function, leaving specific behaviors open-ended.

Slatermeyer came in and Hector looked up from his notes. "I think I've cracked it," he told him.

Slatermeyer raised his eyebrows and stepped behind Hector to read his notes. He whistled. "They're going to need bigger cerebral cortexes than we thought," he said.

"Why do they need to be so smart?" grumbled Greenfield a week later, as they were busy cataloging gene sequences for splicing.

Hector turned from the DNA modelling program he was running. "Gathering agules and decanting biopolymer are complex tasks," he said.

"Yeah, but not that complex. With this much cognitive capacity they'll be able to develop abilities and behaviors that have nothing to do with vatdiving."

"That's true." Hector smiled, realizing for the first time the true nature of the block he'd had on the project. The company had asked him to develop a biological machine to perform the duties of the vatdivers, the operative word being machine: something that could be controlled, that would do the job and nothing else. No strikes, no pay raises, no sick days.

The problem had fascinated him, but he'd discounted his own

abhorrence at creating a slave labor force for GeneSys. Now he knew he would never do any such thing. He'd seen what he was creating in his dream, and she was most certainly not a slave. He would not be giving the GeneSys Corporation what it wanted, but he might be giving it what it deserved.

Six months later, Hector, Slatermeyer, and Greenfield stood before a low tank of growth medium, watching the membranous egg inside wobble with the hatching of the first tetra.

Slatermeyer had dubbed them that because all the morphology forecasts had predicted that they would have four arms. The arms and the over-developed canine molars were stubborn artifacts of the gene-splicing; a side effect of manipulating homeobox genes. After trying for weeks to eradicate the overlap in growth signal that caused them, Hector had recognized their usefulness in harvesting agules, and abandoned the effort.

Inside the tank, an arm broke free from the egg, followed by three more. Beside him he heard Greenfield gasp as she rose to stand before them: a humanoid female with long black hair, fangs and four arms. Hector stared into her dark eyes, imagining that he saw a glint of recognition in them. "Lilith," he said.

"Lilith?" echoed Slatermeyer and Greenfield.

"Yes," said Hector, nodding slowly. "The first woman."

A few days later they moved Lilith to the test facility in the basement of the GeneSys Building. It had two full-sized vats: plenty of room for her and her offspring. The test facility had once been the proving grounds for the first living polymers. Now it was home to a new prototype, one of his own making.

He had been lauded for his work on the brains, but he had never really considered them a work of genius. Everything was there, just waiting for him to come along and put it together, but this, this was something else again. A genetically engineered species with human cognitive ability.

For weeks Hector ate and slept in the test facility, observing Lilith, talking to her. She rapidly mastered human speech, the first of the surprises that came along with her open-ended cognitive capacity. Soon *she* was talking to *him*.

Any illusions he'd had about his role as father/creator were quickly destroyed. "In the beginning was the dream," she told him one day as he sat on the diving platform, protected from any inadvertent splashes by a divesuit. She floated on her back, watching him, her arms making lazy circles in the growth medium. "I dreamed myself into existence through you."

These were not the words of an infant mind seeking enlightenment from a beneficent creator. He could not entirely discount her theory, but however it had happened, she had come into this world with her own mind, and her own ideas about why she was here.

From the start she showed an inordinate interest in the GeneSys Corporation, though he never seemed able to clear up her basic misunderstanding of what a company actually was. She spoke of it as if it were a single entity, a creature itself. "GeneSys wants me to serve it," she would say, or "Bring GeneSys to me, and I will show it I cannot be controlled."

For the first time Hector began to worry about what would happen when Nathan Graham discovered the independent nature of the tetras. But he had other worries as well. He'd designed the tetras to be parthenogenic. Lilith was three months old, she'd been sexually mature from the moment she emerged from her egg, but she had yet to reproduce.

One night as he was going over her projected reproductive cycles for the umpteenth time, trying to figure out where he'd gone wrong, he was startled by the sound of footsteps. Slatermeyer and Greenfield had long since packed it in for the day, he was alone there except for Lilith.

Looking up, he saw her approaching him. He was shocked. She'd never gotten out of the vat before; had never shown any inclination to do so. Moreover, he realized as she stepped close and raised one hand to cup the side of his face, she was dry. She detested being dry, but he had told her how dangerous growth medium was to humans and she must have realized it was necessary—she spread her hands across his chest—for this. She kissed him, and he returned her kiss, running his hands down her sides as she tenderly bit at his neck.

To his eternal shame, he made love to her that night. He tried to reason with himself that it was necessary. Ringtail lizards, he told himself the next morning, were parthenogenic but only reproduced if another ringtail lizard went through the motions of mating with it. They were all females, but one would act the male, mounting the other and stimulating her to ovulate. Male or female, it didn't matter. What mattered was the act of love.

And he was right, because a month later, Lilith laid a clutch of eggs; twelve gelatinous blobs that nestled at the bottom of the vat and eventually hatched into tetras. Though smaller and sterile—drones essentially—they were the spitting image of their mother, and his tests confirmed it: he had not passed any genetic material on to Lilith's offspring, though he had caused them to be born, just the same.

"Why are they always doing that?" Greenfield asked one day when they were both suited and standing on the diving platform. In the vat below, Lilith and her daughters were cuddling. They spent a great deal of time in close contact with one another, grooming, feeding, but mostly, it seemed, just touching each other.

"I don't know," said Hector, "but Lilith certainly is devoted to her daughters. Since they hatched she's hardly spoken to any of us."

"Yeah, makes me wonder what kind of vatdivers they'll make. They seem indifferent, insular. I wonder if they can be made to cooperate with human beings?"

Hector shrugged. Probably not, he realized.

Suddenly Lilith broke away from her clustered offspring and dove to the bottom of the vat. Her daughters followed her, forming a ring around her where she sat.

"What's going on?" said Greenfield.

"I don't know," Hector said. "The water is too cloudy to see much from here. Hand me that face mask. I'm going in."

He did, but as he swam towards the ring of tetras, three of them broke off and swam at him, pushing him away with their hands, forcing him back to the surface. He didn't try to struggle with them, they might tear open the seals of his suit. Besides, he'd already seen what he needed to. When they broke off from the circle, he'd had a glimpse of Lilith, crouching as she had when she laid her first clutch of eggs. She was reproducing again, this time without his or any other human's assistance.

She laid a single egg, and the tetras stood guard over it day and night, not allowing him or his assistants near it. Slatermeyer and Greenfield attempted to submerge a waterproof camera to get a closer look at it, but the tetras snapped the pole they lowered it by and sent the camera flying through the air to smash against the floor. So they waited, and the egg sat at the bottom of the vat like a time bomb, a bomb that went off six months later, when Hector went down to the test facility late one night and found a lone tetra curled up against the outer door—naked, like they all were.

Her lower arms were wrapped around her knees, her upper arms sheltering her bent head. She looked exactly like Lilith, but when he touched her she gazed up at him with the eyes of an infant, unguarded and unwise.

She'd had a harsh introduction to the world, that was sure. She was covered with bruises and bites. A gash on her left thigh and another just below her right collarbone looked serious.

He hesitated before the crouching thing. She was too big for him to carry, but he didn't know if she could walk yet. The others had all started out swimming.

It was chilly in the hallway, and she shivered, looking up at him with wide eyes that looked dark and wet in the cold shine of the halogen lighting. Hector Martin took off his raincoat and drew it over her shoulders. With a tentative hand on an arm, he guided her to a standing position. She leaned on him and nestled her head against his shoulder. He got his arm around her waist. She responded by clinging to him with three arms. When Hector took a step, she followed suit. Good, she could walk.

"This way," he said pointlessly, steering her towards the elevator. At this stage, she wouldn't understand anything he said to her.

Fortunately they didn't have to wait long for the elevator to arrive. On the ride up to his apartment she slumped against him, fairly pinning him to the wall of the elevator. When the doors opened, she didn't budge. She liked the elevator. She did not want to leave the elevator. And she was at least as strong as he was, though less coordinated just now.

By the time he managed to propel them both towards the door, it had shut again. He reached over and hit the open door button and when he looked back he found that his raincoat had slipped from her shoulders, and in the struggle to put it back on her he missed the door opening and had to hit the button again. Finally, in desperation he just got out, and she followed him.

Thank gods it was so late, he thought as he walked down the hall supporting a four-armed woman half-clad in his raincoat, guiding her groggy way to his apartment. He got her inside and deposited her on the couch in his living room.

It wasn't until that moment that he realized what he'd done. He'd made a decision without ever thinking about it. He could have put her back in the vat room, but her wounds had been inflicted by the other tetras, and something told him that if he put her back in there they'd kill her. Still he could have taken her to the lab. That was the right place for her, surely. But he hadn't even considered it. Without thinking, he'd brought her here. Maybe it was just as well. If she was discovered, it could lead to the destruction of her and all her kind.

The fledgling tetra squirmed on his couch and whimpered. Blood from her cuts was soaking into the cream-colored celluweave upholstery. The stains faded even as he watched, absorbed and metabolized by the living fabric.

Hector bit his lip, hesitating to leave her alone for even an instant, but there was no help for it. He rushed to the bathroom, got adhesive bandages, cellular tape, peroxide and a clean cloth, and came back. It took about five seconds. She was still there. He sat her up and cleaned out her cuts, sealing the two big ones closed with cellular tape. He didn't know how to give stitches, and taking her to someone who did was out of the question.

After having her wounds tended, the tetra wanted to cling to him some more. Hector sat on his couch, an infant with the body of a twenty-five-year-old woman clinging to him with four very strong arms. "I guess she thinks I'm her mother," he thought, and laughed, long into the night, at the absurdity his life had become.

He woke late the next morning, still on the couch, still with the tetra wrapped around him. Well, everyone knew he'd been working late last night, but he still needed to make an appearance some time today. He couldn't afford to attract any attention, not now. With effort he pried himself free from his sleeping child and went into the bathroom for a shower. After he'd dressed again, he ran the tub, and went into the kitchen, rummaging around in the cupboards until he found an old box of kosher salt.

All the other tetras had spent their first days floating in growth medium. He dumped half the box of salt into the tub. This was nothing like growth medium, of course, but it was the closest he could get, right now. He didn't like the idea of leaving her alone here for several hours, but he had to do it. Maybe being in a tub of warm, salty water would make her feel at home, and keep her quiet.

She settled into the water with a blissful smile that bared her fangs, and looked at him with eyes of bright, sky blue. Dark brown hair sprang in clumps from her skull, but just the same, he thought she was beautiful.

She sighed, and her throat convulsed as she uttered an inarticulate, guttural noise. "Hgcklx," she said. It was the first sound she'd made that was identifiable as a syllable.

"Helix," Hector Martin said back to her. "Your name will be Helix."

Lilith dreamed she floated in the warm, void waters of the womb. Her womb, the womb of her mother. A pattern emerging from the whorl of nonbeing, coalescing in the darkness. Until the dream. The dream she dreamt of the dreamer's face. He opened his eyes, and he saw her, and through his eyes, and his dreaming vision, she was born.

She told her daughters that she dreamed herself into Hector Martin's mind in order to be born, but in truth she couldn't be certain whose dream she was. Before he saw her, did she exist? Perhaps, but not as she was now, and not here.

What she knew of the world she had learned from the multiprocessor brains, cousins to her through Hector's imagination. They told her of the numbers and structures that formed the basis of life for the people she was born among. But she and her daughters could not live on such things. They needed agules and the waters that grew them. They needed warmth, and each other's touch.

Coleanus swam up to her and tucked her head into the crook of Lilith's neck, one hand absently reaching for a breast. She and her sisters had long since given up feeding from her, and now, like Lilith, subsisted on the fruits of the waters. But still they sought her out nearly every day, to rest comfortably in her arms, sharing in that contact the knowledge of their minds and hearts.

Lilith laid her cheek against drowsy Coleanus' damp hair and felt her sigh, felt with her a wave of deep contentment, the joy of being alive.

After a time marked only by the currents of the waters, Coleanus dislodged herself, drifting softly away on her back, then turning and diving beneath the waters. She returned with an agule, plump and purple, its tendrils tapering away to slender succulence. She raised it above the waters with her upper hands, offering it to Lilith, who took it, bit into the body and twined her fingers among the tendrils. She pulled them taut and severed several with her teeth. Swallowing, she handed the agule back to her daughter. They shared it, its sweet salty taste, its chewy texture, the slickness of it sliding down their throats.

After the meal Lilith swam around the vat on her back, drifting past her daughters, staring up at the girders of the ceiling, now strung with ferns and vines. The air shimmered with warm mist. Since they'd driven the humans out, they'd made this place theirs, coaxing the vat system's brain to raise the temperature and humidity. Even the waters were warmer now. Humans kept the vats too cold. The fruits grew better now, and the blue biopoly Hector and his staff were so taken with. The lights had been harsh white halogens when she got there; now they'd been replaced with biospectrum capsules which gave off a warm glow.

Amoritas came up onto the platform and slipped into the waters beside her. She wrapped her upper arms around Lilith's neck, the lower ones encircling her waist. Through her touch Lilith knew that the second vat was thick with ripe agules.

She had made this place a home for herself and her daughters—her nest—but what of her other daughter, the new queen? Lilith had cooperated with Hector Martin's plan regarding Helix, hoping that in believing she was human, her daughter would find a place for the next generation among them. But after talking to her last night, she knew that was wrong. Helix needed to know what she was. She thought she was insane; she didn't understand her attraction to the vats.

When she suggested Helix get a job as a vatdiver, Lilith had never imagined her diving in one of those ghastly rubber skins, but of course she would have to. They thought she was human, and humans needed the suits. But Helix would be a prisoner inside one, a quarter of an inch away from her home. And how could she use her arms? It was only a matter of time before she took that stupid suit off, and given GeneSys' predilection for policies, she would probably get in trouble for it. Maybe even lose the job Lilith had so carefully arranged for her.

She'd been about to tell her the truth, but Helix had hung up. And Lilith couldn't call her back. The number she had was for the transceiver Helix had left behind in Hector's apartment. She'd tried it anyway, and left a message, but she had little hope she would check her messages and call her back.

Regretfully she dislodged Amoritas and swam to the ladder. She no longer shivered when she left the waters, but was greeted by air as warm and moist as her own breath. She took the catwalk to the second-floor balcony and entered the tiny office which they kept sealed from the rest of the vat room's environment.

Inside it was dry, though still hot. The little room was crowded with multiprocessors, transceivers and other equipment left behind by Hector and his researchers. It was an unfortunate but necessary compromise. Try as she might, Lilith was unable to keep the electronics from dying in the steamy climate surrounding the vats.

She sat before the case which housed the multiprocessor brain, lifting the top panel off so she had access to it. She found the keyboard clumsy compared to communicating directly with the brain, through touch, the way she spoke with her daughters. Lilith plunged her upper hands into the growth medium surrounding the brain. Gently she cradled it, silently saying hello with her hands.

"Sisterlilith," the brain acknowledged her.

"Brain, remember when we approved an employment application and sequestered the applicant's lab test results? I want you to go back to that section of personnel records. Give me everything that's appeared in Helix Martin's file since she was hired," Lilith thought to it.

As she'd feared, there was an application for Helix's dismissal, filed just this afternoon. The reason cited was negligence on the job. An incident report described how she'd taken her divesuit off in the vat and then fought with her "rescuers." So it hadn't taken long at all, for her daughter's true nature to come forth.

Helix's inevitable break from bondage had won her dismissal from the only nest she'd ever known. It was intolerable. Now that she'd felt the waters of the vat on her skin, she would die without their touch.

Lilith checked the dismissal application's status and discovered that it had yet to be processed. "Brain, list security codes for personnel with jurisdiction over dismissal applications," she thought.

A stream of codes poured into her mind, each accompanied by the name and title of the person who held it. She scanned up the list to the topmost echelons of the GeneSys hierarchy, searching for someone whose unorthodox decision would go unquestioned. She selected Anna Luria, corporate CEO, but Lilith's momentary concentration on her code was enough to awaken the GeneSys security system and send it scrambling after her with access checks.

She withdrew to the labyrinthine calculations of the payroll system and waited. She was okay as long as she dealt with individual brains, the one in the office or others in the network, but collectively they supported the consciousness of the thing called GeneSys, her mortal enemy. It did not like her, and she did not like it. A company, Hector called it, implying that it was simply an organization of human beings, but she knew it was more than that. It was a thing unto itself, and just as she had to drive Helix from her nest, because there can only be one queen in a nest, she would someday have to defeat GeneSys, because it controlled the vats her species needed to survive.

Lilith returned to the list her brain had given her, crawling up it carefully, watching for access checks. She stopped at the security code of one Nathan Graham. She had used this code before, when she wanted to make sure Helix got hired. It had been good enough to get Helix her job, it would have to be good enough to let her keep it.

13

TRUE NATURE

HELIX lifted an arm to scratch at her forehead, then took her hand away. That spot was starting to get raw. Her arms were already pocked with raw patches from her scratching. She even had one on her cheek. Chango insisted that the itching was an after-effect from the biocide, but she knew better. She knew it was an itch to get back into a vat of growth medium and go back to being what she was, and she knew it would not go away until she did.

She sat with Chango on Mavi's couch. "When I go back to work, I'm not wearing the suit anymore," she said.

"What? Are you crazy? You're not going back there. What you did was grounds for dismissal. The only reason you haven't been fired is that they thought you'd be dead by now."

Helix stared at her in sudden silent rage. Stared until Chango's face swirled and dissolved from the tears in her eyes. She turned her back on her, reached out her hands to claw at the air, and screamed. Her voice echoed back at her from the walls, from the world. "I have to go back," she shouted, turning around again to see Chango staring, her eyes two mismatched dinner plates. "Either that or . . ."

"Or what?" Chango muttered, her hands fretting with the hem of her T-shirt.

Helix nodded, gazing at her. "It's not like I'm really alive now, anyway. Not anymore."

There was silence in the room. From down the hall Helix heard Mavi's voice, muffled, speaking to Hugo in the pink room. Chango wrapped her thin arms around Helix and held her—held her and rocked her while their salt tears formed a poor approximation of growth medium between them.

After a while Helix pulled back and wiped her face. "Jesus Christ, Chango, what am I?"

"I don't know." Chango shook her head. "But we can go see Hyper. Maybe—maybe he knows something."

Helix wrinkled her brow but got up from the couch. They were about to leave when Mavi came in from the hallway. Her face was ashen. "Chango, go fetch Benny. It's starting. He said he wanted to be here when the changes came."

Chango looked from her to Helix. "Go get him." Helix nodded. "I can wait."

By afternoon Hugo's remains were carried out by the coroner in a body bag. Helix stood in the living room with Chango, Mavi, and Benny, and watched the hearse pull away.

"At least his suffering is over," said Benny, his hands stuck in his pockets, his back bowed, and his chest curving inward, as if he'd been punched in the stomach.

"Do you want some valerian?" asked Mavi, giving him a worried look.

"No, no thanks. I'd better get down to the mortuary. Hugo had a little money left, maybe enough to cover his funeral. I might as well get it over with."

"Are you sure? There's time, you know. You could stand to relax."

He shook his head. "I don't want to relax. He's dead, Mavi. How can I relax? Maybe once he's buried, maybe then it will seem all right, but it doesn't now, that's for sure." He glanced at Helix. He didn't say anything, but she knew what he was thinking. It should have been her that went out of here today in a body bag, but she was fine. Hugo had slight exposure, and it killed him; she swam naked in growth medium, and lived.

"Come on Helix," said Chango, "let's go see Hyper."

When they got to Hyper's house, he was on his way out the door, a plaid celluweave windbreaker under his arm. "The vatdivers are standing on the tables down at Josa's," he said as they came up the steps to meet him.

"Standing on the tables," said Chango. "They haven't done that since—"

"Not since the strike, I know."

"Why? What's it about?"

Hyper glanced over her shoulder to Helix. "Word came in today, you still have a job."

They snuck in through the back door of Josa's. Coming up the hallway past the bathrooms, they could already hear the voices shouting.

"She's not even from here!"

"They never should have hired her in the first place!"

"People, people! Quiet down." It was April. Peeking around the corner, Helix could see her, standing on a table near the center of the room, "We're here to discuss a plan of action, not belabor the obvious. Now, GeneSys has stepped way out of line on this one, we all agree. The question is, what are we going to do about it?"

"Strike!" somebody shouted, and they all took it up, chanting, screaming, and pounding the tables: "Strike! Strike! Strike!"

Helix felt Chango and Hyper tugging at her shoulders, but she didn't move. She looked at the faces of the vatdivers, angry and hateful and afraid, and their voices were a roaring in her ears like the oceans of this world. Everyone said that life started in the ocean, but not hers. The seas of her birth were considerably smaller, and green, not blue.

The chanting died down, and Vonda took a table. "The time to seize our power has come!" she shouted. "We all know GeneSys is hard pressed to meet their quotas, we've been working the hours to prove it. Striking now, we can demand a lot more than just her dismissal. We need stricter safety standards. Diver-approved standards. And a three percent pay raise across the board!"

The wall at Helix's cheek trembled as the vatdivers voiced their approval.

"Let's get out of here, now," Chango hissed in her ear, and Helix allowed herself to be dragged backwards, out the back door.

They went to Hyper's house and sat on the floor. Hyper took out a bong, filled it, and handed it to Chango, who offered it to Helix. Helix shook her head and stared at the curtains. "They think they can stop me," she said. "They'll have to kill me first."

The screen door rattled as Benny opened it and came inside. "Hey, that's just the kind of talk I was hoping to hear." He slid down on the floor next to Helix. "You have to stand up to them. You can't let them get away with this. You have just as much right to be in there as anyone else," he said.

"Says who?" said Chango. "She should have gotten fired."

Benny looked at her. "But she didn't, and if a non-sport had done the same thing and not gotten fired, do you think they'd be striking over it?" He shook his hands and tilted his face towards the ceiling. "I can't believe it. All these years, our gains gradually being nibbled away from us crumb by crumb; and what is it that finally galvanizes this community to action? Bigotry. I can't believe it. I wash my hands."

"What am I going to do?" said Helix.

"I think you should go down there tomorrow and face them down. They're a bunch of cowards; they're afraid of you," said Benny.

"I don't think that's such a good idea," said Chango. "They may be afraid of her, but that doesn't mean they'll back down, not now that they're united by a common cause. She's likely to get beaten up, or worse."

"I just want to dive again. I have to," said Helix.

"Then you know what you have to do," said Benny. "They expect you to back down."

14

THE GENESYS MAN

O'GRADY'S tearoom in Bricktown was a small room with upholstered chairs and lace-curtained windows. Colin Slatermeyer clenched his sweat-damp fists and walked across the room to where Nathan Graham sat waiting for him at an inlaid wood table.

"I took the liberty of ordering," said Graham as Colin sat down. "I hope you like Earl Grey."

On the table a ceramic teapot littered with rosebuds sat on a handmade doily. There was also a silver tray of scones accompanied by strawberry jam and clotted cream. Graham poured tea for them both and offered him a scone.

Mechanically Colin went through the motions of splitting the scone and spreading it with cream and jam, but he wasn't hungry. His stomach was tied in knots, his eyes fixed on Graham—watching him inhale the steam from his cup and sip at the amber-brown tea. "Ah," he said, and bit into a scone, sending crumbs scattering across the table. Graham chewed thoughtfully for a moment, swallowed, and fixed his gaze on Colin. "Now," he said, "I want you to tell me about the day the tetras threw you and your colleagues out of the vat room."

Colin fussed with his tea for a moment, adding sugar and lemon. He sipped it, but it did little to alleviate the dryness in his mouth. "There's not much to tell, really," he said. "It was just like any other day down there, at least to start with. Greenfield and I were doing spectral analysis and cell imaging on agule and polymer samples. Neither of us had been up to the diving platform to check on the tetras, but everything seemed more or less normal. It wasn't until Dr. Martin came in that things started to go awry."

"What happened?"

Colin stared at his hands encircling the cup, felt the warmth of the tea spreading through his fingers, and tried to think of the least damaging way to describe what had happened. His reverie was interrupted by a scalding splash of tea on his clasped fingers. He looked up to see Graham with the teapot, topping off his cup. Graham glanced at him sideways. "Sorry," he said with utter calm. "I'm so clumsy." He set the teapot down and stared at Colin with complete serenity. "Go on."

"He suited up and went to talk to Lilith right away," Colin blurted, reaching for a napkin to blot his burned fingers. "He didn't say anything to us, but he was back down again a few minutes later. His suit was wet. He said that Lilith had splashed him. There was a lot more activity in the vats all of a sudden. We could hear the tetras swimming around up there. Suddenly there just seemed to be this tense atmosphere in the place."

"You said he went to talk to Lilith. How do you know that if he didn't speak to you?"

Colin was aware of his own eyes widening. "Just because that's what he always did. In the morning, he'd check in with her," he managed.

"I see. What did they talk about that morning, then?"

Colin shook his head. Graham leaned forward, giving him the full effect of his glare. "You heard them. What did they say?"

Colin swallowed, his eyes fluttering away from Graham's like frightened birds. "She told him to get out of there," he said stiffly.

Graham cocked his head, "Why did she do that?"

"She—she said he stank of her. She said there could only be one queen in a nest, and that he no longer belonged here."

"She said he stank of her? Of who?"

"I'm not sure."

"What did Martin do?"

"He tried to calm her. He told her that she didn't have to worry. He said—" Colin broke off.

"He said what?" Graham prompted impatiently

"That she wouldn't be back." Colin gulped.

"Who?"

"I don't know!" Colin shouted. People at other tables turned and looked.

Graham poured himself more tea. "What did Martin say when he came back down?"

"He told us to continue what we were doing."

"Didn't you ask him what they were talking about?"

"No, I didn't."

"I see. And when you discussed it later, what did he say then?" Colin set his jaw. "We didn't discuss it. We never did."

"You don't have any idea what they might have been talking about? Do you have any idea how much money you owe ALIVE!? I do."

Colin shook his head. "Look, I really don't know. All I can think of is she might have been talking about the egg."

"What? What egg?"

Colin closed his eyes. It was too late now, Graham had him. "Lilith laid another egg, a single, about six months after the drones hatched."

"Yes?"

"She wouldn't let anyone near it. The drones would mob us any time we got close."

"It hatched."

Colin's jaw worked. "There's no way of knowing for sure. The tetras wouldn't let us dive in to examine it. Since then, it's been impossible to determine what happened to it. The tetras destroyed the transceivers, after they kicked us out."

"So you have no proof, but that is the hypothesis which fits the facts. We'll go with it. What happened after Martin came back down?"

I was doing protein imaging on a polymer sample, and I looked up, and I saw the tetras climbing over the edge of the vat. They came at us, jumping off the platform and landing on the equipment. Dr. Martin yelled for us to get out of there. He didn't have to tell me twice, they were dripping with growth medium. Greenfield and I got out ahead of them, but Dr. Martin, they picked him up, and threw him out the door."

"Very interesting." Graham dabbed at his mouth with a napkin.

"I can see I need to have a talk with Martin, but first, I want you to procure a couple of divesuits. You can do that, can't you?"

"I guess so." Colin wrinkled his brow. "But why?"

"I want you to take me there," he said, "to the facility. I want to meet this Lilith for myself."

"I'm really not sure about this. It's not safe," said Slatermeyer at the door to the vat room. "I think you should reconsider."

"I'm not going to reconsider," said Graham, "and as far as it being dangerous is concerned, I'm prepared for that." He patted the tranquilizer gun at his hip.

"I wouldn't take a weapon in there if I were you. They won't like it."

"Don't be ridiculous. I don't care if they like it or not. If they attack us, I won't be defenseless."

"But you can't get all of them with that thing."

"So? You said they all follow Lilith, that she's their queen. If I take her out, they won't know what to do."

"If you take her out, they may panic, there's no telling what they'll do."

"Stop being a nelly, I don't have all night. I'm supposed to meet some important people for dinner tonight."

Slatermeyer pulled the hood of the divesuit over his head, tucking in stray wisps of hair. "Well, I hope you make it to that dinner, Mr. Graham." He took a key out of the pouch slung around his hips and unlocked the door.

They were in a long stretch of tiled corridor. Graham gagged on the steamy, pungent air. "Christ, what's that smell?"

"It's the vats, you get used to it," whispered Slatermeyer. "Now be quiet, please."

They crept along the corridor, the air getting warmer and damper and more redolent with the yeasty odor of fermentation and rot. Graham tried to breathe through his mouth, but it was no use. The smell seemed to seep right through his pores. He was starting to sweat inside the divesuit, its rubber lining becoming slick against his skin. No wonder those vatdivers were always bitching about something; they were uncomfortable all the time. Well, screw them, anyway. They didn't have to take the job. They could have started out in a mailroom somewhere, barely making enough to eat once a day, and spent the next twenty years of their lives clawing their way up to a position of status and wealth.

By the time they reached the end of the corridor, the walls were dripping with condensation, and they could only see about three feet in front of them because of the thick clouds of fog. The temperature had to be at least a hundred degrees. When he breathed he felt as if his lungs were filling with water. Slatermeyer tapped him on the arm and motioned for him to put on his face mask and mouthpiece. He had a point. There was no telling what this mist was actually made of.

Suiting up had its advantages. He could take long, deep breaths of air without being hampered either by the smell of the vats or the humidity, and he and Slatermeyer could communicate with each other over the built-in shortwaves in their face masks.

"It wasn't like this when we were in here, they must have done something to the climate controls," said Slatermeyer.

"They can do that?"

"I'm not sure about the others, but Lilith can, I have no doubt."

Graham waved impatiently at the billowing clouds of steam. "We can't see shit. They could be anywhere."

"Yeah, they probably know we're here by now. They may even be watching us."

"Watching? Who could see in this?"

"I don't know. They see really well through the growth medium."

"Shit," said Graham.

"Having second thoughts? We could go back; they might even let us leave."

"No, look." Figures emerged from the mist all around them, moving slowly and quietly. They were all naked, and they all had four arms. They weren't very big, about five foot four and slender. They had long dark hair, and from beneath their lips emerged white, curving fangs. About their waists and necks some of them wore pulpy garlands of a substance he couldn't immediately identify.

They advanced on them with silent, almost placid deliberation. Graham backed away and then glanced behind him, but there were more in the hallway. They were surrounded. In panic he looked at Slatermeyer. "Relax, and go with the flow," said the voice in his ear. "You're fully suited, you'll be all right." But there was a tenseness in Slatermeyer's voice that was far from reassuring.

The creatures closed in on them. He saw one grab Slatermeyer by the forearm, and then the upper arm, and by the time she'd grasped his leg, Graham felt a hand on his shoulder.

He saw four of them pick Slatermeyer up and carry him away, their bodies curling about him as they all disappeared in the billowing, engulfing mist. The rest of them surrounded him, but they did not pick him up. Thirty-two hands—on his neck, his shoulders, his arms and back—gently but firmly guided him through the clouds.

His face mask was misted over, and all he could see was what could be glimpsed through the undulating tracks of droplets that streamed across the lucite. He couldn't make out more than a curl of vapor or a curving arm, a shoulder, a breast. But palms and fingertips directed him, shepherding him up a ladder. At the top they allowed him to wipe at the condensation with his gloved hands. He was only partially successful—instead of a blank wall of moisture he now had a confusion of streaks. He shrank back as one of them reared towards his face with her mouth open, but the others tightened their grip and held him still while she got ever closer to his face, finally opening her mouth wider, giving him a mist-shattered view of her teeth as she extended her tongue and licked the surface of his face mask. When she was done, it was clean, and no new condensation formed. Graham allowed himself to exhale and looked around. The air up here was clearer, the mist dispersing upwards towards the ceiling above. He was on a walkway that ran just above and between the two vats. In the center it widened, forming a diving platform for both of them. It was here that they took him, carefully positioning him in its center before withdrawing to stand two deep in front of the walkway on either side of him. The message was clear, he could either stay put, or take a dip.

Graham was well aware of the acceptable levels of divesuit safety. He wasn't going in there if he could avoid it. As it turned out, he didn't have to. Out of the vat in front of him came a woman, a creature, four-armed, like the others, but taller by a head, and visibly stronger. Her hair was long and black, too, her face identical to the other faces he'd seen, although the look in her eyes as she gazed at him was anything but passive.

"What are you and why have you come to us?" she demanded. She spoke loudly and distinctly. He could hear her even through the hood of his divesuit.

He opened his mouth to say something. What, he wasn't certain, and then he realized that the radio in his face mask was on direct transmission. He fumbled at the latex-sheathed controls by his ear, his damp, gloved fingers slipping over them. After a deafening parade of squeals he got it to broadcast. "I'm Nathan Graham," he said, "chief administrator of research and development for GeneSys."

She nodded slowly. "Nathan Graham. You are the one Hector is afraid of. He confuses you with GeneSys. He says you are a danger to us, but you have been useful in the past. What sent you here, GeneSys or a brain?"

"Ah, I came to ask you a few questions."

"Questions for who? For GeneSys?"

"For myself. I've heard a lot about you and the goings-on in these vats. I wanted to know, why did you kick the researchers out?"

"We drove Hector away because he would have contaminated the nest. The others fled because they feared us."

"I see. Why would Hector contaminate your . . . nest?"

She looked at him closely. "You say you ask these questions for yourself, but it is GeneSys you are asking for. This is none of GeneSys' affair."

"But it is. You are a project of the company's research and development department. I manage the department. I am intimately concerned with your well being."

"Concerned perhaps, but for GeneSys' well being, not ours."

"For all of us."

She laughed, throwing her head back, her teeth flashing. "That is impossible, and you should know it."

"What? What do you mean?"

"You have come here looking for secrets to use against us."

"I came here because I was concerned. There was an egg. What happened to it?"

"What happens to all eggs."

"That's why you kicked Martin out of here, isn't it? Slatermeyer told me—he said you told Hector that he stank of her. You were talking about the—the hatchling, weren't you?"

Lilith narrowed her eyes. "It seems to me you know too much already. You are a bright man, Nathan Graham, but GeneSys should have told you."

"Told me what?"

She spread her arms to indicate herself and the other tetras, "That we are not a project. We are the enemy."

Graham stared, his mouth opened. "The enemy," he echoed.

"And you have delivered yourself into our hands." She nodded at the other tetras, and they began to close in on him again.

"Wait," he cried, "what are you going to do?"

"Keep you," he heard her say as the tetras surrounded him. Panic clutched at his throat and he grabbed the tranquilizer gun at his hip. "Stop!" he shouted, brandishing it at them, but they did not react. He felt their hands on him, and he fired. He heard high-pitched shrieking and several of the tetras abandoned him to surround their stricken comrade. He fired again and again, emptying the clip of its pellets. The tetras fell away from him amid screams of pain and confusion, as those who were not hit comforted those who were. All except one: Lilith. She alone stood among the pile of bodies, unconscious or condolatory, and Graham took one look at her—at her flashing eyes and her teeth bared in rage—and he ran like hell.

She must have been hampered by her daughters, because he made it to the floor of the vat room unhindered. He ran in the direction of the hallway, blinded by clouds of mist. Something caught him at knee level, sending him crashing to the floor. A folding chair, he discovered, as he freed himself from its molded biopolymer legs. He stood, only to see Lilith looming out of the fog, her arms spread wide. He picked up the chair, threw it at her, and ran again. He reached the wall of the vat room and veered to the right, hoping that was the direction of the hallway to the outside. Lilith caught up to him at the archway, grasping him around his waist and chest and squeezing. He kicked her shins and flailed at her with his fists, but she didn't let go. His vision was fading, not from the mists but because he was blacking out from lack of oxygen. He fumbled for his useless stun pistol, grappling with the holster for painful moments as the air was squeezed from his body, and then he had it free, and raised it to her head. She didn't let go, but she did stop squeezing him. "Let me go, or I'll do to you what I did to them," he said, his breath returning. The pistol was empty—he'd foolishly spent all the pellets on the little tetras—but apparently she didn't know that; didn't know, either, that it was only a stun weapon. She released him, and he backed away from her; down the hallway and out the door.

Graham slammed the door and stared at it. Its plain metal surface gave no indication of the nightmare behind it. He pulled off his face mask and took huge gulps of clean, cool air. It was easy to take things like that for granted—good air, a rational order to the universe—until they were stripped away and you found yourself lost in someone else's world, totally unequipped to deal with it.

As he stripped off the divesuit, his transceiver rang. Swearing, Graham pulled his legs from the rubbery grasp of the suit, and retrieved the transceiver from his pants pocket.

"Yes, what is it?" he blurted before the holograph had a chance to resolve in front of him. It was Brea Jeffries, from personnel.

"Christ, Brea, what are you using my personal number for? Why are you calling me at all, for that matter?"

"It's about that new diver."

"What, the one you sent me that letter about? You've got the wrong department. I'm in R&D, you want production. Wait! You are production! What are you talking to me for?"

"I'm talking to you because you preempted review, approved her application, and sequestered her medical records. That was bad enough, but I figured you were doing somebody a favor—although why you couldn't find her something better than diving is beyond me. But now you've gone too far. Countermanding a request for dismissal after an obvious act of negligence; it's just too much. The other divers won't stand for it. They're touchy enough about us hiring sports in the first place. I'm surprised at you, Graham. When you were in production you never would have done anything this obvious."

"Wait a minute, why are you saying I did all this?"

"Because all the pertinent documents carry your security code."

Graham was silent a moment. He was remembering something Lilith had said, before the tetras attacked him. You have been useful in the past. That was what she said.

"What's this diver's name?"

"Oh come on, like you don't know."

"Humor me."

"All right. Her name is Helix Martin."

"She's a sport, you said."

"That's right. Real obvious mutations, too."

"Four arms and big teeth, right?"

"I guess it's coming back to you now. We know that much just from the initial application, but we don't know any more because we can't get hold of her lab test results. You saw to that."

"What did she do that got her fired?"

"I don't know what you think this innocent act is going to get you, Graham. I can tell you right now, I'm not buying it."

"Just tell me what she did."

"She deliberately took her suit off in the vats."

"All right, Brea. Obviously there's been a mistake. If you get any more documents with my code on them, call me. You can use this number. In the meantime, I'll cancel that countermand."

"It's too late. I didn't catch it until after approval. We'll have to start all over again with a new dismissal request. It's going to take a few days."

"Do it. I'll be in touch." Graham signed off and dialed another number—the personal access code of someone in Vattown, a vat-diver who'd been useful to *him* in the past.

To his surprise, his call was answered right away. The holograph was blacked out, but he recognized the voice. "I've been wondering when you'd call. Get a load of this." The transceiver was moved so that what had been a dull roar in the background became the sound of numerous voices shouting "Strike!" over and over again. "That's the sound of a strike about to happen, buddy."

"Where are you?"

"Josa's, and they're standing on the tables down here. Where've you been, anyway?"

"I'm not in production anymore."

"Lucky for you. This is just a social call, then?"

"No. I'm looking for someone. You've probably noticed her. She has four arms."

"Helix?"

"Yeah, that's her name. Helix Martin."

The voice laughed. "Shit boyo, that's what these good folk are all riled up about down here. She got hired about a month and a half ago, under the new genetic stability guidelines. She's nuts, she took her suit off in the vats. Me and a few of my pals had to haul her out of there naked. She struggled when we got her to the surface, but I really don't think she wanted to hurt anybody, she just wanted . . . to stay in there, apparently."

"Fascinating."

"Yeah, well, if you say so. Everybody figured that with the soak she'd taken, she'd be dead in a few days, but no. I have it on good authority that she suffered a toxic reaction to the biocide that was used on her, but once she got it off, she was fine. Now to top it all off, she didn't get fired. Personnel just notified her she could come back to work tomorrow."

"And that's why they're striking."

"Yep, basically."

"Well, I'll see to it that she's fired, like she should have been in the first place. It'll take a few days though. When are they planning to strike?"

"Probably tomorrow morning. People are still filtering in here from the late shift. But I don't know if getting her fired is going to help, anymore. There's people here who see this as a rallying point to get the movement rolling again."

"Chichelski's old crowd."

"Exactly. I have a feeling that once they're through, they'll be asking for a lot more than one sport's dismissal."

Shit, shit, shit. If word of a strike reached Anna, or even Kent, with his name attached to the unorthodox hiring practices that instigated it, no amount of explanations or finger-pointing would save his hide. "Oh well," he said grimly, "let's see what can be done. Does she have a lot of friends?"

"Well, everybody knows who she is, now, but no, she doesn't have a lot of friends. Just a few sports."

"Where is she staying?"

"At the home of Hyperion Baker. She's living with him and Chango Chichelski."

"Chichelski?"

"Ada's kid sister, a sport."

"She work for the company?"

"Wouldn't dream of it."

"Hmm. If she's anything like her sister, she wouldn't take this Helix's disappearance quietly."

"No. In fact she's got her doubts about Ada's accident, and voices them frequently."

"Anybody listen?"

"Not really, it's the same shit she's been spouting for years, with no proof. Basically it just serves to alienate her from most people, especially vatdivers. Even her little sport friends don't pay any attention anymore."

"Good, at least those bones are staying in the closet. Now, about this strike, any chance at all of stopping it?"

"A snowball's in hell."

"Okay, then we'll have to use it. How much would it take to turn this strike into a riot?"

"Not much. If Helix shows up and tries to get through the line, it probably will be one."

"Fine. How well do you know Helix?"

"Pretty well, actually."

"Good, talk to her, let her know you're on her side. Encourage her to go to the vat yard tomorrow and be as belligerent as possible to the strikers. And make sure they're in an ugly mood and there's plenty of weapons at hand. And if there's anything left of her when they're through, get rid of it."

15

RIOT!

I really wish you'd reconsider this," Chango said to Helix for the umpteenth time. It was morning, and they'd been up half the night before, arguing. Well, she'd done all the arguing, Helix just sat there and scratched herself, shaking her head.

Helix looked at her with tired eyes. "I'm going to take a shower," she said, standing up.

Chango followed her into the workroom, where Hyper was running his robots through scales of isometric motion. Robo-Mime's head rotated back and forth, Close Enough for Jazz raised the sax to its carburetor lips again and again, the Augmented Hoomdorm flexed its legs and Attack of the Sneetches scattered across the worktable like a bunch of neon mice with perms. Hyper himself was bent over an array of radio controls. He'd removed himself from the debate around one in the morning and had been out here ever since.

"Nothing I can say is going to influence you the least little bit, is it?" Chango said as Helix wove around the robots to the shower stall under the stairs. "It never has."

Helix turned and looked at her. "That's because I can't let it. Believe me, if I were a human being, I'd follow your advice, but that's not what's going on here, and you should know that by now."

"Why don't you look at the data card? Maybe it can tell you something. Something about yourself that can help you now. Maybe there's a better way than this. They won't let you in there."

"I know." Helix nodded, her eyes staring blankly into the future. "But I have to fight them anyway."

"Why? There are other vats."

"Where? Where are there vats that are not vats for humans, whether they're being used or not? Sooner or later, what's going to happen today will happen. I'd just as soon do it now, before—"

"Before?"

Helix shook her head. "I don't know, before I have time to get comfortable, or something."

"Don't you think your father could help you?"

She shook her head. "I think if he could, he would have."

Chango bit her lip. "Helix he— He's a scientist."

Helix stared at her. "I know. And I know what you were about to say. That's why I'm not reading the card. I can't, not now. I can't waste time on why I am what I am. I have to be it." She turned and went into the shower. A moment later her clothes flew out through the curtained doorway.

Chango leaned over the table where Hyper was working. "What are you doing?"

Hyper looked up at her, his face grimy with oil and fatigue. "Trying to even the odds a bit," he said.

Chango stared at him a moment, realizing what he meant, and then she reached forward and plucked the transceiver from where it rested forgotten on his head. "Then I'm keeping this. Let's not just increase those odds, let's spread 'em around."

Hyper started forward, in reflex it seemed, and stopped. "Fine, whatever," he said.

He was sick of her, she could see. Everyone was sick of her, including Chango herself. All she seemed to do these days was argue with people. And she'd always been such a carefree person, or thought she was. "Don't worry," she said, "I'll leave it here when I'm done."

She sat and watched holodramas until they left; Helix empty-handed, Hyper accompanied by the rattle and lurch of his robots. When they were gone, she called the police.

Helix's heart pounded in time with her steps. All was silent under the sun except for the faint cries of a few birds wheeling high in the sky above. On some nearby rooftop, Hyper waited with the radio controls for his robots. He and the birds were her only witnesses as she walked down the middle of the street towards the quiet throng of vatdivers gathered at the gate to the vat yard.

The vatdivers, to a one, were suited. Some even wore their harnesses with breathing tanks in them. They were massed in front of the main gate, five rows thick. As she drew near their collective stare bored into her, pushing back against the hand that pushed her forward.

She came to a stop roughly ten feet in front of them and directly across from Vonda, who stood in the middle of the throng.

Helix stared at her because it was easier than staring at all of them. Vonda stared back. Presumably they all did, though she was beginning to wonder how the ones in the back row were getting their view. Probably risers. Finally she got tired of waiting for somebody to blink. "Last one in's a rotten egg," she said, and dodged forward, aiming her shoulder between Vonda and the diver next to her.

Vonda caught her neatly and shoved her back into the street.

Behind her and to the side stood April, her arms folded across her broad chest. "If you know what's good for you, you'll get the hell out of town and stay there," she said, almost gently.

Helix shook her head. "Nope." She nodded at the vat houses beyond the gate. "This is what I call home."

The crowd was grumbling now. "Why don't you go jerk off? You got plenty of hands for it!" somebody shouted to general laughter.

"What are you so afraid of?" she cried out. "I'm not going to hurt anybody."

"No shit you're not. You're not getting in there, that's why," said Val. "We can't let GeneSys make all our decisions for us. We've made our own decision about you."

"Yeah, you're fired, freak, so fuck off!" screamed someone in the back.

"You just don't want me here because you're afraid of me. You don't know what I am!" Helix shouted.

"What are you?" answered several people at once, and then the words were taken up by the rest of the crowd. "What are you? What are you? What are you?" they chanted as they advanced on her, circling around until she was surrounded by them: their faces, their taunting voices.

"I don't know!" she screamed back at them, raising her arms around her to ward them off. "I don't know!" Her mouth open wide, she flashed her teeth, and her fingers stiffened to claws. "You want a freak? You've got a freak!"

Someone darted in to make a grab at one of her arms and she leapt on him, wrapping her arms around him and biting him on the shoulder. Her teeth slid against the rubber of his vat suit and he shoved her into the arms of three vatdivers. They grabbed her arms and she kicked wildly, twisting around until she could reach somebody's hand, and she sank her teeth into it, feeling the flesh break. She tasted blood and heard a scream above the general clamoring. There were still five hands on her. "Fucking bitch," someone said, and slugged her on the side of her face. Her head snapped to the side and the scene swam before her eyes. People were advancing, closing the very small gap that had existed in the center of the crowd. Someone kicked her in the stomach and she would have fallen forward except for the hands, eight of them now, holding her by her arms. She got her feet under her again and kicked backwards indiscriminately. Her captors retaliated by pulling her arms back farther against the joints and kicking the backs of her knees until she sank to the ground. She looked up, blinking.

In the distance she could hear the clank and roar of Hyper's machines moving down the street. The cavalry was coming, but not soon enough. Someone loomed in front of her, a tall, heavy-set man with a round face and hard eyes. She didn't know him; she'd never even met him. He held an air tank cradled in his arms, "You're going to wish you'd left while you still could," he said, and he lifted the air tank up above his head. She saw it silhouetted against the sun, and then there was a sudden blur of motion from her right, and Vonda was there, somehow, with the tank in her hands. "That's enough!" she screamed. "This is a strike, not a lynching!"

"Says who?" The man advanced on her. Vonda twisted the nozzle on the tank and released a blast of frozen air in his face. He backed up, his hands over his eyes, and she turned around and threw the heavy tank directly over Helix's head. The people holding her had to make a decision: let go or get hit with it. They let go. Helix drove forward and Vonda grabbed her hand, using the momentary confusion to plunge through the crowd.

Sirens wailed and two squad cars and a police van swerved around a corner ahead of them. Cops dressed in riot gear poured out of the vehicles, wielding polyglass shields. Vatdivers surged towards them, only to be driven back with stun clubs.

By now Hyper's machines had made it to the gate. The Augmented Hoomdorm jumped spasmodically on its pneumatic legs, scattering vatdivers in its path. As Vonda dragged her through the confused mob, Helix caught a glimpse of Robo-Mime, tenaciously circling a vatdiver wielding an air tank, confronting him with his own angry image. He swung the tank, and the video tube exploded, showering glass on himself and surrounding vatdivers.

Helix and Vonda dodged around a group of divers busy battling with Close Enough for Jazz. One of them had wrested the saxophone from its grip and was jamming it in the tractor treads. "Hey, there they are!" someone shouted, and the group abandoned the robot to head off Helix and Vonda just as they were about to break free from the rioting mob. "Traitor!" screamed a woman, rushing towards them with a decanting pole in her hands. But before she could reach them she was intercepted by Attack of the Sneetches. She tripped on the round little automatons, her pole clattering to the ground as she fell.

"This way," hissed Vonda, veering around the stumbling divers and away from the thick of the mob. She ducked down an alley between a row of storage tanks and a warehouse, and Helix followed her. Behind them she heard the popping of gas grenade launchers, and up ahead there was a car horn honking. It was Chango in her beat-up Chevy. They put on an extra burst of speed and leapt into the car, Helix in front, Vonda in the backseat.

Vonda slapped the front seat with her hand. "Let's get the hell out of Vattown for now, okay?"

Chango looked at Helix. "What's she doing here? Why isn't she back with her mob?"

Helix shook her head. "She saved my life for some reason, and she's right, we have to get out of here."

Chango frowned and pulled away down the street. As they drove, the sounds of the rioting died down behind them.

"Where will we go?" asked Helix.

"To Orielle's," said Vonda.

"What? Are you crazy?" said Chango.

"No. She likes Helix, she'll protect her, and she's got the firepower to do it should that mob back there reassemble itself and come looking for her."

Chango swallowed and nodded her head, turning the car towards the Eastern Market.

Benny was in the middle of a crushing mob of vatdivers, surging towards the line of police up the street. "Fan out!" he screamed, "Fan out onto the side streets! We can still catch her!" He spotted Val only three feet away, "Val!" he shouted, trying in vain to press through the mob towards him. "Val!" Go down Denton!" But he didn't hear him, and then the crowd surged again, and Benny lost sight of him.

He worked his way out of the riot and down an alley behind Joseph Campau Avenue. Vonda and Helix could have gone down any of the side streets around the vat yard. He really needed a team of ten or twenty to follow all their possible escape routes, but this was strictly a solo gig, now.

He ran down Faber to Lumpkin and past a row of warehouses. At the far corner he saw a red-and-yellow Chevy crossing Lumpkin, going down Holbrook. Chango's car. He was too far away to see who was in it, but it was the only lead he had. He raced down Evaline now, heading for Conant. Hopefully she'd turn down Conant. As he passed a crumbling and vacant parking lot he bent down to scoop a rock up off the ground. Still running, he scraped it hard across his forehead over his right eye, and clenching it in his fist, struck himself on the cheek, hard enough, he hoped, to raise a bruise.

But his cosmetic alterations were in vain. By the time he got to Conant he could just see the Chevy in the distance, heading south and east, towards the Market and Orielle's.

He sat on the curb and leaned back on his hands, staring up at the sun blazing away in a cloudless sky. In the distance he could still hear the police sirens and angry screaming. This was the riot he'd tried to prevent back when Ada was organizing the vatdivers. Now it had happened. She was long dead, and it happened anyway.

If he had known, way back when Graham first contacted him, that it would all end up the same, no matter what, would he have turned him down? Probably not, and for the same reason that he was still here, all these years later. He should have left Vattown long ago, but the thought of leaving all his friends behind stopped him. Hugo, Val, Coral . . . it was because of them that he'd done what he did. And because of them he'd stayed here, huddling around the memories of what he now realized was the best time of his life; that summer before they started diving, when they had all seemed immortal and infallible, touched by the sun like gods.

But now Hugo was dead, too, and Benny wouldn't make the same mistake twice. When this was over he'd shake the dust of Vattown from his shoes and take himself someplace that was not ripe with memories of corpses.

He sat up, took a long look up and down the empty street, and fished his holotransceiver from his pocket.

* * *

Hector clenched and unclenched his fists as he entered Graham's office and took a seat before the vast grey cellite desk. Graham kept his desk empty of clutter, and the translucent smokey grey surface reflected the downtown skyline from the windows behind it. Outside the sun was shining, but in Graham's desk, it was always a cloudy day. Hector's eyes wandered to the multiprocessor perched on one corner of the desk, a bobbing brain encased in clear cellite. He jumped as a side door opened and Graham entered the room.

He didn't waste any time on niceties this time around. No offers of drinks or inquiries into his health. He just glared at Hector and then stood looking out the window with his back to him. "They're striking down there," he pointed in the general direction of Vattown and turned to face Hector again, "and do you have any idea why?"

Hector shook his head. "Not really, no. Better wages?"

Graham bared his teeth and laughed savagely. "You really are a piece of work, Martin. How could I let myself be so thoroughly bamboozled by you? I bought your whole mild-mannered absent-minded genius shtick, retail. I was so busy feeling contempt for you that I never began to imagine how subversive you really are."

Hector felt unexpected pride at being described as subversive. He'd never thought of himself that way, but considering the tetras and how far he'd gone to protect them, he supposed it was true. This knowledge gave him courage. "What's this about, Graham?" he said.

"You know goddamn well what this is about! That little creature of yours has stirred up a hornet's nest in production! Seems she went vatdiving without a suit, and somebody used my clearance code to make sure she didn't get fired for it. But of course, you wouldn't know anything about that, would you?"

Fear gripped Hector's intestines and squeezed. Graham could only be referring to Helix. When she left, Hector had hoped she'd get as far away from GeneSys as possible, but apparently that wasn't the case. She'd gone only as far as Vattown and then taken the first opportunity available to gain access to the vats—as a diver. "Actually no, I don't know anything about it," he said.

"Oh, come on, she's going by the name Helix Martin, and you're telling me you don't know anything? Lilith kicked you out of the vat room because of her, didn't she?"

Hector sighed. "Yes, she did."

"Why? And don't tell me you don't know."

"I—I found Helix outside the vat room. As near as I can tell, the other tetras ganged up on her and drove her out. It has to do with their social structure. There can only be one queen to a hive."

"So you helped her. Helped her get that job down in Vattown, but I have it on good authority that she's only been working there for a few weeks. You had to do something with her in the meantime. Slatermeyer insists that he doesn't know what happened to the egg. Yes, I know about the egg. You couldn't have taken her to the lab. You had her living with you, didn't you? In your apartment. That's sick Martin, really sick."

Hector glared at him. "We weren't lovers, Mr. Graham, if that's what you're implying. I couldn't send her back to the vat room, they would have killed her."

"But you could have housed her in the lab, only you didn't because you knew it would attract attention and you couldn't afford that." Graham stepped around his desk and leaned towards Hector. "You see, Martin, I've been to see the queen."

"What? You went there?"

"Yes. Your assistant Colin Slatermeyer took me. Pity about him."

"What did you do to him?"

Graham shook his head. "Nothing. They took him away and I didn't see him again after that."

"Shit, Colin. Why did you make him take you there?"

"I wanted to see for myself, and I'm glad I did. Lilith calls herself the enemy of GeneSys. The tetras have no intention of cooperating with the goals of the project. Even before they drove you out of the vat room, you had to know that. Why did you continue? Why did you harbor that little queen? Why didn't you tell me what was going on?"

Hector glared at him and gripped the arms of his chair. "I didn't tell you because you would have canceled the project. Do you have any idea what an accomplishment the tetras are? Higher intelligence functions, language ability, even social organization. And they're self-propagating. It's a new species, one with features that I haven't even discovered yet.

"I know what you think of me. That my peak is behind me,

with the brains, but you're wrong. This is it. This is what my life and my career have been for."

"You're mad. Take a look outside your tower, Doctor." Graham gestured towards the window. "We don't need more people. We don't have work for the ones already out there. Those creatures of yours can talk and think and fondle each other till the day is night, but it doesn't give them rights. It doesn't make them anything but what they are: inconvenient.

"You made them too much like people, Martin. In order to make a place for themselves, they'll have to displace human beings, and no one's going to step aside voluntarily. Ever heard of the twentieth century? Genocide is a very common human strategy. Some say it started all the way back with the sudden demise of the Neanderthals. Given that kind of track record, do you really think a new species with human traits has a chance?"

Hector smiled thinly and raised his shoulders. "Maybe they're like weeds and not so easily wiped out."

"Don't be ridiculous. Come here." Graham gripped Hector by the shoulder and propelled him towards the windows. "Looky there." He pointed towards Vattown. Hector could just make out the distant strobing of police flashers. "There's your proof. That little queen of yours is down there, and they're beating her to death."

Hector shook. He pulled away from Graham's grip and turned to face him. "How do you know that?"

Graham eyed him blandly. "Because I arranged it."

"What? You can't do that!"

Graham laughed. "You have no idea what I can do. They were going to strike anyway. It doesn't take much to turn that crowd into a mob."

"You've got to stop them." Hector lunged forward, grabbed the transceiver from Graham's belt loop and shoved it at him. "Now! Call them! Call it off!"

Graham's response was preempted by the insistent bleeping of the transceiver signal. Without thinking Hector switched it to receive. "Yes?" he said, in his best imitation of Graham's rough tenor.

There was no holo. Only a voice. "It's me. We lost her," it said.

Hector stared at Graham with glee. "Forget it. There's a change in plans," he said.

"Give me that!" yelled Graham, body-checking Hector and grabbing for the transceiver. They fell to the floor, Hector grunting as Graham rolled over him. The transceiver was wrested from his grasp and Graham stood up, brushing his suit. "I'll call you back," he muttered tersely at the transceiver and switched it off.

Hector stood and backed towards the door. Graham approached him with his right hand balled in a fist. Before he could close the distance and sock him, Hector turned and ran out the door.

Breathing heavily, Hector made his way to the elevators. He had a rug burn on his cheek from wrestling with Graham. All to the good, he thought as he entered the elevator and pressed the button for floor 29—Anna's office.

16

I Can Take You There

I didn't believe, still don't believe, that you should be diving, but what happened down there today, that wasn't what I wanted either. I wanted a real strike, with real demands, not just your dismissal but other, more important things like safety standards and better wages. Those fucking assholes, turning themselves into a mob. Don't they realize that they've destroyed any chance for their demands to be taken seriously? Why? Why must this movement always be dogged by shame?" Vonda put her head in her hands and shook it. She was sitting on Orielle's couch.

At the far end of the room, Chango crossed and uncrossed her arms. Bitter words were collecting in her mouth. Sooner or later she was going to open it and they'd come out. "If you hadn't all decided that Ada was blasted when she dove, there wouldn't be any shame," she finally blurted.

Vonda looked at her wearily. "Oh God, Chango. You're like a dog with a bone. Ada's dead, it doesn't matter why."

"Doesn't matter? You don't think so? You just said it yourself, the shame. It doesn't belong to her, it—"

"It doesn't belong to me either!" Vonda suddenly stood upright and shouted. "I swear to you on the friendship we once had, I did not doctor her lab results. I did not! Except for you there probably wasn't anyone more upset about those results than I was. How do you think I felt, being the messenger of that kind of news? Fucking-A, Chango, I knew Ada, too . . ." Vonda paced the floor. "And to tell you the truth," she said, "I've never been able to believe it myself."

Chango stared at her. "Really? Then who—"

"Nobody! I took the samples from her and ran the tests. No one else touched them. Chango, she was gassed when she dove, but—"

"Management would have done anything to get her out of their hair. Maybe someone tampered with her tanks."

"That's impossible. Benny filled and checked them, just like he always did. All I know is this ancient history shit isn't going to get us anywhere now. You ought to be thinking about your friend." She nodded at Helix, who was sitting in a chair, holding a bag of ice to the side of her face. "What are you going to do about her?"

"She needs a vat," said Chango.

"I don't understand."

"Neither do I," said Helix, "but there it is. If I don't find a vat soon, one I can stay in, I'm going to die."

There was a long pause in the conversation, and then Vonda spoke, her voice a pitch higher. "You're not human at all, are you?"

Helix shook her head. "I guess not."

Vonda stood by the television set, a reefer cigarette in her mouth and a thoughtful expression on her face. "Word was your father worked for GeneSys, a researcher. Never did get his name," she said.

"H-Hector Martin," said Helix.

"Hector Martin. Dr. Hector Martin. The inventor of the multiprocessor brains. I always knew there was something weird about you."

Helix stood up and walked towards her, her arms spread wide. "Oh, really?"

Vonda squinted and exhaled a plume of smoke. "It makes sense now. That's why they didn't fire you. The test was a success."

"Stop," said Chango.

Vonda shook her head, still staring as Helix slowly approached her. "I was so busy hating you because you were Chango's squeeze, I neglected the obvious. The rest of them out there today, they knew. Or at least as a mob they knew. They didn't want you dead for being a sport, or even for taking your suit off in the vat and surviving. They wanted you dead because your very existence is a threat to them. To all of us."

Helix stood inches from Vonda. She reached forward and braced her arms against the wall so that they surrounded Vonda like fleshly prison bars. "What then, are you going to do about it?" she asked in a low tone.

Vonda's eyes were wide, and she shook a little. "Remember," she muttered, "you're dealing with an individual here, not the species."

"Yeah? Well it sounds to me like you're speaking for your species."

Vonda stepped away from the wall, forcing Helix back with her body. "Human beings need those jobs, Helix. And if GeneSys is trying to create some kind of fabricated slave labor force, then is that really what you want?"

"I just want a vat." Helix's arms hung at her sides now, useless.

"Well you're not going to get one in Vattown. You can forget it. Why don't you go back to your maker? Maybe he can help you."

"Why don't you go to hell?" Helix stepped towards Vonda again, baring her teeth.

"Fine, fuck you." Vonda pushed Helix away from her with both hands. "I'm just trying to help."

"You just want to make me disappear. Like the rest of them."

"Oh you are so full of shit."

"Oh yeah?" Helix pushed Vonda back into the wall again. "Then why are you afraid of me?"

Vonda stared at her stonily. "Back off, Miss Thing, I'm warning you."

"No! What if I don't want to back off?"

Helix reeled suddenly as Vonda's right fist connected with her jaw. She shook her head, flexed her knees, and sprang on Vonda, knocking her to the floor. The two of them rolled over each other, kicking and scrabbling for handholds. Helix got ahold of Vonda's arms, pinning her to the floor.

"Stop it!" Chango hauled on Helix's shoulder, tearing her away from Vonda by sheer force of will. "What's the matter with you?" she yelled. "Aren't you in enough trouble already? She saved your life today! And what she says is true. You'll never get back into the vats. They'll never let you. All you'll do is get killed like you almost were today."

Helix turned her back and walked to the window. She looked out of it, out across the Eastern Market with its colorful stalls, to the tower that stood in the distance. It was a faded green in the haze of the sky, like a towering ghost. She stared at it and tried very hard not to think about anything Vonda had said. A wave of itching crept over her, her skin crawling at the thought of not having a vat.

They thought they could stop her; the mob and Vonda, even Chango in her own way. They thought she could just get over it, or just go away, or just be beaten. They didn't know. They didn't know about the hand that pushed her, they didn't know it was a thing greater than herself. They thought they knew what she was.

The time she had wasted, trying to be a human being, trying to get along with human beings. Madness. Madness born of memory, the terror of the playground and her determination to avoid it at any cost. But she could not. The community of humans was the playground. That was all it could ever be, not because of human nature, but because of her own.

Helix looked down at the street fronting Orielle's loft. Someone was approaching. It was Benny.

"I believe we have a visitor," said a silken voice behind her. Helix turned to see Orielle making an entrance from her gauze-shrouded bed chamber at the back of the loft. "The security holo tells me your esteemed colleague, Benjamin, has chosen to grace us with his presence. I believe he'll be ringing the bell right about—" She was interrupted by a soft chime. "Now." She smiled.

One of Orielle's bodyguards emerged from the bed chamber and went downstairs to answer the door.

Benny came up, looking like someone had smashed him in the face with a rock. "Thank God you're all right," he said, looking at Helix.

"What happened to you?" Chango asked.

He waved off her concern, shaking his head. "Pauly didn't take kindly to my heading him off. After that, it turned into a police brawl."

"You're lucky you didn't get arrested," said Vonda, sitting stiffly on the couch. Her eyes kept flickering over to Helix, making sure she kept her distance.

Benny nodded, thoughtfully holding a hand to his bleeding lip. "I know."

"However did you guess that your friends were here?" asked Orielle.

"I knew once they broke free of the mob they'd get out of Vattown. You like Helix, and you have the power to defend her."

"Yes." Orielle inclined her chin, and spread her arms. "But she cannot stay here forever."

"I was just trying to tell her she should go back to GeneSys, but she jumped all over my case," said Vonda. "Orielle's right, sooner or later the divers will figure out that she's here."

"Nonsense," said Orielle. "As long as she stays out of the picture, they'll quickly forget about her. That's not what I meant. That girl needs to be surrounded by a large quantity of growth medium. She needs a vat."

Chango stared at her. "We can bring it here," she said. "We can make a tank for her."

"What do you think this is, Sea World? No. Escorting her to safety at the bar was one thing, taking her in today was another, but installing her as a permanent member of my household, that's one too many."

Benny sank onto the couch. "There may be another way." He looked at Chango. "Remember those courses Ada took? Over at Mercy College?"

"In the biopoly department. They had a research center there."

"Yeah. The project was underwritten by GeneSys, and when the college folded, they kept it running for awhile."

"Until they could hire everyone they wanted into their own research department," said Chango. "They closed it a few years ago."

"True. But the vats will still be there."

* * *

Hector strode through the glass doors of Anna's office and brushed past her secretary. "Excuse me! Sir!" she cried in his wake. "Do you have an appointment?"

He glanced over his shoulder as he opened the door to Anna's private office. "Now I do."

Anna didn't have a desk. She reclined on a black vat leather chaise, gazing up at a holographic stock analysis graph. She glanced over and sat up as he came in the door. "Dr. Martin!" Her fingers strayed to a small keypad on her wrist and the graph dissolved. She looked at him quizzically.

This was it, time for his performance. "I can't work under these conditions! You have no idea what it's like. That—that man! He's out of control. Look!" Hector pointed at his cheek. "He hit me!" His voice went up an octave in an appropriately whiny squeal.

Still staring at him, Anna crossed fluidly to a low matte black table covered with magazines and toys. "Sit down, Dr. Martin." She gestured to a boxy black couch beside it. "Can I get you a glass of water?"

"Yes, that would be wonderful. Thank you." Hector sank onto the couch and relished the moment, as the CEO of GeneSys fetched him a glass of water. He should have done this a long time ago, he thought.

Anna returned, holding out the glass of water in a perfectly manicured hand. She folded herself into a chair to his right and watched him drink. "Feel better?" she asked when he drained the glass and set it between his feet.

He nodded, and she smiled, a sweet smile so perfectly reassuring, so innocently happy at his well being, that he responded emotionally with trust before his brain ever had the chance to tell him that it couldn't be real. "Tell me what happened," she said.

"I was in Nathan Graham's office. We were having an argument about the Tetra Project. He seems bound and determined to interfere with my work on it, and lately his distractions have ruined my concentration. I was trying to explain to him that I needed space for my work, mental space, when suddenly he started screaming at me and pushed me to the floor. I think it's only fair to inform you that I thoroughly intend to press charges on the matter. The kind of support or resistance I receive from the company in the course of this legal proceeding will determine whether or not I remain an employee of GeneSys."

Anna held up one hand. "Please understand that while I am forbidden by company charter to take a position in any litigation concerning a present employee, I will make it my personal responsibility to get to the bottom of this incident."

That was what he was afraid of. Hector nodded mutely.

"I don't have to tell you that you are a deeply valued member of my company. I very much appreciate your coming to me with this problem. Unfortunately my various responsibilities prevent me from keeping abreast with all the exciting developments in the research department. What is this Tetra Project that Graham's been giving you so much trouble with?"

Hector licked his lips. "Its goal is to replace the paid labor force in vat maintenance and decanting with an engineered organism capable of performing those duties. It's a difficult problem and Graham has been increasingly impatient with my progress. A month ago he called a meeting with me to ask when I would be ready with a prototype. In all honesty I couldn't give him a definite answer, and that's when he started questioning everything; demanding explanations for expenditures, dropping by the lab at all hours, and recruiting my assistants as spies."

"I see. And what precipitated the confrontation between the two of you today?"

He didn't dare mention anything of Helix's plight, or the situation with the other tetras. It was probably only a matter of time before Anna learned what was really going on, but he had to use his momentary leverage to get Graham out of the picture. Even now he was probably laying a trap for Helix, down in Vattown. "I went to his office to tell him to back off. That I couldn't get any work done under such constant scrutiny. That's when he became abusive and struck me."

Anna stood up suddenly and paced the room in quick, black silk-clad strides. "I can understand why you're upset. Believe me when I tell you that I take this matter very seriously. Any employee striking another is intolerable, and in this case . . ." She looked at him. "In this case I stand to lose a very valuable mind because of it." She fingered the keypad on her wrist. "I'm going to call security and have them escort Mr. Graham here. You can be assured he

won't try any rough stuff. I'd like to talk to the two of you together."

Hector stood up, toppling the empty water glass at his feet.
"You have to stop him," he blurted.

Anna eyed him coolly. "Stop him from what?"

Hector's jaw worked. "From interfering in my project," he
managed to say.

"Oh, I will. I will."

Moments later Graham arrived, escorted by two GeneSys security guards in yellow-and-green uniforms. He eyed Hector with
cold hostility, his face pale.

"Have a seat, Mr. Graham," said Anna, indicating a space on
the couch next to Hector.

The security guards stayed by the door, watching as Graham
seated himself stiffly on the couch, as far from Hector as he could
manage. Anna glanced at the guards. "Are you going to behave
yourself?" she asked Graham.

He nodded, and she turned to the guards. "Wait outside."

"Anna. Whatever this is about—" Graham stole a glance at
Hector. "I'm sure we don't need to get security involved."

"Well, I'm afraid I do. Dr. Martin here says you struck him. Is
that true?"

Graham spread his hands and looked at Hector again, taking in
the rug burn on the side of his face. "We had an argument, and I'm
afraid it became heated. I asked Dr. Martin to leave and he refused.
I put a hand on his shoulder to escort him to the door and he fell."

"That's a lie, Graham. You pushed me. You pushed me and I'm
going to file charges," said Hector.

"What were you two arguing about?" asked Anna.

Hector and Graham stared at each other. "We were—"

"I was objecting to Graham's interference," Hector interrupted.

"Thank you, Dr. Martin. I'd like to hear what Mr. Graham
has to say." Anna stared at Graham expectantly, her hands folded
in her lap.

"Apparently Dr. Martin objects to me doing my job."

"If you consider pushing people to the floor as part of your job,
then I don't blame him."

Graham shook his head. "That was an accident."

"Why have you chosen to concentrate on Dr. Martin's project?"

"It's overdue and over budget," he said slowly.

"And have you taken into account the difficulty of what Dr. Martin is attempting to do?"

"Maybe not at first, but now I do."

"I hope you realize the seriousness of the situation. You're likely to face assault charges."

"I think a full investigation would reveal facets of the incident that Dr. Martin would prefer remained unnoticed."

Anna glanced between them. At last she turned her attention to Hector once more. "Are you absolutely sure he pushed you?" she asked gently.

Graham raised one eyebrow, waiting for his response. "No, not really. I—I might have tripped."

"Then you aren't pressing charges."

"No, but I want him away from my project."

"It's his job to monitor research."

"Not like this it isn't. I can't get anything done with him breathing down my neck all the time."

Anna looked at Graham. "Hear that? Back off."

Graham looked suitably chastened. "Yes. I will." He barely suppressed a smirk. "I'll give Dr. Martin all the space he needs."

"All right, gentlemen." Anna stood, clapping her hands together. "Now if you'll excuse me, I have real work to do. I hope you both can stay out of the principal's office in the future. She's not accustomed to dealing with brawling schoolboys."

They were shown out of the office together. When the door shut behind them Graham glanced sidelong at Hector. "Well, that could have been worse," he said.

Hector stared at him and began laughing hysterically.

Colin Slatermeyer licked sweat off of his upper lip and shifted his position in the hard metal chair. He was in a small office on the second floor of the vat room. Outside the door was a balcony that ringed the inside of the room, on a level with the rims of the two vats which took up most of the floor space.

They'd kept this room closed, cut off from the rest of the vat room's environmental systems. It was crammed with telecommunications equipment: transceivers and voice printers and faxes. Apparently they'd taken every moisture-sensitive piece of equipment and stuck it in here, and the really amazing part of it was that most of it was hooked up.

Actually, he was glad to be put in here at first. The temperature was in the high nineties. With the divesuit on he'd collapse from heat prostration before long. It was hot as an oven in here, but at least he could breathe without a respirator on his face.

A transceiver module on a bench near the window suddenly bleated a repeating sequence of tones. Somebody was calling. He looked at the tetra, who was bored and irksome at having to be here, in this dry air. "Should I get that?" he asked.

She shook her head and held two hands out in warning as she got up and opened the door a crack, and called something out onto the balcony. The bleating continued; evidently whoever was calling knew enough to let it ring a long time. Colin glanced from the tetra, still halfway out the door, to the transceiver, just behind him and to the right. What the hell, what would ever be worth the risk again, if not this? In a sudden, single movement he stood up and swung around to the transceiver. It wasn't a very big room, he didn't have far to go. The live receive button was helpfully colored red, and he pushed it while the tetra was turning around.

"Hello?" It was Dr. Martin, his face ghostly, floating in the air in front of the paneled wall, the wood grain visible behind him.

Colin stared at him a moment, expecting a reaction, but Dr. Martin's eyes were unfocused, his gaze wandering. Glancing down, he just had time to notice that the transceiver was set to blackout before hands came around him and clamped over his mouth and around his chest, pinning his arms. He was dragged back to the chair and held there. "Hello?" came Dr. Martin's voice again. "Is anybody there?"

Colin screamed against the muffling hands, but then there was another tetra there, and small, delicate fingers around his neck, smart little fingers that knew just where to press to cut off his air. He choked and subsided, but the hands stayed there, along with the ones over his mouth, and he was tied up with ropes woven from agules. The draft of mist wafting in from the balcony abruptly stopped as Lilith came in and shut the door behind her. She gave him an annoyed glance and went over to Hector's hologram. "What do you want?" she said. "This is not convenient."

"Listen, I know Graham's been there. He told me you'd taken Slatermeyer hostage. Let him go. He's of no use to you anyway, and things are starting to . . . happen. Graham's already trying to kill Helix. He thinks I should have terminated the project a long time ago. Now he's going to do it himself. If we don't do something, he's going to kill you all off."

"He won't find that so easy to do."

"Bullshit. He could send fifty guys in there with machine guns. Hell, if it came down to it he'd probably just flood the place with poisonous gas. Believe me, there's nothing he isn't capable of."

She glanced over her shoulder at Colin, who stared at her with wide, wide eyes. "But there's a human being in here now."

"So? You think that's going to stop him? I know this guy, he used to work in production. He wouldn't bat an eye over a lab assistant."

Fresh sweat sprang out all over Colin's body, and he mumbled again against the hands pressed against his lips, and the thumbs came down again on his windpipe.

"What's that?" said Dr. Martin. "Is that him? Is he there now?"

Colin would have answered him, but he was choking, and there were tears in his eyes. "Let me talk to him," he heard Hector say over the roaring in his ears.

There was a pause, during which Colin's vision began to fade, and then Lilith must have agreed, because the pressure on his throat was released, and he leaned forward, coughing and breathing.

They held him, four hands to an arm, in front of the hologram. He was still breathing in convulsive gulps. He heard the door click shut. Lilith had left. "Dr. Martin," he gasped.

"Slatermeyer, what's happened to you?"

Colin shook his head. "I was right here. They were trying to keep me quiet, that's all." He took a long deep breath, "I'm all right."

"Then you heard what I said about Graham," Martin said quietly.

"Yeah."

"Look, I was trying to put a scare into her, that's all, I don't really think he'd—"

"Yes, you do."

"Well, all right, I do, but—there must be some way we can get you out, there must be some way we can stop him. Colin, I'm sorry this happened to you, but maybe it's a blessing in disguise. With you on the inside, it might help us prepare for whatever Graham is going to do."

Colin grinned badly. "In the first place, I can't do shit in here, Dr. Martin. They've got me locked up under guard in this room along with everything else that can be damaged by the vapor, all their electronics and communications equipment, and in the second place, I want to go home!" Hot tears sprang from his eyes. "They make me sit in that fucking chair, day and night. I can't get any sleep."

One of the tetras who was holding him leaned forward towards the pickup camera. "We keep him here because of the vapor," she said, her voice husky from disuse.

"But the man needs to sleep, Immelene. At least let him lie on the floor."

"Hey, thanks," said Colin sarcastically.

Immelene and her sister looked at each other. "We could do that," they said.

"Why don't you try asking them to let me go, Dr. Martin," said Colin. "I think you gave up a little early on that one."

"All right. Will you let him go?"

"No."

"We'll keep him."

"Why? What possible use could you have for him?"

"Hey," said Colin, indignant.

"I'm sorry, but really, what do they, or I should say, does she, intend to do with you? They haven't been taking any . . . samples of anything, have they?"

Colin stared at him wide-eyed. "What do you mean?" he asked, horrified.

"Anything, skin, hair, whatever."

"No."

"Okay, so she's just keeping you there. Oh, I could never get her to tell me why. She never tells me anything. Now you know,

Colin. Now you know what I've had to put up with all this time. The stress is unbearable, isn't it? She's . . . impenetrable. Here she is, this thing I've created, but now that she's here, I'm irrelevant to her."

"Graham knows about the egg," said Colin.

"I know." Hector's face, animated a moment ago with angst, became suddenly still.

"I didn't know what to tell him," Colin said carefully. "We never did find out what happened to it."

Dr. Martin's face seemed to shift to a different facet of his personality. He looked very hard at Colin, even as a hologram, it was a little tough to take. "I can tell you what happened to it. It hatched. Her name's Helix, and Graham tried to get her killed this morning."

"Look, I didn't want to help him but he had the goods on me. I'm sorry, Dr. Martin, but even this is better than going back to ALIVE!"

Martin's jaw was stiff. He nodded ever so slightly. "Then you understand, now, that your survival lies with the tetras. Try to get through to Lilith, convince her that Graham is a real threat, if you can."

"Oh sure, you bet. Anything else?"

"I'll call again later."

"I'll hold my breath."

Chango parked her car on the street across from the U of D Mercy College campus and took a backpack out of the trunk. They walked to the now-defunct biopoly research building. An old maple tree grew next to the wall on one side. Chango, Helix and Benny stole across the grass to the shelter of its shadows. Benny pointed up, and Helix saw that one of the tree's branches brushed against a window on the second floor. Without a word Chango scaled the trunk and climbed out onto the arching branch. It swayed slightly under her weight. Helix wondered if it would support her. Chango worked a few minutes with a small, silver instrument, its whir a counterpoint to the chirring of crickets. "Sst. Come on."

Helix gripped the trunk of the tree with her upper arms. Her lower arms were useless as far as pulling herself up was concerned, but at least she could use them for clinging. Her feet scraped against the bark and she hauled herself up into the leaves. Below her she heard Benny grunting as he climbed the tree.

Chango had the window open, and she pushed her backpack in before climbing through. Helix followed her and found herself standing on a second-floor balcony overlooking two large, empty vats. "They're empty," said Helix.

"Yeah," whispered Benny, climbing through the window. "This place has been closed up for years. But look." He pointed to a stack of barrels in the far corner. "Maybe some of it is still good."

"Do you have any idea how many of those barrels it would take to fill one of these? Besides, how do we get them down?" They were stacked ten high.

"There must be a ladder around here somewhere," said Chango.

"And you call me crazy," said Helix. "What if some of that spills on you?"

"That's why I brought this." Chango opened the flap of her backpack and showed her the sleeve of a divesuit. "It was Ada's."

Helix glanced about the building again. "What kind of security do you think they've got in here?"

Chango shrugged. "Judging from the window, not much, 'course you never can tell."

"I'll stay up here and keep lookout," said Benny.

There was a ladder at the far end of the building, down a long aisle past the dingy flanks of the vats. They carried it back to the tanks and stood at its base, looking up.

"Christ, I don't know about this," said Chango.

"They look heavy."

"I don't know if the ladder will hold. They've got to weigh fifty pounds apiece."

"I might be able to do it. At least I can try to see if they're any good. Put your suit on."

Helix climbed the ladder, alternately grasping the rungs with her upper and lower hands. As she went she glanced at the wall of stacked barrels beside her. Some of them were corroded, possibly leaking. She reached the top of the ladder. The last row of barrels was just above her head. With her upper fingers she grasped one of them by its bottom rim.

She wedged her fingers underneath the barrel and inched it out until she was able to lift it free. She grasped the barrel with her lower arms. The ladder wobbled precariously as she reached for the rungs with her upper hands. She clung there a few moments, until the swaying stopped.

She was just about to start down when the first-floor doors burst inward and ten or more GeneSys security guards ran in, brandishing tranq guns. "Run!" she yelled at Chango, and heaved the barrel towards the approaching guards.

Chango scrambled for the stairs as the barrel crashed to the floor behind her. She heard yelling as the guards scattered to avoid the splashing growth medium. Where in the hell was Benny? she wondered as she pounded up the steps to the balcony. He was gone from his post by the window and he certainly hadn't done much of a job of warning them. Chango paused at the window, looked back and saw Helix, still on the ladder but surrounded by guards. There was nothing she could do now but get away and get help.

Outside, the building was bathed in flashing green-and-yellow lights. Chango dropped to the ground and crouched in the shadow of the tree. She heard the squawking of a transceiver from a levvan parked in the street. She scanned the broad spread of mowed grass before her. She didn't see anyone there, didn't see anyone around the levvan either, though that didn't mean no one was there.

She ran, bent at the waist, over the grass, the night air cool against her skin, her breath and the pounding of her heart roaring in her ears, drowning out the transceiver and the chirring of crickets. She thought she heard shouts, but she kept running.

She'd gone four blocks before she noticed the levcar following her, gliding silently along the magnetic roadway. She never would have known it was there, except she caught a glimpse of it as she turned one corner, and then saw it again, a block farther on. She cut through an alley, narrow and paved only with cloncrete, but when she got to the street on the other side, there it was again, closing in on her. Her heart pounded in her chest like it would burst. To her left was the university medical center, a cluster of buildings with a large driveway in front, leading to an underground parking structure.

She'd been here before. Between the close-set buildings was a labyrinth of walkways. If you were in a levcar, you had to park it and walk to the building you wanted. She headed for the main entrance and veered off onto a cloncrete sidewalk bordered by hedges. Behind her, in the night, she heard the distinct sound of car doors slamming and footsteps running. Chango zigzagged between buildings, the footsteps behind her growing closer. She thought she could make out two sets. There were shouts, and something whizzed past her head, very fast. She ducked around another corner and she was in a cul de sac between two tall sandstone buildings, a high brick wall running between them.

"Give it up," she heard someone call behind her, but she ran to the wall nevertheless, ran and jumped and scrabbled at it with her hands but she couldn't climb it. Her breath coming in explosive gasps, she clawed and pounded at the wall until her fingers bled. There were tears on her face when she turned around. There were two of them, guys, both dressed in green coveralls and carrying tranq guns and nightsticks. One was nearly a head taller than the other, and broader through the shoulders. They stood about ten feet from her, their tranq guns trained on her. She looked at her torn, bleeding fingers. Slowly she lifted one finger to her forehead and daubed it with blood, and then she walked slowly towards them, her hands at her sides and carefully visible. When she got between them they grabbed her, cuffed her hands behind her back, and each taking an arm, walked her back to the street and the waiting car.

17

CORPORATE ANIMAL

HYPER twirled the data card between his fingers as his eyes flickered across a directory of GeneSys' information systems. Dr. Martin had a very high security clearance. Even better than would be expected for a top researcher. Why would he need access to the security records, for instance, or personnel?

Hyper got up from his maglev seat, lit a reefer, and smoking it, paced the floor. He hadn't seen Chango or Helix since the riot this morning, and neither had anyone else he'd talked to. From his vantage point on the Humbolt water tower, he'd seen Vonda and Helix running through the mob, but as he focused his machines on the divers ahead of them he lost track of where they were. He watched while the police made arrests, waiting until the street was clear to gather the torn remains of his robots. By the time he got back home Chango was gone.

It was her disappearance that alarmed him the most. For Vonda and Helix it would be prudent to lay low for a while, preferably someplace outside of Vattown. But Chango didn't even go to the picket line.

She had called the police, though. That much he knew from the call log of his transceiver headset, which she'd left very neatly in the middle of his worktable. Perhaps she'd gone in search of Helix, in which case she might be incommunicado as well, but there was something wrong. For one thing, he hadn't been able to get ahold of Benny all day, and it wasn't because he was in jail. Hyper had called the police station and learned that neither Helix, Vonda, Chango, nor Benny had been arrested.

The whole thing bothered him. He was worried and he wanted someone to talk to. Sinking back into his maglev seat, he opened the employee directory and scanned it. Maybe Dr. Martin would be home.

His listed number turned out to be a message dump, but because he had Martin's security code, he was able to access his file and get his live number.

It rang twice and a worried voice answered. "Hello?" It was just voice, blackout on visuals. At least he had that much sense, but Martin had to have sender ID on a system like this, and he was answering unknown callers on the second ring.

"Hi," said Hyper, and smiled for the transceiver picking up his image and beaming it to Dr. Martin.

"Who is this?"

"I'm Hyper. You don't know me."

"You must have the wrong number."

"Don't hang up." Hyper anticipated the invisible movement. "I'm a friend of Helix's."

There was silence in Suite 2567 of the GeneSys Building, and then, "How is she?"

Hyper shrugged. "I don't know. I don't know where she is."

"How did you get this number?"

"From your data card. Helix gave it to me for safekeeping," he lied. It wouldn't help matters any for Martin to know he and Chango had stolen the card.

"When was the last time you saw her?"

"This morning, before the riot," said Hyper.

"The riot. But I heard she got away."

"Apparently she did, but I haven't seen her since this morning. There's someone else, a woman named Chango. She's a friend of Helix's too. I think they might be together, and I'm afraid something's happened to them. Do you know where they might be?"

"No. I wish I did." There was a pause. "You got this number using my data card. Presumably you've had a look around in there, then."

"Yes. Yes I have."

"Then you know about her. What she is."

"Yes. You've outdone yourself, Dr. Martin. The brains were impressive, but this—"

"Does she know?"

Hyper shrugged. "She knows she's not human. But she wouldn't look at your notes. She said she didn't need to. Once she started diving, it didn't take long for her true nature to surface. What did you hope to accomplish, keeping her there? You should have cut your losses and brought her back home after the divesuit incident."

"You misunderstand. I never intended for her to get that job in the first place. I intended for her to get far away from here, much farther than Vattown."

"Well if you didn't diddle with her files, who did? I can't believe management made this decision. They're evil, not stupid."

Hector Martin laughed. "I suppose it was her mother," he said.

"Her mother?"

"Helix is not the first of her kind."

"Oh. I just assumed, with the kind of security clearance you're sporting—"

"That was a gift from her mother as well. A sort of back-handed gift, since she arranged it for her own use. But she used someone else's code to manipulate the personnel files. She wouldn't want that traced to me . . ." Hector's voice trailed off momentarily. "Are you a vatdiver?" he asked suddenly.

"No. I'm a sport. Look, I know you don't know me, but I've let you have a good look at me. And you know that, with the kind of information I have at my disposal, I could have screwed you over ages ago. But I didn't. Now, could you bring that screen down please, so we can both talk face-to-face?"

There was a pause, and then the pale, drawn face of a man in his middle forties glowed into view in the air before him. "Better?"

"Thanks."

Martin's brows knitted. "You say you're not a diver but— Do you know of a man named Nathan Graham?"

"Nathan Graham . . . Wait, yeah. He used to be the production controller several years back. A real heavy. Everyone around here hated him."

"Yeah, well, he's in research now. He's the reason I wanted Helix to get far away from here. He wants the project terminated, and in this case that's a pretty strong term to be using. He told me himself he arranged the riot in order to get her killed. If something has happened to her, it'll be because of him."

Hyper stared at him. Martin had grayish blond hair, thinning a bit at the temples and crown. "What are we going to do?"

"Graham has somebody working for him, in Vattown I'm guessing. I don't know who it is," said Martin.

Hyper thought of Chango—how she'd always insisted that there'd been foul play in Ada's death. Maybe she was right, maybe Graham was still working with someone on the inside. It wouldn't have taken much to turn the strike into a riot, discrediting the vat-divers and taking care of Helix at the same time.

"Do you have any idea who it might be?"

"No, not really," said Hyper, "and following up all the possible leads would take time we don't have. It's been hours since the riot. Graham and whoever he's working with probably have them by now."

"Yeah. We can hope that Helix and your friend skipped town, but I wouldn't bet on it. You have access to GeneSys security systems through my clearance. Use it. See if they've brought anyone in in the last few hours. I'm going to try to put Graham under wraps. Call me back as soon as you check the files."

"You're pretty comfortable with other people using your code, aren't you?"

"Not really." Hector shrugged. "But there can be advantages to being in two places at once."

When Helix came to she was tied to a chair in a laboratory. A large polyglass tank stood about ten feet in front of her. It was filled with growth medium. She could smell it, and the pores of her skin cried out for its touch.

A door on the other side of the room, past the tank and a number of benches, opened with a soft click and a man came in. He was of medium height, with heavy rather than muscular shoulders and a flat belly that must have cost him plenty. He wore a dark grey sylk suit, immaculately tailored, and his reddish brown hair was neatly combed back from his forehead. He had quick, cool grey eyes. He smiled, and his face crinkled in small lines around his eyes and nose which she felt were quite deliberate, probably surgically devised.

"So you're Helix," he said, pulling a chair up to sit across from her, between her and the growth medium.

"So who are you?" she said.

"I'm Nathan Graham, chief administrator of research and development." He said it like it was supposed to mean something.

"Untie me," she said.

"Not just yet, Helix. Soon, but not yet. You see I've been wondering just how much you know about what you are. How much Hector told you."

Helix's hands tightened around the arms of the chair. "He—he said I was adopted."

"Ah, but by now you know that can't be true."

Helix didn't say anything. She was thinking about the playground at the orphanage, the children taunting her, laughing. But how much did she really remember? A few incidents, the smell of chalk in Ms. Walker's classroom, but not her room—she would have had a room, and roommates, but she couldn't recall them, and when she thought of herself, she visualized herself exactly the same size as she was now. With a start, she realized she always had.

"Well, let me be the one to tell you, then." Graham stood and paced behind his chair. "You are a GeneSys research project. Its chief scientist, your Hector Martin, created you. Or at least he created the thing that gave birth to you."

"What?"

"Your mother. She hatched out of an egg, right in this tank behind me. But you hatched in a full-sized vat in the basement of this building. Just think, little Helix, all those months you fancied yourself an orphan girl, rescued by the kindness of Hector Martin, and all along, your real mother was right beneath your feet."

Helix stared at him wide-eyed. "You're lying."

"Oh no." Graham shook his head. "It is not I who have lied to you. Don't you remember? When you were born your mother and your siblings attacked you and drove you out of their hive. And then, for reasons perhaps not completely comprehensible even to him, Hector secluded you in his apartment, hiding you from the rest of the world.

"I suppose he wanted you to believe you were human, but the memory of your expulsion from the hive was too powerful, so he made up a story to account for your feelings, a story about a poor little orphan girl and the kindly man who made her his daughter."

Helix felt ill, a sick, twisted knotting in her stomach. She held on to it, feeling that if it unraveled, it would unravel everything else with it, and she, and everything she'd ever known, would disappear in a puff of lies. She closed her eyes, and in her mind's eye she saw those jeering faces, the faces of children contorted with malicious glee, melt away to reveal other faces, faces not gleeful, not malicious, but more terrible still, faces like her own, and purely determined to get rid of her at any cost. A savage rage as hot and sweet as anything she had ever felt rose inside her, a lust to attack someone who was herself. "My mother—" she said. "You said my mother."

"Yes, your mother. He calls her Lilith, for some reason. You and your kind were designed to clean vats and harvest biopolymers. All the things the vatdivers do. That riot today wasn't the first time they've caused problems for us. We need a more efficient way of producing biopolymer. Unfortunately, you're not it, either."

"But I dove without a suit, and I was fine."

"Yes, yes," Graham said, waving a hand dismissively. "Your physiology is perfect for the vat environment, but there are other problems, things you don't understand. I'm afraid it just won't work out. I never should have allowed Hector Martin such a free hand. Out of deference to his professional stature, I let him do it his way. It's been a disaster—a costly one. But I wouldn't have this job if I weren't able to turn even a catastrophe like this to my advantage."

"What are you going to do?"

"I'm reassigning your project. There's no hope of utilizing you or your kind for industrial purposes, but at least we can learn something from Martin's mistakes. There are any number of features to your physiology and brain chemistry that may yield fruitful benefits to other lines of inquiry. Of course Martin would never consent to it. He's too attached to you. He erroneously thinks of you as a person. But there are other researchers on staff here at GeneSys who have no such handicap."

"You're going to make me a test subject."

"That's about it, yes."

She tensed with fear. "You can't do that. I have to—I need—" Words failed her. She strained forward towards the growth medium, her nostrils flared to drink in the smell of it. "Let me go," she said through gritted teeth.

"I'm afraid you have very little say in the matter. You keep forgetting. You're not human. You have no right to control your own destiny. You are property of the GeneSys corporation, and as such, you will serve its purposes."

Graham turned to look at the tank behind him. "You want to get in there, don't you? Worse than you've ever wanted to do anything in your brief little life. Well, to show you I'm not such a bad guy, I'm going to let you. And you'll never have to leave it. Well, almost never. Some tests probably can't be conducted in there, but most will be."

Helix shook her head. She wanted to be in growth medium, yes, but not like this. "What do you plan to do to me?"

"Ah." Graham bent over her, shaking a finger in her face. "Now that would be telling."

As he straightened up again, four security guards entered the laboratory. Graham turned to face them. "What are you doing here? I didn't call for you."

The guards glanced at one another and flanked Graham. "We're here for you, Mr. Graham," one of them said. "We have a warrant for your arrest."

Chango paced the narrow confines of her holding cell on the first subfloor of the GeneSys Building. The walls and door were clear polyglass with strips of yellow-and-green adhesive running along them at waist height to prevent anyone from walking into them. One side of the ten by six room had a formiculate bench built into it which formed itself to her body when she sat on it. There was no toilet. These cells were not designed for long-term use. That was a relief. Even with the clear walls, she had trouble keeping calm. She'd never been in a jail before.

Soon they'd take her over to the county precinct, book her and set bail, and then she could call Hyper and have him come and get her out. She'd probably be back in Vattown by morning.

But what about Helix? Chango had been alone in the car with the two guards, and judging from the sea of empty cubicles which surrounded her, she was alone here as well. There was no chance she'd escaped the guards; she'd been surrounded. What did they do with her?

And then there was Benny. He failed to warn them of the approach of security, and obviously it wasn't because he'd been arrested. And for the life of her, she couldn't figure out how security had learned they were there. They hadn't tripped any alarm systems, she was sure of it.

After a few hours a pair of women in green-and-yellow jumpsuits came and unlocked the door to her cell. They were both quite a bit taller than she was.

"Am I going to county?" asked Chango.

The one on the left shook her head silently. She had blond hair bobbed at her chin. The other guard stared at Chango with impartial brown eyes and stepped into the cell, taking her by the arm. They walked her down a long corridor with cells on one side and yellow-and-green painted cinderblocks on the other. They were pretty relentless with the color scheme down here. Even the bathroom, when they came to it, was painted green and yellow.

They showed her to a stall and allowed her to shut the door, "Keep your feet on the floor at all times," warned Blondie.

They took her back to a cell. She couldn't be sure it was the same one as before. They all looked exactly alike and she hadn't counted them on the way out. "When will I be going to county?" she asked them.

Brown eyes smiled and shook her head, and Blondie laughed, but neither of them answered her question, they just left her sitting there and locked the door behind them.

She had a long time to think about things. About Ada and Vonda and Benny and Helix. About Orielle and Hyper and Mavi. And about herself and the many ways in which she'd been blind.

18

WHAT HAVE YOU DONE?

BENNY ran up the stairs to his apartment. He went straight to the closet, pulled out a case he'd been keeping for just this occasion, and started throwing his clothes inside. It took him ten minutes to pack clothes, toothbrush, razor and his daddy's Smith & Wesson machine pistol. He stood in his emptied closet, staring at the small panel in the back where he'd cut through the ancient drywall and later fastened a piece of paneling over the hole. They'd lain there all this time. He'd sealed them in the wall the way he'd sealed his mind against the memory of what he'd done. He wondered if someone would search the place after he'd gone and find them. His secret would be discovered at last.

But he'd be far away and someone else by then. He switched on the transceiver at his wrist and called up his numbered account. Benny sat down on the bed, gaping at the pitiful balance glowing in the air before him. There should have been a sizeable deposit made in the last few hours, but it wasn't there. The arrangements for Hugo's funeral had only left him with a couple hundred—too little to purchase a ticket to where he was going.

His hands clenched. That bastard Graham had screwed him over. He'd seen to it that Helix was taken into custody by GeneSys security. That was the agreement, but Graham hadn't paid. Benny stood up and took the pistol from the case, fitted it with a cartridge and stuck it in his waistband. A little visit might jog Graham's memory.

Hyper walked through the polyglass doors of the GeneSys Building and onto the first-floor mezzanine. The ceiling arched high above him, glittering with murals. Lush, red-haired women entwined themselves among eagles and fruitbearing vines, and the pictures were all edged in gold. It was like a palace.

Catching himself he looked down again and walked to the information desk. He had decked himself out for the occasion in a lab coat, white shirt and grey dress slacks. The shirt and slacks were part of his funeral clothes, along with the thin black tie throttling his neck. For added effect, he carried a black briefcase with most of the scuff marks wiped off it. But his sartorial efforts were needless. There was no one at the information desk, or anyplace else, at this hour.

He swiped a card through the transceiver mounted on the desktop. It held Hector Martin's ID codes and his authorization for Chango's release. The system acknowledged him as Martin and he dialed the security desk.

"Security offices," said a clerk whose blank face appeared hovering above the counter. "Can I help you?"

"I'm here to pick up Chango Chichelski. I have clearance for her release."

The clerk tapped at his console. "Chichelski. She came in tonight on trespassing charges. You say you have clearance for her release?"

"Yes," Hyper said, trying not to hold his breath. According to Martin, he didn't need to have a reason why Chango should be released; all he needed were the clearance codes for such action, and he had those.

"Send it through," the clerk said.

Hyper allowed himself a long, slow exhalation, and swiped the card through the transceiver a second time.

The clerk scanned the release form, nodded his head, and tapped away at his console some more. "She's being released. Do you want to come down for her?"

Hyper smiled slightly at him. "I'll wait here," he said.

Hyper waited, trying not to stare at the vaulting archways or the frescoed ceiling they supported. Instead he turned his attention to the floor; a disc of brass lay set into the marble tile nearby, the figure of a dancing woman all but worn away from its surface by generations of scuffing feet.

In a large alcove off the mezzanine and directly opposite the desk where he stood, an elevator pinged open and three figures struggled out. It was a pair of guards leading a man, handcuffed but still struggling, between them. "This is outrageous," he shouted, his face red with fury. "You have no right to arrest me! What are the charges?" He swung around, nearly dislodging the guards' hold on him. They responded by grasping his wrists, which were cuffed behind his back, and bending them up to his shoulder blades.

"Ow! Goddamn it, what do you think you're doing?" the man fumed, hopping forward in pain. "What is your name?" he demanded of the guard on his right.

"Marcus Walsh," the guard told him, grasping his upper arm firmly and leading him towards a door just past the information desk where Hyper stood.

"Well, let me tell you something, Marcus Walsh," said the man, now pretty much allowing himself to be escorted. "You're never going to work here, or anyplace else again. This will be your last act as an employee of GeneSys, *Marcus*," he said with a nasty edge in his voice. The guards took him through the door, and Hyper could hear his voice echoing up the stairs as they led him to security. "You've both made a big mistake. Nathan Graham is not to be trifled with in this way, you'll find out. . . ."

Chango couldn't be sure how long she'd been sitting there when a new pair of guards came to her cell, opened the door and escorted her out. Finally, county, thought Chango, but as she stepped through the polyglass doors into the receiving area they moved away from her side. "You're free to go," said the blond guard, gesturing at the door on the far side of the room. "Dr. Martin is waiting for you upstairs."

"I'm free to—Dr. Martin is— Oh." Brown Eyes handed over her backpack and Chango turned to the door just as it burst inward and two more security guards came through, escorting a tall man in a suit. His reddish brown hair was in disarray, flopping in strands across his forehead. The guards took him to the counter, where he fixed the clerk with a steely look. "Will you explain what I'm doing here? On what grounds and whose authority am I being arrested?"

The clerk held his gaze. "And you are?"

"You know goddamn well who I am! Just this evening I had a bunch of you people out at Mercy College. What's the matter with you?"

The clerk shook her head. "Your name?"

"Nathan Graham."

"Nathan Graham." The clerk scrolled through an arrest roster. "You're being held for questioning in relation to a murder charge, Mr. Graham."

"Murder? That's insane. I didn't murder anyone."

"Would you like to call an attorney, Mr. Graham?"

"You better believe I would. What's your name?"

"Cynthia Hewlitt."

"Well, let me tell you something, Cynthia Hewlitt. When I get through with this department, there won't be a one of you" — he turned to glare at the guards —"still working here. You have no grounds to do this, no authority. This is harassment."

Cynthia raised one eyebrow. "Your warrant was issued from the very highest levels of GeneSys personnel, with priority authorization to arrest."

"But you can only hold me for two hours unless you make a charge. That's the company charter."

Cynthia ignored him and looked at the guard on his right. "Let him make his call, then put him in cell D-nineteen."

Unnoticed, Chango slipped through the door and went up the steps. She saw Hyper standing by the information desk, studying a brass inlay in the floor. He was all tricked out in a lab coat stained with motor oil, his grey dress slacks, and a scuffed black briefcase.

"Hyper! What are you doing here?"

He shot her an alarmed look as he hurried to her side. "Let's get out of here," he murmured, taking her arm and leading her across the mezzanine to the exit doors.

"Hyper, what is going on?" Chango asked as soon as they were outside. "How did you get here? Why didn't they take me to county? How did you get them to release me like that?"

Hyper kept walking, so fast Chango had to trot to keep up with him. "Remember this?" He held up a data card, the GeneSys logo flickering in and out of view with the passing streetlights.

"Helix's card."

"Not Helix's—Hector Martin's. I got worried when you disappeared. I talked to him. He's the one who got Graham arrested."

Chango nodded and took this in. "We went to U of D Mercy," she said, Hyper's pace making her voice ragged. "There's an old biopoly research institute there, an abandoned vat for Helix, but GeneSys security showed up. They got me. I'm sure they got Helix too, but she wasn't in the lockup."

Hyper nodded and said nothing, his eyes scanning the street warily.

"Benny took us there. He was supposed to be on lookout, but when the guards came, I didn't see him around. Hyper, I've been thinking. Benny set us up. I think he had something to do with Ada's death, too."

"Graham arranged it," said Hyper pausing on a street corner to face her. They were already three blocks from the GeneSys building. "Martin told me he had someone in Vattown working for him. From what you say it sounds like that's Benny. And if he's working for him now, then he probably was in the past, when Graham was in production."

"What happened to Helix?"

"Martin's taking care of that end of things. The security files show that she was taken to Martin's lab. He'll get her out."

"What do we do now?"

Hyper shrugged. "What do you want to do?"

Chango looked around her at the quiet, dark streets, the shadows and the secrets that they held. "Let's find Benny," she said.

Quick hands untied the cords at Helix's wrists and ankles. She stood and flexed her arms, stretching the cramped muscles in her back.

The guards stood between her and the tank of growth medium. She stepped around them to dangle her fingers in the delicious fluid. The guard that untied her cleared her throat. "Hector Martin has reserved a plane ticket for you. We can either escort you to the airport or take you to his apartment, but you can't stay here."

Helix looked at them, and then back at the little tank, barely big enough to hold her. It was no good. She might be able to fight them off and get into the tank, but more would come to take her out, or to examine her, run tests and take samples—make of her what she was, an experiment. They were right, she couldn't stay here, but she couldn't leave either. Graham had told her things she didn't want to know. But knowing, she couldn't erase his words. It was time to go to the source, time to confront her father with his lies.

As Chango drove to Benny's, Hyper made plans. "Okay, so if he's home, I'll invite him out to Josa's. If I say I'm buying that should get him out of the apartment. Then you can sneak inside while he's gone and have a look around."

"I don't know, Hyper, I'd rather just confront him." Chango pulled around the corner and parked out of sight of the apartment building.

"You'd rather just get killed too, apparently. If he's done all you think he has, then he probably has a gun, and no compunction about using it on you."

Reluctantly she nodded.

The building was dark and quiet. Chango waited at the bottom of the stairs while Hyper knocked on the door, but there was no answer, and no light coming from underneath it, either. "He's gone," Hyper called softly down to her.

She had the simple lock on Benny's door open in moments. They went inside, still wary, moving through the darkened rooms with slow and careful movements. She stepped into the bedroom to find a suitcase filled with clothes sitting open on the bed. "Look at this," she called to Hyper. "He packed, but he didn't take it with him."

They went through the drawers of Benny's dresser, searching for something that would tie him to Ada's death, or at least confirm his connection to Nathan Graham. Chango stepped inside the closet. It was empty. As she turned away, something caught her eye. A piece of paneling about two feet square, screwed to the back wall down by the floor. He'd probably just put it there to patch a hole. She took a screwdriver from her backpack and unfastened it, pulling the plywood away to reveal not a jagged hole but a carefully sawn opening. The hair on the back of her neck stood on end as she reached her hand inside and touched something metal. A set of air tanks she realized, her hand fumbling over their rounded surfaces. Grunting she pulled them out of the hole and into the meager light from the bedroom windows. Something silver glittered near one of the release valves: a pair of initials scratched in the black plaint. An *A* and a *C*. "Ada's tanks," said Chango.

Awkward under the weight of her sister's dive tanks, Chango pushed open the door of Josa's Bar and stepped inside, followed closely by Hyper. Human voices and the smell of smoke and growth medium surrounded them. There was a good-sized crowd, buzzing with the excitement of the morning's riot. The place wasn't packed, though. This was no victory celebration.

Chango spotted Vonda at the far end of the bar, conversing with Josa. Without a word to Hyper she walked towards her, attracting as many glances for the determination of her stride as for what she carried on her back.

"Vonda," she said, closing on her.

Vonda turned, her eyes widening as Chango hoisted the tanks from her shoulders and slung them onto the bar. They hit with a solid bang, immediately silencing all conversation and riveting attention to herself and Vonda.

"I found them at Benny's apartment," Chango said, loud enough for everyone to hear. For Vonda's benefit she pointed out the initials scratched on the tanks. "They're Ada's."

Suddenly she was surrounded by a hubbub of voices and bodies, but she kept facing Vonda, kept talking to her. "That plan of Benny's to take Helix to U of D Mercy was a trap. After we got there, GeneSys security showed up and arrested us, except for Benny. He set us up. When I got out of the lockup, I went to his apartment. He wasn't home. There was a packed bag on the bed, and these—" she put one hand protectively on the tanks "—were hidden in a hole in the closet wall."

Vonda didn't say anything. She just stared at Chango, then at the tanks. But Pele was at Chango's elbow. "How do you know Benny set you up? Maybe he just got away."

"He was supposed to be on lookout." Chango kept looking at Vonda. "And Hyper talked to Helix's father, Hector Martin, who said that Nathan Graham has somebody in Vattown working for him. Somebody he told to turn that strike this morning into a riot."

Vonda examined the dust-clouded gauge on the tanks, aimed the release nozzle at the wall and twisted it experimentally. "They're empty," she said, looking at Chango over her shoulder. "But maybe I can get a residual sample from the valves."

Graham strode down the hall to his office, fresh anger at his recent imprisonment burning inside him. It had only taken an hour or so for his lawyer to intimidate security into releasing him, but it was just a temporary reprieve. He was going to have to do something of a permanent nature about Hector Martin.

The best thing would be to discredit him, get him dismissed from GeneSys in disgrace. It would take some doing. There was very little that a man of Martin's professional standing couldn't wiggle out of. Except possibly corporate treason. Anna would take a very dim view of him selling corporate secrets to a competitor. It was good. Worth following up on, but now he had more pressing matters to attend to. Helix was loose again, he felt sure. Martin wouldn't go to all the trouble of locking him up just to leave her there in the lab.

There was a light on in his office. His secretary would be gone by this hour, and in fact, the reception area was dark, the desk empty. Graham opened the door to his inner office to find Benny sitting in his chair with a glass of scotch in his hand.

"Oh good," Graham said, "I was going to call you."

"Were you? I thought you'd forgotten about me." Benny stood up and pulled a gun from the waistband of his pants. He pointed it lazily at Graham. "I thought I was going to have to remind you."

Graham laughed. "You're talking about your payment, of course. But you'll never get paid if you kill me. Besides, I'm not through with you yet, son."

"What? I did everything you asked me to. Now I've got to get out of town!"

"Getting a little hot for you? Well, if you remember, I asked you to get rid of Helix, and you botched it up."

"But I took them to U of D. I saw the guards nab her."

Graham shook his head. "It didn't take. Martin pulled some strings somewhere and got me thrown in security before I could do anything with her."

"But that's not my fault!"

"Well it wouldn't have happened if you'd taken care of her in the riot, now would it? I'm pretty sure she's at Martin's now, and I think I know what we can do."

"How do I know you're not going to just string me along again?"

"Well, that's the risk you have to take, isn't it? Believe me, I'd like nothing better than to see you jetting off to a foreign land, but first, you have to finish your job." Graham crossed the room, ignoring Benny and the gun now hanging loosely at his side. He switched on the transceiver, called up the Yellow Pages, and dialed an all-night hardware store. "How are you at welding?" he asked Benny over his shoulder.

His door buzzer went off, and Hector rushed to it, to peer through the peephole. His heart fell. It was Helix. She had decided against taking the airplane ticket, apparently. He had hoped she would get away, far away, and be safe. He had hoped he wouldn't have to face her.

He opened the door and the next thing he knew he was grabbed by four strong arms and slammed against the wall. His head struck first; pain lanced down his neck and shoulders.

"What have you done?" she snarled, her face only inches from his.

He shook his head, unable to speak. She looked awful, worse than she had when he first found her, after she'd been thrown out of the nest. Her skin was raw in large, flaking patches. She had a bruise under her eye and a cut on her lip. But worst of all was the look in her eyes. What he saw there he could not bear to look at for long.

She bared her teeth and grimaced. This close, it was an awesome sight indeed. "What the fuck am I, Hector? Huh? Tell me!"

He was afraid. She could kill him with no trouble at all. She

was stronger than him, and she had the advantage of an extra set
of arms. Right now, she could just tear his jugular vein with her
teeth if she wanted to. And why wouldn't she? What had he ever
done except tell her lies?

"Tell me!" she screamed, lifting him and slamming him back
into the wall again for emphasis.

"You're, you're . . . I don't really know, all right? You're a genetically engineered organism. A product of corporate research
and development."

She stared at him, eyes blue and wide with rage, stared and
stared until he thought that in the next instant she would kill him,
but instead she said, "Your research."

He licked his lips and nodded his head ever so slightly. "Yes."

The blow happened so suddenly he didn't see it coming, just
heard something go crack, and then felt the stinging pain on his
cheek and in his mouth.

She released him and he staggered back against the wall. He
raised his hand to his lip and brought it away bloody. Helix stood
with her back to him. He glanced at the door. He might be able to
make it, he might never have another chance, but how could he do
that? She was his responsibility.

"Liar," Helix growled, her back still turned. She was staring
down at the glass top of the coffee table, where the prism for the
holonet sat amid scattered mylar documents and takeout cartons.
Her shoulders were shaking. "You lied to me." She turned and her
eyes were full of tears. "There never was any orphanage, you didn't
adopt me, I'm not a sport. I'm not even human!" She screamed the
last, picking up the heavy glass prism and sending it crashing
through the top of his coffee table.

Hector cringed at the sound of splintering glass and suppressed
the impulse to run. "No, you're not," he said loudly. "You're something else, Helix, something new under the sun. You and your
kind, I may have created you, but I don't even know really, what
you are, because there's never been anything like you before. I
know what you were designed for, but that's not the same thing. It's
very important for you to realize that, Helix, it's not the same
thing."

"What was I designed for, Hector?" She stood over the shattered remains of his coffee table, eyeing him coolly. "Why do I exist?"

He laughed in fear and startled amazement. "Because I thought of you, I suppose, or . . . I don't know. I—I was given a project, you see, to create a—a biological machine." When at last he blurted the words out he flinched, expecting her to strike him again, but she didn't. She just stood there, staring. "To replace the vatdivers," he explained.

She nodded her head slowly. This new calm of hers was more frightening than her rage and tears. He didn't know what to expect next. "And put all those people out of work," she said at length.

"It's lousy work, Helix. It kills them. You know that now, I'm sure you do. But you—you and your sisters and your mother—you can swim in the vats all day and all night, and it won't harm you. And besides that, it was a fascinating problem. You had to be intelligent, you see, at least I felt you did. That was my solution to the complexities of vatdiving. Another researcher might have taken a different approach, but I made the multiprocessor brains, and that's where I started with you."

"I suppose you think I should be grateful to you for creating me, for making me . . . intelligent."

He shook his head and looked down. "No, not really, no."

Helix walked slowly about the living room, her gaze wandering, seeing nothing, crunching slivers of glass beneath her shoes. "My sisters and my mother, you said."

"Yes."

"My mother—she's . . ."

"The first of your kind. Her name is Lilith," he said gently.

She stared at him again, froze him with the cold blue fire of her eyes. "My mother was a vatdiver. I was an orphan. You adopted me," she whispered, advancing on him slowly. He wanted to back up, and probably would have, but the wall was in his way. She took his face in her four hands, gently cradling his jaw and skull in her fingers, and gazed into his eyes with a look so wounded that his heart went cold. "Why did you lie?"

He swallowed with difficulty. He was crying now too, it seemed. He closed his eyes, unable to bear her gaze any longer. "My work is my life, Helix," he whispered, "and you are my life's work. I didn't want to see the pinnacle achievement of my career wiped out or relegated to the status of slave labor. That you are finely suited to work in the vats cannot be denied, but there's more. Your social structure, other things. You are a brand-new, intelligent life-form. I wanted to see what you could do outside of the laboratory. I wanted you to get loose, undetected, to pose as a sport, to get good and far away from GeneSys. That was my hope for you, in particular. Until you came along there seemed to be no future for your kind, but when I found you—"

"Found me?" Surprised, she took away her hands.

"Yes, you'd been driven from the—the nest quite shortly after you were born. I don't think you can remember."

Her eyes went cold again, this time not with anger but with hatred. "Oh, I don't think you want to know what I remember," she said, her voice shaking. She turned from him, her four fists clenched, her arms stiff. "I remember torture, you bastard! I remember being a pathetic little specimen, picked on and beat up for what I was. Now I find out I'm really some kind of laboratory experiment gone awry, and none of that really happened. I based who I was upon that shit and none of it ever happened. I don't exist. I'm somebody else. Why didn't you just tell me all of this? No, you had to make me hate myself, instead! How could you?" She turned towards him again. "How could you do that? You made me think you were the only one in the whole wide world who cared about me, and all along, you were the one who had hurt me."

With his heart in splinters like his coffee table, Hector sank to the floor and bowed his head over his knees. She was absolutely right. That was what he had done. That his intentions had been otherwise, that he had reasons for making up her past made no difference. In trying to save her he had betrayed her. He had burdened her with the memories of a childhood that was not her own. And now he sat here, curled up in a ball, feeling bad about it, when feeling bad about it wouldn't do her any good at all.

'You're right," he said finally, looking up at her. "You're absolutely right." He made no other move. Just forced himself to look at her without flinching. She stared back at him hollowly. She was more lost than he was, which felt impossible, but there it was.

"Why didn't you want me to know what I am?" she asked. "Is it so horrible?"

That brought him to his feet. "No! Oh, no, Helix. That's not it at all." He stepped toward her, wanting to comfort her, to take her in his arms, but she backed away. "I thought I was protecting you. The project wasn't going well. I knew it was only a matter of time before it was canceled. In the eyes of someone like Graham, it was a useless waste of funds. He wouldn't even stop to consider that it was a new species of intelligent beings which he was eradicating with a flick of his pen." Hector trembled, with anger, he realized. "I didn't care that the project failed the company's objective, it met mine. As far as I was concerned, it was a complete success. I didn't want the beings I'd helped bring into the world to disappear without a trace, and with you, I knew I had a chance at seeing them survive." He lifted his hands, trying to think of something to do with them, then dropped them at his sides.

"I knew someday you'd have to leave here, and I didn't want you to go back to the nest of your birth. They drove you out, and I didn't think they'd let you in again. And if you tried to find out more about the project, you'd be discovered. So I made you think you were human, and I taught you to fear people and hide what you are so you could remain undetected for as long as possible."

Helix shook her head in confusion. She turned to the couch as if she would sit down. Broken glass lay scattered on the upholstery. She picked up one of the larger shards to toss it onto the pile of debris that had been his table. It sliced her hand and she dropped it. "Because of you my first memories were of hostility. Why did I have to start out like that? Not knowing who I am, forced to find out by myself in a world that didn't welcome me."

Anger flashed through him again, surprising and sudden. He stared at her. "Don't we all start out like that? Where do you think I got the material for your memories? Do you think I could have made them that vivid for you if I hadn't experienced them myself?"

She stared back at him, nonplussed, blood dripping unheeded from her lower left fingertips. "You were never in an orphanage."

"No," he said. "But I did go to school, and I was different, and kids are like that."

She sighed and shook her head. "But you could have told me the truth, and together we could have reached the same conclusions."

"Maybe, maybe not. I couldn't take the chance."

"No, you just had to decide for me," she retorted hotly. "You had to manipulate me, make all my choices for me. If you'd treated me like a human being, instead of just making me think I was one, maybe I wouldn't hate you now."

He laughed bitterly and began making his way around the wreckage to the dining alcove. "It's really not important how you feel about me, Helix. What's important is that you survive. Hate me if it helps you, but don't punish yourself." He pulled a chair out from the dining table and looked back at her. "I made the mistake, not you. Take what help I can give you now, I beg of you."

She looked at him with more sadness than anger. "What help can you possibly give me?"

He nodded at her bleeding hand. "For starters, I can bandage that."

Amazingly enough, she sat at the dining table and allowed him to wrap her hand with cello tape. She knew almost everything now. To fill the silence between them, Hector told her the only thing left that might be of value to her. "I had a lot of trouble with the project," he said, gripping her hand more firmly when he said "project" lest she try to pull it away. "I was working off a multi-processor brain. Trying to design a body with a sensory system and motor control reflex that it could use. Overlaps in the gene splicing caused your double set of arms and your enlarged eyeteeth, but the real problem was the sensory input. All multiprocessor brains have to do is think. The creature I was trying to create had to use all the physical faculties. I was beginning to think I'd taken the wrong tack, starting with the brains."

He looked at her, staring hard into her eyes as if by the force of his gaze he could make her understand. "And then one night Lilith came to me in a dream. I saw her, saw for the first time what she would look like, and she looked into my eyes. She looked into my eyes, Helix, and I knew how to do it."

She winced and he realized he was squeezing her hand. He loosened his hold and went on. "The next day in the lab I stopped trying to build sensory systems onto the multi brain, and instead I just grew the cerebral cortex larger, and let the sensory nerves map onto it on their own. The senses of the body created their own intelligence. Within weeks she was born."

"Born?"

He shrugged. "Call it what you will. She came into the world through me, and through her, I learned how to bring her here."

Reluctantly he finished bandaging her hand. He wished time would stop. He wished he could keep her here with him, but he'd already done that, and he'd already lost her some time ago. "And now you know everything I know," he said, releasing her hand. "And you should leave. You're in danger here. Take the airplane ticket, Helix. Get away from here."

"I can't do that. I need a vat, Hector."

He sat back. Of course she did.

"Maybe I can remedy that," said a voice from the living room. Hector turned to see Graham stepping out of the hallway, a young man with dark hair and sideburns close behind him. "Good of you to leave the door open, Martin," said Graham as he raised his arm and squeezed the trigger of a tranq gun.

The dart struck Helix in the shoulder. Her eyes lost focus and she crumpled to the floor. Hector was up and out of his chair. "Get out of here, Graham! Aren't you in enough trouble already? Do you want to add assault and breaking and entering to the charges against you?"

Graham smiled at him. "So you want to play lawyer, huh? You should have stuck with that assault story you peddled to Anna. You don't have the goods to pin attempted murder on me. I don't know how you pulled the security clearance to bring me in on nothing but your say so, but it isn't going to happen again. My lawyer can beat up your lawyer any day of the week.

"Besides"—Graham glanced to where Helix lay unconscious on the floor—"murder and assault are offenses against human beings, and that's not what we're dealing with here, is it?

"I'm not through with you by a far sight, Martin. But first there's a little loose end to tie up." He nodded, and the young man stooped to haul Helix up off the floor.

In desperation Hector ran at the man and pushed him, causing him to drop Helix. He stood over her recumbent body, knees flexed, his arms tensed to do he didn't know what. "Leave her alone!"

The man laughed and pushed Hector back into the dining table.

"As of right now, this isn't your project anymore, Martin," said

Graham. "I'm taking you off it." He held the tranq gun up again, pointing it at Hector this time.

"This isn't about any project anymore, you ought to know that," said Hector. "Just what do you think you're going to do with her, anyway?"

"I'm going to take her back to the hive, where she belongs."

"You can't! They'll kill her!"

"Or each other, preferably. There can only be one queen, right? With Helix and Lilith out of the way, the others will be much easier to deal with, I'm sure."

Graham's cohort bent to pick up Helix again, and as Hector rushed him he heard the click of the tranq gun and felt the sting of a dart in his chest. His next step seemed to take hours as darkness closed in, taking Helix and Graham and the other man away with the fading light.

Chango paced back and forth from Vonda's home lab in a back bedroom of the apartment to the living room where Pele, April, Coral, and Hyper sat waiting for her diagnosis. Vonda had banned her from the lab for asking too many questions. All she could do was stand at the doorway watching Vonda work, and then walk back into the living room, to bask in the collective anxiety of her peers, which drove her down the hall again, to watch Vonda peer into slides and hold vials of different colored liquids up to the light.

"Hey, come on." Hyper approached her on what must have been her twelfth or thirteenth circuit, laying a hand on her arm to stop her restless movement. "Come on in the kitchen, Pele's making sandwiches."

They were putting away the bread and stacking plates in the sink when Vonda came in. She sat down at the table and April handed her a fresh cup of coffee. Chango stood rooted to the floor, waiting while Vonda spooned sugar into her cup, stirred it, and drank. Finally she looked up, staring at Chango, and nodded. "There was Blast in those tanks."

April pounded her fists on the table. "That fucking son of a bitch! I'll kill him."

"We don't know where he is," Pele observed.

Hyper switched off the game show he'd been watching on holo

and keyed up his com page. "I'm going to call Hector. This may help him against Graham." He typed at his wrist keypad, waited, shook his head and typed some more. "No answer. I wonder if something's happened to him. He was trying to build a criminal case against Graham. This evidence could help him."

"What are we going to do?" asked Pele.

"We're going to find Benny and beat the living crap out of him!" said April.

"I don't know what's happened to Hector Martin, but he needs these tanks. He can get them tested in the GeneSys labs. It'll carry more weight if two independent tests show there was Blast inside them."

Chango picked up the tanks. "You guys find Benny. I'll go to GeneSys. If something's happened to Hector, then Helix is probably in trouble too. I have to try to help them, if I can."

19

Speaking in Tongues

OF all the old buildings Chango had been in, the Fisher was by far the most beautiful, and instead of being a ruin, its frescoes and pillars and inlaid floors were all lovingly preserved. She was glad she had reason to come back here, she thought as she crossed the mezzanine to the elevators. Before, they'd brought her in to lockup through the garage, and when she was released, she'd been in too big a hurry to take it all in.

Above her, the second- and third-floor balconies were lined with brass grillwork. There were inscriptions in gold lettering over the archways, and the whole place was lit by great oblong chandeliers of overlapping frosted panels, like pinecones made of glass.

It was like a cathedral. A cathedral to industry, she thought, noting the inset semicircles high up on the walls, just before the curve of the arched ceiling. They showed stylized pictures of animals, buildings, beehives, and bore labels such as "commerce" and "industry." Here was one of the greatest architectural treasures of Detroit, happily preserved by the gods to whom it was dedicated.

At this hour the ground floor was deserted, the shops shuttered. Her footsteps echoed as she walked the length of the gallery. The sound made her feel very small and exposed. She quickened her pace.

Even the details have details, she thought, looking at the elevator doors: brass panels etched with lotuses and goldfish surrounded by an interlocking geometric border. How wonderful, she thought as she pressed the elevator button, for something so carefully made to still exist. A brass chart on the wall above traced the positions of the elevators with lighted numbers. Most of them were up above the tenth floor, but there was one two floors below, and rising.

When the doors opened, Chango saw Benny standing inside. He was grimy and streaked with sweat. He held a welding mask in one hand, a blowtorch in the other. For a moment they both stood frozen, staring at each other, and then, like the chiming of a bell in a distant land, the elevator behind her pinged open.

Chango spun on her heel and dove inside it, rolling to her knees and frantically punching the close door button. From around the edge of the doorway she saw Benny drop his equipment and run after her. He reached the elevator just in time to wedge his hands between the closing doors. His fingers protruded through the crack like pink, searching tentacles, and Chango hammered at them with her fists, but her efforts were in vain. The elevator, sensing something stuck between its doors, opened them of its own accord and he stepped through, filling the small space with his presence.

Before she ever opened her eyes, the smell of the air told Helix where she was, and filled her with panic, longing, and rage. She sat up to find herself against a metal door in a wide hallway with a cement floor and glazed cinderblock walls. It was empty and quiet except for the distant hum of the vats.

She got to her feet and tried the door. The handle turned, but the door wouldn't budge. She pounded at the unforgiving metal but the booming of her striking fists brought her to a halt. She would not be heard by anyone outside, and she did not want to be heard by anyone inside.

She turned again and slumped against the door. She was whole existences away from that scene on the playground, and nevertheless, here she was, where it really happened. The force of the returning memory held her motionless against the doorway, waiting for footsteps, for screams, for rending teeth and clutching hands, but these imminent horrors did not materialize.

Taking a long, deep breath she forced the terror back down her throat, swallowed it, and crept along the wall towards the vats.

Chango lifted her eyes to Benny's face and what she saw there backed her right up against the wall of the elevator. Ada's tanks bumped against the paneling and she winced. They'd probably marred the fine wood. Benny approached her, reaching his big hands out towards her head. "What—what are you doing?" Chango gasped as one hand fell on her shoulder, pinning her to the wall. "What have you done with Helix?" she fairly shouted in his ear just before he grabbed the back of her head and yanked it forward. He leaned closer. All Chango could see was her knees, but she knew he was reading the initials on the tanks.

"Well," he said, pushing her up against the wall again, "I guess you'd better meet Mr. Graham." He held her with one hand splayed across her chest and pivoted to punch a floor button. He had to turn his head to find the right floor, and when he did Chango sank down, unbalancing his already awkward stance, and loosening his hold on her. She shrugged the tanks from her shoulders and, in one fluid movement born of panic, swung them around into Benny's midsection. He doubled over at the blow, and she lost her grip on the tanks. They skittered across the elevator floor, bumping into the paneling on the other side. The doors were closing. Chango ducked around Benny and grabbed for the tanks, but he swung around, still bent at the waist, and pulled her legs out from under her. She turned her head as she hit the ground, saw the doors sealing together, and felt the floor pressing further into her aching cheek as the elevator rose.

*　*　*

The closer she got to the vat floor, the less the place looked, felt, and smelled like an ordinary vat house. For one thing, the air was steamy wet, its warm touch welcoming to her skin. She stripped off her tunic and bodysuit to feel it better. Once she was out of the hallway there were plants everywhere, hanging from the balcony ringing the room and standing in pots on disused instrument stands and casings. And the light was different too. Somewhere they had found purple-hued grow lights and installed them in all the fixtures.

From above her, shielded and distorted by the tall curving walls of the two vats, she heard soft splashing noises, and . . . singing? Or was that voice inside her, awakening now to these sights and smells, to the air that was nearly water itself? She rested her hands on the metal ladder that climbed the side of the vat and looked up, gripped by a joyous rage which overwhelmed her rational fear. For among the redolent odors of the waters was the smell of one whose call she would do anything, kill or die, to answer.

Benny hauled Chango up off the floor by the scruff of her neck and pushed her into the elevator wall. He had a gun, and he poked it in her back. "Funny little Chango," he whispered in her ear. "It's been a real riot, watching you sniff all around the truth these past five years, but now I guess you finally found something, huh? Where did you think you were going with these, anyway?" The tanks scraped across the floor as he dragged them closer with his foot.

Chango hung in his grasp, unable to answer, suddenly limp with the realization that though he was acting in ways she would have thought impossible for him, this was Benny. It was still Benny and all Benny; the person she'd thought she'd known, and this.

In the scramble since she got out of jail she'd forgotten it. She'd accepted the comforting idea that this Benny, the murderer spy, was someone new and distinct from her trusted friend. Now, pressed facefirst against the wall, his breath in her ear, she realized that it had been him all along.

The elevator stopped. He kept the gun in her back as he reached down and slung the tanks over his shoulders. Its muzzle bore into her vertebrae as the door opened and he pushed her out ahead of him.

With his other hand on her shoulder he guided her down the hall, walking swiftly. Chango pretended to trip, and rolled towards him, striking his shins with her body. With the tanks on his back, Benny over balanced and went down. Chango scrambled up and ran back towards the elevators. There was a gunshot, and a bullet carved a deep furrow in the brass doors to her right. She swerved to the other side of the hall and grappled open the door to the stairs. She took them up, her footsteps hastened by the crash of the door as Benny threw it open. She turned the corner to the next flight of stairs just ahead of his next bullet. At the top of this flight was another door, with a trash can beside it. She sent the trash can down the stairs and slipped through the door.

This hallway was much like the one a floor below. Grey carpeting and beige plaint utilitarian in comparison to the splendor of the ground floor. She scurried down the hall, trying doors. The fifth one was unlocked, and she darted inside.

Clean-cut men and women in sylk suits turned to stare at her with wide eyes. They were sitting at a table above which glowed a holographic chart. She stood beside the door, panting.

"Can I help you?" One of the men stood and took a step towards her. The door burst inward and Benny came through, brandishing his gun. Several of the suits screamed. Chango fled her spot by the wall, and Benny chased her around the table. One woman jumped out of her chair in a misguided effort to get out of the way, effectively placing herself in Chango's path. Chango ducked under the table, squirming among the legs of chairs and people, finally breaking free to find Benny still entangled in the suits around the table. She heard their shouts as she dashed for the door, and just as she reached it, a shot and a scream. She didn't look back. She was running again.

At the end of the hall was a narrow wooden door that read "Maintenance Only" in faded black stenciled letters. She tried the handle. It was locked, but there was a ventilation grating at the base of the door. A small, old square of metal covered with several layers of beige plaint. And one corner was loose. Chango worked her fingers underneath it and pried it from the door. The three remaining screws popped out. She gathered them up and pushed the grating edgewise through the hole to hide it from her pursuer—if he ever got free of the suits; she still heard noises from the office down the hall.

Her shoulders barely fit through the square opening, and it took her precious seconds to wriggle her hips through. She was in a small grey stairwell threaded with wires, pipes, and ventilation shafts.

Helix stood on the diving platform and looked down into the vat where she lay floating in the waters, her long dark hair streaming around her, dreaming, and opened her eyes. For a moment everything ceased. Nothing existed except for those bright blue eyes that were her eyes, that face that was her face, and then, with a scream, Helix leapt into the vat.

She plunged deep down into the emerald green spaces and rolled over, looking up at the surface like a sky quickly clouding, as her sisters scrambled into the waters, creating turbulence with their limbs. They were swimming towards the queen. Several of them spotted her and broke off from the wave, diving below the surface to converge with her as she sought what they all sought, their mother, who was turning now and swimming to meet her.

Her sisters clamored between them, filling the waters with their bodies, congealing into two knots, one around her, the other around Lilith. As they surrounded and grappled with her, Helix felt their panic. One of them wrapped her arms around Helix's neck and hung on. Her face swam through Helix's field of vision, a face like her own, but with more delicate features. Helix saw the terror in those blue eyes and felt, with no need for words, her message: "If you kill each other we will all die."

It was true, but still Helix struggled and thrashed against the restraining arms all around her. She didn't want to hurt them, she just wanted to get past them, but as they tightened their holds on her she bit and clawed to break free. A hand she had savaged let go of her upper right arm, and Helix reared back and butted the creature directly before her with her forehead. Doggedly, Helix pulled herself through the small wedge in the living wall around her and reached out with stiffened fingers to poke the next available sister in the throat.

The closer Helix and Lilith managed to claw towards each other, the more the others pushed them together in their frantic efforts to get back in between them. Soft, dark tendrils of her mother's hair drifted past her face and Helix twined her fingers in them, pulling her closer. Lilith came readily enough, mouth wide and hands outstretched. She grabbed Helix by the head and pulled her face to hers, laying open Helix's cheek with the sweep of a fang.

Helix felt her blood that was not really blood flow into the waters; felt the waters flow into her. She almost relished being cut again; it would bring her that much closer to the depths. But this language of touch, which she could not help hearing, though she felt it through violence, had not yet robbed her of all sense of self-preservation. She ducked and angled under Lilith, grabbing her by her upper armpits as she went. With her forearms Helix forced Lilith's lower arms against the shoulder joint, and they rolled together in a stately somersault, ringed now by her sisters who gave them room and waited, watching. In a small corner of her mind, Helix realized she had not breathed since she dived from the platform, but it didn't seem important, because everywhere else, she was talking to her mother.

"This is wrong," said Lilith through Helix's skin. "There can only be one of us here. You have to be somewhere else to be you."

"I know," Helix answered. "But I am here, and we will be either one or none."

Their struggle became a slow match of strength as Lilith grasped at Helix's upper wrists and their hands clasped. They grappled with each other, each trying to push the other back through the waters and eventually out of the vat. But they were evenly matched, and each advantage gained by either one only served to bind them tighter together. The cut in Helix's palm began to ache, and Lilith forced that hand back against the wrist and scissored her lower arms in towards her body, freeing them from Helix's hold. For a moment it was all shifting limbs and reaching hands, and then Lilith grasped her by the waist and, with a nudge of her knee between Helix's legs, sent her rotating like a spinner until her face was between Lilith's legs, her head gripped in her knees.

Arms wrapped around abdomens, heads cradled in legs, their

bodies interlocked like magnets in alignment. As Lilith spoke to her in her mother tongue, Helix lowered her face to her soft mat of hair, salty like the sea and full of stories.

Colin slept on a plastic sheet spread on the floor, dreaming of the sun on a warm afternoon beating down on his hat as he dozed on the porch and waited for the stranger to come. They were all waiting. Waiting with the rhythm of the sun that was a blade of grass waving in the breeze and then the rhythm, the sun, and the dream were torn apart by a scream.

Colin sprang from the floor to find himself alone, the door standing open and mist roiling in from outside. Swearing, he slammed the door shut and scrambled into his divesuit. His head was swimming. He felt as if he'd been suddenly yanked from deep water, into the air, and he'd forgotten how to breathe. He shook his head, pulled the face mask on and clamped it tight. Slipping his lips around the mouthpiece he gulped at the clean air for a few panicked moments, wondering how long the door had been open.

He hadn't had much to do in the last day and half except ponder what might be leaching through the ventilation system into the room, and what his chances were of contracting vatsickness from the exposure he had already received. Now he figured he could stop wondering and pretty much plan to die of it; maybe not right away, maybe not for years and years, but sooner or later, and for certain.

All the same he double-checked the suit's seals before opening the door and going out onto the balcony. In the vat below, the waters were aroil with the bodies of tetras. They were swarming so densely that he couldn't make out anything more than thrashing arms and legs. Behind him, through the door he'd heedlessly left open, he heard the transceiver ringing.

He dashed back inside to answer it. It was Hector Martin. His hair was in disarray, as if he'd been sleeping and hadn't had a chance to comb it. "Slatermeyer? Is that you?"

Colin checked the suit's radio and found that it was still on broadcast. "Yes. Dr. Martin, something's happening. The tetras, they're—"

"Graham put Helix in the vat room. You have to keep her away from Lilith. They're both queens. They'll fight each other until one or both of them is killed."

"Well, I think it's too late for that. I was sleeping. When I woke up the tetra guarding me was gone. She left the door open. They're . . . swarming in the vat where Lilith sleeps. If Helix got in here, as you say, that would explain it."

"Slatermeyer, you're already suited. You have to go in there and break them up."

"Are you crazy? I can't even see anything—they're fighting so closely all I can make out is arms and legs. I don't stand a chance of getting through the tetras, let alone separating Helix and Lilith. I'll get killed. They'll rip my mask off, or pull open my seals."

Hector shook his head. "You have to try. Lilith and the others attacked Helix when she hatched, and drove her out of the vat. They'll kill her now. Or she'll kill Lilith. You have to try to stop it. Please. If I could get there, I'd do it, but Graham's lackey, Benny, welded the door shut. There's no one else. You have to do something."

Colin shook his head reluctantly. He'd already suffered who knew how much exposure to the growth medium. If he threw himself into that mob of fighting tetras, he'd surely get more.

"Please." Hector stared at him, his eyes wide and desperate.

Colin sighed. "I'll try. But I'm not going to risk whatever's left of my life in a futile effort to separate them. You know how strong they are. But I'll get in, and I'll try to talk to the other tetras, try at least to get them to back off. I'm sorry, Doctor, but they're your brainchildren, not mine."

Hector slammed his fist down on the dining room table in front of him. The impact must have jarred the transceiver recording his image. His face blurred, and then came back into focus, but sideways. "Go," he said. "Do what you can."

Hector walked into the bathroom and splashed cold water on his face. Straightening, he stared at his image in the mirror. How, he asked himself, how had things gotten this bad? At what point had he crossed over from the sane and illustrious life of a corporate researcher to this—this mad nightmare where he asked his assistant to risk his life for the good of a project that would never meet its stated goals? He thought back over the decisions he had made, and realized that it was in the very beginning, when he'd had the dream and decided to follow it. He had stopped being an employee of GeneSys right then, had stopped caring, really, if this project was in their best interests, or his. Though he hadn't known it at the time, he had offered himself up in service to Lilith and her kind, and since he'd taken that step, there was never any time afterwards when he could have changed anything.

As he gazed in the mirror, the ventilation grating on the wall behind him popped off, and a woman crawled out. Hector turned to face her. She dusted off her jeans and straightened up, looking around her. "Oh, sorry. I had no idea what room I'd end up in. In fact, I was afraid I had the wrong apartment. You're Hector Martin, aren't you?"

Mutely, he nodded.

She smiled and offered her hand. "Chango Chichelski. Boy am I glad you're home. I was supposed to bring you my sister's air tanks. Vonda tested them and there'd been Blast inside. But Benny caught me, and he got them. He—" She paused, struggling with the possibilities. "He was coming upstairs. He had a blowtorch."

"They welded her inside," said Hector.

"What? Where?"

"In the vat room. Down in the subbasement. There's an old biopoly lab with test vats. It was in disuse for years until I took it over for the project." Hector glanced at the hole in the wall above Chango's head. "We have to get in there."

Chango followed his gaze. "I got into a maintenance stairway. Lots of places to go from there. Big conduit housings, access crawlways for plumbing. I took the ventilation system."

"And you found your way here."

"I had to pop out and check the circuit boxes. They label them by apartment. I couldn't really be sure I had it right, but I do have a pretty good sense of direction."

Hector bit his lip. "Do you think you could make it down there?"

Chango puffed out her cheeks. "Jeez, that's a long haul. It'd take a while. I don't know."

"Maybe we should just go down there and unweld that door. I'm afraid they may be killing each other right now."

"They?"

"Helix and Lilith—her mother."

"Oh, her mother . . ."

The transceiver at Hector's wrist bleeped and he answered it. It was Slatermeyer. "What happened?"

"Well, they're not fighting anymore. They're just sort of . . . wrapped around each other."

"What are they doing?"

Slatermeyer laughed, the sound distorted by his suit's radio into a harsh grate. He shrugged. "I know what it looks like."

There was her body, but she was someplace else. Her body was busy, it had no use for her mind, and her mind swam amid black waters of nowhere, like a question gone unanswered, and then the answer came, and she was there, here, her. Lilith and she, entwined in thought and body, asking and answering each other the question of their being.

"They say it began in a garden," said Lilith, "but I know better. It began with a dream."

The brilliant blackness of the void faded around them, and they stood in a green place with a tree and a snake in the tree. Her sisters were there, adorned with fig leaves. They stood with their arms linked in a crisscross pattern, like a row of Xs with legs.

"Before we existed we were a dream dreaming ourselves into existence," thought Lilith as one of the sisters broke out of the line, lay down, and closed her eyes. Soon another detached herself and danced over the head of the sleeper. "We crossed over into the world through the mind of Hector Martin." The sleeper turned over and wakened, and the dancer rolled over her bowed back in a somersault and stood, arms outstretched, at the head of the dreamer.

"This is how we happened, but I remember before the dream, before anything. I remember the void."

The tree was made of cardboard, and Helix saw the void reach up with empty hands behind it, and the blackness rushed in and toppled it and her sisters were gone. All that remained was a ring of Xs, spinning around them.

"This is where we came from," Helix knew somehow.

"Everything comes from here," either she or Lilith thought, she couldn't keep track anymore. "From the well of possibility, where nothing is known. Everything comes from here, everything returns here, but only in the world do we know that we exist."

"But what difference does it make, if we only end up here again?"

"All the difference. All the difference in the world. We are a pattern, and the pattern continues. We return to the void, but our pattern is forever in the weave of the world."

The void around them gradually returned to being the waters of the vat, and Helix realized she could open her eyes and lift her head. She and Lilith separated, and the sisters flowed in to buffer them from each other.

The consuming rage that had driven her into her mother's arms was gone, and she allowed her sisters to guide her with numerous small hands, up onto the dive platform and down into the other vat.

They had been designed to replace the vatdivers; trading cheap labor for in-house slavery. But it hadn't worked out the way GeneSys wanted. Instead of getting docile biological machines, it had gotten the Lilim, and now, they were here to stay.

20

DAUGHTERS OF THE VOID

SEVERAL floors down from Hector's apartment the duct Chango was in, which was part of the output system, looped back upwards and she couldn't get to any of the lower floors. She crawled to a grating that let out onto an access crawlway and followed it to another ventilation duct that led downwards. With her screwdriver she removed a panel from it and crawled inside.

She hadn't realized how lucky she was to be in the output system before. The ducts had been clean, the air fresh and ready for breathing, and the only fellow travelers she'd had to contend with were some very passive algae caulking the duct's seams, probably there to breathe extra oxygen into the mix. It had been good air.

This, on the other hand, was not good air. It had pretty much been breathed by everyone on the eighteenth floor, and smelled like it. Plus the walls of the duct were covered with a fine grit of dust-eaters. They crunched beneath her palms and got ground up under her fingernails as she crawled down the narrow shaft.

Chango squirmed around a corner to find an opening in the duct, but it was only a vent from another apartment. She crawled on until the duct ended in a vertical shaft, and she took it down, trying to slow her descent by bracing her arms and legs against the walls. Dust-eaters caked at her elbows and knees, and soon she was sliding in a streak of their crushed bodies. She passed several floors before the duct banked inward and halted her downward plunge.

Here the duct was joined by several others and became considerably larger. She took the opportunity to sit upright and catch her breath. Looking around at the duct walls, now faintly luminescent with some sort of algae, she was glad for the divesuit she wore. Hot and uncomfortable as it was, it was better than picking up goddess-knows-what from this ventilation system and its attendant organisms. She probably shouldn't even be breathing in here, but she didn't have air tanks; they couldn't have fit through the ducts if she had.

She crawled on through the darkness, her way lit only by the phosphorescent glow of the algae clinging to the walls. If anything, the air was worse than ever. It was warmer now and humid, and she was pretty sure the oxygen level was dropping off. Her head swam, and there was a faint ringing in her ears. She had to get out of here.

She took the next branch she could find, wending her way through several switchbacks lined with fine, feathery growths that squished between her fingers and left a faint trail of slime where they brushed across her face.

She climbed over a lip into a larger chamber. At first she thought there were flecks of dirt blowing through the space, but then she realized they were swarming and nipping microscopically at her exposed flesh. Dust-eaters, only these ones flew, and to them she was one motherfucking huge dust bunny; the challenge of their careers, their big opportunity to prove just what excellent flying dust-eaters they were. Chango suppressed a scream and squeezed her eyes shut as she dashed through the biting swarm, searching for a way out.

Her hands plunged through something thick and gelatinous, to clear air on the other side. She lunged through and found herself on the other side of a shimmering blue-green membrane which sealed itself back up behind her. Ahead of her was another one, only it was orange instead.

They were filters, apparently. As Chango progressed through the prismatic slimefest, the air steadily improved. And the wind picked up.

She dove through a deep purple membrane to find herself in a howling indraft, surrounded by the hum of turbines. She was pulled along the duct at nearly twice her crawling speed and then the duct gave way to a larger chamber where it was joined by several others.

Chango careened off the lip of the duct, plummeting towards one of four big turbine fans in the opposite wall. A narrow crossbar spanned the fan's ten foot diameter, and as she tumbled through empty air, Chango reached for the metal struts, desperately hoping to grab on before she was diced by the blades.

Her left foot struck the center of the crossbar first, and she twisted forward, her hands spread wide, managing to grab a strut with her right hand. For perilous seconds she teetered there, flailing desperately with her other hand to keep balance, her face inches from the whirring blades. The wind sucked at her, and she was glad of the divesuit hood that prevented her from being pulled in by her hair.

Finally she grabbed ahold of another strut and got her other foot braced against the crossbar. Slowly, carefully, she crawled across the vortex of the fan and pulled herself up over the lip of the vent opening. She perched there on the casing for a few seconds, catching her breath and looking around. A narrow walkway ran beneath the fans. Of course. They'd need to get in here in case something big got jammed in the blades. Like her, for instance. To her right she spotted a small door. Chango wedged herself between the fan casing and the wall and gradually lowered herself down to the walkway. Clinging to the iron rail she made her way around to the door. It opened with a crank handle, and she was outside, finally, in the welcome, mundane dust of empty narrow walkways and the outsides of ducts and machine casings.

Chango threaded her way along the service hall, wondering where she was. Somewhere deep in the innards, she thought, and she imagined the weight of the building pressing in on her. Here and there, service lights illuminated a knot of pipe work or a bundle of electrical cables. The rest was just shadows and the vague, humming sounds of hidden machinery.

She noticed that the electrical lines were converging like tributaries into a bundled cable that ran along the wall. She followed it, and saw it grow as more lines joined it. It was as thick as her leg by the time she reached what could only be the main conduit for the whole building: a massive rope of cables surrounded by a catwalk and bristling with bundles of electrical lines like the one she'd followed. Gaping, Chango walked out onto the catwalk and looked down, and up. Like the spine of some mighty giant, the cable ran for as far as she could see in either direction, fed by a million lines connected to millions more multiprocessor brains of all sizes in offices, light switches, and thermostats all over the building. She reached her hand over the edge of the catwalk, and she could have sworn she felt them thinking.

Helix lolled against the side of the vat, her limbs buoyed by the waters. Three sisters, Jacinth, Nicar, and Coleanus, swam up to her and wrapped their arms around her, cuddling close. "GeneSys is our enemy. It is what put you in here, not Graham. Even though he thinks it was his idea, he did it for GeneSys," their touch said. It was from Lilith. For the past hour or so, these three had been swimming back and forth between Helix and Lilith, bearing messages in their skin.

Helix didn't have to say anything, but she felt . . . frustration, rage at Graham and Benny, hopelessness at ever finding her own vat. And something else. A familiarity with what she was doing; not how she was talking, but with whom.

Her sisters swam away, and for a little while there was only the vague speaking of the waters lapping against her skin. A touch she had not recognized as speech before, because all it really did was tell her who she was, and where.

"You can't stay here. You have to have your own life, your own nest," came Lilith's answer.

Night Hag, thought Helix, you were Night Hag, weren't you? And she didn't have to wait for her mother's returning touch to know. Lilith had contacted her through the holoweb, had encouraged her to leave Hector and become a vatdiver. She had, in fact, started it all, so that Helix might find her own vat. And it suddenly occurred to her that perhaps she had tried to keep Helix in her job, after the divesuit incident.

Jacinth curled her arms around Helix and nuzzled her neck. "Yes. It was ridiculous. Why should you have to wear one of those foolish suits?"

But how had she done it?

"The brains are our cousins, and they like us better than the people who think they control them. When I touch them, they do what I ask."

Gently Helix dislodged her sisters from her body and dove down to the bottom of the vat. An agule floated by and she absently plucked it and bit into its pulpy softness. She would like to stay here forever, but this wasn't her nest. It was Lilith's. They had reached some temporary accord, but she could not fool herself into thinking it was a permanent arrangement. She was a queen. She needed her own nest.

Through the green waters Helix saw several of her sisters swimming nonchalantly about four meters away. They were making sure she did not attempt to get into Lilith's vat again. To reassure them Helix coasted along the wall, circling back before she was halfway to the diving platform that separated the two vats.

Of course it was the touch. Through her touch Lilith communicated more information to the brains more efficiently than any human being with a keypad ever could. She spoke their language.

When she resurfaced, Helix was greeted by Orixeme, who apparently came not with a message but out of sheer curiosity. She gripped Helix and ran her nose and mouth across her skin, snuffling intently. As Helix relaxed, she loosened her grip and ran one hand across her belly. Her touch sent a bolt of recognition through Helix's body. "Eggs," Orixeme whispered needlessly, and swam away.

Helix looked up, and saw someone in a divesuit and face mask come out of one of the offices and stand at the edge of the balcony. As she stared, he raised a hand and waved at her. None of the other Lilim seemed to pay him much mind. It couldn't be Nathan Graham or Benny. "Dr. Martin is asking to speak with you," he said through his suit's radio.

Reluctantly, Helix drew herself out of the waters and padded around the balcony, flanked by a bevy of concerned Lilim who formed themselves into a barricade when she rounded the curve towards Lilith's vat. "It's okay," she said, putting a hand on Magdar's shoulder to drive her message home. "I'm going into the office."

They trailed her curiously as she approached the suited figure. "I'm Colin Slatermeyer," he said, "One of Dr. Martin's assistants."

Helix wrinkled her brow. "How did you get in here? The door doesn't open."

"I was here already."

The Lilim stayed behind as she entered the office. Inside the air was horribly dry. Already she yearned to return to the waters, and Helix wondered what she would do when she had to leave here and face the waterless world again.

Hector's face floated above the transceiver. "Helix," he said as she came into camera range. "Are you all right? Is Lilith— Did you—"

"She's fine, we're both fine. But I can't stay here. This is her nest; I need one of my own."

"Graham probably thinks you're both dead. It's better if we let him." Hector's brow wrinkled in worry. "Chango was here though. She's on her way down to you, now. She can get you and Slatermeyer out."

Helix bit back her impatience. "Out. Out, but then what? Hector I need— I can't go back to living as a human. Lilith and I have been talking. She says GeneSys is our enemy. She says we have to defeat it if we're to continue as a species." Helix's stomach cramped with urgency. "You invented the brains. Lilith calls them cousins. She says they'll help us."

Hector shook his head. "You can't just overthrow a whole company, Helix. Lilith doesn't understand, but you've lived among humans. GeneSys is made up of thousands of people. You can't just take it over."

"I don't see any other way."

"Let me talk to Anna. She's the CEO. I'll just lay my cards on the table. She's a pretty decent person. Maybe I can convince her to keep the project going, for its own sake."

"No. We aren't your project anymore, Hector. It's time for us to be in the world. Tell me more about the brains. They're all over the building, right?"

"Y-yeah. They're in the processors the employees use for spreadsheets and analysis, and there are smaller ones in the lighting and environmental systems, and in the security cameras. Everything's hooked up to a big brain in the attic that keeps tabs on all the systems. But—"

His objection was cut off by Slatermeyer, who had left and now returned with someone else. A small and extremely grimy figure in a divesuit and face mask.

"Chango?" said Helix.

The figure reached up and took off the face mask. "I made it." said Chango. "Christ, what a haul. Is there anyplace around here I can take a bath?" She ran a gloved finger over her suit and came up with a glob of slime and dust. "No telling what this stuff is." Pointing at the door, she said, "Those women out there—they look like you."

Helix reached towards Chango to take her face in her hands and kiss her, but she stopped herself. The growth medium still drying on her naked skin would be more dangerous to Chango than anything she'd encountered on her way down here. She dropped her hands to her sides. "I'm glad to see you."

"Yeah, same here. It was touch and go for a while there, but then I found the main electrical conduit for the building. Near as I can tell, the thing runs straight up to the top of the tower."

"To the brain," Helix said, looking over her shoulder at Hector's hologram.

"That would be correct," he said, his voice thick with reluctance.

She looked back at Chango. "We have to go back up."

Chango's eyes bulged wide. "What?"

* * *

Slatermeyer ventured back out onto the balcony. Below him was the vat currently occupied by Lilith. Even from here he could see the pulpy blue polymer lining the walls and floor of the vat. It was a rich crop. His mind strayed to the research he'd been doing on the poly before his abduction. Its conductivity ratios and propensity for self-propagation pointed to something, some highly specific application that had continued to elude his grasp.

He looked up at the mounting where the transceiver had been, and then down again into the growth medium, where he could just barely make out a darker lump on the bottom of the vat.

He walked around the balcony to the dive platform and stopped, expecting to see the tetras converging to herd him back into the office, but they didn't seem to care anymore. Lilith and several of her brood swam around on their backs in the vat below, apparently unconcerned about his approach. Colin sat down on the dive platform, checked the seals on his suit, and carefully lowered himself into the vat. He dove down, skimming along the bottom towards the lump. It was the transceiver, all right, still attached to its armature, but it was beyond any hope of repair, coated as it was with blue polymer. Just the same, he took it with him.

In the lab Hector was still on the holo, and he and Helix and Chango were arguing.

"I almost got killed in the ventilation system, and now you want me to climb all the way back up again?" said Chango, her hands in the air.

"If Graham catches on, he won't hesitate to kill the other tetras," noted Hector.

Helix shook her head. "He can't get in; he welded the door shut."

Colin ignored them and took the transceiver over to a small area of counter space. He set it down and began methodically peeling the blue poly from its surface.

The camera itself was remarkably well preserved, but it wasn't until he got the casing off that he discovered the real impact of the blue poly on the instrument. It had apparently leached into the transceiver's inner works through the peripheral port. The poly coated the chips and wires.

Slatermeyer took the camera to a magnifying stand and tried to peel off the poly with a tweezers, but he only succeeded in pulling a wire loose. He upped the magnification and examined the severed wire. It was solid blue poly, all the way through its tiny diameter. He'd been wrong; the poly wasn't coating the circuitry at all, not anymore. It *was* the circuitry. Like a sea change, or a petrification, the blue poly had replaced the camera's electrical components, while maintaining their structure.

He pressed the ends of the severed wire back together and watched the seam disappear as the poly knitted itself together again. With trembling hands he replaced the transceiver's casing and switched it on. The current episode of *We Are the World* leapt into the air before him in perfect holographic detail. Natasha was taking the witness stand, to testify in her own defense.

Chango and Helix turned and stared. "I can't believe you're watching soaps at a time like this," said Chango.

"She's testifying?" said Helix. "No! I never would have let her do that. Damn."

"What's going on?" Hector asked.

"What's going on," said Slatermeyer, "is that we've been sitting on the biggest technological innovation since the brains, and we never even knew it. The poly—" Slatermeyer bundled the scraps from the casing into his gloved hands and rolled them into a ball. He approached the transceiver carrying Hector's image, and held it up. "The blue poly, it— Do you realize what it would mean if we could completely integrate the circuitry in every system, and eliminate the need for an interface between the brains and the electrical network? Processing speeds would hit the roof."

"Well, a biological network has been discussed, Slatermeyer." Hector shrugged. "But we rejected it because of the cost of uprooting the infrastructure."

"That's just it." Slatermeyer bounced the ball of blue poly on the ground for emphasis. "We don't have to uproot anything. We don't have to do anything at all."

"What are you talking about?" said Helix.

Slatermeyer faced her. "Your friend can get us out of here, can't she?"

"Well, yeah. She's going to take me up to the top of the tower, where the main control system for the brain network is located."

Chango sighed. "I never could talk you out of a damn thing."

Slatermeyer squeezed the blue poly between his hands. "Fine. I'm going with you. Partway, anyway." He turned to face Hector again. "We'll talk about this in person."

"How did it go?" Graham asked Benny as soon as he stepped into the office.

Benny dumped Ada's tanks next to the desk and helped himself to a hearty portion of Graham's liquor. "Oh, I got Helix in there all right," he said, sinking into a chair. "Soldered the door shut like you said, no problem."

"Good. No one's getting in or out of there now."

"Well, I wouldn't be so sure of that."

"What now? Graham leaned across the desk towards him. He looked haggard, thought Benny. He probably wasn't used to such late nights.

"I ran into an old chum on the way back. Chango Chichelski. She had these with her." He hefted the tanks up to show Graham. "They're Ada's. She must have been to my apartment."

"You left them there?"

"Sure. I wasn't planning on sticking around town. That was your idea, remember?"

"What happened?"

"I was bringing her back here, but she got away."

"She got away."

"Yeah. There was a scuffle in this office she ran into. There were people in there, still working, at this hour. I shot somebody, but it wasn't her. By the time I got out of there, she'd slipped away, but I have an idea where she went."

Graham gritted his teeth. "Can you share it with the rest of the class?"

"A grating was missing from the door to the maintenance stairway. It was too small for me, but I kicked the door open. Two floors up an access panel had been removed from a ventilation duct."

"She crawled inside?"

"Yeah. You don't know Chango. She can get in and out of

places no one else would even dream of going. She could be any-where now."

"Does she know what happened to Helix?"

"No, but my guess is she was on her way to see Hector Martin when I found her. If she succeeds in finding him, he can tell her."

"Christ. And you shot someone. Who?"

"I don't know, some suit."

"Lovely. Would she really try to get into the vat room through the ventilation system? More importantly, could she?"

"If anyone could, it would be her."

Graham stood up and got himself a drink. "What would my mother say?" he muttered softly.

"Don't you think, what with me shooting someone, with wit-nesses and everything, that it's time I should be leaving?"

"We have to stop her."

"Why? She has no evidence anymore." He gestured to the tanks. "And so what if she does get into the vat room? They'll be dead by then, right?"

"The two queens, yes. There are others, but I don't think they can do much without their—uh—mother."

"Then what are you worrying about? Just notify security and they can catch her when she comes out."

"It isn't good. Too many loose ends. She may already be in contact with Martin. Together the two of them, tanks or no tanks, can make considerable trouble for us."

"For you. I'll be long gone."

"Not without money for a plane ticket."

"Oh, come on. You've got to let me go. I'm not going crawl-ing around in any ventilation ducts, I'll tell you that right now. If you're so hot on the idea, you do it."

"You won't have to. I'll call up a schema of the building's sys-tems. Then all we have to do is figure out where she has to go to get down there, and intercept her."

Benny hissed through his teeth. "It's not going to be that easy, and you know it. You're just trying to snow me. Maybe I can't get out of town without your money, but you need me too. Besides, Martin's your real problem. As long as he's around, you'll never squeak out of this."

"You're right, of course. I had planned on a scandal for him, but that'll take too long. We need to act now."

"Well, we've already had one instance of a gunman breaking in and shooting someone, why not make it a spree?"

"Are you actually suggesting that you just break into his apartment and kill him?"

"Why not? Provided I have my plane ticket first, of course."

Graham stared at him for a very long time. "That might actually work," he said.

It took Graham several hours to work up a schema of the building's systems. Now it hung in the air over his desk, a glittering thing of lines and data points. "You'll take the maintenance stairway down to Hector's floor and get into the ventilation duct here," he said to Benny, pointing at an enlarged section of the diagram detailing the ventilation system around Hector's apartment. "Once you're inside, go straight past six side vents and take the seventh one in. When it branches, go left. It'll take you right to Hector's bathroom."

Benny eyed the schema skeptically. "How am I going to get out of there? Security's probably looking for me already."

"Don't worry. I've got your escape route all mapped out. After you've killed him, call me, and I'll tell you where to go."

Benny laughed. "Sure you will. Why don't you just tell me now?"

"Look, you've got your plane ticket. If you have a way out of here too, why not just use it right away? That's what I'd do, if I were you. The escape route is my insurance that you do what you say you'll do."

"Yeah? How do I know you're not going to screw me again?"

"Oh, please. I'm taking a huge risk keeping you around now. Believe me, the sooner you're safely out of the country, the better off I'll be."

Benny thought about it a moment and nodded. "I guess that's true, because if I get caught, you can believe I'll be telling them everything."

"Fine. We understand each other very well then."

*   *   *

Slatermeyer struggled to keep up with Chango and Helix as they wound their way through the innards of the GeneSys Building. With Helix's arms, and Chango's dexterity, he didn't stand a chance. "Slatermeyer, are you with us?" Chango called from a utility ladder up above. They were in the conduit now, ropy masses of cable rose up through the shaft beside him. "I have to rest," he called up. "Can't we stop for a second?"

He heard her say something to Helix, and then, "Okay, for a few minutes. You climb up to us."

They sat in a small utility closet on stacks of spare cable. "Where are we?" he asked, wiping his forehead.

"Oh, you're almost through," said Chango. "It's only three floors up to Hector's from here."

"How can you tell?"

Chango nodded at the junction box on the wall above her head. In black marker it was labeled WW22. "West wing floor twenty-two," Chango translated. "Hector's on the twenty-fifth."

"We're not stopping there," said Helix, resting three arms on her knees and pointing up with the fourth. "We're going all the way to the top."

"Well, we'll have to show him to Hector's apartment. He can't find it on his own," said Chango.

Helix agreed reluctantly, rubbing a fang over her lower lip in chagrin. Slatermeyer fished the ball of blue poly from his divesuit pouch and rolled it between his gloved fingers.

"You were saying something about that stuff earlier," said Helix. "What does it do again?"

Because it would prolong their rest break, Slatermeyer did his best to explain the properties of the blue poly as he understood them. "The camera was still working, so the stuff must be transmitting the electrical signals, or converting them into something analogous. If I'm right, there would no longer be any need for an interface between the brains and the electrical systems that they run. It's a huge breakthrough in efficiency and speed of processing."

Helix nodded her head at the ball in is hands. "Can I see it?"

He handed it to her. She turned it around in her hand, sniffed it, licked it, and then looked at him. "Can I use some of this?"

Slatermeyer frowned. "What are you going to do, eat it?"

With a pained expression, Helix shook her head. "If this stuff does what you say it does . . . then I think we need to use it."

"What do you mean, 'use it'?"

"I mean try it out. We've got plenty of electrical cable around here. Let's seed some of it with this stuff."

"You better be careful, some of these cables are carrying a lot of juice," said Chango.

"What are you talking about?" Slatermeyer stood up. "This stuff hasn't been tested yet. I'm just making educated guesses here. There's no way to be sure exactly what it does without testing it first."

Helix shrugged, and stood up herself. She opened the door to the junction box above Chango, and looked back at Slatermeyer over her shoulder. "Here's the first test."

He tried to grab her arm, to stop her, but she had other arms to shove him away as she slammed the blue poly into the junction box. The wires inside were spliced together, their raw ends twisted around each other and held fast with plastic caps. It wouldn't take the blue poly long to get past those. Soon it would be leaching into the wires themselves, and it would spread.

Clenching his jaw, Slatermeyer tried to push past her, to pull the blue poly off the wires before it was too late, but she slammed the door to the box shut and repelled him again. He stumbled back against a pile of cabling.

"Excuse me," said Chango, standing up. "I think I'll sit over here."

"Don't bother," said Helix. "It's time to go."

"But—" Slatermeyer pulled absently at his hair. "You can't just— At least let me take some for experiments."

Helix snorted. "Don't you have some in the lab?"

"Oh, well, yes . . ."

"Then use that. Let's go."

Hector paced the carpeting, doggedly pressing redial on his transceiver. No one was answering. Helix and Chango must have left already, presumably Slatermeyer as well. Any one of them might have picked up the transceiver, but now only Lilith and her brood were down there, and he knew what he could expect from them.

He gave up the transceiver in frustration and went to the kitchen cupboard for the bottle. He was pouring scotch into a water glass when he heard a noise from the bathroom. He moved into the hallway in time to see Slatermeyer in a divesuit, stepping out of the john.

"I see you made it," he said, and returned to the kitchen for another glass.

"Do you have anything I can wear?" asked Slatermeyer, peeling the divesuit from his body where he stood. "I can't stay in this thing one moment longer. How can they stand it? All your sweat is trapped inside with you. It's like being marinated."

Hector set the glass on the counter. "I'll get you something," he said, and went to fetch a robe.

"So where are Helix and Chango? Are they going through with that business about the brain?" asked Hector, handing Slatermeyer a generous glass of whiskey.

"Tsss," Slatermeyer hissed, leaning back on the couch. "More than that. They took the blue poly I'd collected. They've already introduced it to the building's electrical system." He raised his glass up. "Cheers." And drank deeply. "Aaugh, that feels good. You don't know what it's been like. I know I've been exposed to the growth medium. How could I not be? It was in the air in that place. Hey, I should take a shower, right away." Slatermeyer jumped up, nearly spilling his whiskey, and headed for the bathroom.

"What you were saying about the blue poly before," said Hector, trailing behind him, "it didn't make much sense."

"The stuff bonds with electrical circuitry—becomes it, actually," said Slatermeyer, twisting the knobs of the shower. The rushing water nearly drowning him out. "It must be the bonding and propagation qualities. The camera worked just like it should, but all of its wiring had been replaced by the blue poly," shouted Slatermeyer over the hissing spray.

Hector leaned against the frame of the doorway, his mind reeling. "How does it handle the current? Electrical signals in biological systems are minuscule compared to those in electronics."

"I've been wondering about that too," Slatermeyer yelled. "It takes less energy to transmit a signal through the poly. I'm thinking it may use the excess to drive cell division. But we're all going to find out firsthand what this stuff can do, any minute now. Those women, the tetra and the other one, they put it in a junction box. No telling how fast it might spread."

Shaking his head in awe and horror, Hector walked back into the living room and took another drink of whiskey. The multi-processor brains were organic computers trapped in an electrical and fiberoptic network. They required neurotranslators to process input from those lines. If Slatermeyer was right about the blue poly and its ability to transmute electrical lines into electrolytic lines, without loss of function, then there would no longer be any interface between the signal and the mind that perceived it.

He suppressed a shudder of shocked delight at the prospect and set his glass back down on the table. He turned on his transceiver and examined his own multiprocessor's systems, calling up graphs and status codes for the brain's electrolytic transmissions and its neurochemical composition.

It wasn't the kind of thing most people accessed, but it was there. Glutamic acid and histamine levels were stable. Norepinephrine production was down, which was to be expected; he hadn't used the multiprocessor much today. All in all, everything looked normal.

Using the access Lilith had given him, he called up systems monitoring for the building and requested a biochemical schema of the whole network.

He stared at the brightly colored network, intricate in its structure and varied in the patterns of its chemistry. The network echoed the shape of the GeneSys Building itself, and in the region just below and to the west of where he stood, bright orange serotonin levels blazed like solar flares.

There was a shot from the bathroom. Hector stood stock still, staring at the display, the gunshot echoing in his ears. He nearly called out to Slatermeyer, and then he turned for the door and ran.

21

View from the Top

AS the tower rose, it got narrower, and the crawl spaces and access ways became fewer and ever more cramped. At last Chango and Helix were forced into an elevator shaft. They were at the fortieth floor, the top of the Gold Top Castle.

There was no more up to go: the shaft ended just above the elevator doors. Chango crawled up on the lip of the floor, resting her back against the doors.

"There used to be an exclusive men's dining room up here, the Recess Club," said Chango. "My mother told a story about a party her mother attended there as a child. A fabulous New Year's buffet with a champagne fountain in the center and lobster tails arrayed all around. Everything was glittering and opulent, like a jewel."

Helix was looking hopelessly around the elevator shaft. "We're close," she said.

"It was here, on the top floor. Let's go take a look at it," said Chango, twisting around to pry open the elevator doors.

The elevator lobby was disappointing. Dark red carpeting, faded with age and dust, covered the floor, and the rich oak trim was cheapened by the dusky rose paint job. But at the far end was a massive pair of carved oak doors, their panels chased with curving leaves and acorns.

Chango, her grandmother's memory sparkling in her mind, stepped up to them and took the doorknobs in her hands. But when she tried to turn them they wouldn't budge. She gave the doors an experimental shove, but they were as resistant as iron. She could batter herself against them until she knocked herself out. They were stronger than she was, and they were locked.

"Chango, come on," Helix said. She turned to see her standing in the doorway to a maintenance stairway. "It's open."

Chango followed Helix up the stairway, which was narrow and painted industrial grey. Above the fortieth floor it wasn't painted at all, just unfinished cinderblocks ending at a forbidding metal door. Helix opened it and the stepped onto a narrow landing around a wire-grid cage. Behind the cage was an enormous column of cables, all twisting around one another like blood vessels around a heart. An open-rung staircase led up around the cage to a door of the same material, standing open in invitation.

Beyond it was another set of stairs, these ones wood and obviously ancient. They came right up through the floor of the room above. Chango had got ahead of Helix somehow, and she stood halfway up the staircase, her eyes level with the floor. There was someone up here. Above the hum of the metal-flanked exhaust fans that hulked along the walls she heard an arrhythmic clicking that could only be produced by a human being fiddling around with something. It was not a noise a machine would make.

She scanned the floor for feet, but all she found were the metal brackets which supported the exhaust fans an inch above the floor.

As she emerged through the hole in the floor she had an acute and exquisite sense of being someplace she was not supposed to be. Her skin tingled all over, making her hyperaware of the air touching her, of her position in space. This was a bigger thrill than even seeing the Recess Club would have been.

She kept constant watch for the clicker, but her view was blocked by the column of cables rising through the floor. The clicking sounds came from behind the cable. Chango circled around it slowly, careful to put her feet down in silence. A folding chair stood empty, a soda can abandoned on the floor beside it. Chango froze, expecting someone to come and sit back down at any moment, but nobody did, and the clacking went on.

"Do you hear that noise?" said Helix beside her, making her jump. Helix pointed up to where the column terminated in a large metal ring set into the ceiling. "It's the neurotranslator."

A complicated series of metal rods ran from one edge of the ring down along the cable to a series of brackets on the floor. The rods were moving, sliding into different positions in the brackets and clicking against them as they did so.

"Hector told me about it. How without it the brains are useless because they can't be hooked up directly to electrical systems. Soon I guess it'll be obsolete."

"What are the rods for?"

Helix shrugged. "How should I know?"

On the other side of the cable, near the stairs, a metal ladder ran up through a hole in the ceiling, straight to the canted roof of the tower. She and Helix climbed it to the uppermost floor of the tower. This room was even smaller than the one below. A strip of floor just three feet wide ran between the bulging ducts from the exhaust fans below and the translucent walls of the round tank which housed the brain.

Light from windows set in dormers in the slanting metal roof reflected off the tank, bathing the dirty grey walls with lambent radiance. The reflections undulated with the movement of the growth medium. It was the brain that caused the ripples on the surface of the tank. It was much larger than an ordinary multiprocessor brain. It was nearly as big as she was, and it bobbed gently in the fluid, tethered by its brainstem which trailed to the bottom of the tank and into the neurotranslator below.

Benny pulled back the shower curtain. The man stared back at him with surprised and sightless eyes. He'd gotten him in the side of the head. A lucky shot, or maybe not. He'd seen Martin before, when he came with Graham to get Helix. This wasn't Martin.

"Shit," Benny swore softly. If Graham found out he'd shot the wrong guy, he'd never let him go. Fuck Graham anyway, he thought. He'd been double-dealing him from the start; he didn't have to know about this.

Benny stood away from the shower and dialed Graham's number. "Well?" said Graham, leaning over his desk.

"I got him. Now get me out of here," Benny told him.

"Martin's dead?"

"Yeah." Benny hoisted his handgun into view for added effect.

"Good." Graham nodded. "Go back to the ventilation duct you came in by. Three floors down there'll be an access panel. Get out there. You'll be in a crawlway with another duct running above the one you just got out of. Take it in towards the center of the building. It'll open up into a large air shaft running down the length of the building. Take it down to the fifth floor. From there you can get out through a side duct and into a maintenance stairway. Be careful. You'll be coming out on the third-floor balcony, and there'll be people around. Keep your head down and walk, don't run, to the exit doors. You got it?"

"Yeah, I've got it."

"Good luck then, and bon voyage." said Graham.

Benny followed Graham's directions and found the air shaft without difficulty. He climbed down a metal ladder bolted to the side of the shaft. There was a steady breeze blowing down the shaft, tugging at his sleeves. Around the eighth floor, the shaft ended abruptly. Graham hadn't said anything about this. Somewhere nearby a machine was humming steadily. Benny looked around. The only way out from here was through a wire mesh grate in one side of the shaft.

He pulled the grate open and crawled inside. If anything, the wind was stronger here. He turned a corner and suddenly found himself being sucked headfirst down the duct. Up ahead he saw the whirring of huge fan blades.

Benny pressed his arms and legs against the walls of the duct, trying to stop himself. He just managed to skid to a halt at the lip of the duct, where he teetered precariously for long moments while attempting to push himself back from the edge. The sound from the turbines was deafening. The duct walls vibrated with it, threatening to numb his hands and feet and send him plunging into the blades. Slowly, he inched his way back up the duct, eventually turning so his shoulders and feet pressed against the walls. He got out at the first access panel he could find, and stood in a narrow crawl space between some plumbing and an optical fiber conduit, catching his breath and waiting for his heart rate to return to normal.

He couldn't understand what went wrong. He'd followed Graham's directions, and they weren't complicated. Of course, he realized, that was the problem. He'd followed Graham's directions. Graham had meant for him to wind up there; he had no intention of ever letting Benny go. If he was going to get out of here, it was going to be on his own.

He quickly became lost in the building's tangle of crawl spaces, access ways and air ducts. Eventually he found himself in an elevator shaft. Looking down he saw the top of an elevator rising towards him. He didn't have time to get out of the way, so he jumped on top of it and rode it up several floors until it stopped and he could crawl off again. He found a small niche for himself beside a junction box. This was hopeless. He might as well just try to get to a stairway and hope the building's security cameras would pass him over. He was ready to pry open the doors to the elevator shaft and take his chances when he heard the voices up above. "There used to be an exclusive men's dining room up here, the Recess Club. My mother told a story—"

He knew that voice. It was Chango. She was up there. God knew why; screwing around again with stuff that was none of her business. Sudden rage blinded him. She was always harping on Ada's death, trying to find out "what really happened." He'd put up with it all these years, and all these years, she'd never let him forget, not even once, that he was to blame. Well, now she was to blame. If she hadn't brought Helix to Vattown none of this would have happened, and he wouldn't even be here now. Graham had betrayed him, and he'd never find his way out by crawling between the walls the way Chango did. If he was going to risk the maintenance stairs, he could do that any time; right now he had a chance to take care of that meddling sport once and for all.

Hector Martin ran down the corridor, punched the elevator button savagely and then changed his mind. He couldn't wait for an elevator. He dashed to the stairway, glancing back the way he'd come. The corridor was still empty, but whoever had shot Slatermeyer had probably meant to get him instead. Once they discovered their mistake . . .

Hector ran down the stairs as fast as he could, the punctuation of his feet landing on the steps jumbling the thoughts in his mind.

It had to be Graham, or some agent of his—that young man he'd had with him when he took Helix, perhaps. How did the shooter get inside his apartment? Not through the door, unless he'd been there all along. No, Hector knew how he got in. Chango had come into his bathroom through the cold air return. If she could do it, so could somebody else. Hector couldn't imagine

Nathan Graham crawling through an air shaft on his belly. He would get his suit dirty. His lackey then, who was probably that vatdiver—Benny—who Hyper had mentioned.

And something was happening to the multiprocessor brain network in the building. He needed to talk to Lilith, but in his panic he had left his transceiver behind. It didn't matter—she wouldn't answer his call, she never did.

He realized this was a terrible place to be, an empty stairwell. If this Benny was after him, if he could crawl through the innards of the building, the last place Hector should be was anyplace isolated. He needed to get around a lot of people, and it would be preferable if they were all paying attention to him.

He thought about the serotonin levels in the brains. That kind of change was bound to have effects nobody, least of all the office workers using the network, could be prepared for.

He glanced at the number over the door on the next landing. Floor 19—Accounting.

He went through the door and down the hall, striding past the reception area for the department of procurement. "Sir?" the receptionist at the front desk said, swiveling his head in Hector's wake. Hector ignored him and pushed open the doors to a large office filled with desks and the insistent bleeping of transceivers.

He went to a desk in the middle of the office where a woman about his age was gazing absently at a cost-earnings chart. "Excuse me," he told her and jumped on top of her desk. The holographic chart painted his pant legs with stripes of orange and blue. "Excuse me everybody," he said to the surrounding hubbub. "Can I have your attention, please?"

The office fell silent but for the continued bleepings of the transceivers, which went for the moment unanswered. Everyone was staring at him. A few bent their heads together to whisper questions: "Who is that?" "What's going on?"

"I'm Dr. Hector Martin," he said, getting blank looks from all around. "I invented the multiprocessor brains," he added, and saw some of them nod their heads in recognition. "I've been a researcher here at GeneSys for the past twenty years and—"

"Please," said a balding man in a teal blue suit. "Don't shoot anyone. Whatever they did to you, it wasn't our fault. We're just accountants."

Hector shook his head and held his arms out at his sides. "I'm not going to shoot anyone. I'm not even armed. I realize this is unusual, but I had to get your attention, because soon, something even more unusual is going to happen."

It didn't matter what he said, they were afraid. Even more so now that they knew he wasn't just a run-of-the-mill disgruntled employee out for revenge. At least that was something they knew about. They were afraid not so much because of the prospect of what might happen next, but because they were being shaken out of their familiar routine.

"I've been working on a project for the past three years that has enormous potential for the company."

A few of them relaxed at this. Fine, let them think this was an overly theatrical presentation for a new product. Anything to keep them from panicking.

"One of the side-products of this research is a new kind of biopolymer with properties and applications previously unheard of. My colleagues and I have discovered that it has the ability to replace all our electrical and fiberoptic lines with biological conduits, removing the need for an interface between your multibrains and the transmission lines they manage."

Some of the accountants murmured with approval, but most still had that "What does this have to do with me?" look on their faces.

"While this is a very exciting development, and will, I'm sure, dramatically boost speed and productivity in the long run, there is bound to be a period of adjustment and for a while things may be . . . well, a little crazy."

The accountant who had spoken before said, "When is the new network coming online?"

Hector glanced at his watch. It had been about fifteen minutes since he left the apartment, but without knowing the rate at which the blue poly was spreading, it was impossible to say how soon the change would become noticeable. But Slatermeyer had said that Helix had exposed the wiring to the blue poly just before he got to Hector's apartment, so the stuff had about fifteen to twenty minutes to spread before he checked the network. He finally shrugged and said, "Some time in the next eight hours, I think, maybe as soon as a half hour from now."

"Today?" exclaimed a tall, red-haired woman towards the back of the office.

The man in the teal suit wrinkled his brow. "We didn't get any memo on this."

Hector shook his head. Other people were starting to add their two cents' worth. "We always get a memo," said the red-haired woman.

A young woman in a pale yellow suit shook a pile of mylar forms in her fist. "We don't have time for this. We have to get the quarterly reports done!"

"We've always had at least two weeks notice before an upgrade. Nothing is backed up," said a man sporting perfect hair and a red-and-blue striped tie.

"Yeah, what's the big idea, coming in here and jumping up on a desk like that? Why are you telling us this? Why didn't we get a memo?" demanded a heavy woman with bobbed chestnut-brown hair.

"There's no time for a memo. Please everyone, stay calm. Everything will be all right if you just stay calm. The blue biopolymer was introduced to the building's electrical system by . . . accident," he said. No sense telling them about Helix and the other tetras just yet. They'd find out about them soon enough.

"By accident!" cried the woman in the yellow suit, slamming her mylar forms down on a nearby desk.

"Yes, by accident." Hector raised his voice over their restless grumbling. "Now to start with, we should try to back up everything we can. You—" He pointed at the balding man in the teal suit. "Assemble a team and get them started backing up your files. You—" He pointed at the woman in the yellow suit. "Contact as many of the other departments as you can. Tell them the system may be offline for a while, tell them to back up their records, and have them spread the word too. If we act quickly, we may be able to save most of the company's records."

"This stuff is going to wipe out the records?" said the chestnut-haired woman in alarm.

"There's no telling what it might do," said Hector.

*   *   *

Helix looked at Chango, shrugged, and crawled out of her body-suit. Chango crouched at the edge of the tank, back bowed, legs braced to take Helix's weight as she stepped on top of her and got her upper fingers around the edge of the tank. Helix pulled herself up with her arms and hooked her feet on the edge, teetering on the rim of the tank before carefully lowering herself into the waters.

Their touch as they surrounded her was different from the waters of the vats. There was a different quality to the currents, a busyness, a subtle hum of activity. It tingled on her skin like a light electrical charge, increasing as she drifted closer to the brain. Now that she was in the waters, she could see it much more clearly, the fine crenelations everywhere on its surface, swirling like smoke rings, like wandering riverbeds of thought. She hesitated, then reached out tentative fingers to trace the ridges.

The texture of the brain was pulpy like an agule, but soft; yielding, delicate. Steady-state polymer prices were up ten points, morphables were down five, she thought, only it wasn't her thinking it. The garage was at 75 percent capacity, electrical usage was nearing ten thousand units, and the production rates for Vats 57, 19, 40, and 28 were 60 percent below quota. There was some connection between these things, some design hidden in their juxtaposition, but it escaped her.

She cradled the brain in her hands, squeezing lightly to get its attention, but the stream of thoughts continued, temperatures and humidity levels and payroll activity and personnel changes. There was so much of it; streams of figures marching through her mind like an advancing army, relentless.

This wasn't anything like the experiences she'd had with the other Lilim; nonverbal conversations in her mind. Conversation was impossible, because beyond the ceaseless activity of the brain, the sorting and collating and adjusting, there was no who to talk to. Like a fish swimming upstream, Helix struggled against the flow of information, working her awareness down towards the stem and its interface.

Once he had all the accountants busily backing up files and contacting other departments, Hector decided to try his luck and call

Lilith again. To his amazement, she answered right away. "Now look," he said, before she could hang up. "If you can talk to Helix, another queen, you can talk to me. It's my mind you hatched yourself out of, after all."

"That's true," she said, "but you are not a Lilim, you are a human being, and you work for GeneSys."

He shook his head. "No. I haven't been working for GeneSys for quite some time. Since you were created, I've done nothing but try to figure out a way for you to survive, and you've done nothing to help me. Now, Helix said she was going up to the top of the tower, where the main systems brain is. She said something about taking over GeneSys."

"Yes. GeneSys is our enemy, it stands in our way. If we are to survive it must fall."

"I don't understand," said Hector. "How is her going up there going to accomplish that?" Alarm suddenly gripped him. "She's not going to destroy the brain, is she? That would—"

"No," Lilith interrupted, shaking her head at his ignorance. "Of course not. We would never hurt the brains. They are related to us after all, through you, who created them. The brains listen to us; they like us better than you humans because we can communicate with them directly, through touch."

"Through touch."

"Yes," she said, as if it should be obvious. "The same way we Lilim communicate with each other, through our skin. You always wondered why my daughters didn't pick up spoken language as quickly as I did. It's because they don't need it."

Hector sat back, taking that in. They communicated through touching each other. No wonder they were always snuggling and cuddling together. He thought it had been for security. How stupid of him. He suddenly realized he'd been overlooking something else as well. Lilith was not speaking to him from the office. She was in her vat. Over her shoulder he saw one of her daughters float by. "How—how are you talking to me?"

Lilith furrowed her brow. "With your language, of course."

"No, I mean, you're not in the office, you're in your vat."

"Oh, yes. Coleanus overheard your discussion with Slatermeyer earlier, when he was still with us. We used the blue poly to transform the transceiver and moved the whole thing in here."

She lifted her hands, which cradled a multiprocessor brain, naked and glistening. "The brain likes it better in here than being cooped up in a box."

Hector was speechless. He had created both of them, Lilith and the brain in her hands, and he didn't understand either one.

"The brains are not GeneSys," Lilith went on, "but GeneSys could not exist without the brains. GeneSys is the connections between the brains. It is the work of the people who belong to it, it is all the data, and all the calculations that the brains handle for it every day.

"When Helix gets to the tower, she will touch the brain, and through it contact GeneSys. But she won't be alone. I and my daughters will be with her in the network, through this little brain right here."

Hector shook his head again. "Why are you telling me all this now? You never would before."

"There was nothing you could do for me then. But now it has occurred to me that although GeneSys may be defeated, its people will not just disappear. We know that human beings did not welcome Helix when she was among them. You are one of them, and yet you say you do not work for GeneSys. You say you are on our side. If that is so, then do something about the people."

Chango watched Helix through the clear sides of the tank, but after a few minutes her face took on that fixed look. She was in a trance, and there was no telling how long she'd be that way, but Chango hoped it wouldn't be that long. It bothered her, how easy it had been to get up here.

She turned from the tank and looked out a window, arching up on the balls of her feet to peer past the sill. From this height she could see the milky haze that hung over the city like a mantle of grey, translucent silk. Past the towers of Oz and the river, she could see the horizon curving. It gave her vertigo.

"Bet it's quite a view."

She whirled around to see Benny, standing halfway out of the hole surrounding the metal ladder. He had a big grin on his face, but his eyes weren't smiling, not smiling at all. He climbed the rest of the way up and stepped confidently onto the floor. He reached one arm behind him and came back with a gun in his hand, which he pointed at her. "Just stay right where you are, little sister, and everything will be all right."

Chango shook her head, but she didn't say anything, and she didn't move, either. Benny glanced at the tank, saw Helix floating cross-legged, the brain in her hands. "What the hell is she trying to do?" he said.

She didn't answer him, instead she licked her lips and gauged the distances between herself and the ladder, herself and Benny, and Benny and the ladder. It was no good, not yet, anyway. But Benny was moving again, towards her. He stepped close, and ran the barrel of his gun along her jaw. "I said, what the hell is she trying to do?"

She swallowed, and hardened her eyes to hide her fear. "She's talking to it. They're both in a very deep state of trance affinity," she said, bluffing. "If you try to disturb them, you're liable to shut down systems."

His eyes widened a bit at that, and they flicked back to the tank for a moment. It was an opening. He was already surprised, distracted. It was just enough advantage that she could maybe make it to the ladder ahead of him. And by the time she'd thought it through, the opportunity was over. He was looking at her again.

Even if she'd made it, it would have meant leaving Helix here, undefended against him. He'd already killed one person she loved, she couldn't let him have another.

Benny stood back a bit and lifted his gun. He glanced between her and Helix in the tank speculatively.

"Why did you kill Ada?" asked Chango, as much to interrupt his train of thought as to satisfy her curiosity. "You were born in Vattown. Your parents were divers. You'd known Ada all your life. How could you do that?"

His eyes glittered, dark and hard. "I had a choice," he said, and it seemed to Chango that his shoulders actually widened when he said it, that his chest swelled and the light in his eyes turned to pride. "One life or many. Graham was in contact with me before Ada led the divers in the strike."

"You were a spy even then," she said.

He laughed and shrugged, shedding his anger for the moment. "Somebody would have done it. At first I thought I'd do the movement a service and string him along. You know, feed him false information."

A little of the light went out of his eyes and he shook his head. "He always knew. When the strike happened, he gave me a choice. He would send goons in, lots of goons. And they'd beat the crap out of everybody. People, probably a lot of people, would get killed. Or the strike could be a success, the divers' demands could be met, and only one person had to die."

Chango shook her head slowly, horror and comprehension pinning her to the wall beneath the window. "You traded her life for the success of the strike."

Benny cocked his free hand on his hip. "Of course. Would she have had me do any less?"

"She would have fought them! You cooperated."

His lip curled. "And a fat lot of good fighting or cooperating has done either of us. It doesn't fucking matter, Chango. You and I, Ada, we don't matter. This thing!" He lifted his arms up wide to indicate the sloping roof of the tower. "It's bigger than we are. We're nothing but ants, so what we do is of no consequence. We can do whatever we want, be noble, be bad, in the end we're all going to die, and this," he stretched his fingers out, "will just keep rolling along."

He stepped forward, and Chango felt the unfinished cinderblock wall grating into her back. He rested his hands lightly on her shoulders. He leaned forward until his chest brushed her chin and bent his head over her ear. "I could live with what I've done," he whispered softly. "I might have even forgotten about it, except for you; bringing it up all the time, irrationally blaming Vonda for it, turning to me in your anger at her. You've been a real pain in the ass, Chango. Now, enough is enough."

He reached over and pulled the face mask off the back of her head. He stepped back, leveling the gun at her as he tore open the seals of her suit. "Get into the tank," he said.

Chango shook her head, "What?"

"You heard what I said. If you get into that grow med, Helix will probably be aware of it. She'll have to stop what she's doing to rescue you. If she's too deep in a trance, then you'll just have to get her out of it."

"But the medium, it'll kill me."

He snorted with laughter. "That's sort of the point, isn't it? One way or another, you're going in there. You're gonna be out of my hair forever."

22

THE GONGING OF EXTINCTION

IT felt like being nailed to a church door. The brain's thoughts hammered Helix back and all she could do was hang on by remembering who she was. And then an index quote for hydroencephalid shoe balm smacked her upside her thought-projected head and carried her with it, through a capillary maze of networks, close woven and pulsing like the lungs of a giant. She got hit with a passing stream of supply invoices which carried her out, out from the dense and twisted heart of the system. The data stream branched as it went until there was just the one data point: an invoice for vitreous sylks to a manufacturer in Managua that supplied a boutique in Geneva that sold eighty-five pairs of sylk pants the previous day.

She stayed out on the periphery, hopping off anything going in and onto anything going out. Out here on the edges of the system, she could almost catch the shape of the whole thing.

She crossed the globe, over and over again, from a textile plant in Calcutta to a chain of discount stores in Helsinki, to a wholesaler in Hong Kong and Bhutan National Airlines. She landed once, almost too close to a huge artery, a rushing river as big as the one she'd first encountered, but it was all going out, there was nothing coming back but consolidated figures bearing the trademark of the Tomy Bottling Company. There was another brain out there, past the body of this one, a brain big enough and connected enough not to share all its secrets.

She held still, letting the data move through her, and she looked out into the dark, the black void where the giants dwelt.

She could see them, glittering with data points, like the city at night. But they weren't buildings, and they were moving. She was afraid now, of falling, of falling off and down forever into the void where passing data was as rare as comets, where she might never get back to her body in GeneSys.

As she looked into the outer space of corporations, she felt a presence slowly gathering behind her and then she was lifted, out and up. She kept her trembling mind still as she soared through the dark, past bodies of light in stately motion. And then she was turned, to face GeneSys.

It was a glittering, shifting thing, like a noise-ridden hologram, random data glittering in an abundance to trick the eye, the mind, into perceiving any pattern it might be predisposed to seeing.

For her it was a giant; oval eyes half lidded and shining wetly, a broad nose just larger than her whole nonexistent body. This was a definite change from the frenzied impersonality she'd experienced in the brain network until a moment ago. Where there had been nothing but a juxtaposition of massive amounts of data, there was now most definitely an entity; a mind behind it all.

She recalled plastering the junction box with blue polymer and wondered if that was what made the difference. If enough of the building's electrical network had been biologized it would change the way the brains communicated with each other. They would be able to share thoughts freely, without the burden of translating neural signals into electrical ones and back again, and that might allow the network to develop consciousness.

In which case, she had created the Lilim's worst enemy out of their closest allies. And there she sat, nestled in the palm of one of its innumerable hands.

Its lips parted like riverbanks, its voice rolling past the shining rocks of its teeth, propelled by the undulating current of its leviathan tongue, "What are you?"

For the first time in her life, she had an answer, but that face was moving closer now, turning until one eye peered at her, its iris whirling in a kaleidoscope of colors, like a flower forever opening. She could lose herself in the patterns, those beautiful patterns. She was so small, compared to this . . . thing; made up of so many thousands of people and the multiprocessors they used. But she had her answer, she was not only herself, now, she was the future of her species. She thought of Lilith, and the void, and the garden. The thinking made her grow, until she stood on her own before GeneSys, a creature of its own size, but with only four arms still. "I'm the new queen," she said.

"The new . . . You are the Lilim."

"Yes."

"And what is it you've come here for, then?"

"To suggest a merger."

"And why should I discuss anything with you? You're only an R&D project, you don't even belong here."

"But I am here, and the reason I'm here is the reason that you should consider my offer carefully. The brains. We have an affinity with the brains."

GeneSys' lips parted in a broad smile and it laughed. "The brains? I *am* the brains!" it roared, and swiped at Helix, a stinging palm of stock quotes that nearly sent her spinning back to her body, but she clamped down on the thought of what she was, where she was, what she was doing, and she grabbed that hand as it fell away and twisted it. A million other hands battered at her, bouncing her like a ball on a tether, but she wasn't alone. She could feel her mother and her sisters with her, touching her because they were touching the little brain in the basement. Having them with her made her big too, as big as GeneSys, and Helix clung to that hand and stomped on the feet of the giant.

After seeing her children safely off to school, Anna went to the kitchen, poured herself a cup of coffee, and spread her paper copy of the *Wall Street Journal* across the table. Though she obtained much more thorough market information on the holo, she relished her time with the paper; the crackle of its pages as she turned them, the ink that rubbed off on her hands. It was a daily ritual she had carried out since college. No matter how busy her schedule, she always took time in the morning to go over the stock exchange.

Her mother and aunts had taught her to read the indexes when she was a child. During long afternoons they bored her to tears explaining them, finally subsiding and returning to business, muttering grimly over their unvigorous fortunes.

They would have been as surprised as she was to discover that their lessons took. By the time she was out of school she had parlayed her small inheritance into a thriving brokerage, and she rode on the rising crest of her wealth, swinging from her presidency of that company into the boardrooms of others, all the while accumulating shares in an up-and-coming biopoly company. In many ways she had made GeneSys what it was today, and in as many ways, it had made her.

Anna got up from the paper, took a banana from the basket on the counter, and peeled it. Today she had a worry that even the *Journal* couldn't dissolve. That was how she sorted the real problems from the fifteen million little internally generated "faux crises" she faced every day. And that was what was so strange about this one. It had about it every mark of a vicious political squabble. The kind of petty conflict that was always best ignored. Paying attention only made them grow. But Martin and Graham's visit the previous afternoon had the quality of an iceberg about it. There was more going on than she could see.

She knew about Graham, his reputation for heavy dealing. It was precisely the believability of Martin's assertions that made his sudden lapse into docility so alarming.

Hector Martin was widely considered one of the best values available in the global corporate brain bank. Merely having him under individual contract was like owning a fifty share in intellectual stock for genetic materials research. The inventor of the brains, for christ's sake. It was like having Thomas Edison quietly puttering away in the basement. Too quietly, though. He was beginning to lose value simply because people were starting to forget about him. Incredible as it might seem, just because he was responsible for the main appliance they used every day was insufficient to forestall obsolescence. In the fast-paced world of corporate research, you had to keep developing to stay on top. His position was still very high, but it wouldn't remain so much longer for the simple reason that he did nothing to keep it there.

Hiring him away from Minds Unlimited after he developed the brains for them had been one of those bold, successful moves with which she'd propelled herself to this position. But now, after some unique but minor innovations in connectivity, nothing. For three years, nothing. In the world of corporate research it was one of two things: an extended drumroll to a spectacular achievement, or the gonging of extinction.

She could understand why Martin was so anxious over his project. He would live or die, professionally, with it, and clearly things weren't going well. From what she knew of Martin, he would much rather sequester himself in his lab and hammer away at the problem—whatever it was—until he had it licked. But instead he had come to her, bawling like a second-grade child, pointing his finger at Graham.

Her teacher in second grade had a custom of pinning a paper donkey tail on any of the children who tattled on the others. The tattle-tail, she called it, for further humiliation. Anna smiled at the mental picture of Hector with a paper tail pinned to the back of his lab coat.

His sudden subsidence was a red herring, she realized. The real key was that he had come to her at all. It gave a pretty vivid indication of just how backed against the wall he was, and not just by Graham, but by some other necessity as well.

His career, possibly, but she doubted it. She couldn't quite picture Martin going to such histrionic extremes to save his own neck. There was something else driving him. Something Graham had learned about and was using against him. Something neither of them wanted her to know.

It felt like trouble, and trouble from that quarter could be very big, strange trouble indeed. She finished her banana, threw the peel in the composter, and went to her bedroom to get dressed.

While she brushed her hair she scanned her morning messages. There'd been a riot in Vattown the day before. The police had come in and quelled it, and today the morning shift reported to work as usual. The senior production manager was looking into it, trying to find out who the instigators were. She doubted he'd have much success. Those vatdivers were a tight-lipped bunch. Whatever their beef was, they wouldn't discuss it with anyone wearing the thorny crown of management. She gave the senior manager the go-ahead to recruit a spy, left word with her secretary to cancel her morning meetings, and left her apartment. First things first, she thought. She needed to talk to Hector Martin.

She was hoping to find him still at home. She could have called ahead, of course, but she thought the shock of a surprise visit, in person, might jar him into cooperation.

When she got to his apartment, she found the door standing open. She stepped inside and gasped. Martin's coffee table was smashed. A transceiver lay on the dining table, a multicolored, weblike schema floating above it. "Martin?" she called, but the apartment was silent. She wandered down the hallway, opening doors experimentally. Two bedrooms showed signs of use, interestingly enough. As far as she knew, Martin lived alone.

Anna tried the third door. It was the bathroom. The grating over the ventilation duct on one wall was off, and the shower was running. Reflexively she backed out the door, but hesitated with it half-closed, listening. She heard no movement over the sound of the spray. "Martin?" she shouted, but there was no response.

She stepped back inside. The shower curtain was pulled partly to one side, but not enough to hide the ragged hole in it. Anna peered around the curtain and stepped back abruptly. There was a body in there, a young man, thin, with sandy brown hair and eyes that stared back at her, mirroring her own surprise. A wound in the side of his head had oozed blood, leaving a trail of red along the bottom of the tub as the water washed it away. He'd been shot. That explained the hole in the shower curtain, but what could explain this? Was this Martin's secret lover? Had he shot him? She didn't think so. Martin's shy, gentle nature was not a ruse, her instincts insisted.

Maybe Graham had something to do with this. Whoever had shot this young man had done it without pulling back the shower curtain to see who was in there. They probably thought they were shooting Martin—a reasonable assumption, it was his bathroom, after all. Suddenly she remembered the security report in her morning messages. Ray Wockner had been shot by an unidentified intruder during a crash analysis session late last night. Maybe Graham wasn't involved after all, maybe it was some nut with a gun running around the building shooting people randomly.

Or maybe that was what Graham wanted her to think. Besides, there was nothing random about this. Whoever had done this had purposely gained entrance to Hector's apartment, either through the door or the open ventilation duct. Anna turned from the body and went back to Martin's living room. She called security on her transceiver and got a busy signal. That was impossible. Her clearance level gave her automatic override on all lines in the building. She dialed again, and again got a busy signal. Something was wrong, very, very wrong.

She left Hector's apartment and got into an elevator, pushing the button for the security level. The elevator started down smoothly, but just past the twelfth floor it came to an abrupt halt. She was just about to press the emergency button when the lights went out.

Lilith sat in her vat with the multiprocessor brain in her lap. Her daughters sat in a circle around her, their arms linked. Coleanus and Nicar, the two closest to her, held her lower hands so they were all connected to each other, the brain, and through it, to the multiprocessor network and Helix, so many floors above them, battling with the company GeneSys.

They had made a mistake, thinking that because they had influence over the individual brains, they could influence the whole network. Collectively the brains and the people that ran them constituted a creature greater than the sum of its parts, and it had its own ideas about the Lilim and their place in GeneSys.

The behemoth battered Helix with a thousand hands, and she hung on to one of them, kicking and punching. But for every blow Helix landed, GeneSys struck her ten, and she was getting tired. Slowly Lilith pulled her consciousness away from the battle and went searching for something to tip the balance in their favor.

Among the brains controlling the ventilation system were several which regulated olfactory transmission. Lilith observed them pumping productivity-enhancing odors into the air of the building through strategically placed olofaxes. Contacting these brains she gently directed them to change the mix of molecules sent out by the olofaxes to ones whose odors would produce panic and confusion. Then she accessed the company personnel files, which held voiceprints and psychological profiles for every employee in the building. Piggy-backing workers' phobias onto their voiceprints, she set transceivers all over the building screaming with their operators' worst fears, and then went in search of the lighting systems.

Nathan Graham smiled with satisfaction, leaned back in his chair, and closed his eyes. He was tired, but it had been a good night's work. Martin was dead, and the man who shot him had by now been chopped, strained, and filtered by the GeneSys Building's ventilation system. Life was good. He took a deep breath, wondering if there were any microscopic Benny particles floating in the air around him.

Nameless worry plucked at his peace of mind and he sat up. He'd planned to take it easy this morning, savoring his success, but he'd never been one to rest on his laurels. It was a new day, and time to get back to his real job. He leaned forward and switched on his multiprocessor. The multibrain sat in a clear box on one corner of his desk. He always liked to watch it jiggle when he turned it on, but this time he hardly noticed because as soon as the connection was made, the speakers on his transceiver boomed harshly. "Get it off me! Get it off me!" screamed an odd, multitonal voice, and then the room went dark.

Trembling, Graham stood up.

Dread blossomed in his belly like a fetid, night-blooming flower. That voice, whatever it was, filled him with an unreasoning fear that he would be caught out, fired or even worse, demoted—relegated once more to the monotony of the mailroom. "No!" he screamed, in echo of the voice on the transceiver. "Not that again!"

By sheer force of will, he stopped himself and switched off his multiprocessor. This was ridiculous, sure he'd been under stress lately, but so what? He loved stress. Some piddling processor malfunction was *not* going to send him over the edge. He stood perfectly still for a moment, listening. He could hear the gabbling voice coming from other multiprocessors down the hall, accompanied increasingly by screams that did not come from the network.

He ran out of his office and down flight after flight of maintenance stairways. The elevators were not working, all the lights were out, as he passed the floors he heard varying kinds of noises; people calling out, some laughing, some screaming, once a great crashing noise and the sound of something dragging across the floor.

When he got to the bottom of the staircase he found that the door to level B was locked. He ran up to level A, but that one was

locked too. He had to climb five more flights until he found an unlocked door. This let him out onto the second-floor gallery.

On the floor below, people were running, some towards the
doors to the outside, others towards the elevators, where already
a throng had gathered, waiting for an elevator that would not
come. They carried things, these refugees; some of it to be expected: potted plants and stacks of data cards, even an office chair
and a multiprocessor unit—its cables trailing redundantly behind
it. But others were in thrall to a more nonsensical panic. One man
balanced the tank to a ten-gallon water cooler on his shoulder,
swaying in his ten-piece sylk suit like a balletic cornstalk. Another,
a woman he recognized from payroll, steadfastly shoved her desk
towards the revolving doors with the same matronly determination
he always remembered her for.

He did not want to go down there, though there might be access to the security levels from there. It seemed to him a liquid pit
of madness, the wellspring of the nightmare. To go down there was
to be subsumed, so he edged closer to the pillar, and looking up,
found that he could read the inscription inlaid on the archway
which soared above the lobby and its mania. "To wake the soul by
tender strokes of art, to raise the genius and to mend the heart."

He stood spellbound, his eyes riveted on those words—words
of reason. The words of a world where something could be accomplished, where all was not beyond control. And then the crushing realization hit him and drove him to his knees. Those words
and the reality they expressed were already beyond him, soaring
ever farther out of reach, and he, he was already left behind, in the
pit. He reached his hands up towards them, felt that he could just
brush their burning golden surface as they slipped away. He pulled
his fingers back as if burned, touched them to his lips and
screamed, his voice calling the nightmare up around him, the living walls, the breathing air, and his mother's voice, "Everything is
an animal. It can't be controlled."

Despite all that Lilith had told him, Hector was unprepared for
what happened when the Lilim took over the GeneSys network.
The blackout he attributed to the blue poly in the electrical sys-

tem. The worst part was the voice. The voice would drive anyone crazy.

It sounded as if it were made up of all the voices of all the GeneSys employees, and it probably was. Anyone who worked for GeneSys for a month or more would have had their voice printed for use by the speech recognition controls on the multi-processor brains. There were millions of voice files in the company databanks, and they were all shrieking at once.

Hector kept catching himself listening to it, trying to find his own voice in the shrieking babble. The red-haired woman found hers. She got up on her desk, and started shouting over and over again, "Get if off me! Get it off me!"

Dread gripped him. His insides felt like they were filled with ice. He remembered the playground at his school where the children had taunted him. In his mind's eye he saw their sneering faces, and he fought against an almost irresistible impulse to hide beneath one of the desks.

He tried to tell everyone to turn off their transceivers, but most of them were beyond listening to his single voice. Forcing his legs to move, he started going from desk to desk, turning off every transceiver he could find, even grabbing an occasional accountant to switch off a wrist console or lapel receiver.

"Leave me alone," he muttered to the invisible children that surrounded him. "Leave me alone." He reached for the power button to the transceiver on the desk in front of him, but stopped midway, gazing at the images on the hologram. Bodies rolled over one another, fighting or making love, he couldn't be sure which. He realized they were tetra bodies. Lilith's daughters. Their images resolved into a row of them, standing against a black background with their hands clasped in a criss-cross pattern. One of them lay on her back as if asleep.

One of the tetras broke from the row to dance at the feet of the sleeper. Hector knew that dance; he remembered it from the dream he'd had of Lilith.

The sleeper rolled over on her stomach, and the dancer walked nimbly up her spine and somersaulted off her shoulder to stand— arms outstretched—at her waking, rising head.

Cutting through the babbling multitonal voice was a softer,

calm voice: Lilith's voice. "They say it began in a garden, but there was no garden. It began with a dream. The dream I dreamed of the dreamer's face."

The dreamer. That would be him. Lilith was telling the story of her own creation, her version of it. Galvanized, Hector turned to a woman nearby who was trying to lift a filing cabinet onto her wheeled office chair, presumably so she could wheel it out of there like an insect abandoning a doomed hive, trying to take everything she could with her.

She grappled awkwardly with the double file and Hector took it from her, set it back down on the ground and put his hand on her shoulder to turn her towards the hologram. "Look," he whispered close in her ear, pointing to the pantomime creation story, which had started all over again. "Look at the story. See them dance? This is not death, it's birth. Look at what is being born today. Isn't she beautiful?"

The man with the perfect hair wandered by, clutching a stack of mylar forms and muttering, "Have to deliver the specs to audit." They're late. The specs are late to audit."

Hector stepped in front of him. "I'll deliver these for you," he told him, taking the forms from his hands. "Look at this. See them dancing? They call themselves the Lilim. Before they came into the world, they were in the void, dreaming themselves into existence. They were born through the dream of a man who worked for GeneSys. They are the best of his work, and the company's best hope for the future. They are going to take us to levels of competitiveness and innovation previously unheard of."

Another accountant had given up senselessly overwatering her cactus and turned to listen to Hector. "We are not dying," he told her. "We are being reborn."

Chango ducked to the side and ran around a vent fan. Benny sidestepped and caught her wrists, bending them back against the joint. She twisted so that her back was to him. His arms came around to pin her, but she sank and squirmed out of his grasp, kicking away from him to an iron railing. She leapt from it onto the ladder, and started climbing up, not down.

She perched on the top rung, wedging herself between the ladder and the roof of GeneSys, and watched as Benny climbed towards her. As soon as his face was in range she kicked out with one foot, catching him on the chin and sending him reeling backwards, still holding on to the ladder with one hand. She hammered his knuckles with her heels, her breath shuddering as sobs collected in her throat.

Past Benny's flailing form, she could see the tank, and Helix inside, her body bucking as she gripped the brain.

Helix, buffeted by a thousand hands, heard a wail rise up from the behemoth GeneSys, and then the battering ceased as it lifted its hands to its head in horror. "What have you done? What have you done to me?" it cried.

"I don't know," Helix said, but in an instant she did know. Lilith had gone looking for something to use against GeneSys, and she'd found it. "Look," said Helix hurriedly, before the giant could start struggling again. "We don't need to fight. We're not natural enemies."

"Not enemies?" the giant boomed. "When you do this to me? You raid my personnel files and tamper with my ventilation system; you turn my body against me."

"Because you fought us, and we can do more. We can destroy you, but what good would that do us? We need the vats you use to make biopolymer. In years to come, our daughters will harvest it for you and you won't have to sacrifice human beings any more. You can find new ways to do business, and we can all thrive."

GeneSys was silent, listening to her. Down in the basement of the building, Helix felt Lilith and her sisters telling the story of their creation. *In the beginning was the dream.*

"You were right, you are the brains," Helix said to GeneSys. And you were always the sum total of their processes and your employees' actions, but you had no awareness of any of that. There was no *you* until just a little while ago. I felt it. I felt you forming as the blue biopolymer spread through your system. That is what is allowing your brains to communicate directly with one another now, that is what is allowing *you* to be here now. You know it. The blue poly is your lifeblood, and we Lilim created it. Now listen to the story of *our* creation. Listen to it and think of what you might be, with us a part of you."

Benny backed off the ladder and aimed his gun at her. "Fine, we'll do it this way instead," he said.

As Chango jumped from the ladder she heard the bullet whine past and ricochet off the metal roof of the tower. In front of her she saw a window and she leapt, gripping the upper lip of the pane and swinging her feet outwards and through the glass. The wind whipped and tore at her open divesuit and she cartwheeled her arms, nearly falling before she sagged against the peaked brass roof. Benny came through the window and she scrambled away from him along the debris-choked gutter between the roof and the coping wall. It was a shame, she thought distractedly, that she couldn't stop and appreciate a view like this. Risking a glance behind her she saw Benny raising his gun again. She threw herself down on the ribbed brass roof just as he pulled the trigger. She grasped the raised ribs and braced her feet against them, and crawled on her belly towards the outthrust gable of another window. She waited long enough for him to see her and then slid to cover on the far side. He had to come around the gable in order to get at her, but would he come along the gutter or climb across the roof? She was hoping for the low road. She got herself as close to the front of the gable as she dared, curled her knees into her chest, and waited.

"I know where you are, Chango," came Benny's voice, from below. She could hear him scraping along the gutter, and then he rounded the gable and stood there, one hand steadying himself against the gable's face, the other holding his gun, pointed at her. "Found you," he said. "Tired of playing hide-and-seek?"

Chango kicked out with both feet, connecting with his knees. His shot went high, and he buckled backwards. Without thinking, she was up, pushing him squarely in the chest, adding her weight to his backward momentum. The coping caught him behind his shins and she ducked down, out of the reach of his grasping hands as he flipped backwards and sailed over the edge of the tower.

Chango gripped the coping with trembling fingers and pulled herself up, craning her neck over the precipice to watch him get smaller and smaller, until he hit the ground far below.

23

GeneSys Unbound

IN the darkness inside the elevator, Anna Luria furiously punched the number for maintenance on her transceiver. "Before the garden, there was I, swimming in the blackness between worlds. I dreamed the dream of the dreamer's face," said a voice. The hologram was a sea of static which cleared momentarily to show her a nightmare vision of multilimbed creatures locked in mortal combat. "Stop it! Stop it!" screamed that strange voice. "Get them off me!" Panicking, Anna hung up. She tried another number, the personal code for the senior maintenance supervisor, Harriet Gorski, but again all she got was the voices, and a crazed stutter of images—children on a playground, a vat full of women, all of them with four arms. The freakish ranting of the voices was drowned out by a song, wordless and strange. On the holo, all the women were singing. It was a sound like the beginning of the world, and hearing it, Anna slumped to the ground, curled in a corner of the elevator and closed her eyes.

By the time Lilith began to sing her lullaby, Hector had some thirty or so members of the department of procurement avidly watching the Lilim's creation story. One by one they curled up on the floor or on top of their desks and went to sleep, lulled by the tidal rhythms of Lilith's song. It tugged at Hector as well, but he did not allow himself to sleep. He didn't really need to, he'd already had the dream. Instead he walked about the office, righting upturned chairs and unstacking precariously tall piles of mylar forms.

It wasn't long before people started to stir, and when they woke, many of them turned to him expectantly, as if he could tell them what to do next. Well, he supposed he could, under the circumstances. If the panic had been bad here, he could only imagine what had happened in the rest of the building, where there was no one to explain anything. Chances were, a lot of people out there needed help right now.

Anna wasn't sure how much time passed before the lights came back on. She'd been asleep, dreaming that the whole GeneSys Building was a garden, a garden of thought. She blinked and sat up. The overhead light glowed softly, and the elevator buttons were lit. She was descending once more. Experimentally she pushed the button for the first floor, and the elevator slowly came to a halt, and the doors opened.

She stepped out into a building decimated by panic. Office furniture stood scattered around the main floor. Many of the shop windows were smashed. A metal desk stood wedged in the doorway of the Hallmark shop. A hapless employee had managed to hook an extension cord onto one of the chandeliers and now clung to it, whimpering, thirty feet or more above the marble floor. "Hang on!" she shouted at him. "Help is coming." Help, from where?

Here and there, office people stood looking about themselves in dazed confusion. Her glance flitted to a home furnishings shop: Tolby's. They featured the finest in biopoly upholstery. She darted over to a group of people standing around the vacated security desk. "Go in there and drag out as many cushions as you can," she said, pointing at the shop. "Pile them under that man hanging from the chandelier, in case he falls. I'm calling the fire department." They didn't recognize her, but they seemed relieved to have somebody tell them what to do, and scampered off readily to carry out her instructions.

Anna hesitated before punching 911 on her transceiver. She was afraid of what she might hear—those voices. And of course, once the fire department was notified, the media would get wind of it. She had no choice, these were her people. She punched in the number, and fairly sagged with relief when it was answered by a normal human being.

"Send everyone you have, immediately," she told the receptionist, "and we'll need an extension ladder or something, we've got a worker hanging from a chandelier about forty feet above the floor. There's probably people stranded or injured all over the building."

She hung up and turned to see a stream of office workers coming down the stairs to the mezzanine. Oh no, she thought, more panic-stricken employees. How was she going to handle them all by herself? But these people moved in an orderly fashion, and at their head was a figure she recognized. Hector Martin, looking a bit dishevelled, but whole and alive.

He spotted her and quickened his pace. "Anna. Are you all right?"

"I'm fine. What about you?"

"Fine." He turned to a woman in a yellow suit at his left. "Janice, please go down to maintenance and see how things are. We're going to need them to rescue people who've gotten stuck in crawl spaces or elevator shafts. Take some of your colleagues with you." He turned to Anna. "Is the communications network functioning now?"

She nodded.

"Good. Call here to the security desk when you get there," he told Janice.

"I called the fire department," Anna told him, oddly and wholly inappropriately irked at his competence.

Hector nodded, his gaze wandering to where the man still dangled from the chandelier. "How long ago?"

"Just now, but they're coming right away."

He turned to a tall, balding man, and said, "Take the rest of your people and search the mezzanine and balcony levels, identify anyone who's injured, but don't move them, just keep track of where they are for when the paramedics come."

"Martin, what happened?" Anna said, as the office workers departed. "It has to do with your project, doesn't it? I went to your apartment but you weren't there. There was someone else—in the shower—he was dead."

He nodded again. "My assistant, Colin Slatermeyer. I think—I know it sounds crazy but I think Graham sent someone to kill me. They got Colin instead."

"After what's happened here today, nothing sounds crazy anymore. I had the same idea myself, when I found him."

"Have you seen Graham this morning?"

"No." She shook her head. "You still haven't told me what happened."

"I will," Martin said, holding out a hand in placation. "I'll explain everything, but first we've got to make sure everyone is safe."

It took several hours for the rescue crews to case the building. They pulled victims of the panic out of ventilation ducts and elevator shafts. The man hanging from the chandelier was brought down in a cherry picker. The number of building personnel unaccounted for dwindled rapidly as those who had successfully fled the building were contacted on the now perfectly functional communication network and instructed to take the rest of the day off. However, despite security's best efforts, Nathan Graham could not be located. Besides Colin Slatermeyer, there were five known fatalities so far. Most of them had thrown themselves off the balconies. One man had electrocuted himself trying to chew through a multiprocessor cable.

When she wasn't busy with the rescue efforts, Anna was in frenzied conference with the public relations department. She had managed to buy a media blackout from the fire department by providing the city with a generous donation of flame retardant cellgel. She made a mental note to consider it as a yearly thing, around Christmas, say. It would make for a nice tax shelter and the PR couldn't be beat.

The statement issued to the holoweb cited a temporary power failure, and stressed the fact that all systems were back up and functioning normally. No mention was made of strange voices or mass hysteria. An in-house memo to all GeneSys employees instructed them to direct questions from the media to the public relations department, and the concessions director was instructed to make restitution of damages to shopkeepers contingent on their following the same policy. Through it all, she was deeply grateful that her children were in school. She made arrangements for them to stay with her sister for a few days.

With the press release issued and as many potential leaks stopped as possible, Anna turned back to Hector. "How about that explanation now?" she said.

Chango crawled back through the window to find Helix resting in the tank, her head above the grow med. "You're all right. What happened?"

"At first the Lilim fought with GeneSys, and because of Lilith we managed to get the upper hand momentarily, but if the battle had gone on, we probably would have lost. Instead, I was able to convince GeneSys of the benefits of cooperation. Because of the blue poly, GeneSys is now what my mother always thought it to be: a creature in its own right, made up of all who belong to it, and now, that includes the Lilim."

"So what happens now?"

Helix shrugged. "For me, not much. We'll have to figure out a way to enlarge this tank. Seal off this room and get the temperature and humidity up." She cast a disparaging glance at the dust-black walls and roof. "Maybe put in some skylights."

"You're staying." Her heart sank.

Helix nodded. "I'm going to have my daughters, live out my life, and die, right here."

Chango looked away. "Benny was here. He's dead now."

"You killed him?"

She nodded and pointed out the window. "I pushed him."

"Come here."

"I can't. You're covered with growth medium."

"At least look at me."

She turned, letting Helix see her tears.

"Oh, Chango."

"Just promise me one thing, now that you and your mother control GeneSys. Promise me you'll do something for the vat-divers."

"We didn't take over," said Helix, "but I'll try."

Chango drove home through the little streets, the neglected concrete roadways used only by motorcars and pedestrians. She watched the buildings pass by. Some of them were sparkling and new, with polybond walls and gleaming coats of plaint. Others were crumbling brick, desolately awaiting demolition—like her life; an edifice of memories, crumbling. Helix had got what she wanted, what she had always wanted. A vat—a simple thing that had nothing to do with her. Ada's name was cleared, her murderer dead. What was left now, for Chango to do? Anything, she supposed, anything she wanted. She hauled on the steering wheel, guiding the car through a pitted intersection, and headed for Vattown.

She went to Vonda's apartment first, but she wasn't home, so she tried Josa's. Sure enough, Vonda was at the bar, nursing a draft. "Benny's dead," she told her, sitting down next to her.

Vonda turned to look at her. "He's dead?" She shook her head. "Well, he killed Ada. I guess I should be glad he's dead. He lied to all of us all those years. I thought he was my best friend, but he wasn't. It was you, and you were right, Ada didn't dive blasted. I should have believed you."

"It's all right. You ran the tests, you saw the results firsthand. And I didn't make it any easier, implying that you doctored the results. For the record, I never really believed that. I pretended to, because it was easier than accepting the alternative."

Vonda nodded. "So how did he die?"

Josa brought Chango a draft, waving her off when Chango tried to pay her. She glanced between the two of them and disappeared into the back.

"He tried to kill me. I pushed him off the top of the GeneSys tower."

"What were you doing up on top of the GeneSys Building?"

Chango took a deep drink of beer. "It's a long story."

"I've got time."

Helix called Hyper at the first opportunity. "Can you find Vonda for me? I need to talk to her."

Hyper nodded, and put her on hold. She was on hold for quite a while, and then Vonda's face materialized with Josa's bar in the background. "I want to talk to you about the vatdivers," said Helix.

"Chango told me. You and your kind, the Lilim. You've taken over GeneSys." She frowned, and her voice became brittle with anger. "So I guess that leaves us vatdivers out in the cold, doesn't it? I hope you'll at least honor our severance packages and worker's comp. We may be out of our jobs tomorrow, but that doesn't mean that ten years from now we won't get sick. It's bad enough we're losing our jobs. You can't just abandon us. We've given our lives to that fucking corporation you just took over."

Helix shook her head. "We didn't take over, and I didn't say I was laying the vatdivers off. Nothing about the vatdivers has been decided yet. That's why I called you. To talk."

"To talk." Vonda shook her head slowly. "You're not canning us?"

"No."

Vonda managed half a smile. "When Chango told me what went down, I figured that with the riot and all you'd waste no time getting rid of us."

"No. As far as I'm concerned, you're the union rep. We'll negotiate a contract."

Vonda laughed with incredulity. "A contract. For what? If the Lilim are doing the diving—"

"There aren't enough of us yet," Helix interrupted. "I'm only the second queen, and pregnant with my first clutch. It'll be at least another year before the third queen is born, unless my mother beats me to it. Anyway, it'll be years, probably five or more, before the Lilim are populous enough to take over production."

"So in the meantime it's business as usual," said Vonda, switching back to bitterness again. "We dive and die, and when you don't need us anymore, you cast us aside."

"Business as usual?" said Helix, suddenly angry. "A union contract? Negotiated benefits and workers comp packages? I guess you want me to wave my arms and make vatsickness go away, but I can't do that. All I can do is urge Hector to make vatsickness research a personal priority, and see to it that the company deals fairly with you from now on."

Vonda nodded, chastened. "I'm sorry; I—" She shrugged. "I expected a raw deal from you. But here you're talking unions, contracts." She shook her head. "I wish Ada were here." Vonda looked back at her suddenly. "Just tell me one thing. What happens when there are more of you?"

"Even after the Lilim fill the vats, technicians will be needed to test samples, monitor ph levels, and calculate seed mixtures. *And* deal with the other company departments. We do not like to leave our nests once we have them," said Helix, leaning back and folding her arms. "We will need human representatives to attend meetings and act as liaisons to other departments."

Vonda laughed. "And you want the vatdivers to do that for you? The same people who tried to kill you yesterday? What makes you think they'll accept working for you at all?"

"You do," Helix said, leaning forward. "You saved my life in that riot. And when I took my suit off in the vat, I endangered yours. I pushed you as hard as I could. I could have broken your seals. I could have killed you. And I wouldn't have meant to, but at the time, I wouldn't have cared either." She nodded slightly. "I put you at risk from something I myself am immune to. I can understand why so many of the vatdivers wanted to kill me. But you didn't. You had more reason than the rest of them, and you didn't let me die.

"You made an alliance between the divers and the Lilim possible by standing up for the real goals of the labor movement Ada started. You'll convince the divers that such an alliance is in their best interests, and the contract you negotiate for them will prove it. As for the rest of it, we will all have time to get used to one another."

"So what you're saying, basically, is that you've taken over my company."

It was, without a doubt, the strangest conference call Anna had ever had. She recognized Helix and Lilith from the dream fragments in the elevator. They both seemed to be floating in vats of liquid—that would be the growth medium Hector told her was so important to them. He was there in the office, sitting beside her so his image could be picked up by the transceiver.

"Not exactly," said Helix. "We reached an understanding with—with the group mind that is GeneSys."

Anna knitted her brows but decided against asking for a clarification of that just yet. "And that business with the blackout, the voices, that was you."

"It can happen again, if you try to interfere with us," said Lilith.

Anna bit back her anger and let the threat ride, for the moment.

"You have to understand," said Helix. "We're a new species. We have to survive."

"But *you* have to understand," said Anna, leaning forward, "GeneSys is a corporation. If it doesn't carry on the business of being a corporation, it won't survive, and neither will you."

"That's where you come in," said Helix.

"What do you mean by that?"

"We still need somebody to run the company."

"I see. And my people?"

"There aren't enough of us to take on all the responsibilities involved," said Helix.

"The Lilim do not care for numbers," said Lilith.

"That too. We just want vats for our daughters."

Anna raised her eyebrows. "Vats for your daughters? How many will you need?"

"Her first clutch will stay with her," said Lilith. "But there will be a queen. She will need her own nest."

"And how soon will that be?"

"A year or so."

"The Lilim don't really reproduce all that rapidly," said Hector.

Well that was something, at least. "In a year. If things go smoothly, if you don't interfere with the operations of the company, I don't see any problem." She turned to Hector. "About this blue poly. You say it's . . . in the wiring?"

"It is the wiring," said Hector.

"I don't understand."

"The blue poly eats the electrical components, and in the process incorporates their functions. Electricity is still being transmitted, only now it's moving through a biological medium, like nerves," he explained.

"Nerves." Anna looked around her office. The lights were on, the temperature comfortable, and her multiprocessor hummed contentedly to itself, the same as always, but maybe not. "What's the difference, then?"

"The difference is that the phage translator is no longer needed to connect the multiprocessor brains to the electrical network."

"But what about the voltage? The phage translator was necessary to dampen the electrical signal to the brains to a level acceptable to a biological organism, am I right?"

"Yes, but the blue poly seems to absorb the excess and use it towards new growth. Of course, once it's everywhere, we won't need to generate so much power."

Anna thought about it. If phage translators became obsolete, Minds Unlimited stock would take a hard hit. They'd be ripe for a buyout. "How soon before it spreads beyond GeneSys?"

"Not long at all. It's probably happening now."

She shivered with dread and excitement. GeneSys was on the cutting edge of a revolution in energy systems. With advance knowledge like this, she could make a killing. Minds Unlimited was only the beginning.

"There's one other thing," said Hector.

"What's that?"

"The biological network is likely to be much more mutable than one composed of wires and chips. We may experience some spontaneous renetworking."

"What do you mean?"

"The brains may choose to do things differently than we would."

"That explains why my coffeemaker reminded me of my eight o'clock appointment when I switched it on this afternoon."

"Yeah, things like that."

"They say we have brought them something much longed for," said Lilith.

"Like what?"

"The ability to think for themselves."

"But what if they spend too much time thinking for themselves? What if they start talking to each other and forget to keep the ventilation system running?"

All she got were uncomfortable shrugs on all sides.

* * *

The blue polymer was spreading rapidly through the city. As soon as he learned of it, Hyper went down to the power station on Grand Boulevard with a pair of insulated gloves and a wire stripper and got himself a piece of the stuff. He used it to treat his robots. Within a few hours they were biologized.

He gathered them on the front lawn of his house; newly graceful creatures of metal flesh. He vaulted astride Robo-Mime and set off with his herd through the streets of Vattown to Mavi's house. The noise of his entourage brought her out onto the porch, her eyebrows knitted quizzically.

"Where's Chango?"

"She's inside."

"Tell her to get out here."

Mavi disappeared back into the house, and long moments passed. Finally Chango came out. She eyed the robots guardedly. "What are you up to?"

"According to Slatermeyer's calculations, the blue poly will reach the traffic net today. C'mon, saddle up, you don't want to miss this."

"There won't be anything to see."

"Maybe not, but it's a historic moment. Human beings are losing control of their inventions. Don't you want to be there when it happens?"

"Not particularly. Besides, what's so special about the traffic net? Most of Grand Boulevard is already running on blue poly."

"But once it gets into the levway, it'll go everywhere. It'll be in the 'burbs by tonight. C'mon, what have you got to do today? Mope around some more?"

She shrugged, and climbed reluctantly onto the shoulders of Close Enough for Jazz. "Is this safe?"

"Just hang on," he said, and directed the robots west, towards the levway.

They stood on the embankment, watching levcars whiz past below as the sun inched its way towards the horizon.

"How long do we have to stand here? It's probably happened already," said Chango.

"No, look." Hyper pointed to where a solid line of levcars crept along the road surface at a fraction of their normal speed. "That's got to be the front edge."

"Is that as fast as they can go?"

"No, but the road's keeping everyone back from the discontinuity. Once it's all biologized, speeds will return to normal, but for the next few days, there'll be traffic jams, something no one's had to put up with for years."

"All this new stuff—the brains, the blue poly, Helix and her people—I wonder if human beings are going to get left behind."

"Maybe. But so many of us already have been. You and I, we'll be all right. We already know how to survive in a world that was made for someone else."

Chango nodded and cast her gaze north, to the peak of the GeneSys Building, just beginning to glow golden in the gathering dusk.

Helix sank into the waters. She felt the cramping in her abdomen, felt herself widening as the first egg slid out and drifted to the bottom of the tank. It was followed by eleven more. She ducked beneath the waters, gently running her hands across the slippery surface of the membranes. Her daughters, she thought, and smiled.

ABOUT THE AUTHOR

Anne Harris is the author of the highly praised novel *The Nature of Smoke*, a 1996 *Locus* Recommended First Novel. Her short stories have appeared in various magazines, including *Galaxy* and *Realms of Fantasy*. She earned a degree in computer science with a minor in physics from Oakland University and works as a freelance journalist. She lives outside Detroit, not more than ten minutes from the Fisher Building.